CONTROL MY NIGHT

THE SHADOW CAGES SERIES
BOOK ONE

SARAH L RICHHELM

THREE LANE PUBLISHING
AUSTRALIA

First edition, printed: 2024

Edited by: Emma O'Connell at Emma's Edit
Proofread by: Sharon Strahand
Cover Design by: Jaqueline Kropmanns
Formatting & Interior Design by: Stacey Blake at Champagne Book Design

Paperback ISBN: 978-1-7635195-1-0
Ebook ISBN: 978-1-7635195-0-3

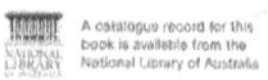
A catalogue record for this book is available from the National Library of Australia

AUTHOR'S NOTE

Thank you so much for choosing *Control My Night*. This is the first book in an interconnected, standalone series featuring different main characters. I hope you enjoy Keanna's journey and this introduction to the world I've created.

Before we begin, I wanted to make you aware of some content and/or trigger warnings for this story. They're listed below if you'd like to read them, otherwise please skip ahead.

Control My Night is a new adult fantasy for mature audiences and contains strong language and content some readers may find distressing including profanity, violence, alcohol use, graphic sexual content, disordered thoughts around food and self-image, death of a family member, and mentions of death during childbirth (off-page). A full list of content and/or trigger warnings can be found on my website. If there is something not included on the website that you as a reader found distressing, please contact me so it can be added.

ALSO BY SARAH L RICHHELM:

Control My Night

Shatter My Night

For the people pleasers (if that's alright with them).

CONTROL

MY

NIGHT

PART ONE

AN INSTRUMENT OF CHAOS

PRAGUE

CHAPTER ONE

I WAS USED TO PEOPLE WATCHING ME, BUT TODAY FELT different.

Zeina's stern 'on-duty' expression hovered beside my shoulder as we carved a path around the crowd of peak-hour shoppers. I'd psyched myself up to face the world for one hour to buy my father's present, my determination to achieve this most basic of goals only inhibited by the pricking finger of unease skirting the base of my spine. Given it was the first time I'd ventured out in public since my attack two months ago, I should have expected to feel this way.

In fact, Zeina had told me I'd feel this way—to be kind to myself during this 'period of adjustment'. Strangely enough, my anxiety hadn't listened to my bodyguard's platitudes. It's great like that.

We cut through a cross-section of humanity, my heeled boots clacking on uneven cobblestones. Upbeat, contagious music filtered down the steps of the shopping mall beside us. A thin breeze ribboned between curved multi-storied buildings, carrying with it the scent of warm bread and apple pastries, and reminding me that in my eagerness to achieve normalcy, I'd skipped breakfast. And lunch.

Normalcy should be Saturday morning shopping in Prague's Old Town, not suffering dark memories of a blood-soaked hotel room. Of a dead coworker surrounded by glass I'd shattered with my screams. Those had been my constant companions for two months, holding me back from living my life, and dammit, *today* I'd move past it. I refused to dwell on that night any longer, just as I suppressed the pressure rising beneath my sternum. It unfurled toward the base of my throat.

I swallowed hard, as if to push down the reptilian head of the beast trapped in my chest. *Nice try,* I told it, slamming the cage shut.

Instead, I indulged in the heat from the sun peeking above the pleasant beiges, sage-greens and grays of the surrounding buildings. Beyond them loomed the contrasting dark brick, sharp spires, and steep, sloping roofs of the gothic Powder Gate. Taking in the mixture of textures and colors never got old, especially in this part of the city. I'd missed it.

More to keep my hands busy than anything else, I accessed the emails on my phone to double-check the confirmation of my order. My father's present gleamed in the attached photo.

"What made you go for cufflinks?" Zeina asked, observing the droves of shoppers reveling in the last remnants of summer. She led me around the horse and cart combo sweeping tourists through the square. "Your father already has some, doesn't he?"

He did. In neat rows next to his folded ties, organized in a drawer I'd Marie Kondo-ed for him during my self-inflicted isolation. Naturally, this sent my pulse fluttering like hummingbird wings. Nothing like a comment from your bodyguard to revive insecurity over purchasing a redundant gift for a man who has everything. This was the best idea I'd come up with.

"Cufflinks are like socks. You can't have too many. And he doesn't have bespoke ones from his daughter," I replied, injecting bravado into my voice. "These ones have diamonds, *dahling.*"

Zeina's eyebrows rose above her narrow cheekbones and prominent jawline. "I stand corrected." She studied my posture, no doubt tabulating the effort of this venture against my level of visible angst. "Are the wheels on the bus, or off?"

Am I freaking out, or am I okay? "Wheels on. I promise."

"Hmm. Don't get me wrong, Keanna, I'm glad we're here, but you don't have to do this if you don't want to." Her wry smile creased the tawny skin around her light brown eyes. "I'm sure this place can afford to deliver diamond cufflinks, right?"

I sighed, relaxing shoulders that had found their way back up to my ears. "Figured I should engage with society again." I couldn't wait for the trauma to heal. My father was celebrating his milestone 5-0 in a week whether I got my act together or not. "But first"—I steered us to the end of a queue in front of the drink cart propped on the sidewalk—"a smoothie."

I'd allowed time and calories for the berry goodness that, before my attack, had been a staple of my Saturday mornings. The woman ahead of me shifted up the line, her Salvatore Ferragamo shopping bag banging painfully across my shins. My pointed look went unacknowledged—seriously, she must have felt it hit me—but at least the child accompanying her proved distractingly cute. My father didn't allow any of our employees to bring their children to the estate or our company office, making any interactions with mini humans rare. I pulled a face, eliciting a giggle from the russet-haired little girl and some serious side-eye from my bodyguard.

I stuck my tongue out. Another giggle. Approval, even from a child, lightened my heart. For a moment, I wasn't a murderer with a guilty conscience. The tension in my chest released, schedule forgotten. "She won't bite, Zee. And her pink tutu is *adorable*."

If I'd had it my way growing up, I'd have worn a tutu daily. They matched well with most shoes in my wardrobe. They were also a terrific social distancing tool.

"That's something my ex-girlfriend would say," Zeina said. "Children do, in fact, bite. Frequently. And tutus are aesthetics over functionality. Like beige leather car seats." She stepped back as the girl made a grab for her jeans with sticky fingers. "I'll go stand over here."

I hid a smile as she took her position next to the florist behind me. Less than twenty feet, but the most distance she'd put between us since we'd exited the car—and a testament to her level of discomfort.

Soon, the woman dragged Little Miss Tutu away. I shuffled forward and placed my order. The almond milk and berry smoothie wouldn't do much to stop my hunger, but I chose it anyway. The dress I'd bought for my father's birthday ball in a week couldn't be altered, and shapewear only did so much. I'd dedicated a lot of energy to working out its limitations.

I waited under the eaves, shielded from the midday sun, and ticked through my task list while scanning for Zeina. She'd merged into the crowd as she'd been trained to do. I paused, the beast in my chest stirring as I noticed a man sitting at a tiny two-seater cafe table across the street, facing the smoothie store. Alarm coursed down my body. Was he looking at me?

Get a grip, Keanna. Of course he's not.

The server called my name. I accepted my drink and straightened my posture, raising the straw to my lips. Acting casual, I gazed over the crowd again.

After observing him, tendrils of dread squeezed my stomach. Oh, he was watching me alright, but not in the way that I—a horrifically single girl nearing her twenty-first birthday—should be excited about.

His attention wasn't obvious, like in those cheesy spy movies my father always chose on our movie nights. It was actually what the man *wasn't* doing. Zeina had shared some of her wisdom during the long days of accompanying me in our estate, teaching me how to make Knafeh and play badminton. "Look for lack of authenticity," she'd said. "People going about their lives, even sitting and drinking coffee, have a sense of purpose and vulnerability in their movements. Look for someone performing. Being too careful." I hadn't understood what she meant until now.

A book lay open in the man's lap, pages unturned. His smooth, unlined features lacked interest and was carefully neutral—not bored, like the woman sitting at the table in front of him, shooing off the wandering pigeons; not hopeful like the teenager near her, checking his phone and those around him like he was waiting for someone. No, I'd bet the smoothie I'd just purchased, that behind those stylish Ray-Bans the man's gaze tracked my every movement.

Tightening my grip on my tote, I spun, searching again for

Zeina's uniform: black jeans, white shirt, black blazer. Normally I'd commend her functional style and use of neutrals, but right now her efforts to blend in were totally unhelpful.

The spot beside the florist was empty.

I grabbed my phone. No messages; just the smiling portrait of me and my father, green eyes side by side, his short graying hair fighting with my own blonde strands for dominance in the frame. Today's schedule didn't allow for loitering. Perhaps Zeina had gone ahead to the jewelry store to check it? She could have misjudged how long my order would take. Besides, I only needed five minutes to pick up the present. I had to make it to my father's office at noon to help his assistant prep for the board meeting on Monday. Which was … I checked the time. Soon.

I sent Zeina a message asking where she'd gone and if the tutu had scared her off. While I waited, I chewed the straw, mindful of my lipstick.

She didn't reply.

Zeina *always* replied.

I searched the crowd again. The reassuring blanket of her presence slipped off my shoulders. *Where is she?*

Zeina was a step up in security. Had my father hired this man? Then again, if that were the case, they'd have been introduced so I wouldn't be freaking out like this. My father wouldn't have called Zeina away and not told me.

My unease was enough to act on. If, for whatever reason, I was being monitored and Zeina wasn't around, then I could only assume something had gone wrong. Wrong at home, or wrong here? The paper straw crumpled between my teeth. I needed those cufflinks. Then I needed to get to the office. I needed …

Calm down. The last time I'd panicked, I'd filled a room with blood and death.

I breathed deep, trying to stop my anxiety from taking over. Zeina was probably at the store. If she wasn't, I'd reassess. If the man followed me, I'd have my answer. And if he did, my bag was heavy. In a worst-case scenario? An effective projectile.

Plan decided, I walked ahead. A subtle glance showed he hadn't moved, though the lenses of those sunglasses followed my every step.

☙

My smile stayed polite but fixed as the store assistant wrapped my father's present with care. Internally, I bounced from one thought to another, a *ratatatat* I couldn't turn off. I locked and unlocked my phone, checking I hadn't missed any calls. Nothing. Why hadn't I asked Zeina what her security company was called? I'd messaged my father too, letting him know I'd lost her. Also nothing. My calls to both had gone unanswered. No taxi yet. The sickening tendrils had expanded to fill my stomach.

I swung from confident to not-so-confident with every lock/unlock, assuring myself that if I'd felt watched during my first venture into the city in two months, I had a reason for it. One minute I was proud of myself. The next, convinced I'd overreacted. Zeina was probably searching the square in a panic, thinking I'd expired in a haze of anxiety.

The yellow taxi arrived. If I was followed to my father's office, security would intervene, and I'd be safe. In the meantime, I would *not* entertain any of the horrible possibilities the radio silence might suggest.

Taxi. Taxi. Get to the taxi.

I crashed into someone outside the store. Slick with condensation, my drink slipped onto the patterned sidewalk, along with my phone. Blended berries splashed over my beige ankle boots, staining one side purple.

"Gosh, I'm so—"

My knee-jerk apology cut off. My face, slack with shock, was reflected in Ray-Ban lenses. Above, short brown hair sat styled and neatly pushed back. Below was ivory skin, a symmetrical nose, and sharply tipped lips.

Before I could say anything else, the man ducked. His slender fingers swiped my phone up off the ground.

And put it in his pocket.

I swallowed, backing away. I bumped into another shopper, then stumbled, ignoring their cry of annoyance as I considered the distance between the man and the taxi. How did that saying go? Better paranoid than in trouble. Or dead.

I fled in the opposite direction.

"Miss Backhus!"

A guttural, cutting accent sounded in my ear, a hand pulling me to a stop. I yelped, looking up—*way* up—at the man speaking. It wasn't the Ray-Bans guy, but that didn't make me feel much better. The beast rattled inside its locked cage as I glanced to see if he still stood behind me.

He was gone.

"We cannot locate Ms Farouq." The man holding me flashed identification that resembled what Zeina carried, his grip tightening around my arm as if to quell the squeal loading behind my lips. He looked to be late twenties, perhaps early thirties, and his face was all harsh angles—cutting cheeks, jutting, clean-shaved chin— as he scanned the street.

I managed to choke out a response. "Zeina? What do you mean you can't locate her?"

He nodded at the shopping mall. "Please. Come, miss." He tugged at my arm.

I planted my feet as best I could. "*No—*"

The man relented, squeezing my shoulder in what I assumed he thought was a comforting gesture. "My name is Matej," he said. "I work with Zeina, but we have lost contact with her. Your father wouldn't want us to leave anything to chance. I must get you back."

"My father—"

"Let me get you to his office first, then we'll investigate. We have a car parked nearby."

The mention of my father's office helped, but it wasn't enough. Not with Zeina missing. "'I'm a little teapot, short and stout …'" My voice trailed off expectantly.

Matej's sigh was barely audible above the bells tolling a few streets over. I prepared to wrench my arm free.

"'If you don't drink Earl Grey, count me out,'" he finished. Zeina's remixed nursery rhyme passphrase sounded—quite frankly—absurd coming from this giant man, but I let him pull me forward. What had happened to Zeina? She'd been right *there* while I lined up for my smoothie, and then …

Gone.

Matej's strides across the white reflective tiles reeked of practice and professionalism. He guided me past the glittering storefronts and toward the elevator accessing the parking garage. Zeina had never mentioned who she worked with, but I was thankful she had someone looking out for her. And me.

My grip tightened on my father's present. I exhaled, trying to stay calm. It was going to be fine. There had to be an explanation that didn't end in something bad happening to her.

Matej led me to a late-model black BMW spaces from Zeina's empty white one. My gut churned. He ushered me into the back. Icy air-conditioning and sterile disinfectant washed over me as I sank into the leather seat.

The driver nodded. "Miss."

I murmured a response; Matej sat beside me and spoke to the driver in Czech. I'd moved from Australia with my father while he settled a new company branch and hadn't lived in Prague long enough to learn the notoriously difficult language past the basics, so I only recognized Zeina's name in the stream of words.

Heavy silence fell as the doors locked, the driver screeching the car up the spiral ramp toward the street. Matej opened the bag on the floor.

I spied a matte black gun barrel, rope, handcuffs, and black zip ties that almost blended in with the material. Almost.

Without thinking, I gasped, grabbing for the door handle. Zeina carried a gun, even if she'd never used it in my presence, but this bag looked like it belonged to a serial killer.

I sensed violence in the air as I moved. Spearing pain lanced through my temple. I cried out as my head slammed against the car door. Pressure clawed at my chin as Matej shoved the side of my face against the cold glass, jamming my mouth shut.

His other hand tugged at my hair. I flailed, pushing against him, my feet tangling in my bag. Tears spiked the corners of my eyes as he overpowered me. Numbness blossomed beneath my ribs from where the armrest dug into my side. Familiar, panicked thoughts rose like a reflex: *stuck-confined-can't-breathe-can't-move have to get out out OUT*.

No. No. Not this. Not *again*. Adrenalin compressed my throat as his fingers caged my jaw. A muffled, pained squeal managed to escape.

"Oh no you don't." Matej's peaty cologne was as overwhelming as the rest of him. Material with a leathery, sandpapery consistency pushed against the lower half of my face, forcing my mouth closed just as effectively as his hand had.

A muzzle.

CHAPTER TWO

THE SEDAN PAUSED IN AN ALLEY A FEW STREETS AWAY.
Matej dragged me from the vehicle without ceremony.
I fell, one knee tearing open on the cobblestones. Handcuffs
pinched my wrists. Leather rubbed abrasively against my chin, my
clenched jaw aching under the too-tight straps of the muzzle.

He banded an arm around my waist and forced me toward a
gray van parked between the close-set buildings. It was exactly the
kind of gray van people go into and don't come out of. No *way* was
I going in there. Zeina would have a brain hemorrhage if I let myself
get thrown into a *secondary* vehicle at a *secondary* location.

Curved lampposts, dark brick on either side of the shaded alley,
and the empty road beyond were our only witnesses. I thrashed as
tears blurred my vision. My chest grew tight, pressure rising in my
throat again, unable to escape.

One of the van doors swung open, revealing a gutted interior.
I kicked furiously. *No. Freaking. Wa—*

With a heavy grunt, Matej tossed me inside like a sack of flour.
Fire ignited my side as I rolled across the metal floor and the door
slammed shut. Darkness swallowed me. The van lurched. I careened
forward, my cuffed hands breaking my fall. Alongside the sharp, searing pain of my right shoulder, one of my knees was bleeding, mixing
with the sticky smoothie already coating my bare legs.

Muffled sobs pounded in my head as I shifted onto my good
shoulder, adjusting to the darkness.

I could just make out Matej sitting beside the van doors. The
gun in his bag now rested on his lap. He'd known to silence me in

the car immediately. How? Outside of my father and his trusted executives, no one knew the truth about that night two months ago. *No one.*

Unless …

Was this revenge for the man I'd murdered?

Using the momentum of the vehicle, I pushed myself into a seated position against the wall, keeping my eyes on Matej and his gun while trying to inhale through my rapidly congesting nose. A red light—a camera?—glowed above the bare doors. Slivers of light seeped through the cracks in the hinges. The interior was all metal, dusty floor, and peeling gray paint.

A shifting noise sounded from the back corner. I squinted then inhaled sharply, clutching my skirt. It had bunched up, exposing a great deal of thigh, but it was the side furthest from Matej, so I hadn't prioritized smoothing it down. I did now.

Through the gloom, another man slid his black boots across the floor, stretching his legs out until his feet nearly touched mine. Below his broad shoulders and thick torso, his hands sat bound in his lap.

I was trapped with *two* strange men. Anyone in the back of a van probably wasn't someone worth meeting—and yes, I included myself in that category.

"A muzzle, Matej? Really?" the man murmured as I froze. "This is the level he's sunk to?"

Matej tapped his gun on the floor. "Quiet."

The floor swayed. Movement of the van, or was I about to pass out? The man's handcuffs reflected the dull light as he gestured to the floor panels, as if encouraging me to grab them.

The van jolted up and then down, like we'd passed over a raised pedestrian crossing. I fell to the side.

Despite myself, I started crying again. It was a stupid thing to do—I could barely breathe as it was, and these men were watching my humiliation—but I couldn't stop. My stomach clenched like a vice, fear clouding my brain. Everything hurt from being tossed around in this metal cage, like I was a doll inside a washing machine.

The other prisoner developed a milder tone. Kinder. Or secondhand embarrassment. I somehow heard it above the purr of the engine. "You can sit back here. You'll move less in the center of the vehicle."

Man I didn't know. Enclosed space. *Not appealing.*

Matej barked again for him to be quiet. My fingers curled around the metal panels on the floor as I considered his suggestion. This other prisoner knew my kidnapper by name, hadn't attempted to escape and didn't seem as scared of the gun as he should be. He could be trying to gain my trust, lulling me into a false sense of security before he …

Before he, what, kidnaps me and throws me into a van?

I swayed as we slowed to a stop. My shoulder, screaming at the movement, decided for me. If it meant preserving some semblance of class and control, I'd take it.

Mindful of my skirt, bare legs, and damaged knee, I used the opportunity to move. Judging from the chatter of pedestrians, passing cars, and the *ting* of tram bells, we were at a set of traffic lights. Where were they taking us?

I crawled to the back corner. Could I bang my restraints to get attention? Leap on Matej to see if our combined weight knocked the doors open? The thoughts disappeared as Matej raised his weapon, a finger held to his lips. I sank into the space beside the man to distract myself from the gun casually pointed in my direction.

Though it was still dim, the prisoner's features were clearer. Black stubble lined his jaw. A thin cream sweater covered his stocky build. Pallid skin stretched tight over a wide, mature face that had seen at least twenty-five, perhaps thirty years. Wisps of brown hair curled around the edge of his navy beanie. He must have been somewhere with heavy air-conditioning recently, because the September sun retained its heat, and the need for knitwear during the day was weeks away. He had to have been uncomfortable, but aside from a raspy, rattling cough, he remained silent for the rest of the journey.

Sweat streaked my hairline as the van shuddered to a halt,

engine silenced. The temperature of the panel above us had risen to an almost unbearable level. Adrenalin had long worn off, leaving behind a painful awareness of my injuries and a desperate need to go to the bathroom.

Surely by now my father would know something was wrong. The tracker inside my phone would lead them to Ray-Bans man. People would be dispatched to find me. I held on to this with everything I had, because the alternative was to admit I was on my own and I had no other installed coping mechanism for being abducted. My father was capable. He had capable people at his disposal. He'd find me. Somehow.

Surrounded by uncertainty, there was one thing of which I *was* certain: if I escaped this, I'd happily go back behind the walls of my father's estate and stay there. I didn't need a social life. Or a boyfriend. Or friends, or anything normal people my age did. I'd be bored, but I'd be *safe*.

The van doors opened with a whining creak, and I winced against the sudden onslaught of afternoon sun. Matej hopped out. With his golden-bronze complexion and shoulder-length dark hair, he looked similar to many men I often saw walking the streets.

No one would remember me leaving with him.

The two guards behind him were even more intimidating. Scars punctuated their umber scalps, cheeks, and foreheads. They aimed weapons toward us, making my chest tighten to the point of pain. The beast in my chest did *not* like being on the other side of a gun. It prowled inside its cage, banging the bars and demanding I do something about it, muzzle or no muzzle.

"Come," Matej ordered.

The prisoner ducked his head as he shuffled out of the van. He stood with the armed guards, his eyes on my face, always my face.

Matej repeated his demand. I swallowed and rose, limping for the opening, my hands trembling even as I tried to keep them steady. I hated that my fear was so transparent.

Impatient, Matej grabbed my arm, hauling me out. One of

the scarred, weapon-wielding guards marched the other prisoner forward.

We were in a courtyard at the top of a valet circle in the shadow of a large, sprawling mansion. A hundred feet away stood a gothic-style wrought iron gate, black spear tips tearing into the sky, armed guards standing either side. A high stone wall curtained the gate, penning us in.

Zeina would have wanted me to try and remember everything, but these were the only details I could take in before we veered toward a separate, single-story building flush against the stone perimeter. I shuddered, the breeze tossing my hair and gravel crunching beneath my boots as the gun barrel pushed against my back.

They marched us inside, through a meeting area filled with a prestigious wooden table, high-backed chairs, and another set of open doors. A seated businessman waited for us underneath fluorescent lighting; a black-walled room visible behind him through a large window.

He stood as we entered, straightening his vest. He was large and well-built, in his mid-to-late forties. Perhaps around the same age as my father, if the gray dusting the temples of his close-cropped blond hair was anything to go by. His tailored suit hinted at understated wealth. Tom Ford? I eyed the navy lapels, then dismissed the observation. Nothing mattered less right now.

The man's handsome face, lined at the corners of his mouth and forehead, remained otherwise expressionless as he assessed my muzzle, my bloody legs, and stained shoes. It was all I could do not to quiver and sink to the floor. I'd spoken to men like him in my father's company, but I'd always worn my own kind of armor when I'd done it: makeup, tailored skirt, my hair perfectly tamed into a bun or up-do. I withered beneath his critical gaze as it swept over me, like he'd taken stock of my value and deemed me without merit.

The prisoner from the van bristled, his thick, defined shoulders shifting inside his sweater. "The muzzle. Take it off. It's not right."

"You'll have the chance shortly." The businessman's steady

accent contained enough of a clipped American inflection to reveal his roots.

A moment passed between them. The prisoner's posture deflated. In relief? Fear? "So, this is it, then?"

The businessman turned to the guards. "Take him in."

They led the prisoner into the black room, but he kept looking back. As if he was worried about *me*.

"I apologize, Miss Backhus, for taking you," the businessman said.

I tilted my head at the way my name rolled off the man's lips. Did I know him? He was vaguely familiar, in the sense that I'd probably seen him on a panel at a conference or his headshot in *The Financial Review*, but—

"Arwood Sayer," he said, obviously seeing the cogs turning. His name snagged my memory, slipping away before I could grasp it. "As much as I regret today's events, they've become necessary." He nodded to Matej. "Put it on her, please."

Put *what* on me? I tried to turn as Matej subdued me in an uncompromising grip. Someone tugged my hair to the side—*ow*—and a cold band clasped around my neck.

I flinched at the metal against my skin. Arwood extracted a chain with a silver cylinder. He clutched it between his fingers, leaning around me, and *who was this man*?

There was momentary tension on the band, the sound of metal scraping against metal—a lock clicking into place?—and then he pulled back, hanging the chain around his neck and tucking it beneath his buttoned shirt. "This collar is one of those necessary things. You'll get used to it."

My cuffed hands nudged the edges of the metal band. A rectangle of pressure formed at the top of my spine. *What the hell has he—?* I pushed it upwards. It moved half an inch, but that was all.

This, on top of the sweet, earthy scent of the muzzle, was too much. I inhaled broken half-breaths, blinking and swaying beneath

Matej's grip as he forced me inside the room where the prisoner waited. Thick industrial black plastic crunched beneath my boots.

The shock of that was enough to distract me from an impending panic attack. I turned to a closed door, the handle unmoving beneath my palm.

Click. Arwood's voice flowed into the room from an intercom. He stood on the other side of the window, observing us both. "Remove her mask, please."

I didn't like the sound of that at all. The prisoner took a step forward. I darted back, pulse leaping. I'd seen enough *Dexter* to know what a room lined in plastic meant, and it was nothing good. The tang of bleach permeated the leather of the muzzle.

"Now."

My legs tingled, prepping to run, but there was nowhere to run *to*. Aside from us and—strangely—a row of four glass vases sitting on the floor against the far wall, the room was empty.

The prisoner took another step forward, heavy eyebrows raised. They'd removed his cuffs; he stretched his hands out like he had in the van, as if to show he wasn't a threat. A matte black band wrapped around one of his wrists. I dug my fingernails into my palms but allowed him to come closer, swallowing hard.

Weariness stamped the prisoner's features, washed under the suspended lightbulb. Whoever he was, he'd had a hard time. Not just today or yesterday, but for months, perhaps years. Below a nose that had been broken at least once, his mouth softened with apology. He loomed above me, reaching around my head.

Cool air hit my cheeks as the muzzle came away, the stench of bleach and metal becoming even more overpowering. I passed my forearms over my face, dispersing the moisture and working my jaw, but I didn't relax. The room was filled with the foreboding sensation of an axe hanging above us.

The prisoner threw the muzzle to the side. "What's your name?"

I pressed my lips together. Without knowing what was about to happen, I didn't want to give anything to this man. Yet … the longer I contemplated his hopeful, open expression, the more I relented. He'd already seen me crying and undignified. In the grand scheme of things, a name was nothing.

"Keanna," I whispered.

"Pleasure to properly make your acquaintance, Keanna. I wish it was in better circumstances. I'm Ri." It must have been a nickname from the way his pale, chapped lips quirked, as if sharing a private joke. "I must say, the leather muzzle was poor taste. I thought blatant misogyny had gone out of style. Don't let them put it back on if you can help it."

Was he being sarcastic? Despite our situation, the lightness in his tone suggested it, which was nuts because of all the occasions to be funny, now wasn't ideal.

The intercom clicked again. "Miss Backhus. I've been told you're quite competent."

I frowned at Arwood, but all questions about who had told him that dissolved at his next words.

"Please kill this man for me."

CHAPTER THREE

H E—HE WAS KIDDING, RIGHT?

Arwood stood at the window, looking completely unaffected by what he'd said. Had I misheard him? Kill him? Kill *Ri*?

"I'm sorry?" I sputtered. "What did you s—"

"I need you to kill this man, Miss Backhus."

Behind me, Ri exhaled heavily. I kept my gaze on Arwood, confused as all hell. Did he know what I'd done to that man in the hotel room two months ago? Was he trying to trick me into admitting it? This must be some kind of test.

I didn't realize I'd said the last part out loud until the speaker clicked again. "This *is* a test," Arwood said. "But not one pertaining to your ethics."

"But … I can't *kill* him."

Arwood's steely expression cracked, a hint of a smile emerging on his broad, aristocratic face. No, not a smile. His lips pulled to the side and his eyes narrowed, as if observing something mildly interesting. "I have it on good authority you can."

My mouth slackened, and I glanced back. Ri's countenance held no fear, only acceptance.

"I—" I swallowed. "I don't know what you've been told, but I'm not that kind of person."

I thought of Zeina training in our gym. The swiftness with which she disarmed her opponents, the ligament-tearing holds she performed with ease. Had they abducted me thinking I was her?

Get real. Arwood wore a five-thousand-dollar suit. His attention to detail belied the chances of him getting something like that wrong. And he'd said my name. So had Matej.

"I'll be the judge of that," Arwood replied. "Kill him. *Now.*"

The way he said this incensed me. We were discussing someone's *life*, not requesting a coffee. What would my father do if he were backed into a corner like this?

"I can't." I tried to keep my voice steady. "I don't have any weapons."

One of Arwood's eyebrows rose. When I continued to blink at him innocently, he pressed the small black device in his hand. A tiny click responded in my metal collar.

Heat forged a quick, precise path down my spine. I cried out, back arching. As quickly as the jolt had come, it vanished, leaving behind a trail of singed nerves.

Oh, no.

No, no, no.

He knew.

"Please." I tried to tug the collar away from my skin. "I can't do what you think I can."

My whimpering achieved nothing. "If you fail in here, you have no use to me, and your life is forfeit," Arwood said. "For your sake, I hope your abilities haven't been exaggerated."

He knew. Oh God—he *knew.* The beast waited inside the cage of my chest, watching with interest. Memories of the coworker who'd attacked me bubbled up like the blood that had fallen from his lips.

His screams. My sobs. Glass and ripped curtains and upholstery smeared with blood, *so much blood,* so much *fear*—

Tears sprang to my eyes as another jolt wracked my body. A blowtorch to my bones. An electrical current racking my limbs. I clamped my mouth shut as I fell to my knees, contorting until the collar clicked off.

"You're a piece of shit, Sayer. Is nothing sacred to you?" Ri let loose another guttural cough, then crouched before me, heavy eyebrows meshed together. He gently wiped the tears rolling down my cheeks. His hands were cold, but his eyes were warm.

"Keanna." He murmured my name in a breathy roll. "It's alright. It might not seem like it, but whatever you're here for … you're doing me a favor."

Doubtful. "You wouldn't say that if you knew what I am. It's monstrous."

Ri swept my cheeks again. "A monster wouldn't cry, the way you are." His smile extended wide, revealing a chipped incisor. Assurance emanated from him, the kind that came from years of knowing yourself. Like he could look in the mirror without needing to look away. It was a smile I didn't deserve. "You're not one. Be brave."

I was a bomb, moments from detonation. Ri was moments from death, but comforting *me*.

My collar clicked. I shuddered again, backing out of his grasp and doubling over as fire rippled to my toes.

It didn't stop.

The creature in my chest struggled to get out. *No.* I couldn't. *I can't.*

"Whatever he wants from you, Keanna, give it to him." Ri still knelt before me. I tried to push him away, but he wouldn't move. "I'm not worth what you're feeling, sweetheart. Just do it, and then find a way to get yourself out of here."

A moan worked its way out and, oh, *it hurt*. Everywhere. My skull ached from holding it in.

But I couldn't hurt another person again.

If I kept my mouth shut …

My lungs—on fire. My throat—expanding. I couldn't breathe, couldn't feel anything except pain, *pain—*

I screamed.

⌒

For the second time in my life, I witnessed the power of the beast inside me.

My scream sliced through the air. The vases against the wall and the lightbulbs above shattered in synchronization, dimming the room as Ri stumbled backwards, clasping his ears, his head, like he was coming apart.

Because he was about to.

Any color in his face drained away. He gritted his teeth.

Pressure exploded from me like a wave. The room shuddered. Ri flew backwards, colliding with the wall and crumpling to the floor. His crimson mouth opened like a gaping fish, his head lolling to the side. Blood tracked from his ears, marred his cheeks, staining his sweater and dripping onto the plastic below. And his eyes—*oh God, his eyes.*

The shocks from the collar dissipated. I fell silent as Ri jerked, his fists melting into flat palms.

His body lay still.

I shuddered with a sob. The plastic crinkled as I fell beside Ri, pressure of a different kind building inside my head. I cast a shadow across him as I forced myself to take in the bloody, hollow pits where his eyes had been. Reconcile myself to what I'd done. What I'd stolen.

He was dead. Gone. He'd never speak or smile again because *I'd killed him.*

I had no right to even touch him, but I gripped his hands anyway, repeating the same two meaningless words over and over. He couldn't hear me anymore, couldn't feel me, but I squeezed him tight.

I'm sorry. I'm sorry.

The door opened to hesitant footsteps. Matej. The emotionless façade worn during my capture gave way to shaking hands as he gathered my discarded muzzle. I made no attempt to move as those hands reached for me. I wanted to tell him that—despite everything—the very idea of harming him too made me want to swallow the shards of glass littered across the floor. But I didn't. I couldn't guarantee his safety. He should be scared of me.

I was scared of me.

I welcomed the muzzle that Matej strapped back into place. He touched me like a grenade with its pin out. I turned back to Ri, knowing I'd see his haunted face in my dreams as I'd shredded him inside out.

Calm flooded my strangely empty chest. A few months ago, I'd never known I could do this, that a beast existed within. When I'd screamed for the first time during my attack, I'd been too overwhelmed, too distraught, to realize the change in myself. I recognized it now.

I felt … better. *Stronger*. The beast sat silenced. Content.

I really was a monster.

Arwood entered the room, pristine shoes scuffing the plastic. "Take this as an example of what happens when your usefulness runs its course."

If I could have, I would have gaped at him.

"Matej." He gestured to Ri's body. "Please deal with this."

I made a muffled murmur of protest, refusing to let Ri go, searching for humanity in Matej's face. How had it vanished so quickly?

He tugged Ri toward the door like a broken toy. My grip slowed him down. With a grunt, Matej pulled Ri free and dragged him from view. Where would they take his body? Would his family learn what had happened to him?

I couldn't stop picturing his hollowed eyes. They matched those of the dead man in the hotel room. In the aftermath, my father had held me, rocking me back and forth, telling me that I was okay, I was safe. I hadn't deserved his comfort, but I'd leaned into it all the same. Now, stagnant air chilled me while Arwood dispassionately observed my sorrow over the top of his phone, tapping at the screen. A guard stood behind him, weapon at the ready.

Is nothing sacred to you?

A shuffle outside alerted us to another armed guard leading someone else through the door. I saw dark hair and for one optimistic moment, I thought it was Ri—but no, this guy was younger, dressed in ripped jeans and a shirt that had probably been black a hundred washes ago. Brown tousled waves haloed around his head, the same color as the stubble shadowing his—*wait*. I squinted against the stark fluorescent light filtering in from the next room, leaning forward, concentrating on the scowl twisting his features.

No way.

My heart lifted. It couldn't really be him, could it? And yet …

His dark gaze ran over me. There was no recognition, only defiance toward the guard pushing him into the room. The triangle of freckles below his right eye … it was *him*. I tamped down on the frisson of excitement that erupted. What was he doing here? What had he done to become entwined with these people?

I pulled back at his hard expression, ashamed of the necessity of my muzzle. I wished I'd never realized who he was. It wasn't that I didn't want to look at him; I didn't want him to see *me* like this.

I remembered him as the beautiful boy with the beautiful smile. He wasn't smiling now.

CHAPTER FOUR

ONE YEAR AGO

THE TERRACE DOORS OF THE REPURPOSED OPERA HOUSE were flung wide, marking the start of the launch event. My father's central European branch had opened two months before, with tonight concluding my first assigned task as an intern. Technically, the executive assistant was responsible for such things, but I had two hands to help and two years to prove myself while I finished my business degree and applied for a permanent position. If I was going to sit in the same room as my father, I wanted to earn it.

An hour passed, champagne flutes were distributed, and I introduced myself to every couple, esteemed business partner, and prospective client on the guest list.

Elegant dresses and sharp tuxedos drifted beside the draped pearls and black silk covering the walls. Crisp flower arrangements adorned each circular table. I'd made no missteps. My dress was appropriate. My hair cascaded in perfect waves around my shoulders. I was in corporate schmoozing heaven.

I was … bloody hungry.

My father motioned for me. I gave one last look at the crowd—as if I was worried they'd suddenly stop enjoying themselves without my supervision—and paused. A boy wove between the attendees with the grace of a dancer. I stood on my tiptoes, trying to catch his face beneath his brown curls, but lost him behind senior executives taking a photo.

Probably for the best. I *was* working.

My father's arm came around me in a half-hug. Pink splotched his fair cheeks. He'd had too many late nights this week; it was good to see him enjoying himself.

"Well done, princess," he whispered. "You and Mariel nailed the brief."

His praise momentarily distracted me from my empty belly as he acknowledged my dress—an A-line affair of emerald-green satin with a hidden slit, making it 'the right amount of intriguing without losing classic appeal,' or so the shop attendant had said.

"Why, the dress looks lovely." Surprise colored his tone. "Not too small after all?"

Actually, it had been a smidge tight around the waist, but I'd made it fit. What was a few weeks of additional Pilates, cardio, and minimal calories if it meant sparing the humiliation of admitting I needed tailoring or a larger size?

"No, it's fine," I said, warming at his approval. "I must have been bloated on the day. Perhaps it *is* gluten."

"I'm not saying 'I told you so.'" He winked, nodding sagely at the circulating trays of canapes. "But skip those pastries, just in case. I know I am." His years-long dedication to the Atkins diet was rivaled only by his man-crush on Rob Lowe. He even looked a lot like the Hollywood actor. I'd picked up on it during a rewatch of *The Outsiders*, and it was a comparison my father had encouraged since. He patted his vest buttons, as if making a solemn promise to Dr Atkins and Rob Lowe himself. "This European food can be so heavy."

We'd built a roster of reliable dinner go-tos during our ten-year stint in Sydney; it would take some time to do the same here. "I organized light vegetarian dishes as the main course for both of us. No carbs."

"Excellent." He kissed my hair, then paused as the classical band played the opening notes of a song from our favorite ballet production. With a sigh, he relaxed. "You didn't."

"I did." We held *Giselle* sacred between us, revering the occasions we'd sat in the audience together, utterly transported. We

played Act one: Andante before client proposals, presentations—
or large events like this, when he had to address his staff. The slow,
smooth strings soothed our souls more effectively than a glass of
wine and an hour-long massage combined. "This is a big night for
you."

"Careful." He chuckled, wiggling his empty flute. "Another of
these and I'll start conducting the band you hired."

This happened often during our drives through the countryside: my father pretending to stand before an orchestra, his palms
waving above the steering wheel. In another life, he'd have been a
composer. Instead, he directed his company with the steady hands
of strategy and vision.

"I'd pay to see that," I said.

"You'd be the only one." He gave me a squeeze. "Shall we dance
once I finish my speech?"

My smile bloomed as I agreed, even while he raised a finger in
response to the person catching his attention. His "Get out there
and socialize, princess" trailed off as he strode toward them.

Though I'd met everyone in the ballroom, I knew no one well
enough to hitch my cart to them conversationally. His assistant
Mariel was nice, but even I could tell she wouldn't appreciate the
CEO's daughter hanging around. Besides, I was content to recharge
alone. My cheeks ached from smiling, and my lower back was stiff
from the posture I'd maintained over the last couple of hours.

When I turned, one of the attendants with a tray of those
damned mini pastries was heading for me, like a shark smelling
blood. I had five seconds to deliberate upholding my father's recom-
mendation versus the lure of consuming empty calories. It would
help suppress the light-headedness creeping behind my eyes. If
memory served, the healthier canapes had done their rounds; dinner was at least another hour away—the music would increase in
tempo soon, and I'd planned to amuse myself watching the crowd
dance—but I had no idea if I could last that long. Sweat prickled
underneath my hair.

Passing out? Probably not the best way to close out an otherwise successful night. Screw it. Pastry it was. Checking my father wasn't looking, I swiped one off the plate and made a beeline outside.

Glittering fairy lights enveloped the stout, manicured trees, lending an ethereal glow to the balmy evening. Behind the high stone wall encasing the garden stood a newly constructed theater with brightly lit upturned eaves; beyond it, the lights of Prague sprawled like an undulating blanket across the hills, halved by the dark swath of the Vltava river.

Tinkering violin strings followed my descent down the stairs and onto the plush grass. I smiled sweetly at the guests milling around the fountain and walked in the opposite direction between the hedges to the darkest, quietest corner of the property.

I'd no sooner taken a bite, moaning appreciatively at the fatty, dense mixture of bacon, spinach and cheese—and yes, lots and lots of gluten—when I noticed a reflective pair of black shoes. A figure leaned forward into view, silver moonlight highlighting his mischievous smile. He'd perched on a garden bench mostly hidden by the shrub wall. No wonder I hadn't seen him.

I squeaked, my hand going to my mouth.

Brown eyes sat above tanned, sloping cheekbones and defined lips. Tousled curls flowed about his face, blending into the darkness of the garden. "So, this is the official hiding place of the socially reclusive? I must have known something."

I immediately regretted my decision. Grease coated my fingers. Could anyone eat a pastry gracefully? He made a noise of protest as I threw what was left into the plants, running my tongue over my teeth.

"Hey—no! I didn't mean to interrupt. You looked hungry."

Wishing I had my mirror—I'd left my bag in the storage room—I dabbed my lips and fingers with a napkin, self-consciousness pricking my skin. I tried not to let it show as I offered my hand in greeting.

"I'm terribly sorry. I don't remember receiving you. I'm Keanna Backhus." *Please don't let me have spinach in my teeth.*

He stood. His tuxedo fit well, but he'd loosened his tie and unbuttoned the top of his shirt. A finger trailed over the inside of my wrist as we shook hands, sending a shiver across my body that wasn't unpleasant at all. He was the kind of attractive you couldn't help but stare at. I tried not to.

"Silas." His introduction came soft above the muffled swell of the orchestra inside the theater next door, a husky invitation to lean closer. "We came late. My father was supposed to attend but he's unwell. My mother's somewhere."

Mention of his parents had me glancing at the dregs of beer in the glass dangling from his other hand. I raised an eyebrow.

"Your staff checked." He smirked. "I'm legit."

At least eighteen, then. Early twenties, most likely. Though his voice rang deep, his cheeky, youthful confidence appeared at odds with his mature features. His accent was hard to place, a flat American delivery underscored by the slightest of European lilts rounding his vowels. It was a charming enough combination to spark an answering smile.

"I'm sorry your father's not well," I said, spinning my mental conversational wheel. Health: always a winner. Anything to stop me from gaping at him. "Does he work for Backhus Development?"

"I think he's a client of an associate's associate. Or something." Silas gestured to the bench he'd risen from. "These kinds of events give me a headache, but duty calls."

I sat beside him, mindful of my dress. "It was nice of you to accompany your mother, then."

"More like she needs to accompany *me*. She found her people as soon as she arrived, and I found my escape route. But it hasn't been a total loss ..."

His gaze caressed my face. Was he about to give me a compliment? My emerald dress was really nice—it brought out the color of my eyes—and he seemed pretty appreciative—

"I'm getting some decent horticultural inspiration out here," he said. "I mean, my geraniums are thriving, but I'm always on the lookout for ways to improve."

My expression must have revealed my dismay because he threw his head back, laughing.

I had to recover, fast. "Geraniums? Those plants basically take care of themselves. You'll have to do better than that if you're trying to impress me."

"Okay, you caught me." He straddled the bench, taking a final swig of his beer and placing his glass down. "Gardening isn't my forte, but I promise I have other talents."

I smiled slyly. "Like chatting up innocent, pastry-eating girls in dark corners?"

His grin came quick, his hand passing over the back of his neck. The ends of his hair brushed the tops of his ears; my fingers curled from wanting to touch it. "You win that round," he admitted. "Tell me one of yours."

We were cut off by the repetitive tinkle of tapped glasses in the ballroom behind us. I instinctively sought the non-existent watch on my bare wrist.

"Is that your cue?" He fished his phone out of his pocket, flashing the time in my direction. According to the run sheet, it was too early for dinner, which meant—

"Speeches. Yes."

Silas rose, buttoning his shirt, tightening his tie. "I'll escort you. I take my introvert duty of care very seriously."

I gasped in mock horror. "But someone might steal your hiding spot!"

He sighed, closing his eyes for a beat, then nodded solemnly. "You're worth it." He extended his elbow. "Shall we?"

His words made my stomach clench—in a good way. Which was silly. Right?

My musings quietened as I slipped my arm through his. This close, his spicy cologne invaded my senses. This close, my pulse was racing … but the nerves binding my body had settled. It was a strange but not unpleasant combination.

Silas scooped up his empty glass as we set off for the steps. He didn't expect the staff to clean up after him? I might be in trouble here.

My father stood on stage in front of the band, champagne flute in one hand, microphone in the other. His lips thinned as I entered, before unfurling into a movie-star-worthy smile for the audience. He must be nervous. Or …

I released my hold on Silas, realizing my proximity to him, and crossed my fingers as my father pushed the button. His smooth voice filled the room. Phew. I'd tested the acoustics five times, but still.

"Welcome, everyone, and thank you for welcoming Backhus Development's newest branch. The Czech Republic has long been thought as the crossroads of …"

He continued quoting the speech we'd prepared for him as I scoped the audience. Smiles, nods. Periodic polite applause from executives and prospective clients alike. Mariel, standing on the other side of the ballroom, gave me a discreet thumbs up. I returned it as my father recited his thanks.

"… my EA, Mariel Sinclair, who always goes above and beyond for me each day." My father met my eyes. "And of course—Ondra Laurant for allowing this event to happen. I promise, we picked the second-most expensive champagne for tonight." Chuckles resounded as our born-and-bred Czech CFO flashed his palms up, shaking his head. "And now, ladies and gentlemen, feel free to take to the dance floor. Supper begins at eight-thirty."

A frown creased my forehead as the band took over, disappointment puckering in my stomach like the edges of paper set alight. I swallowed it down, biting my lip. I was just an intern. Not even a paid employee. I shouldn't have expected acknowledgement. After all, I hadn't included myself in the speech; I'd felt a little vain doing so. Without that to prompt him, he'd probably forgotten.

Unless I'd done something wrong? He hadn't said so, but he

may not have wanted to draw attention to anything while we were in public. I'd have to do a post-review tomorrow.

My father made no move toward me. Instead, he swooped over to a couple, offering a healthy handshake to both and settling in for a lengthy chat. No dance, then. Was it because I'd left, rather than talk to everyone like he'd asked? Had he seen me take the pastry?

I glanced up to find Silas watching me. I feared he'd seen my thoughts all over my face, but he pointed in the direction of the swaying couples. "Come on. Dancing makes the time go faster. It'll be dinner before we know it."

Reserving another look for my father, I allowed Silas to lead me into the crowd. What if my father changed his mind? Was I even allowed to dance with others? I suppose this was a ball, and it might be a good look if I was seen getting into the spirit …

"Is this okay?" Silas's deep voice pulled my attention to the palms hovering beside my body.

Right. Dancing meant touching. Silas. Touching me.

I nodded. A hand settled on one side of my waist, the other scooping up my opposite hand. Even through the material of my dress, heat shot across my stomach. His spicy cologne played under my nose again, mixing with the leftover tang of his beer.

"I haven't danced in a while," I warned. I'd loved to dance when I was younger, but being shoved at the back of ballet class was a humiliating hint that my form—and curvy figure—didn't reach the desired standard. Watching had proved less disappointing. I shifted to the left and placed my hand in the correct position on Silas's shoulder. "And I know exactly this much."

His fingers tightened as cello strings bounced off the arched mural ceiling and the band transitioned to an instrumental rendition of a Coldplay song. "Conveniently," Silas said, "I know the rest."

With a small kick and a squeeze of his hands, he knocked the folds of my dress to the side, freeing up my legs and shifting us into a slow rumba box-step. Only four moves. Bless him. I watched our feet for the first few sets, getting a feel for moving from side to side, before I became confident enough to look up. He stood a head taller than me, his movements guiding and strong.

"One of those hidden talents you were referring to?" I guessed. He had a triangle of freckles under his right eye, emphasized by the glow of the cascading chandeliers. My fingers twitched with the urge to brush them. His brown gaze held something I didn't recognize. A … warmth. Like he enjoyed looking at me too. I swallowed, trying to offset my nerves and anticipation by focusing on stepping in time to the pitching flute chords.

"Blame my mother. She was intent on embedding some classic skills into the family. My older brother wanted to play football, but middle child syndrome made me a sponge in the worst way. You can thank her for my lightness of foot."

"That doesn't sound too bad."

"The teasing at school stopped once the jocks realized I was dating more girls than they were. And you didn't answer me before," Silas murmured, his breath tickling my temple as he readjusted his grip on my waist. Such a small movement, yet it still sent a flush across my chest. "Aside from executing kick-ass events, what else do you do?"

"How did you know I helped organize tonight?"

"I didn't, but thanks for confirming my hunch. What's important to you?"

Any answer that came to mind was somehow work or study related. I began to panic. "You go first."

"How about this: I ended up following my father's footsteps into chef-dom. I make mean gnocchi. The best you've ever tasted, guaranteed." He raised two fingers up from our clasped hands. One of them bore a signet ring. "I make it two ways. With a ragu—I prefer lamb, because why wouldn't you?—or in butter and sage. Gotta have the sage. And a little bit of parmesan."

Some guests had taken the invitation to dance with enthusiasm, whirls of material darting beside slower-moving couples like us. Thankfully, Silas seemed content to talk over joining them, our conversation flowing between passing snatches of German, Czech and accented English. No one had tapped me on the back, asking me to stop. My shoulders loosened, the knot of uncertainty releasing in my gut as my smile returned. This was … fun.

"Just a *little bit*, huh?"

"Absolutely. Contrary to popular opinion, you shouldn't overdo the cheese."

"Microwave brownies are the extent of my culinary talents. The kind you make in a mug?"

"Rustic. I like it. You bring dessert, and I'll bowl you over with my gnocchi."

"Appreciate the pun. Your style of pick-up line?"

His smirk became wicked. I could swear he'd drawn me a little closer. "If I was pulling out those lines, you'd know it. Besides, if we're going to be friends—garden buddies, to be more precise—small talk isn't going to cut it. I have specific selection criteria."

"As in, we must be able to engage in basic ballroom dancing and/or witty banter?"

His eyes lit up. He was enjoying this, too. "See? You're halfway there."

I couldn't stop smiling. My cheeks ached in the best way. "Now, that's setting me up for failure. I can hardly be expected to fulfill the requirements of exchanging witty banter if my dancing partner isn't witty."

He laughed. Something flipped inside me at the sound.

Another tinkle of glass accompanied the aroma of roast duck and sweet honey lacing the humid air. The couples around us swayed to a stop. "Thanks for the dance," I said, my grin turning coy. "Shall we trade blood types later?"

Silas led me to my table, releasing me but reaching for my hand instead. "You bet." He turned it upwards, planting a kiss in the center of my palm. Sparks shot down my arm. My breath hitched. "I hope to speak with you again soon, Keanna."

My stomach lurched, filling me with the sudden urge to grab

him. Keep him close. Like I was magnetized, unwilling to part with him. Startling, considering we'd just met.

I curled my fingers, as if capturing the remnants of his kiss in my palm. "I do, too." I hesitated, then added, "Garden buddies for life."

"I'll hold you to that." With a nod, he strode for one of the tables lining the back wall.

All through dinner I resisted the temptation to search for him, second-guessing my response and whether I should have given him my number. Would he have even wanted it? Had he been merely seeking a distraction to pass the time? Afterwards, I couldn't spot him, but with some of the attendees leaving, I could only assume he'd left too. Disappointment lodged deep, but I told myself it was for the best. And if the hours moved slower, well, at least the start of the night had flown by.

Once we returned home, I sat on my bed, my fist resting against my chest. The beautiful boy with the beautiful smile. My pulse fluttered, remembering how close he'd stood while we danced, even as I tried to keep a grip on reality. I was infatuated, that's all. Placing too much importance on a fleeting, flirtatious exchange.

But I still wanted to see him again. I hoped I would. Butterflies filled my belly as I fell asleep, excitement coursing through my blood …

PRESENT DAY

For months afterward, I'd scanned the room at events, hoping to see those flecked brown eyes leaping with amusement. I'd even roamed outside, searching the darkness for the boy who liked to hide. But I'd never found him. Months had passed. Silas had become a phantom of that night, a night I'd pedestalled in my mind and remembered to be more than it was.

Seeing him now was almost more surreal than what had just happened with Ri.

I held my breath. Silas regarded me, too, confusion replacing his scowl.

"Why am I here?" His voice was like that night in the garden, a husky burr inside the confining room.

Arwood slipped his phone into his jacket pocket. "I have a tool I require your special skills to help wield. She screams, and people die. Find a way for me to control it."

My eyes darted to Silas in horror, but his expression remained unchanged as he scratched his chin. He had a black band around his wrist, just like Ri's. "I'm … not following."

"You're smart. You'll figure it out." Arwood moved to the door. "Solve my problem, or I'll put a bullet through both of your heads."

The door dragged across the plastic until it closed, leaving me and Silas in unforgiving silence.

CHAPTER FIVE

Y STOMACH WAS A STONE, THE ROOM TOO SMALL FOR the tension filling it. Arwood might have said something about 'special skills,' but Silas wasn't doing much of anything. Those once-laughing eyes were now flat, focusing on the puddles of Ri's blood at his feet.

A guard tapped the window and tilted his gun at us.

Silas reached for the straps behind my head, undoing the clasp and lifting the muzzle away from my face. The skin around his eyes tightened, but his features remained otherwise still. I searched for any sign of recognition. There was none.

He didn't remember me. I wasn't sure if that made this better or worse. I decided on worse.

I passed my palms over my nose, removing the remnants of my tears. "You shouldn't have done that," I whispered.

"Didn't have much of a choice," Silas replied, glancing at the guard.

The collar clicked.

More shocks were coming.

Not him.

I rose and ran for the window, panic drawing my chest tight as I smacked my handcuffs on the pane. I'd expected glass; it wobbled, a thick crack in one layer. Plastic. That was why it hadn't shattered earlier, like the vases and light bulbs had.

"Please! Turn it off. I'll do anything you want."

Arwood stood beside a woman. Both monitored me with the

detached nature of scientists. Thick red hair contrasted against the woman's black shirt.

"Mariel?" My father's assistant. The split-second thrill of recognition faded. "Why am I here? Where's my father? Does he know where I am?"

Though she exchanged glances with Arwood, she made no move to help me.

Had she told him what I'd done to Thomas? Betrayal choked me.

"Mariel, please!"

Still nothing. I made eye contact with Arwood and the guard, appealing to whatever soul they had left. "Whatever you want from me, you can have." My vision wobbled through my tears, but I brushed them away. No crying. Tears had no effect here. "But *please*. Don't make me do this." *Not to him.*

My father would have detested my pleading, but I didn't care. My pride meant nothing in here. If I was a puppet, Arwood held my strings.

I didn't realize how much I'd banked on him changing his mind until he gave a single, condemning shake of his head and looked past me to Silas.

Silas blinked, like he had no better idea of what Arwood wanted than I did. My panic alarmed him—as it should have. Ri's lifeless body flashed in my mind.

I went to the door. It didn't move. I tried again. The handle rattled. I kicked it, aiming the heel of my boot at the center and—hopefully—the weakest point of the door.

Silas stepped closer. "What's about to happen?"

I ignored him, my knee jarring from the impact. I had no time to explain. Another kick. No give. Ramming the door with my shoulder sent pain flaring up into my skull.

Nothing was working. *Nothing was working.*

His words turned into white noise as the shocks started from my collar, squeezing my brain like a vice. I fell to my knees. My help-lessness only enhanced the pain. No, no, *no*.

Inside my chest came a purr from the beast. *Set me free.* If I screamed, the pain would stop.

If I screamed, *Silas* would stop.

Stars crossed my vision. My chest heaved, like it was about to tear open. An ice pick lanced my spine, vibrating my bones. I no longer felt the cold, bristling plastic floor underneath my knees.

The beast roared. I screamed, releasing a wall of pressure toward Silas.

It happened in a split second, but his brown eyes—originally wide with bewilderment—narrowed. His stance shifted, as if bracing himself, and a ribbon of violet swept across both of his irises. He threw his hands between us.

An egg-shaped, sapphire barrier curled over his body, protecting him from the onslaught of my bone-crushing explosion. The room shuddered, black plastic ripping away from the concrete beneath. Silas stood behind the transparent shield, forehead furrowed and teeth gritted. *Alive.*

The heat consuming me faded. I sagged, my scream dissolving into a whimper. Silas lowered his hands, and the barrier fell. Perspiration dotted his forehead. A strangled sigh escaped. He braced against his knees, panting like he'd run a mile.

The intercom clicked. "Looks like those bullets won't be necessary after all," Arwood said.

∽

The familiar weight of my muzzle returned. I was blindfolded and marched outside—the gravel scattering from my boots—then into another building.

Scents of hardwood and furniture polish crept underneath the leather, the temperature fluctuating as they led me down corridors and up flights of stairs. The guiding hand pulled me to a stop as a *beep* sounded, then pushed me forward, unlatching my handcuffs and removing my blindfold. I blinked, adjusting to the bright room, as the door shut behind me with a *clunk*.

I wasn't sure what I'd expected. My day had taken a downward trajectory into depths from which I'd never recover. But … this?

The room had the cold, clinical efficiency of a jail cell. Wafer-thin carpet lay over freezing concrete. A metal bed frame held a single mattress, white sheets strung tight. One chair and table, both metal, both bolted down. The only concession to 'atmosphere': vertical teal blinds framing the barred window. The solid white door I'd entered had a peephole on the outside. No handle.

I strode to the window. A small electronic box with a flashing red button sat on the sill. I reached through the bars. Locked, of course.

The purple-orange sunset glowed above the perimeter, casting long shadows over the garden hedges and the paneled greenhouse tucked between them. From my vantage point, I probably stood in the large mansion I'd walked past earlier today. The fact I couldn't see the smaller building I'd been taken to, or the gates, told me I probably overlooked the back of the estate.

A lot of 'probably's there. Too many for my peace of mind. I indulged myself and tried the window again. It was a token gesture. Even if I could get it open and squeeze past the bars, the multi-story drop on the other side ensured an escape attempt would result in broken legs.

My muzzle remained in place, the lower half of my face hot. I tugged at the straps until it released, trailing my nails over the unblemished leather. It represented so much. My capture. Demeaning protection against others. Arwood's ownership.

The man I'd murdered.

At once, my stomach curdled and the tightness behind my eyes returned. I'd killed someone today. Another someone.

The hardest part with Ri would be not knowing who he was and why he'd been there. I'd known Thomas, the man who had attacked me months ago. He'd worked for my father for years. We'd inferred he'd either been working for someone else or had wanted to ransom me to pay off his debt. Afterwards, I'd held on to this like a life vest in my sea of guilt: Thomas had sought trouble first.

Ri hadn't done anything except be in the same *room*. If he was guilty of anything in his life, it wasn't from deeds done to me.

And Silas. I would have killed him too, if not for … well, what the hell had that been, exactly? The way violet had rippled across his irises wasn't human. What he'd summoned to shield against me hadn't been human.

But then again, neither was I.

The possibilities Silas presented hurt my head. I hadn't fathomed that there could be other supernatural capabilities in the world. That would have meant acknowledging my own, and I hadn't wanted to. Had Arwood been coached by Mariel on what to expect, or he was like one of us, with power hidden from the world? Or worse, was he a collector of freaks, the more broken the better? I certainly fit that category, though I wasn't sure about Silas. He hadn't appeared scared. More … resolved.

And he hadn't recognized me. After months of hoping I'd see him again, I now felt completely irrelevant. He'd been a meteorite, soaring into my life; I'd made barely a blip in his. I'd been naive to think otherwise. I hardly knew him, and if today was any indication, he was caught up in everything I should steer clear of.

Keanna, seriously. Priorities.

My knee ached, a dull reminder of my injuries and how filthy I was. That was something I could control. A door adjacent to the entrance stood ajar. Behind it revealed the set-up of a low-class gym locker room, the kind I wouldn't enter without shoes, bleach, and a prayer against germs: cheap, white vinyl bench tops, blue tiled floor, a toilet and a shower separated by a rusting grate. This door shut, thankfully; I hadn't seen any cameras in the room or in here, but I took no chances.

After showering, I glanced in the mirror. I knew I wouldn't like what I'd see, but I still inhaled sharply and gripped the basin. My green eyes were too bright in my pale face, bloodshot and rimmed with tears.

This is what a killer looks like. It didn't matter that I hadn't wanted to kill them. They'd died all the same.

The black collar around my neck was just over an inch wide, clashing with my wet blonde hair. I'd paid it no mind as I'd washed, numbly figuring that if it electrocuted me in the shower, I'd get what I deserved. I slipped two fingers beneath it, but the extra leverage did nothing. Whatever it was, however it was secured ... it wasn't coming off.

An animalistic urge rose: to scream, destroy, try to escape. I swallowed it. The beast had no restraint, wouldn't hesitate to kill again. I refused to feed it.

The sun had set once I emerged in my flimsy white towel. I had nothing to change into, having shoved my stained, bloody clothes and boots under the sink. I'd burn them before I wore them again. Worse, whether by stress, hormones from my contraceptive implant, or bad luck, my period had started early. The wadded toilet paper in my underwear threatened to steal whatever dignity I had left.

The bed sank like a sponge under my butt as I stared at my reflection in the darkened window. Somewhere out there, my father would be searching for me. My heart ached at not being able to contact him. To tell him I was alive, if nothing else.

The beast sat still, my companion in all emotions. *Murderer.*

I had no idea what to do. For now, I curled into a ball on the bed and pulled the sheet up, hunger and despair lulling me into an uneasy sleep.

BEFORE

Blood and death surrounded my birth.

My father found me nestled among the bodies of my mother and those who'd come to her aid during labor. I'd torn into this world too early and too quickly, forcing her to trade her last breaths for my first.

Whenever I questioned my right to exist, my father reminded me my mother would have considered the trade worth it. I'd been clutched in her lifeless arms, my health and well-being her only priority in her final moments.

Of course, it wasn't until two months ago that my father had finally shared the full story. I'd never known the truth of why my mother had passed, alone and vulnerable and exposed. How the others had met their deaths, forming a radius of broken bodies around her. After my attack, I understood why.

She'd killed them.

A beast had been trapped inside of her, too.

CHAPTER SIX

What felt like a minute after closing my eyes, a sharp rap came on the door. I rose from the bed like a soldier at attention, shivering and yanking the sides of my towel closed.

"I can see you're awake," said a feminine voice. "I'm coming in." A beat passed. "I'm not gonna hurt you."

The door opened to a young woman flanked by armed guards. She wore black leggings and a white cut-off shirt, black hair skimming her dainty shoulders. Our single similarity was in height (not much of an accomplishment; wearing boots, I hit five foot six).

She waltzed inside alone, kicking a doorstop into place.

"Sorry you've had to wait so long," she said, tossing her black jacket onto the floor. "'Twas asshole day on the roads." She perched on the edge of the bed, folding a black-booted foot underneath her butt.

I had no idea what to make of her casual disposition. Since I'd been kidnapped, I'd been treated like a bomb that was seconds from going off. Yet this girl didn't appear remotely concerned about being in my vicinity without my muzzle in place.

"I'm Anika," she added.

I sank onto the chair, glancing between Anika, the entrance, and the guards on the other side facing the hall. I wasn't an idiot. The open door didn't mean anything—they wouldn't go to the effort to lock me down only to make it so easy for me to escape now. "What does Arwood want with me?"

Anika laced her fingers around her knee. Black, shaded tattoos coated one of her olive-toned arms. Like Ri and Silas, a black band covered her wrist, blending with the serpent tattoo circling her forearm. "Cutting out introductory pleasantries? I thought you business types thrived on small talk. Arwood needs your help."

Her response was so matter-of-fact, I snorted. "Don't people usually ask first if they need a favor?"

"Arwood's more the 'beg for forgiveness' sort—and before you jump in," she said as my mouth opened, "I know, okay? Typical white male with questionable methods. I'm not here to defend him. I'm here to chat."

"I want to go home. *Please.*"

"How's this: I'll trade you. Clothes for a conversation. And something cute to sleep in?"

My grip tightened on my towel. I was growing more and more uncomfortable with how much skin I was showing. It overrode my instincts to be accommodating. "I shouldn't have to trade anything. He kidnapped *me.*"

"This isn't a trick. You've got nothing to lose right now. If you want to tell me to go fuck myself afterwards, all power to you, but hear me out first."

I squirmed in my seat, weighing up the staying power of the toilet paper wadded in my underwear. New clothes would definitely help, if not a single hardy tampon. "Okay. Fine. I assume you're one of Arwood's cronies, so tell me: where am I? Why did he take me?"

Her tongue poked the inside of her cheek. "I get you're doing the wounded animal thing, but make no mistake: I'm no one's bitch, Backhus."

I pressed my lips together, jutting out my jaw and feeling about three inches tall. Anika could have been my ticket out of here, and I'd just blown it. "Sorry."

"We're in Arwood's estate, and what I said before is true: you're here because Arwood needs our help."

Our help? "As in—yours too?"

"You got your thing." She pointed to the muzzle sitting in the corner. "I've got mine."

What the hell did she mean by that? I shifted, swallowing my question. Was Anika hinting she extended beyond human capability, like Silas? Or … was she like me and my mother, a ba—

No. Naming something made it real, gave it power. The beast in my chest didn't need any more of that.

As politely as I could, I asked, "Why does he want *me*?"

"Arwood manages multiple territories across Prague. He either owns businesses in these zones, or they pay taxes in exchange for his protection and other crap I won't go into." At my bleak expression, she went on. "It's not an easy existence to maintain. We operate on the edge of a knife, and sometimes people try to upset the balance. Someone was stolen from him recently, and he hasn't been successful in locating her."

"My father has lots of money. He'll give anything for—"

"You can't *buy* the leverage your supernatural juice gives Arwood. That's the point. Some people collect Bentleys and Rolexes. Arwood has people like us working for him. And now—you. Though we already give him a hell of an advantage, he hopes you'll tip the scales in his favor while we search."

One of the guards in the hall readjusted their grip on their gun, but otherwise stayed put. I swallowed, lowering my voice. "Why not involve the police like a normal person? Did he report her missing? Unless …" I trailed off as Anika maintained unapologetic eye contact. Mentions of territories, my abduction, the killing of Ri … "Unless he can't. What is Arwood, some kind of gangster?"

"I wouldn't call him that to his face, but potato, potahto."

Oh, God. He *was* a collector of freaks. "What makes you think I'd work for someone like that?" Even as I said it, I knew it was redundant. People like Arwood didn't ask. I sighed, trying to smooth my hair. Without a brush, it would be a snarled mess in a few hours. "I don't want to do this. I don't want to be involved." *Please, let me go home.*

"I'm sorry you weren't given a choice. Not many of us are."

Hope inflated my ribs. "He kidnapped you, too?"

Anika shook her head.

"Then why are you here?"

"Because I wanna be," she said. "Now, Silas is working on a solution to the whole muzzle shebang. If he's successful, you'll be able to do what Arwood needs you to do. *But*—your cooperation is gonna make the whole experience much better. For yourself."

A solution? Talk about being cryptic. "What do you mean, *if* Silas is successful?"

"He will be."

My pessimism reared its head again, reminding me of Arwood's words about bullets and heads. "But if he's not?"

"He's motivated. He will be."

"What are you? What is *he*?"

"Simplest explanation? We're mages. *Maspotem*, if you wanna get all official."

"What is *that*?"

"A different sort to you, babe. And that's all Arwood cares about."

Anika's tone had become clipped, as if she was losing patience with my questions. Her foot wiggled as she popped a piece of gum in her mouth. I wanted to ask her how Silas came to be here, if he'd always been with Arwood, but pride and suspicion stopped me. I couldn't trust Anika or Silas without knowing all the facts, and something told me I wasn't going to get them in this room.

"Seems like extreme measures to find someone. Who is Arwood looking for?"

"His daughter."

I bit my lip, sympathy and irony whirring in my thoughts. I couldn't imagine what it would be like to lose a child. But *I* am someone's child, and he'd kidnapped *me*. My father would be losing his mind.

"Look." Anika gave a gusty sigh. "I know this is a lot, but this is how Arwood operates, okay? He enforces compliance, but he's also aware he'll get a better outcome if people cooperate. And he's open to negotiating with you."

Willingly scream? Willingly kill people? "I can't do that for him. I—I won't."

"You're gonna be here regardless. Don't you wanna be more comfortable?"

"I want to go home."

"Well, you have until Silas does his thing to reconsider. For now, a deal's a deal. This house looks ancient, but we have access to high-speed internet and overnight delivery like everyone else. So"—she pulled her phone from her bra—"what can I get for you?"

I pressed my thighs together. The wadded toilet paper would fail me soon, and I'd leak everywhere. Yet the idea of admitting this discomfort proved more challenging than enduring it. What if she'd asked this question so she knew what to withhold to make me more miserable?

Underneath immaculate winged eyeliner, Anika's dark brown eyes assessed me from head to toe. "A brush, perhaps?"

My hair obviously looked as good as I felt. I nodded.

Again, she studied me. "I can gauge everything but your shoe size. What is it?"

I told her, and she punched notes into her phone. A shiver wracked my body, my lip trembling as I tightened the towel around myself.

Anika rose, using her foot to kick her jacket up off the floor. She shrugged it back on, her face softening. "Look, I'm sorry this happened to you, Backhus. Life sometimes serves steaming piles of shit you don't deserve. But you have a choice here. I hope you'll take it."

I was in danger of crying again. I avoided her eyes so she wouldn't see how uncomfortable I was, even as years of conditioning kicked in, forcing me to respond. "Thank you."

Within thirty minutes, I had a tray of food and a bag of folded clothes—presumably someone's on lend—on top of some grooming products. *And* tampons. She may have been working for some crazy mafia boss and not the least bit trustworthy, but in that moment, Anika was an angel in Doc Martens.

CHAPTER SEVEN

THREE DAYS. THREE DAYS OF MISSED SCHEDULES AND work, three hopeless mornings watching the sun rise. Three days without my father.

Time passed, crawling, then lurching. I barely slept, alternating between embracing my deserved misery and resenting it, making bargains to the universe for my escape. For someone action-oriented, the inability to leave the confines of my room became a different kind of torture. I missed my phone and the soothing email *dings* more than was probably healthy. The beast, frustrated I wouldn't consider using it, stayed silent while I checked every inch of the room for a way out. The changeable September Prague weather assaulted the window I stared out of for hours on end: rain, sun, fog, rain again. I cried more in those three days than in my entire life, and the only person I saw was Anika when she delivered meals. I barely touched the food with my daily movement so reduced—I didn't need the calories, and I still had that dress to fit into when my father rescued me—but it was a good excuse for interaction.

True to her promise, the morning after I'd arrived in the room, so did the packages. My despair temporarily succumbed to the shallow joy of trying on clothes and finding ways of styling them. It wore thin quickly.

Though Anika kept reminding me I could cooperate, she wasn't insufferable about it. Her brief visits became bright points, along with the novels she brought me to read. Arwood's decision or hers, I appreciated the distraction all the same.

Mid-afternoon on the fourth day, there was a knock on my

door. It was out of sync with Anika's usual timetable, so I leapt to my feet.

Anika kicked the door stop in, but she remained in the hallway, alone. "Silas's finished."

My stomach dropped.

"And Arwood wants you."

⌒⌒

"So, are you a psychic, as well as a banshee?"

Anika's casual summation of what I was—a *banshee*—made me stumble in the heeled beige sandals she'd purchased for me as we walked down the hallway. It was a supernatural label I'd resisted putting on myself. It was a label I'd resisted, period. I had no room in my head for it.

"What do you mean by that?"

She gestured to my hair and clothes. She'd ordered me basics like jeans, pants, skirts and shirts. Some were more casual than what I'd normally reach for, but in the absence of anything else, I'd made do. Today, I'd paired one of the nicer black A-line skirts with a crisp white shirt and the chunky gold necklace I'd worn the day I was abducted. It was the closest match to what I'd been wearing while shopping; if I managed to escape for even a second, dressing like this would help civilians recognize me against the details my father was no doubt circulating about my appearance.

"It's as if you knew today would be the day," she said. "You look ready to meet the Queen."

Someone who lived in black leggings thought I was over-dressed? I could deal with that. Armor came in all forms, and mine was looking my best and being prepared. "Wishful thinking?" I replied.

I'd half expected to be forced back into the muzzle, but Anika wasn't even holding it. We passed hardwood doors and jutting win-dow-filled hallways bathed in the afternoon sun. The atmosphere depicted old wealth; the paintings lining the walls were a mixture of landscapes and abstract designs inside gilded gold frames, and the thick mahogany carpeted floors sank underfoot. Anika charged forward. I struggled to keep up.

"Making a quick detour," she said. "Gotta grab Silas."

His name twisted my gut. I tried to ignore it. "It feels like a museum here. Where is everyone?"

"It's got that vibe, right? The house was built late-1600s in the Baroque style, extended three times, and restored a decade ago by Arwood's late stepmother with modern interior features. At the risk of sounding too *Beauty and the Beast*"—she grinned—"we're in the west side of the manor. It's rarely used. Anyway, Arwood needs you outside."

Arwood needs you, like I was something he could fetch. I gritted my teeth, my collar a constant reminder of his influence, the pain he had caused me. The possibilities of what he wanted me for iced my blood.

I tottered—there was no other word for it—after Anika as she speed-walked down two narrow staircases and through three sets of doors into a room with sterile white concrete walls.

It had the design of a lab, but instead of scientific equipment and white coats, a small queue of guards stood before a table supporting a silver machine. A man and a woman clothed in black, guns and knives strapped to their thighs, faced a third person bent over the table. His faded mauve T-shirt stretched across broad shoulders and brushed his black jeans. Even without seeing his hair, I recognized him.

"How goes it?" Anika asked.

Silas was threading a silver chain through a metal loop that held a white gemstone, his forehead pinched in concentration. "Did you bring coffee?" he asked as he lowered the necklace over the guard's head.

"Negative."

A beat of disappointed silence passed as Silas inspected the pendant, then gave the all-clear. "But I asked nicely."

The guard turned, his eyes widening a fraction as he noticed me standing behind him. I met his striking blue gaze, recognition flaring. Short, neat brown hair framed his carved cheekbones. A light dusting of stubble coated a strong, angular jaw. I'd remember the phone-stealer outside of the jewelry store any day, wearing his Ray-Bans or not.

He nodded to Anika and strode for the exit. At least I'd been right about him. Zeina would have been proud of me, spotting a tail like that—

Zeina.

Was she alright? I hoped my father had found her, at the very least. Had that been Mariel's fault, too?

"It'd be an irresponsible use of caffeine." Anika handed Silas another necklace. "Any more and you'll keel over."

Silas said nothing as he lowered the chain, inspecting the pendant, then dismissed the female guard.

"We've got a date with Arwood. And"—Anika gestured toward me—"I brought a friend."

Our eyes met, anticipation making my heart race. Silas's hair looked like he'd been running his hands through it, his face pale under the harsh fluorescent light, eyes bloodshot, but still just as stunning to me as the night we'd first met. Twelve months had broadened his shoulders and filled out his chest. His shirt pulled in all the right places as he offered a handshake.

"I'm Silas."

His palm was callused in a way it hadn't been a year ago. A shiver stole down my body as one of his fingers grazed the inside of my wrist … but his greeting was perfunctory, the kind you'd give a stranger you assumed you'd never meet again. I'd hoped he was pretending not to know me in front of Arwood, but the remoteness in Silas's gaze couldn't have been more different than the dancing warmth in the ballroom.

He really didn't remember me.

"Keanna." I swallowed my disappointment, releasing him. It

was better this way. I needed to stay objective. "Sorry about … the other day."

Silas gave a casual shrug. Medical tape and a thatch of cotton wool nestled in the crook of his elbow, like he'd taken a blood test. "Perks of the job."

On the table behind him lay necklaces on black material; the pendants were plain white gemstones, with either leather or silver chains threaded through a hole at the top. Anika trailed a crimson fingernail over the gem closest to her. "That's the last? Everyone's got one?"

"Everyone's got one," Silas confirmed. "With one notable exception."

She prodded a silver chain, smirking. "Pass. I prefer gold, anyway."

"Anika mentioned you're working on something?" I came closer. "A solution?"

Silas nodded. "This is it."

The milky gems reflected the artificial light overhead. They were cleaved into circles a few inches in diameter, sides smooth like a coin. "White jade, right?" I leaned in. "What are these for?"

It grew so quiet the persistent buzzing from the fluorescent bulbs swelled to fill the room. "In a nutshell," Silas said, "they're supposed to protect everyone. From you."

I fought the sudden, childish urge to run away. I wouldn't consider myself socially adept with people my own age. Most didn't appreciate discussions on agile methodology, and my idea of a good time tended to clash with theirs; mine didn't involve staying up late, or partying. Yet … in a place where I couldn't trust anyone, and nothing was certain—not even my own body—I needed to adapt *somehow*.

"Huh." It took everything I had to keep my voice nonchalant. "I've already got one necklace on; another might overdo it. Do these come in earrings? I don't want to be left out of the anti-Keanna bomb squad."

The tension popped, and Silas smirked.

Anika's phone rang. She brought it to her ear. "I'll send someone to escort you guys. Liss, hey—" Her words faded as the door closed behind her, leaving Silas and me alone.

"Are you okay?" he asked.

Of course not, but there was no point telling him so. He studied my face the way he had in the ballroom. Did he really not remember? The ends of his hair caressed two leather cords disappearing underneath his shirt. One of the necklaces he was moving from the table into a box, perhaps? My cheeks flushed as silence unfurled between us like smoke.

"How did you do it?" I asked.

He raised both eyebrows, gesturing to the machine beside him—a gem cutter, I realized now—but I shook my head.

"No. In that room. You're ... different."

"So are you."

I swallowed. "Until recently, I didn't know I was."

The door swung open, revealing Matej. A black band circled his wrist and a jade amulet hung from his neck. "Come," he ordered, letting the door swing closed. Either Matej wasn't a fan of waiting, or he had other young women to abduct from the streets in a time-sensitive manner.

Silas grabbed the box, then held the door open. I passed by so close his spicy, clean scent flew up my nose, adding to my general awareness of him. I could *feel* him, my skin sparking from his proximity, like heat from a fireplace. Just like the night at the ball, the sensation proved both comforting and confusing.

Once we emerged, Matej took off for the brightly lit double doors at the end of the hallway. Our footsteps echoed in his wake. I'd followed Anika in an overwhelmed daze earlier; I had to start paying attention if I was going to get out of here.

"I shielded myself," Silas said, belatedly answering my question, his tone soft. "Diverted the energy of your scream. Anika and I, our kind ..."

"*Maspotem*, she said?"

"We have three different capabilities." His husky voice delivered this matter-of-factly, like we were discussing the synopsis for a TV show. "I'm a defensive mage."

I shoved aside my disbelief. I'd seen him do it. There was no point bargaining with my memory, trying to convince myself this wasn't real. I couldn't have made up how he'd doubled over afterwards, as if he'd been sprinting. "It looked like an effort."

"Our magic is like a muscle, I guess. The ability to shield against something isn't infinite. That day in the room more so, because I had no idea what to expect—kind of like when you're preparing for someone to give you an uppercut and they hit you with a truck instead."

"You said the necklaces should protect people against me. Like you did."

"Arwood tasked me with transmuting that protection. The stones absorb my power, and I've linked them to, well, *me*. Whoever wears them borrows my abilities when a banshee scream triggers it."

There was that *b* word again, chipping at my soul like an ice pick. "Sounds like there's a catch in there somewhere."

He shrugged. The hand closest to me went into his jeans pocket, his arm nudging mine. The space between us felt heavy, like the humidity from an incoming storm. My skin prickled at the contact. I angled my body away in a subtle attempt to add some distance.

"There is," Silas said, "but it doesn't affect you. Or them. If you scream again and his people are in your proximity, they're protected."

Protective amulets for ordinary people? The side of me engaged in business acumen contemplated the commercial and military implications. The other side of me—the human side, the side not swayed by numbers—was unsettled for what this could mean for Silas. For others like him. "Did you know you could do this with your power?"

"No." He delivered his answer without inflection, nodding to the security as we came closer. Warning me to watch what I said?

These guards, too, had raised scars across their faces. They'd opened the glass doors for Matej, standing to the side to allow us through.

Warmth rushed in, the breeze tossing my hair as we made our way outside. Though it was late in the season, the air smelled of summer—of hyacinth and heat. We'd exited from the right side of the mansion, near the gardens, heading toward the small building against the perimeter I was unfortunately very acquainted with. I focused on the repetitive crunch of gravel under my sandals to keep myself calm.

Once out of earshot, Silas spoke again. "I had to amplify my power in a way Arwood could use. It took a while, but I figured it out in the end."

There was a lot he wasn't saying, but he didn't need to. His drawn expression, his tense shoulders when we'd found him in the lab ... he was tired. Bone tired. Like it had been days since he'd slept properly. I had the strange urge to cup his cheek, offer him some kind of comfort. I kept my hands to myself. "What would have happened if you couldn't?"

Silas remained silent for a few moments, his curls shifting in the wind. "It doesn't matter. I did."

The emotionless way he spoke bothered me. Did he willingly work for Arwood, like Anika? My fingers went to my collar again, smoothing over the blunt edges.

Everyone was protected against me. I wouldn't have to wear the muzzle again. A win, but something about it felt wrong. Silas watched as I tugged at the metal band, worrying at it like you would a chipped tooth with your tongue.

"Can you control it?" he asked. Eyebrows drawn together, he almost looked concerned.

But was he?

I thought back to how my chest had pulled tight, like it would break open if I didn't scream. The beast purred, delighted at the memory. "Control it?"

"You know that muscle analogy? Magic has the potential to

expand, and you can grow stronger with repeated use. If you learn your limitations, you can start to work within them."

We walked out of the shade cast by the seventeenth-century mansion and into the orange glow of the setting sun, passing by the weapon-toting security team. A juxtaposition of past, present and now—the supernatural. I pondered how crazy this all seemed. How the world I'd known could co-exist with the reality Silas presented. Him, a mage. Me, a myth. *A banshee.*

I'd had days to get used to the idea I wasn't alone in my strangeness, and months to reconcile with being different to other humans in a way that wouldn't benefit me at all. The idea of trying to find a way to rein in the beast was too much. Leashing it meant I would have to—at some point—let it out on purpose, and I didn't want to do that. If I could help it, I'd never do it again.

If the beast sat inside a box in my chest, it was shut and padlocked, thank you very much.

"I don't want to." The faces of Ri and Thomas floated in my mind. "You saw what it does."

"All the more reason to try. Or someone's gonna find a way to control it for you." His eyes fell to my collar again.

I changed the subject. "I assume you know why Arwood's summoned us?"

Silas's throat bobbed, his voice turning emotionless again. "Arwood's been suffering guerrilla attacks in his territories for the last two weeks. One of his businesses was broken into this morning. They attempted to destroy the server room."

I didn't miss the choice of words. "Unsuccessfully?"

"Indeed. Aside from having an apparent death wish, Arwood wants to learn why they tried at all."

A sickening sense of foreboding washed through me as we reached the building.

CHAPTER EIGHT

BEFORE MY ABDUCTION, BLACK PLASTIC WAS MERELY AN industrial tool. Painters use it. Construction workers use it. I certainly paid it no mind in my day to day. Now, it will forever mean something else to me.

Death has a smell. It's the furnace of bleach up your nose. The rusty tang of blood in the air. The sharp vinegar of crunching black plastic, concealing sins.

Plastic rustled beneath the knees of five thieves inside the walls of what I'd come to think of as the 'execution room'. It was an ugly place to be, and ugly places deserve ugly names.

The five—two women, three men—were bent over on their knees, wrists raw underneath zip-ties. Everyone wears primal fear differently. Three unabashedly revealed theirs in wide eyes, slack mouths. The other two were different. One was sweat-slicked, rage pulsing beneath his flushed skin, accusing gaze sharp like a knife-blade. The woman to his right stared at a point on the floor like she'd already ascended beyond this life and was waiting for her body to catch up.

There was no way in hell I wanted to go back into that room, but Matej forced me and Silas inside. My muscles locked up as Matej moved behind one of the men, resting the gun against his sweaty scalp.

Opposite the thieves, Arwood stood with Anika, flanked by guards on either side.

At Arwood's nod, Matej's gunshot sliced through the air. My inhalation caught as a wet spray of blood and the sickening thud of a falling body followed in quick succession. The woman beside the dead man shuddered, her sobs the only other sound in the room.

I couldn't swallow past the horror coating my tongue, couldn't think above the ringing in my ears and the pounding of my heart. Watching Matej take a life with practiced ruthlessness made me complicit. If I left this room, I'd never be the same.

Matej went to the crying woman next.

I gasped, bending into the beginnings of a lunge. Silas's hand shot out, grabbing my forearm. He answered my glare with an intense one of his own, shaking his head an infinitesimal amount. *No.*

How could I do nothing? How could *he* stand there, allowing this?

As Matej placed the gun against the woman's head, Arwood asked her what information they were trying to steal from him. Who had hired her.

Tears thickened the woman's voice as she shook her head, desperation clipping her words. "I don't know! Please, I wasn't told, I just had to wait in the ca—"

A gunshot cut off her pleas. Her body slumped.

I flinched, tears in my eyes.

Arwood beckoned in my direction. For one terrifying moment I thought he was pointing toward me, but he said, "The necklaces, please."

Silas squeezed my arm before he pushed away from the wall. His scuffed Timberlands stepped over the dead bodies in his path like they were nothing more than garbage.

I wanted to wash my arm under scalding water to remove his touch—until I noticed the stiff way he passed the box to Arwood. Tension corded his neck and hardened his mouth. Nose flaring, he squeezed his empty fists as he walked back.

Oh.

Arwood fished a necklace from the box, snapping it shut. Everyone in the room already wore one, except me and Anika. And the three remaining prisoners.

I froze. Like a small animal in headlights, if I just *didn't move*, Arwood wouldn't see me. If I *didn't breathe*, he'd forget I was here.

"Who hired you?" Arwood asked the trio. "You're a message. I want to find out who considers you so expendable."

They said nothing.

The amulet skidded across the plastic. Any one of the three could reach it, even with their wrists tied in their laps.

"The person who tells me what I need to know will be allowed to live. Whoever wishes to survive this room needs that necklace."

Oh no. *No no no.*

Confusion won over their fear. The meditative woman on the end was the quickest; her eyes flitted to the necks of the people in the room before giving a single negating toss of her head. The man in the middle muttered, "Fuck you." The shuddering man on the other end observed the amulet with wide eyes.

Arwood gestured again. Matej steered me to the three prisoners. Tension pooled at the base of my skull.

Anika moved in front of Arwood, shielding him. Her black hair swung over her shoulders as her lips pulled downward.

"Remember," Arwood said. "That necklace. Only one of you can have it, and you'll need it momentarily. Think fast."

He took in my crossed arms. My entire demeanor screamed *No*. I wouldn't be a spectacle for him. I didn't want to add to the terror and lack of humanity coating these walls.

I wouldn't.

"Miss Backhus?" Arwood prompted.

Once he pressed the button, the outcome would be inevitable. I was under no illusion of my capacity to withstand pain like that for long. I'd give in, just as I had previously.

It had been a week for firsts, and this was another—crossing my arms, saying no. My father would have been horrified at my rudeness. Given the circumstances, I liked to think he'd forgive me for it.

Arwood triggered my collar. I fell to my knees, moaning. The pain was no stranger, but it hit me as if it was the first time, my nerves igniting like a heated steel blanket constricting around my body.

Through slitted eyes, I watched the sweating man grab the amulet. He clutched it like a holy object, gaping at me like I was a creature crawling from a swamp.

I didn't cry. But as I opened my mouth to scream, to add to a list that I'd never wanted to grow, I gave Arwood the most hateful expression I could. One that, in my cosseted existence, I had no practice giving. *I hate you*, it said. You *deserve to be on your knees, not them.*

A raised eyebrow was his only response.

∽

Silence filled the office next to the execution room, save for the wooden ticking clock sitting above the oak bookshelves. So wrong, that such a grand room could abut one of such terror and death.

The guards had dragged the four bodies away while Matej steered the shaking, weeping survivor into the opposite room. Arwood paused at the threshold, instructing Matej in a low voice to interview and release him. His employer wouldn't let him live, but he'd spread word about what had happened. The right people would find out. They'd learn the consequences, should they try again.

Me. *I'd* happened. A weapon Arwood could discharge whenever he pleased.

Arwood dismissed Matej and sat at the mahogany desk. Guards flanked me; my limbs were still twitching from the collar shocks. Silas stood behind us, his presence like a fire. Anika had excused herself back to the mansion once it became clear Silas's amulets had done the job they'd been built for. She'd stood in front of Arwood for one reason: in case they didn't.

I was learning who Arwood was. I didn't like it. He never allowed himself to be at a disadvantage, executing primary and secondary plans in tandem to avoid vulnerability from potential incompetence. How was I going to escape this man?

Arwood issued orders to the guards. I barely listened, gathering the courage to interrupt him. Deciding if I should. I had things I needed to say, and I might not get another chance.

With such a small audience, I decided to. "You made me kill them."

Arwood broke off his spiel of instructions. If he was surprised by my decision to speak, his broad, chiseled face didn't reveal it. He reclined in his leather chair, interlacing his fingers across his immaculate suit. So much blood surrounding him, yet none of it had landed on the material.

My father had a name for people like Arwood. *Teflon.* Nothing sticks.

"And it will have the effect I'm after," Arwood said. "I won't apologize for my methods."

The guard to my left, the man who'd steered me from the van all those days ago, cleared his throat. "Sir, we can—"

Arwood silenced him with a hand. What was going on behind those hazel eyes? What belief structure embedded into his psyche had justified his actions and given the figurative nod of approval? "Let her continue."

"They didn't have to die. They were scared." Definitely after the first death. Especially so after the second. "They wouldn't have done it again."

He allowed a beat of silence to pass.

"Perhaps they did," he said, as if he'd considered my words. Already, I knew better. He was humoring me. "The world takes from you only what you allow it to, and the people in this world only listen to a compelling argument. I've just made one."

"You're—you're *horrific*, making me do that! I—"

"And *you* had a choice, Keanna."

"I don't have a choice! You've taken it with *this*." I gripped my collar, his calling card for the world to see. I hated it and I hated him. Heat surged. The beast had been silent, sated, since I'd screamed. It stirred again, yawning.

"You can't hold me accountable for your inability to control what happens when you wail."

My hackles rose. The beast rose in my chest, too; I imagined it narrowing reptilian eyes.

I took a steady breath. Teflon. If you had the bad luck to be thrown into the pan, then, in Arwood's system of justification, it wasn't his fault you got burned. Even if he did the throwing. Because people should wear fireproof suits. Obviously.

This guy was insane.

"You criticize me for using you," he continued, oblivious to the pressure building, "and yet you let yourself be used so easily."

This was the kind of rationale I'd listened to growing up. Since my attack, I'd begun to wonder at the fairness of it all. Why was *I* the one being warned about a man's tendencies, as if his behavior was my responsibility to regulate? The hard surface of my conditioning had cracked that night in the hotel room, and Arwood's words were tremors shifting tectonic plates, igniting my soul.

"I can see from your expression you've decided I'm wrong. You condemn yourself with ignorance, and that's not my problem. I have someone out there relying on me to get her home safe, and I'll do anything I can to accomplish that. Whether by willingness or force, you *will* help me."

My entire body shuddered, like it was a firecracker, lit and moments from ascension. It was different from when my collar caused me pain and the beast responded to it. This time, the beast was as affronted as me.

When faced with difficult circumstances, back to the wall, people fight or flee. I'd always assumed I'd be the fleeing kind (never mind that I'd never actually run for anything in my life. Did runners actually *enjoy* running?). I'd never imagined fighting someone. Then, two months ago, I'd fought my attacker with a strength I'd had no idea I possessed. Today, the beast and I reached an agreement: *Stand. Our. Ground.*

I exploded, my sob of frustration rising into a scream. Arwood remained in his seat, the amulet around his neck glowing and sheltering him from my slicing wail. Had he done it on purpose, to see if there was mettle under my exterior? Was he as sickly curious as I was about the beast inside my skin?

Controlled by an urge I wasn't sure was mine, I slammed the stack of pretentious books—no doubt for decorative purposes; this entire room appeared to be a showpiece instead of functional—off the desk. They crashed into the wooden bookcases, pages ripping from their bindings. Table lamps shattered against the walls. The black-paneled windows behind Arwood vibrated on their hinges before the wave of pressure belched them into the afternoon sun. If shards from the pendant lights above rained on my head, I didn't feel them.

I wanted to decimate everything in this room. I probably would have, too, if not for Silas.

I hadn't looked at him once. He represented so much I didn't understand, emotions I couldn't deal with and didn't want to. He worked for Arwood, and that outweighed all else in my ledger of opinions about him.

But when he staggered, sinking to his knees, his white face a stark contrast against his brown curls, I faltered. My screams stopped as quickly as they'd begun.

He collapsed onto the carpet, twitching. My stomach seized. *I've killed him.*

As I raced over, reaching for his pulse, his chest moved. Thank God. Relieved tears rose as the guards hauled me upright.

Arwood had the look of a parent who'd sat through a tantrum and was *not* amused. "I won't applaud your childish efforts to make yourself feel better." He jerked his chin to the vortex of glass, wood splinters, and shredded paper. "Clean this up, and then get yourself presentable. You're working tonight."

CHAPTER NINE

DESTROYING EVERYTHING AROUND YOU IS ONE THING. Cleaning it up afterwards is quite another.

Light from the adjoining rooms sprawled across the office carpet as I navigated piles of paper and glass, using a flashlight to guide my way, shimmying open yet *another* garbage bag. Arwood hadn't been joking when he'd told me to clean up. The sun had long fallen behind the horizon, an orchestra of cicadas taking over as I swept. I'd already returned the shredded books back to their shelves and straightened what furniture remained intact, but the carpet still crunched beneath my sandals regardless of how much I cleaned.

"Forget the broom. You'll need a Dyson on full power to sort that shit out."

Anika stopped at the threshold, phone light washing her angular face gray. Dressed head to toe in black, she'd pulled her hair into a spiky ponytail, the ends splaying like palm fronds.

I paused in my pitiful efforts of trying to juggle the flashlight, the garbage bag, *and* the broom. "There's a vacuum?" Damned Arwood. "No one told me there was a vacuum."

"Come on. I've gotta get you ready to go."

I laid the broom against the wall, rubbing my bare arms. With evening setting in, the refreshing breeze snaking through the empty windows made me shiver. "Is this your life? Fetching for Arwood?"

"I *choose* to fetch for Arwood, banshee, don't ever forget it. You need to be wearing this."

A canvas bag socked me in the stomach. Inside contained … lots of black. "What's this?"

Anika pushed the corner of her phone into her chin, studying me. "Let's make you a little less politician's wife and more 'you're meeting people you might need to run away from.'"

I brushed my skirt protectively. It was a little dusty from cleaning but had held up. A good wash and I'd happily wear it again.

"I need you dressed for comfort," Anika went on. "And warmth. The weather's a mixed bag this time of year and it could be a long night."

I eyed her leggings, her leather jacket. They fit snug to her frame. "You make it sound like we're performing a heist, or something."

Her laugh came quick and high-pitched. Something about her reaction told me not to discount the idea that perhaps she'd done just that. Maybe even twice. Who *was* this girl?

With her trademark efficiency, Anika ordered me to change before I had the chance to ask any more questions about where we were going or how Silas was. Self-consciousness chafed as I forced my hips and butt into the high-waisted jeans, laced up the Docs, and pulled the sweater over my head. They all fit, but that hardly mattered if I couldn't check *how* they fit. Next to Anika, I probably looked like a hulking, blackened peanut shell.

When I'd finished, she turned back around. "Come on. We've got a few minutes to eat."

With how tight these jeans were? "I'm not hungry."

"You clearly haven't cleaned a day in your life, and you're a bad liar. I'm really getting to know you." I shut off the flashlight and fantasized about throwing it at Anika's head, especially as she said, "Let's go, howler monkey. The pasta here is a full-body experience."

As I followed her, I pondered the choice of clothes, hope drowning my sorrow. *Dress for warmth*. Were we leaving the estate?

If so, my chances of escape were rising.

My chances of escape were diminishing.

Anika led me to the mansion's entranceway and through the

bodies milling around the grand staircase. At least two dozen guards in padded vests, some I recognized from being stationed outside my room.

I spotted Silas standing to the side, head ducked in conversation. The woman holding his attention was stunning and posture-perfect in a white silk blouse tucked into white high-waisted trousers. An even, olive complexion complimented her straight nose and high cheekbones, features shown to advantage with her rich brown hair pulled into a low ponytail. I paused, clutching the hem of my sweater.

Were Silas and this woman related? Side by side, their features and coloring were similar. They looked comfortable with each other. Then again, that could also mean …

No wonder he didn't remember me, when there was someone like *that* here.

Ray-Bans man—minus the sunglasses, but the nickname had stuck and 'phone stealer' didn't have the same ring to it—headed straight for them. They exchanged a few words and the woman nodded. Ray-Bans man touched her elbow, then faced the guards. I joined Anika, leaning against the wall under the balustrade as the man cleared his throat.

The room fell silent. In a deep, gravelly voice at total odds with his clean-cut appearance, he directed the group into smaller teams.

"What's going on?" I whispered.

"Steadman's in charge of running us all," Anika told me, continuing to watch the man speaking.

Steadman. With his aquiline nose, short brown hair devoid of grays, and stoic, sculpted features, his age could have spanned anywhere from early to late thirties, though his commanding presence hinted at the latter level of maturity and experience.

He pointed to the guards standing beside the door. "You five—Branik." Then he addressed the group closest to where Anika and I stood. "And you four—head to Zizkov."

"Why is he sending people to different neighborhoods?" I whispered.

"Arwood's territory. It covers districts north, west, and south from Wenceslas Square, give or take some shared zones."

When I'd moved to Prague, I'd obsessed over the way it was divided into neighborhoods. It had helped me understand how to navigate the city and get a sense for the vibe of my new home. Twenty-two administrative districts were further broken into ten municipal districts encompassing Prague. Prague One—well known for its tourist hot-spot areas like Lesser Town, the astronomical clock, and Wenceslas Square—and Prague Two—an expensive expat area with bars, theaters, and nightclubs—were right beside each other in the center, with the remaining areas circling outwards in an almost carousel-like fashion.

From what Anika had said, Arwood controlled much of it. Branik was beside the Vltava in Four; Zizkov was in Three.

"Come on." Anika pushed herself away from the wall. "You're with Steadman."

I followed her across the foyer, passing a guard securing a knife behind his vest while another strapped a holster to her thigh. Around each of their wrists sat a black metal bracelet.

"Stead," Anika called as we approached. "You wanted Keanna?"

"Correct." His sharp gaze roamed my neck and attire and turned to Anika. "We're heading east. Do you know where you're assigned?"

Anika winked at me. "Stay with Steadman, and don't do anything stupid." She was gone before I had a chance to respond.

Arwood appeared at the top of the staircase, clad in his suit. He whistled as he descended, slow and steady, and tossed a small black remote toward us. Steadman caught it. My leash, transferred. Arwood kissed the woman with Silas on the cheek and headed out the door. A group of guards followed him.

"Behave yourselves, everyone," the woman said, an Italian lilt softening her words. "Let's focus on outcomes with minimal disturbance."

Like Arwood, she beckoned to the four guards assigned to Zizkov and walked outside.

"Why are we going east?" I asked Steadman, feeling incompetent and like I was missing something obvious. Usually, when decisions were made for me at work, someone explained those decisions. Here, I felt like a farm animal waiting for a sheepdog. Was Steadman the sheepdog in this scenario? It seemed like it. "Anika said Arwood doesn't own the eastern districts."

Steadman's blue eyes probed my face, as if deciding whether to answer me. Instead, he jerked his head toward Silas and exited. I supposed my following him was implied. This chafed, my collar a reminder I had no power to argue.

Silas avoided my gaze. Although pride prickled my insides, I couldn't push down my concern. I caught up to him as we followed Steadman to the matte black G Wagon outside.

"Are you alright?" I asked, loud enough for Silas to hear over the crunching gravel and shutting vehicle doors.

"I'm fabulous."

His shoulders were slumped, and his gait held the fatigued movements of someone who needed a day in bed. Had this been the 'catch' he'd referred to with the necklaces? "You passed out, you looked—"

"Don't worry about it."

Pride took over. He didn't want to talk to me? Fine. Any lasting kinship from this afternoon faded, reminding me of my purpose. I needed to pay attention; I could miss an opportunity for escape if I focused too much on Silas.

Steadman swung into the passenger seat of the Mercedes, and one of the guards slipped behind the wheel. I found myself sandwiched between Silas and Matej, wishing for some personal space. Headlights illuminated the valet circle. A collection of gleaming sedans accompanied an exiting Aston Martin and Maserati, Arwood and the woman presumably in the latter two.

"They're not coming with us?" I fished.

Steadman nodded to the driver, who steered us toward the gate and the departing line of taillights. "No," he answered in his rough, American-accented voice. It was flatter than Arwood's, the origin just as indistinguishable to my ears. "Never all together."

"And the place we're going to?" I prompted. I was already sick of being nudged here and thrown there without context. After the day I'd had, my threshold had worn thin. When Steadman didn't answer, I pushed on, temper hijacking my delivery. "You clearly have an intended purpose for me tonight. Keeping me in the dark will only prove counterproductive to your end goals, whatever they are."

Silas smirked.

"You're more talkative than I anticipated," Matej murmured. I avoided his elbows while he retied his ebony hair into a ponytail. "It's interesting."

My burly kidnapper's countenance gave nothing about his mood away. His way of telling me to shut up, perhaps?

Steadman lifted two fingers in farewell to the security at the exit. In the rear-view mirror, I watched them close the gate behind us. "Your friend from this afternoon." His tone remained infuriatingly calm as he answered me. "We're going to visit the man who hired him and have a chat. Short or long, it'll depend on him."

"Where I come from, conversations don't usually involve guns." The sharp lines of the thigh holster Matej wore dug into my hip.

"Where you come from, I've heard you do as you're directed. You'll reach optimal performance"—was Steadman making fun of me? It felt like he was making fun of me—"if you stay quiet and follow any instructions I give."

He *was* making fun of me.

I suppressed the urge to kick the back of Steadman's leather seat. Honestly, I was surprised that was my first instinct. I'd never gravitated to violence before meeting Arwood. Clearly, being abducted and forced to kill innocent people had done a number on my character.

The first hint to the location of Arwood's estate came about forty-five minutes later as we snaked down the freeway adjacent to the Vltava River, passing a racecourse I'd visited with my father. He loved horse-racing and attended as much as his schedule allowed during the season. With how long we'd been driving, combined with our northern direction toward central Prague, Arwood must live somewhere in Western Bohemia, the province filled with forests and farmland. I filed this information away.

We were silent, save for Steadman murmuring the occasional instruction to the driver. My shoulders remained jammed between Silas and Matej.

The warm cinnamon scent clinging to Silas crept up my nose. Heat emanated from his body even through our layers of clothing. Not that it mattered. We weren't allies. We weren't even *friends*. He'd made that pretty clear with his distance. Even so, I stole glances at his turned head more times than I cared for, especially at the way his hair brushed his neck. When I started to wonder what that hair would feel like to touch, I resolutely focused on the passing pastel Lego-block buildings of differing heights, the thin tram wires webbing under the night sky, and how the wet cobblestones reflected the streetlights. A billboard with a ballet dancer advertising the performance of *Giselle* my father and I had tickets for snagged my heart.

Somewhere out there, my father was searching for me. I hoped he'd recovered Zeina and somehow got a lead on my abduction. I had to believe that.

It was mid-week, but the tram platforms in the center of the streets were full. The people lazing at the packed restaurant tables lining the streets would never guess that, beneath our tinted windows, I was being held against my will. How often had a vehicle passed by me with someone inside suffering the same fate? Last week, I wouldn't have considered the possibility. Today, it was all I could think of. Between Silas and Matej, I'd be incapacitated before I had a chance to hit the windows and alert the outside world.

Panic fluttered my stomach, but this also gave me pause. I just had to be careful. Play along. What was it Steadman had said? Follow his instructions.

I'd do *exactly* as he said.

And the moment he—and Arwood and everyone else—let their guard down, whether it be tonight, tomorrow, or next week … I'd run.

∽

We pulled up outside the nightclub, a multi-story affair of exposed brick ensconced between two bars. The driver remained in his seat as the rest of us piled out onto the wet street. I tugged at my sweater as the car drove away.

Our attire contrasted against the sophisticated grace of the waiting patrons, but if the bouncer had the urge to dismiss us, it was overridden as Steadman and Silas raised their fists for inspection. At first I thought it was some odd signal—but no, their black wristbands stole his attention. Whatever Steadman said to him must have won us entry, because the bouncer moved aside with an unhappy grimace. His eyes locked on my collar and stayed there as I passed, and despite the situation a bubble of laughter rose. I'd never entered a nightclub before, and Steadman had me walking into this one like I owned the place. What a trip.

Prague is famous for many things, and its nightlife is one of them—not that my father had allowed me to explore it. Everything I knew was from Googling. Bars and nightclubs across the city catered to every taste to entice both locals and tourists. This particular nightclub reflected the city around it, like an animal with two skins: the exterior shown to the world—refined, timeless, a burning phoenix at the crossroads of east and west Europe that would keep rising— and the true one underneath—watchful, unsurprised, appreciating the true grit of life and preferring things a little bit rough and dirty.

We ascended two flights of stairs to the main floor. I followed Silas's broad, leather-jacketed shoulders as he weaved through patrons after Steadman. The interior was coldly industrial, a repurposed warehouse full of concrete and steel. Purple-white circular lights hung from high ceilings, haloing above a central U-shaped bar. Strobe lights from the adjacent dance floor flashed off the glass-paneled catwalks and staircase we headed for, throwing streaks of purple and blue across Steadman's frame. Club-goers either moved out of our way, shouting to each other above the steady house music, or turned as we passed, ravenous eyes roaming over the men in front of and behind me. Any temptation to melt into the crowd and flee was waylaid by Matej's hand on the small of my back.

I was torn between intrigue and terror as Steadman led us to the second floor. We weaved around those milling about on the balcony, sipping from oversized cocktail glasses. Bombs of perfume made my eyes water as we continued to a door almost indistinguishable from the black paint coating the walls. Steadman nodded to Matej, then proceeded inside to the concrete hallway beyond.

The music muted as the door closed behind us, the vibrations from the bass creating a hollow thumping that accompanied our echoing footsteps. Three doors cornered the end of the hall. Steadman went for the one straight ahead. When it didn't open, he shifted to the side. Matej pushed past me. He fired some well-placed bullets between the lock, the handle, and the door frame, and then plowed a booted foot into it.

The other side revealed a larger square, concrete space with circular lights embedded into an atrium-style ceiling. The smell contrasted against the rest of the musky club. A familiar smell. It had clung to Ri. Wafted under my nose while Arwood and Matej interrogated the five thieves. A cloying sweetness with a sharp edge, like sugar sprinkled on razor blades. The rusty, metallic tang of blood and fear.

If danger had a scent, this room was coated with it.

The opposite door opened, revealing six men and an office beyond filled with monitors.

Silas stepped between me and the converging men holding

weapons, shooting a warning look over his shoulder. *Stay behind me*, it said.

The man facing Steadman spoke first. The lights overhead gleamed off his smooth, bald head, and he had the rough appearance of a professional fighter on television. "I'm not negotiating. Leave."

Steadman, unsurprisingly, shook his head. "You pulled the trigger on us first. Ferko, I assume?"

Narrowed eyes answered his question.

"I'm here to discuss some things with you," Steadman said. "Shall we take a seat in your office?"

The other armed men penned us in, blocking the exit. One pointed a gun at my head. I moved closer to Silas on instinct, grabbing the back of his jacket. He shifted again, angling his body toward the man closest to us.

"Not negotiating," Ferko repeated. "And I don't have to. This is a shared zone. No one owns me."

"Arwood *did* own the building your team infiltrated this morning. Their explosives had your signature style," Steadman said. "Unless you were ignorant of who you were paid to sabotage?"

"Everyone knows who Arwood is and where he does business. We aren't stupid."

"I'm inclined to disagree with you there." We were surrounded by weapons. Only he and Matej were armed. How was Steadman so calm? "You *are* stupid, or dispensable. Which is it?"

Stop baiting him.

"Neither," Ferko said. Boots squeaked across concrete as the men crept closer. Silas's hand went to my wrist, squeezing. "You shouldn't've come here—but I'll give you free passage this one time if you and Arwood never come back."

"How long did it take for Claus to return after we let him go?"

Ferko smirked. "He's been handled."

Claus. The man Arwood had spared. His actions had bought himself mere hours. Even if I hadn't been the one to kill him in the end, I added his name to my growing list of sins.

"Did he share what happened to the others?" Steadman gestured to Silas—wait, no, to *me*.

"Do as he says," Silas whispered, releasing my wrist.

Knees as unsteady as the peace around me, I came forward. Ferko's grip flexed on his gun as he noticed my collar. I froze.

The smell inside the room turned my stomach. Sweat pricked my palms. The beast was agitated—hackles up, ready to pounce.

Ferko finally spoke. "She's just a girl."

I was too terrified to take offense.

"Are you willing to risk it?" Steadman asked. "Claus would have no reason to lie. Tell me who you're working for."

Ferko's fist clenched. Silas sucked in a breath.

The men surrounding us fired.

And, right in the crosshairs, I screamed.

CHAPTER TEN

AROUND ME, BLUE SHIELDS ERUPTED. I FELL TO MY KNEES to avoid the gunfire.

My scream and the correlating wave of pressure released, quick and piercing. Concrete crunched. Bullets diverted and bodies flew backwards. Monitors in the room beyond exploded. Blood spurted. Somewhere between my scream and oozing down the walls onto the floor, the armed men breathed their last.

The shields winked out, including the one surrounding Steadman. He'd pulled Ferko against him, protecting him from the blast.

Ferko swayed, his gun slipping from his damp fingers. The beast preened inside my chest as I shook, rising.

"*Silas*," Steadman barked. Silas stood beside him in an instant. They shared a look as Steadman extracted the gun from his holster and aimed it at Ferko.

A gunshot echoed along the blood-stained concrete walls.

Ferko didn't fall.

Between Ferko and Steadman's gun, the bullet sat cushioned in a sapphire-tinted pillow of air like a stone within a slingshot, suspended inches from Ferko's heart. Silas's hand remained outstretched. He slowly contracted his fingers, as if gripping a basketball.

The bullet inched closer.

Ferko stumbled against the wall in a half-crouch, his eyes on the hovering bullet. Silas's fingers paused. So did the bullet.

"Who bankrolls you?" Steadman repeated.

"Johan Matousek."

A beat of silence. "Is he still trafficking for the Kohnstamms?"

"I don't know." Ferko flinched, but the bullet didn't come any closer. A bead of sweat slipped down the blue diamond tattoo covering the side of his neck.

"Claus said your men mentioned a name while delivering the last lot: Isobelle." Steadman brandished a phone, the screen filled with a photograph. "Were they referring to Arwood's daughter?"

"I don't know. Maybe. I honestly don't know." Ferko's voice inflected upwards, catching on a sob. "Johan doesn't tell me much, just that he took delivery of thirty girls last week. She coulda been any one of 'em."

I couldn't see Steadman's face, but I wondered if it mirrored my disgust.

Or perhaps not. Perhaps this was just another day on the job for Steadman.

"Tell me where he's operating now," he ordered.

Ferko blanched, looking between the bullet and me. He swallowed. "He has places near Kbely …" He listed various addresses while Steadman recorded them.

When he finished, Steadman nodded to Silas, who flipped his palm. The bullet soared to the side, slamming into the wall behind Ferko.

We left him alone but alive in that room, a boneless puddle surrounded by his dead men.

☙

I greedily inhaled the fresh night air in an attempt to tame my churning stomach. Bile sat in my throat. I wasn't convinced it wouldn't come up at the first opportunity.

Steadman turned to me. "You did well in there."

My conditioning kicked in, and the part of me that thrived on the approval of others helped dispel some of the nausea. Thankfully, my tongue remained anchored, so I didn't utter anything stupid like

'Thank you'. I concentrated on the slick pavement, rebelling in my own special way by not responding.

I'd *chosen* to scream. No coercion, just a plain *get-me-out-of-here* split-second analysis that had me embracing the beast and opening my mouth to save myself.

I had no idea how to come to terms with that, so I focused on breathing. The damp air, laced with the peppery notes of cigarette smoke from patrons standing outside the club, cleared my head and helped me refrain from vomiting on my boots. Barely.

Steadman pulled out his phone, murmuring instructions to the driver in Czech. His tone grew incensed as he ordered Matej down the street ahead of us. We stopped at the intersection, Silas shifting in front of me. The sidewalks were more crowded than before, with pedestrians in varying states of rowdiness. Steadman watched Matej's departure as he continued his phone conversation with guttural start-stops.

A high-pitched squeal erupted from a passing bachelorette party, jolting me out of the angsty pit of self-hatred I was wallowing in.

Not all opportunities are presented with ample time to dissect them, my father had told me once. You have to act and hope your instincts will guide you.

I melted into the group of eager women celebrating their friend, a cloud of excitement, perfume, and hair floating around me. My expression must have spoken for me, because the woman closest switched places to push me further into the center.

A frisson of hysterical laughter threatened to seep through my lips, but I kept them shut, resisting the urge to look up and see if my sudden disappearance had been noted. I kept my head low, hoping my all-black ensemble would camouflage me under the kaleidoscope of color.

No shouts came from behind. I expected someone to grab me, but nothing happened.

Had I really done it? Could it have been that simple? I was in an unfamiliar part of the city, with no phone and no mone—a *phone*!

I tapped the tall, slim blonde beside me on the shoulder. Understanding my request, she whipped her phone out of her clutch, keying in her passcode—

—and I went down.

My collar activated, liquid heat searing my spine. My knees hit the ground. I clamped both hands over my mouth to stay quiet. The wave of revelers parted, bags and shins smacking me.

The pain vanished. A hand snatched the hair at the base of my neck, hauling me upwards. The woman who'd offered her phone had stopped, seeing me fall, but something behind me made her flee into the crowd.

"That was a mistake," Steadman growled into my ear. He dragged me into a narrow dumpster-filled alley and slammed me against the wall. My head connected with brick. Lancing pain shot through my skull.

His fingers pushed underneath my jaw. "You still don't understand, do you?" Steadman said. "You're permitted to live so long as you prove useful to us." His cold blue eyes locked on mine, backlit by the generic fluorescent 'closed' signs in the cafe window opposite. I tugged at his wrist fruitlessly. His lean figure was deceptive; the man packed serious strength. "I can do anything I like, short of killing you—Arwood only cares that you can function. There's plenty of room between the two. Don't push me."

Silas rounded the corner, skidding to a stop. "James, *no*—"

Steadman squeezed tighter. "Understood?"

I whimpered, nodding as best I could. His fingers were like pincers, cutting my air to an almost unbearable minimum.

"Steadman, stop—"

He released me. I sagged against the graffiti-coated wall.

"Same goes for you, kid," Steadman said, pushing a gun barrel flush against Silas's jugular. "You can't shield against *this*, and we both know what happens if you don't toe the line."

Silas swallowed.

With a final heated glance, Steadman headed for the curb where the car idled. "Matej!" he called, pointing to me.

I'd been manhandled so much in the past week, you'd have thought I'd be used to it by now. I still flinched as Matej entered the alley, gripped my upper arm, and forced me into the Mercedes.

CHAPTER ELEVEN

WE RETURNED TO CHAOS CHURNING INSIDE THE mansion. Uniformed paramedics addressed wounded guards while Arwood's household staff ran around fetching items. Ahead, Anika led a hobbling, burly guard from one of the vehicles to an empty spot on the tiled floor, his Scottish brogue as thick as his torso.

What the hell happened?

Once we jumped out of the car, Silas made a beeline upstairs. The stunning woman who'd been in Zizkov was at the base of the grand staircase. Steadman strode over to her, leaving me alone in the doorway.

Dark red blood slashed across the woman's white outfit, but from the way she stood without assistance—and away from the medics—it wasn't hers. Steadman showed the most amount of animation I'd seen all night. His hands flitted over her shoulders while he ducked to make eye contact with her. She kept shaking her head, but his features remained hard, a muscle leaping in his jaw as they spoke.

"You made it, banshee." Anika, having deposited the Scottish guard, sashayed her way to me.

"I assume this"—I gestured around the foyer—"doesn't happen often?"

"Nope. It was a standard check-in, and it went to shit. Brothel owner's dead—bad for business, right?—and we lost Wen and Scott. Two of our best, for fuck's sake." She picked russet flecks out from under her fingernails. It took a moment to register it was blood. "We got Lissandra out, though, so … coulda been worse."

"Lissandra?"

Anika pointed to the woman Steadman was talking to. "Arwood's wife."

It didn't surprise me a man like Arwood was married to a woman like Lissandra, but … really? From the way Steadman was holding her, I'd have assumed—

"How was your first excursion?"

I gave Anika a droll look she smirked at, as if a single expression could convey that I'd slaughtered five men, terrorized a local gangster, and then failed to escape afterwards. Would the first two balance out the last in Arwood's scales? The sickening sensation of something lodging in my throat had accompanied the entire drive home while I imagined all the creative ways Arwood might punish me.

Then again, with this thing around my neck, was there much else he *could* do?

Okay, probably a lot.

As if conjured by my thoughts, Arwood stormed toward Lissandra. Steadman stepped back. I caught Lissandra mouthing "I'm fine" until Arwood relaxed.

Anika swayed from side to side, fidgeting like she'd consumed a six-pack of energy drinks. "Are *you* okay?" I asked.

"Babe, it'll take more than an assault rifle to keep me down— oh, Steadman wants you."

When I met Steadman's gaze, he jerked his head in the direction of Arwood's retreating form. I hoped he'd get a crick in his neck one day, summoning people like that. I sighed, leaving Anika behind.

⁓

"Watch yourself, girl."

My surroundings blended together as I tried to keep up with Steadman. "What do you mean?"

Steadman stopped in the middle of the hallway. He'd removed

his bullet-resistant vest. His black button-up looked fresh. You'd never guess he'd been interrogating someone an hour ago.

"I'm talking about the stunt you pulled tonight." He plucked at the sleeves of his shirt, re-rolling one of them and exposing a toned forearm and a black band beside an Anderson Geneve watch. That arm had pinned me against the wall with ease. Was his strength a supernatural ability, or was he just a very capable human? "You're not irreplaceable. If you keep your little runaway episode quiet, I'll forget to mention it to Arwood. Understood?"

He continued without waiting for an answer, distaste rippling off his shoulders. I knitted my brows together as I followed. I had to give the people-pleasing side of Keanna a swift kick and remind her it didn't matter if Steadman liked me or not. His threat was loud and clear, but something in his delivery gave me pause. The fact I'd slipped away for even a minute exposed weakness Arwood wouldn't tolerate. Later, when I was alone, I'd dissect this, but for now I stayed silent and hoped he'd perceive it as acquiescence.

Like the king of crisp white shirts and tailored vests, Arwood sat regally behind his hardwood desk. Steadman led the way into the office, announcing my arrival.

Arwood leaned back in his leather chair, clutching a pen and pushing the cap up and down. "Steadman told me you were useful tonight. I'm pleased. I don't enjoy coercing people to work for me."

I kept my mouth shut.

Arwood gestured to the empty seat. Steadman had already taken the one adjacent, a leg crossed over his knee. He had cactuses on his socks. That fact was so removed from my perception of the stoic Steadman I had to do a double take as I sat.

"I know you don't care for me, Miss Backhus. I don't blame you," Arwood said. "But someone out there has my daughter. Isobelle was stolen nearly a month ago, and for all my resources I have no clue why or how. There are certain … things you expect once someone you love has been taken. None have occurred. No ransom, no proof of her life. Or death." He paused. In a less serious situation, the parallels would have been humorous. Had any of those things been issued to *my* father? "On top of their peace-keeping responsibilities, my team—like my second in command, Steadman"—Arwood gave him a nod—"have assisted my efforts to locate her. Until today, we had no leads at all."

I needed to reset expectations; my behavior hadn't done me any favors, and tonight might have ruined any future opportunities for escape. I couldn't count on Steadman staying quiet forever, and I needed Arwood to believe I was willing to comply.

I fidgeted in my sweater and tight jeans, feeling horribly under-dressed and longing for my nice clothes and shoes. "Anika said you were willing to negotiate the terms of my cooperation."

"A deal that expired the moment my mage created those amulets," Arwood said.

Speaking means a degree of willingness, my father always said about negotiation. *You just need to establish how much.* "I wouldn't be here if the deal had expired." My heart raced as I said the words, but they came out steady. Arwood and Steadman locked eyes, confirming my hunch. "As you said, until today, you had no leads. I'm willing to help."

"You'll help regardless."

I'd never negotiated with someone before. This wasn't an ideal time to start. *Think.* I had an opportunity, I just needed to figure out what that opportunity *was.*

Steadman keeping a secret from Arwood revealed much more about their operations than just Steadman himself. They weren't impenetrable. If Arwood's right-hand man was a crack in the proverbial door, the attacks Silas had mentioned and the one on Lissandra's team tonight could be the crowbar.

"Do you believe this Johan guy took your daughter?" I asked, remembering the name Ferko had given.

Steadman cut in. "Do you know anything about him or the Kohnstamm family?"

"No."

Arwood's eyes didn't leave mine as he rounded the table, standing before me. "Are you sure?"

I ran Johan Matousek and 'Kohnstamm' past my mental contact list and came up empty. "I'm not certain why you think I would. Until last week I had no idea you or your operation existed. I think most people in Prague are the same." *And they're better for it.*

"You work for your father, Miss Backhus, that's why." Arwood laced his fingers together, resting them against his pelvis, his black wedding ring stark against his warm ivory skin. His commanding presence intimidated me; Arwood had the wide shoulders, chest, and torso of a football player. After Steadman's surprise display of strength, I no longer counted them among the weedy or bloated men I dealt with at my father's company. I dropped my gaze, unnerved by Arwood's prolonged eye contact. "There's not much in this city Edson Backhus didn't once have a hand in," he said. "I know that personally."

There was subtext there, but I wasn't connecting the dots. He must have realized this because he added, "Edson and I used to be business partners."

I sat back in the chair and dipped my chin, narrowing my eyes.

"I didn't think you remembered me, and I can see now that you don't," he said. "Your father used to host me and my late wife at your properties here and in London."

If Arwood was telling the truth—which I doubted—this made sense. Who recalls dinner parties from when you were ten? Especially when you were relegated to the nanny.

"All I remember is that we moved to Australia," I said, "and we stayed there until I graduated."

"Did you ever wonder why?"

I'd been eleven, and I hadn't cared why. All I'd cared about was leaving London, leaving everything I knew. Then, suddenly, life 'Down Under'. Australians were strange, and for the first six months, it was as if we spoke two different languages. "Three seasons a year!" our gardener had crowed. "Hot, bloody hot, and holy fucking shit."

To a native Brit, it had been hellishly humid and 100% true. Just to enrich my personal growth, puberty had hit around the same time, coinciding with weight gain I couldn't prevent. My father had despaired over the impacts the move had caused. I went from perfect-A Keanna to a failing little fat girl almost overnight. It was a hell of a wakeup call. I did whatever I could to trim my thighs and keep my grades high. My difficulty adapting was the reason I'd heeded my father's advice and chosen online learning upon moving to Prague, instead of enrolling in university here. Why I'd interned at his company instead of working for someone else.

If only he'd seen how I'd managed everything this past week. We had a *lot* to discuss when I saw him again.

"I'm sorry. My father isn't caught up in this kind of thing, and I've never heard of Johan or the Kohnstamm family before tonight. You must be misinformed."

Steadman rubbed the underside of his lips with his fingers, observing us silently.

Arwood smirked at his second-in-command. "Or you are."

"My father's a good man." My voice developed an unnecessarily pleading tone—I shouldn't care what these men thought. "Our corporate social responsibility agenda is off the charts. His staff love him. He's a terrific father. I'm sorry your daughter is missing, but he's got nothing to do with it."

"I wasn't suggesting he took her. He no longer has the means. But he probably knows who did."

No way. No way, *ever*. "Is this why *you* abducted *me*?"

"A reason, but not a decisive one. It's your abilities I need. And I can already see it was a gamble that paid off."

Almost too late, I saw an opening and dived on it like Claus, the thief, had dived on the amulet in the execution room. "An engaged employee is more likely to go the extra mile. You said yourself, you had no success until I helped deliver a lead." My voice was steady. *Go, Keanna.* "Imagine what might happen if I'm *trying* to help you. If I participate in your operations, will you release me?"

Arwood's penetrating eyes were hazel with gold flecks. They remained steady on me as he said, "I will release you once Isobelle is found."

Common sense kicked in. "Regardless of whether she's alive or dead?"

His broad face tightened, but he gave a single nod. "Yes. I will honor our agreement should she be found, regardless of outcome. Who knows, you may find you prefer to stay. Many have."

I swallowed my retort. Hell would quite literally have to freeze over before I decided to stay. "And where will I be living?"

"You will reside here with my team."

He was still talking. A great sign. How far could I push him? "I would also like my collar removed, please. It's no longer necessary."

"No."

Well, I honestly hadn't believed he'd go for that. "Then may I request a proper room with heating and a door that locks on the inside?"

"That can be arranged."

"You're on call to work tomorrow night," Steadman said. "I assume this isn't an issue?" I shook my head, thinking Steadman was being almost amicable. Then he had to ruin it by adding, "Hopefully that's enough time for you to wash your hair. There's blood in it."

Once again, I had the urge to kick his chair. I'd read that people dislike ten percent of those in life they meet, often for no logical reason. Steadman definitely fit into that category.

I gave a very restrained, "I'll be ready."

Steadman stood, his stupid cactus socks disappearing under the hem of his pants. He held out a hand toward the door, a clear directive for me to move.

"Oh, and Miss Backhus?"

I paused, facing Arwood. He was still watching me.

"Either your father is lying to you, or I am. It's too soon for you to know this, but I don't lie. There are very few people in this city who can say that with absolute conviction. Think on it."

CHAPTER TWELVE

I F DEATH HAD A SMELL, GUILT HAD A TASTE. I WOKE SOON after falling asleep in my new bedroom, a choking sourness coating my tongue.

Faces floated in my mind, a reminder of all I'd stolen. Even worse, I hadn't looked at the men I'd killed in the nightclub, so they adopted the properties of Arwood's guards. Hopefully that was my imagination filling in the blanks and not a premonition.

I was so wired my skin prickled, like the beast was trying to escape. Chills coursed down my body as I sat up. Sweat coated my forehead and pooled underneath my collar. This bed might be more comfortable than the metal frame I'd slept in for the last few days, but I still couldn't breathe properly in here.

I dragged a robe on top of my silk nightgown. The light from the bedside lamp flooded over the cream Chesterfield three-seater opposite holding my measly pile of belongings. I got an eyeful of myself in the mirror above it. My clean but unstyled hair was full of serious cowlicks, and under normal circumstances I'd never allow someone to see me like this. Right now, I didn't care. It was late— so late it was closer to sunrise than midnight.

Thick mahogany carpet absorbed my footsteps. I unlocked the door, moving the curved golden handle. Everything was still, the ticking of a grandfather clock the only sound on the second floor. Its steady, repetitive *tocks* faded as I walked past one closed door after another. The housekeeper who'd led me to my room had mentioned I was in the main quarters; useful should we need to assemble quickly. Which door was Silas behind? Anika?

The silence was comforting … and unnerving. I wrapped my arms around myself, trying not to look at the camera lenses as I exited the wing. No one stopped me as I passed the grand staircase and continued down another hallway filled with windows that stretched toward the ceiling. My disheveled appearance reflected off the dark glass. I came across a window with a cozy built-in seat overlooking the side garden and sank onto the teal cushion, expecting an alarm to sound.

When it didn't, I repositioned, tucking my knees up and resting my temple against the pane. The glass fogged from my breath. Outside, spotlights illuminated a guard and the garden hedges he patrolled. This sight wasn't a new one—my father had hired protection for our home, too—but his automatic weapon was a step up from the small guns our security wore.

My new room and the ability to leave it was welcome, but a cage is still a cage. I'd merely negotiated myself into a bigger one.

What am I going to do?

I didn't trust Arwood. Even if we found his daughter, what was to stop him from keeping me forever as his personal executioner? I was a heck of a supernatural trump card. Willingly working for him chafed my moral compass in every way, but it had been the only way to wrestle back some control. On the flip side, I faced a terrifying future.

My throat burned and I pushed the tears down. Crying wouldn't solve my situation. If I was at work, how would I approach this?

Cause and effect. A problem in business often meant an opportunity. My problem wasn't so simple. My ability had caused—and would continue to cause—an effect I couldn't live with.

Ri, the thieves, the men at the nightclub, would have had people who needed them. Parents. Siblings, possibly. Partners, perhaps. Children. My analysis was pretty simple. If I remained here, subjected to Arwood's machinations, others would continue to die. If I didn't escape soon, there'd come a time I wouldn't be able to live with myself. The wheels on my bus would come off.

Shoes scuffed on the carpet.

"A fellow nightcrawler. Can I join you?" Silas tugged at his worn black shirt and, seeing my bewildered nod, sat on the other half of the window seat. As he slumped against the wall opposite and straightened his legs out beside me, I swept my fingers across my face, checking for sleep in the corner of my eyes and if there was crusty drool, well, anywhere else. My hair was a lost cause. I pulled my knees closer. Thankfully I'd shaved my legs recently, even if one of them was covered in a bandage. God, I was a mess.

Silas placed a paperback with a cracked spine to the side and leaned his head back, looking out the window. Although he still had dark circles under his eyes, he wasn't as pale as earlier in the evening. The smoke from outside the nightclub lingered on his black jeans.

"Trouble sleeping?" he murmured.

"Yep."

"I can't sleep either."

We didn't speak for a few moments. I was trying to pin down just *one* question to ask him when I had hundreds. Unfortunately, I wasn't confident he'd answer many, if any.

"Tonight …" I trailed off until he nodded. "Is it always like that?"

"People dying? Sometimes."

"Do you get used to it?"

Silas fiddled with his silver signet ring. He twisted it around and around, pushing it past his knuckle. "Never."

"I … I thought you were here by choice." I'd been playing over Steadman's words in the alley all night. "But you're not, are you?"

He finally met my gaze. What did I look like, sitting in front of him? A scared little girl? A potential ally?

"No."

One word, but it was everything. Even if he wanted nothing to do with me, at least I wasn't the only one held against my will. "How long?"

"Ten months."

I couldn't do this for ten months. I wouldn't. Emboldened by his apparent willingness to chat, I said, "The necklaces—they sap your energy, don't they?"

"Using in general saps my energy."

"And the necklaces expedite that process?"

"Compound it. There was no other way to do it."

From what I'd seen of Silas, he tested his limits constantly. He'd warned someone would find a way to exploit my abilities. Arwood had. If I couldn't control what happened when my voice went an octave too high, the amulets would remain. Silas would suffer. Regardless of why he was here, I couldn't have that.

"You made it sound like my power could have degrees." The confidence in how he wielded his abilities inspired a competitive edge—along with hope. "I have to find a way to stop killing people." Silas said nothing, but he tilted his head to the side, as if encouraging me to go on. "Can you teach me?"

I held my breath, but I didn't have to wait long. "It's not like for like—but I can try."

"I appreciate it." Having a plan helped. "Arwood and Steadman. Matej. Do they have abilities like … us?"

"They're human. As far as I can tell."

I almost snorted at the irony. "Yet they hold more power than we do."

Silas gave a weak tug of his lips. "You can use anyone if you know how to leash them."

His defeated silence threatened to pull me under again. "I wanted to say … thank you for standing up for me tonight. Against Steadman."

Silas shifted, his foot brushing my hip. I tucked my legs closer. His presence alone sent goosebumps down my arms.

His gaze dropped as he turned his ring faster.

"Had to. After all"—he looked up at me through his eyelashes in a way I would have characterized as bashful in any other person—"we're garden buddies, remember? That stuff's in the job description."

My breath caught. I gripped my robe in my fists, trying not to look as shocked as I felt. "I didn't think you remembered me."

"How could I forget the person who outwitted me in a dance-floor conversation at her own party? You were so unexpected. And stunning. Green eyes. Green dress. I couldn't stop watching you."

Warmth flooded my chest. I suppressed a smile by biting my lip. It had bothered me more than I'd realized, thinking he didn't know who I was. But he did. And he'd thought me witty *and* unexpected. "Why didn't you say anything earlier?"

He watched the moths flying in and out of the spotlight. "It wouldn't have done us any favors that day. These people ... they learn what you want, and then they make sure you can never have it. Besides ..." He shrugged. "Time changes everything, doesn't it? It's been a year. That part of my life is over."

The hope that had blossomed cooled with rapid speed. This wasn't the Silas I'd met in the garden. If the smiling, charming boy who'd danced and regaled me with his cooking skills was still there, I hadn't seen him yet. The last twelve months had changed him irrevocably.

When we'd reunited, I'd thought him not remembering me was the worst thing. I'd been wrong. *This* was worse. My meteorite had burnt out. I'd lost the beautiful boy with the beautiful smile before I'd ever had him.

I nodded, my throat full and sorrow weighing my heart. I needed to leave. Ideally, before I did—or said—anything I'd regret. I moved to the edge of the seat, dangling my legs over the carpet, gripping the sides.

"I understand," I whispered, offering him a small smile. "No one needs to know."

This close, the undercurrent of tension sparked between us. His jaw clenched tight, but his gaze roamed slowly over my hair (would it have killed me to brush it?!), the exposed part of my shoulder where my robe had slipped, and settled on my lips. His own parted, like he was about to say something else. Or *do* something else.

I sat, expectant, the air growing heavy. For every second that passed, my pulse raced, arms prickling in anticipation.

His eyes dropped from my lips to my collar, then rose to the camera on the ceiling. This had the equivalent effect of dousing me with a bucket of water. I realized too late I'd leaned closer, my traitorous subconscious giving me away. I pulled back, feeling all kinds of an idiot.

We were both trapped here. I didn't know Silas anymore, if I'd known him at all. I had to focus on escaping. I couldn't afford to form any attachments. Just because he'd said, *once*, that I was stunning—that meant, well, nothing.

My mind screamed at me to leave. My body—the beast, the heathen—wanted to straddle him on the window seat and see if his lips really were as soft as they looked.

Which would be a mistake. Probably.

No—definitely.

"Good night, Silas," I whispered.

I didn't wait around for his response.

CHAPTER THIRTEEN

I WOKE LATE MORNING TO A SCRAWLED NOTE PUSHED underneath my bedroom door.

Meet me outside, 3pm.

The idea of training to control your abilities when you're spiraling at 4am sounds like a terrific one. After all, the urge to proactively tackle life's issues is strongest before the sun rises.

But when you're bleary-eyed, head throbbing like a rubber band is snapping around it? Not so appealing. Something about the day starting makes your fears in the small hours feel, well, *small.*

I chewed my thumbnail, waiting for the water splashing the gold-flecked shower tiles in the bathroom to turn hot.

My chest fluttered whenever I reflected on how close Silas had sat, the way the corner of his lips had curved while admitting to remembering me. As much as I didn't want to dwell on his words, my mental terrain had split into two. The focused side insisted any attachment was incompatible with escape and rendered it out of scope, thank you very much. I needed to learn what I could from him and move on. Then there was the other side, the young girl who'd daydreamed about Silas long after meeting him in the garden. Had often wondered what became of him, how he was doing.

Thanks to our chat, I knew the answer: not good.

I styled my hair, taming the cowlicks, and applied the makeup Anika had delivered. They weren't my usual products, but it was just another strange thing in my otherwise strange existence. Nothing about the marble counter and brass furnishings felt familiar, nor the wary look in my green eyes and the puffiness beneath them. I patiently contoured and applied blush and mascara. Slowly, the Keanna I knew reappeared in the mirror. When Silas next saw me, it would be at my best. And yes, I shouldn't care what he thought—but, dammit, I did.

I missed my reformer Pilates machine. I missed my phone. I missed my schedule. I pivoted, my lips a grim line above the plain matte black collar marking me as Arwood's. At least my stomach looked flat. I would have fit into my dress this Friday easily.

A dress I wasn't going to wear, for a ball I would no longer attend. Arwood had taken that from me, too—

Perspective reared, hot and shameful, saving me from another spiral. *What the hell is wrong with me?* I had no right to get upset over dresses and reformer machines when I'd *murdered* people.

The presence of those I'd killed watched me like a third eye, solidifying my resolve, as I left my room.

∽

"You could have been more specific." I'd finally located Silas seated on a wooden bench in the garden we'd overlooked from the window, his face tipped to the sky. He could have been asleep, if not for the lines of tension cording his neck. "'*Outside*' is … not."

Silas cracked open an eye. "Didn't wanna leave much detail. Besides, you figured it out. No harm done."

Incorrect. My watch read 3:15pm. I was never late for anything.

Unsure of what one wore to wrangle their internal beast, I'd decided on a simple white T-shirt, dark blue jeans, and Converse sneakers. Heeled sandals would have made my legs look nicer, but I couldn't get Anika's "What if we need to run?" out of my head. Seeing Silas's black jeans—knees ripped in a way that would have made my father despair for the youth of today—validated my choice.

"Where do we start?"

Silas stood, gesturing for me to follow him. "First, some distance between us and the mansion. I don't know what Arwood's gonna think of you training, but this leads me to point number two—getting away from breakable objects so we don't piss anyone off."

He led me deeper into the garden until we were boxed in by emerald-green hedges, their disciplined leaves maintained within manicured boundaries. A white-painted concrete seat filled one corner. This kind of neat space calmed me. I couldn't imagine Arwood in his blond number two haircut and Berluti suit, sitting here, taking in the peace, while observing the perimeter wall he used to fence us in.

"Third, I ask you some questions. What does it feel like when you scream?"

Silence stretched while I contemplated that. The rattlesnake-like quivering of trees surrounding the estate replaced the frenetic exchange of cars and horns found in the city streets. External peace clashed against the anxiety within. This conversation was anything but soothing.

"Give me a moment," I murmured, searching his features for a hint of impatience. "It's hard putting something into words when I've spent months trying to ignore its existence."

"Which is your first step: it exists," Silas said. "It's a part of you, whether you like it or not. Ignorance and denial are walls between you and your abilities, and if your magic is anything like mine, it resents barriers."

"You think yours is sentient?"

"Isn't it? Magic flows through us. Affects our well-being like a vital organ. It's as much a part of our bodies as our brain or lungs are."

How appealing, to be so at ease with yourself. "Mine feels like a reptilian beast sitting behind my heart. I've certainly thought of it as one."

A smile tugged at his lips. My fingertips tingled as the trio of freckles on his cheek bunched together, a constellation I wanted to smooth out. "It probably resents that, too. Think of your beast's personality. How would you describe it?"

Instead of slamming the door on the beast, I approached it.

Prodded it. I imagined it opening a sleepy eye, peering between the cage of my ribs. Slumbering my entire life. Recently awoken through circumstance and fear. Assured of its own strength and superiority, even trapped. Wanting to roam free. Hating that I wouldn't let it.

And seriously unimpressed that I wanted something from it after ignoring it for so long.

I had my answer: *proud*. No way I'd tell Silas that, though. I'd sound like a lunatic.

"I don't think this is working." The urge to curl into a ball and hide from the world flooded my limbs, making me restless. I should be in a meeting taking minutes on a new acquisition, not acknowledging *this*. "Should we try something else?"

"Do you want my help or not?"

I straightened my posture. "I'm not sure how discussing this thing has anything to do with controlling my scream."

"It has everything to do with it. Stop thinking about it as the enemy. It's not. It's *you*. It's a part of you." The afternoon sun illuminated the gold around his irises, turning his brown eyes a dark amber. Normally, I'd enjoy being this close. Instead, his gaze pinned me down. "Each part of your body wants you to survive. Its sole purpose is to keep you in that state. Why would your power be any different?"

He painted a beautiful picture of a reality I couldn't participate in. Frustration bubbled, amplifying the headache I'd woken with. "You feel that way because your power doesn't kill people. Unless you've intervened—*every* time I've screamed, I've killed someone."

Silas absorbed my shaky outburst, his expression smooth and open. Too open. Too accepting. "You're unwilling. That matters."

He didn't get it. "Murder is murder."

"They would have died anyway. This world, people like Arwood … it's brutal and unforgiving. You're a weapon, yes, but it's not your fault."

I couldn't keep standing for this. I crunched over to the seat, so he didn't have such a clear view of my face—except he followed, the material of his jeans bristling as he sat beside me. I nudged white gravel with my toe. With a sneaky side glance, I could see him squinting into the sun, watching a bird soar above the estate wall keeping us prisoner.

"You have to find a way to forgive yourself," he said. It might have been my imagination, but I could have sworn his hand reached for me. I blinked; his hands were resting on his knees. "No, really, Keanna. It'll eat you, inside out, if you don't. You won't be able to fight back."

Tears seared my eyelids as I passed my fingers through my hair. I'd styled it into perfect waves and used it as a curtain while I composed myself. The heaviness in my stomach wasn't going away, and I felt as caged as the beast inside me. Even before I'd learned my screams were deadly, I'd never had the urge to cry out like this. *Girls don't make a scene*, my father had ingrained into me. *They process their emotions in a composed state because they have the maturity to.* I'd collected these foundational beliefs like flowers. Prided myself on maintaining composure, always. Now all I wanted was to unleash like I had in the office yesterday. I wanted to kick things over, break things. Howl at the top of my lungs. But I wanted to do it without consequence, and those two things were mutually exclusive.

There was something to be said for finally touching the bars in a cage of your own making.

I launched to my feet. "I didn't realize training involved this much talk."

"Which takes me to my original question." Silas didn't look impatient, but I'm sure he was. I was being annoying. I was irritating myself. "What does it feel like when you scream?"

I sighed. "Ever watch a champagne cork pop?"

"I take it your scream is the champagne in this scenario?"

"Correct. There's so much pressure inside me. And when I *do* scream, it can't come out of me quickly enough, like the beast is forcing it out. I can't stop it."

"Wrong. You can. And you've just shown yourself the way: visualization. How are you feeling right this second?"

Despite my agitation, I no longer wanted to run. There was something in the matter-of-fact way he addressed my capabilities that made me almost … comfortable. Since my attack, I'd felt isolated in my otherness. He was the first person I'd met who was different, too. He wasn't scared of it. He wasn't scared of *me*.

I wanted that self-assurance. I needed it.

"Champagne bottle," I whispered. "Shaken. Barely corked."

Silas walked backwards with outstretched arms. Only the hedges surrounded us. Even the birds gave me a wide berth. "I can handle anything you throw at me. What you'll need to do is try to control the flow of that champagne." He winked. "Come on, Keeks. Do your worst."

Keeks. I wasn't one for nicknames, but I liked the way this sounded, coming from him. I inhaled.

The beast screeched in elation.

I clamped my mouth shut, shaking my head.

Silas exhaled. "You can."

"I can't."

He bit his lip, cocking his head. "Aren't you an overachiever?"

"What's that supposed to mean?"

"You know exactly what I mean."

"Uh, well, I suppose, to some people I could be classified as—"

"Excellent. Glad we got that out of the way." He smirked, bringing his palms together. "Keanna, my sweet overachiever, I need you to scream. We don't have all day."

Heat licked up my throat. "Are you trying to annoy me into screaming?"

"Is it working?" He drummed his fingers against each other, eyes sparking with mischief.

I took a step forward. "No."

He, too, stepped closer. "You *are* a bad liar. Do you need me to get the remote from Arwood?"

"That's a low blow."

"Incorrect," he said. "I could demonstrate a low blow, but I don't hit people." Another step. "Even overachievers."

"Goading me won't help my focus at *all*."

"Are you always this stubborn? You were so lovely when we first met."

Step, step, step. "And here *I* was, thinking you were charming." I poked his chest, appreciating how my finger rebounded off muscle. Not that I should be focusing on that detail. "I won't make that mistake again."

"I *am* charming." He grinned. For a moment we were back in the ballroom again, his face lit up. Toe to toe, I was in his space, and he was in mine. I took a shuddering breath, my lower abdomen tightening at the cinnamon notes of his cologne. His gaze slid to my lips.

Is he—?

He stepped back.

"Don't you want to learn control? Only one way to do it." The cadence of his voice remained deep, unaffected. *Learn control.* Something he had, and I clearly didn't. Showing my cards. Again.

I fisted my hands and screamed.

Like a snake poised to attack, the beast struck. My scream split through the air.

Violet flashed across Silas's irises as a translucent sapphire shield shot over his body. Pressure billowed against the hedges like a wave crashing up a rock.

I stopped, sucking a breath. His shield winked out, torn leaves falling on us like confetti.

Color dotted Silas's cheeks as he exhaled, eyes bright and no longer bloodshot. He looked—he looked *exhilarated.* Like he'd just ridden a bike downhill and jumped from it while it was moving. Like he was, uh …

My abdomen twisted again.

"See?" he said. "You're fine. How'd that go? Any different?"

To be honest, I'd been so keen to get back at him I'd forgotten why I was screaming in the first place. "I don't know. You distracted me."

"I have that effect. Let's try again."

I tried to concentrate on the sensation right before I opened my mouth. There it was, the feeling of too much being forced through a funnel too small. *Visualization*, Silas had said.

I could do hard things. I smiled at men who called me 'honey' instead of by my name. I reminded people paid triple my wage how to open a .pdf without a hint of sarcasm. I'd learned about the law of attraction in *The Secret* at my father's insistence, even though the book had nearly put me to sleep.

Looking at Silas, ready to deflect me, proved too distracting. I shut my eyes and inhaled.

The beast no longer shoved at the bars, making it easier to focus. This time, pressure rose steadily. A shaken soda bottle, rather than a champagne cork. I cracked the bottle top, gas hissing as it escaped, the sucking, devouring sound of the liquid consuming airspace. Up it came, then—

I kept my eyes shut, trying to dampen its speed as it hit the neck of the bottle. It was like gripping a rope as I skidded across the floor.

My scream spewed out of me like an uncontrollable tidal wave. Silas's shield reappeared.

I cut it off, sighing.

Silas dropped his hands, his shield dropping with it. He shortened the distance between us, so he no longer had to raise his voice. "You tried. It's progress."

Sure it is. I rubbed my eyes, scowling, then regretted it because—mascara.

"You'll get better. You just need to practice."

I peered up at him. The sun bore down; a delicate breeze tickled my exposed skin. "I'm not used to things being so difficult for me." The words came out before I considered them. I cringed. I might be presenting at a high standard today, but Silas was getting a front-row seat to the 'Best of Keanna: Internal Edition'. "How long did it take you to learn control?"

"A single day. I'm *spectacular.*"

I raised an eyebrow as he caught his tongue between his teeth.

"A few years," he amended. Seeing my face fall, he added, "But my situation is different. As an *avertat*, a lot of our learning curve is discovering what's possible and what's not. A *ferox* is similar—they can't create a weapon from nothing, but they can amplify the environment around them. A well-trained one can be quite lethal."

"What's Anika?"

"A *subicite.* She neutralizes energy."

No wonder Arwood had stood behind her in the execution room. Silas could weave defensive shields—Anika was a *walking* shield.

My mother hadn't left details about where she'd come from or if there were many others like her, so my father hadn't had anything on banshees to share. I lapped this information up like crazy. "How did you practice? Did you go to some mage boarding school, or something?"

"Family members are responsible for passing down knowledge. My father taught me."

His words had lost their inflection, their edges sharpening. I recognized the shift in tone. It was something my father did, too, when I hit a boundary. Obviously, Silas's family—or his father—was a place not to pry.

I changed the subject. "It costs a mage energy to use their abilities?" Silas nodded. "Which is why you passed out yesterday while I was ..."

"Redecorating?"

"Does that happen a lot?"

"It's a fine line. When I use, I feel *alive.* But too much too quickly strips you. Too much over a long period kills you."

With Arwood's team wearing his amulets, the drain on him would increase. Arwood was using Silas just as much—if not more—than he was using me. What hold did he have on Silas to make him willing to do this to himself?

"There's a price for using your power. Always?"

At his nod, I exhaled, a familiar thickening inside my throat. I swallowed it down. I'd been so careless in my retaliation after killing the thieves.

"I'm really sorry I hurt you yesterday." Another domino, pushed by Arwood.

Something flitted across Silas's face, too quick for me to catch. "Please stop apologizing for what you are."

"I need to. Me being here just makes everything worse for you."

He was watching me intently. His lips parted—

Gravel crunched. We shifted apart as Steadman rounded the hedges.

"Sorry to interrupt," Steadman said, not sounding remotely sorry at all. "Let's go."

Silas turned, but Steadman clicked his tongue. "Not you, kid. Her."

My gut clenched. I followed Steadman, leaving Silas behind.

CHAPTER FOURTEEN

Another night, another black outfit in Steadman's car. Lissandra and Anika accompanied us as we followed the stream of taillights through winding country roads. When Prague filled the windscreen, the other vehicles veered off the freeway to their respective destinations. We continued south-east. The gritty clash of glass and historical brick of the inner city gave way to neat tree-lined streets and monochromatic matchbox buildings.

Anika spent the entire drive playing Candy Crush, fingers darting across the screen as her head bopped to the 80s rock music Steadman was playing. The familiar songs reminded me of cooking dinner with my father, evenings with clashing guitar and drum solos flavored with medium-rare filet mignon and Italian wine. I clung to those memories as Steadman navigated us over tram lines, through countless traffic interchanges, and past Chodov shopping center.

The landmark helped anchor me: looming above were properties we leased, buildings I recognized. My fingers flexed for a phone I no longer held all hours of the day, palms itchy at the missed notifications and unanswered emails. The deadline for the procurement presentation had come and gone. I'd helped close on a massive portfolio sale last quarter, and I didn't even have the platform to showcase it.

Lissandra's painted nails tapped on her beige purse to Electric Light Orchestra's repetitive beat. No weapons, apart from what Steadman had pushed into his holster and behind his padded vest. One mage, one banshee, and two humans. It didn't seem like enough, but I clearly wasn't here for strategy.

A vehicle overtook us, leaving the neighboring lane empty. It invited intrusive thoughts of opening the car door and throwing myself onto the road. How far did I have to be to lose signal to my collar? I'd been at least fifty feet away last night, and Steadman had still brought me down. I'd have to move fast. A linear graph formed in my head, where I plotted the speed of the car versus the likelihood of sustaining serious injury. I wore a leather jacket and jeans, so that had to count for something. If I cradled my head as I rolled …

I prodded the interior. Steadman's G Wagon was the same brand as my father's sedan. Would Steadman have disabled the automatic locking doors? If so, wasn't there a way to override it by opening the door handle twice? Was that a thing?

Steadman cleared his throat, his blue eyes meeting mine in the rear-view mirror. I raised my eyebrows innocently as he wiggled a black object.

The remote.

The linear graph dissolved, along with fantasies of leaping, action-man style, toward freedom. I sat back, trying to keep my expression unaffected against the crawling sensation of his surveillance.

"May I ask where we're going?" I couldn't stop the apologetic inflection, even as the beast reminded me it was a valid question, considering I was now their 'employee'. "What's the plan?"

Steadman's deep voice added to the music filling the car. "I prefer to run these excursions with minimal detail."

Irritation flushed my skin. "Minimal implies quantity. You've dispensed none." The words were out before I could stop myself.

"Where you're concerned, I plan to keep it that way."

His self-assured tone reminded me why I hated him, and his socks, all over again. The memory of him squeezing my throat in the alleyway silenced my response.

Anika paused. "Don't be an asshole, Stead. Just answer the poor girl."

Lissandra laid a hand on Steadman's forearm and acknowledged me for the first time. Her thick hair, slicked into a bun, matched the color of her large, expressive brown eyes. Her eyeshadow was one of the best makeup jobs I'd ever seen. If things were different, I'd have asked her for tips. Everything about her, from her tailored black high-neck jumpsuit to the marquise diamond earrings hanging from her earlobes, screamed Old Money. "This neighborhood is a shared zone with the Kohnstamm family. We're treading lightly on a lead."

Finally, the link I was after. "We're visiting one of the locations Ferko mentioned."

"We have a well-placed mutual associate who may be able to provide information on Johan Matousek and who he's currently doing business with."

The lack of guards accompanying us made even less sense now. "Why didn't we bring a bigger team?"

"We're not expecting this to be a violent exchange."

If words determined reality, we were in for a peaceful night indeed. Unfortunately, my fledgling—but impressionable—exposure to their world indicated this to be unlikely.

"You probably said that last night, too," I retorted, remembering Lissandra's ruined white outfit.

Anika snorted. Steadman's grip tightened on the steering wheel. I cringed. What was *wrong* with me?

The corners of Lissandra's perfectly lined lips rose. "You're right to be wary," she murmured, humor and approval underscoring her Italian accent. It warmed my stomach. Annoyingly so. "Though our peace was hard won, we never assume it will last. We've taken appropriate precautions."

I didn't see any knives hidden underneath her long black sleeves but didn't comment further.

"Be careful," I whispered to Anika.

Anika smirked, streetlights dashing across her face like warpaint. "*You* be careful."

"Our priority," Lissandra said, "is to scout for Isobelle. Second: Objectively assess any information provided by our associate. Waldemar is a veritable chatterbox, but he may reveal something useful. And, Keanna?"

We'd driven into a tree-lined street; foot traffic had dropped off, and we were the only moving car for at least a hundred feet. The street name tugged at the threads of my memory, but nothing landed firm. I tore my gaze away.

"I look forward to working with you. Tonight, our goals are the same."

Was Lissandra threatening me, or confirming she knew of my deal with Arwood? I nodded, mostly to stop her from looking at me. The idea we might locate Isobelle sped up my pulse. Could it be over so quickly?

Minutes later, we pulled up beside a row of connected buildings, demarcations visible in the patchwork of colors; golden-yellow brick to the left, weathered beige to the right. Recessed windows stacked three stories high, some lit and showing hints of the rooms beyond. Most had curtains drawn shut, the businesses lining the ground floor closed for the night.

Anika unbuckled, pulling her hair into a haphazard bun, and shrugging on black fingerless gloves to complete her stretchy pants and black-knit ensemble. She darted from the car and disappeared into the shadowed alley next to the beige building. A few minutes later, a black figure slithered across the roof, halting at the cornice above a third-floor window sitting ajar.

Like, *barely* ajar. Surely she wasn't going to—

With acrobatic ease, Anika folded over the edge of the roof and slipped her Converse-clad feet through the gap. She hooked her ankles inside the window frame and allowed her upper body to recline. Then, displaying a feat of abdominal strength akin to a trapeze performer, she rose upwards, pushing the window up along with her.

Steadman and Lissandra sat like spectators used to such feats. Me? Well, aside from motivation to increase the resistance coils at my reformer classes, I wondered what else Anika had done in her twenty-something years. Was this just another Thursday night for her?

My inexperience with breaking and entering meant I had no

idea what to expect. I watched the dark window until Steadman's phone lit up with a message.

"'Five men on the top floor,'" he read aloud. "They're repackaging jewels. Counterfeits?"

"Unsanctioned activity, if that's the case," Lissandra replied. "Think Waldemar's flipped on us?"

"Men playing both sides are often ripped apart. You'd hope he was smarter than that."

They exchanged nuanced expressions like a dance they were both familiar with. Steadman's head tilted to the right, Lissandra's shifted to the left. His eyebrow rose, her mauve lips pursed.

Just as I started feeling like I'd intruded on an intimate moment, Lissandra said, "Let's go."

A street over, a dog barked, accompanying the train screech from the nearby Metro station. A cool breeze snaked between the buildings, agitating the fallen leaves coating the thresholds as our car doors slammed shut.

I wiped sweaty palms on my black jeans, following Steadman and Lissandra to a set of ornate Baroque-style wooden doors covered in wrought iron filigree. Beside the hinges sat two white plaques: one featured a black line drawing of a distinctly feline animal; the second was a capital C formed by two intertwining lines, like the iron vines on the doors. Above them in intervals were carved stone faces with gaping mouths. Their eyes seemed to follow Lissandra as she reached for the handle, leading us inside.

Waldemar Givozdy-Porath, a compact but debonair salesman in his fifties, swanned around Lissandra like a bird trying to attract a mate. First he complimented her outfit, then her earrings—"One of my favorites from our summer release!"—and once he sensed Lissandra was tiring of his flattery, he invited us to the adjoining room—in a dramatic, singsong dip of his voice—for an exclusive view of one of his newest designs, "if we are agreeable to this, of course."

The ground floor of the building was laid out like a traditional jewelry store, with walls of glass separating fingers from the sparkling treasures behind them. The Keanna I had been a month ago would have walked around this room in a distracted, superficial bubble. That Keanna would have inspected the antique chandelier rather than the cameras in the ceiling tracking our procession through the set of double doors. That Keanna wouldn't have noticed the bulkiness of Steadman's jacket concealing a weapon, nor the way he studied the windowless 'client conversation room' Waldemar led us to. She wouldn't have sought the exits on the likely assumption she'd be running for them before the night was finished. No, *that* Keanna would have only cared about the pretty items in the rectangular cabinets flanking us in H-formation, and whether she could have some of the champagne Lissandra accepted.

Arwood's statuesque wife was either used to gushing compliments—I mean, who could blame him? She really was stunning—or suspected Waldemar's sincerity went as deep as the pockets on his waistcoat, because she placed her half-empty flute on the client desk a little harder than necessary, interrupting him.

"We have some questions you may be able to assist us with." His face fell until she added, "Then, if time permits, a quick browse before we leave."

Steadman had taken up position at the doorway we'd entered. To his right, the outline of a black door blended into the black-painted brick walls. Thick crimson carpet sank under my boots, contributing to the claustrophobic sensation of being in a bank vault.

Anika waltzed into the room, making loud excuses about how she'd gotten lost finding the store. She locked eyes with Lissandra as she moved to stand beside me, the pop from her bubblegum ringing throughout the quiet, enclosed room.

As for me, I was hiding my eagerness.

I *knew* Waldemar Givozdy-Porath.

He knew me, too. Irritation at Anika's obnoxious gum chewing faded as he noticed my black collar. His eyes widened with recognition, his smile turning brittle. Just as quickly, he focused his attention back on Lissandra.

I felt Steadman's gaze on me. He'd noticed. Dammit.

Disappointment and urgency flooded my gut. My father had done business with this jeweler. We'd met at the ball last year. The contents of these cases confirmed the origin of the diamond necklace I'd received for my twentieth birthday. Had my father known Waldemar was caught up with people like Lissandra? Or was this just how the world worked, with mere degrees of separation between honest business and crime?

Either way, he was still a connection to my father, and right now I didn't care how. Could he see I was here against my will? Perhaps that was why his movements had stiffened, the pitch of his voice ringing higher. I hoped his nervousness wasn't because he thought I wanted him to interfere. Steadman noticing us had knocked my chances of slipping a message to Waldemar, but I wasn't ready to give up. I just had to find another way to get near him.

"I assume Ivan continues to be a client?" Lissandra asked, her fingers trailing over the satin couching the bracelet presented to her.

Waldemar nodded. "I am extremely appreciative of your support, and that of my other clients." He pointed to the bracelet.

Lissandra shook her head. "It is our pleasure to maintain the livelihood of those who assist us. Such is the intention of our visit. We have reason to believe a man called Johan Matousek has established headquarters in this neighborhood."

Waldemar made a show of wrapping the bracelet in cloth, a noise of agreement gurgling in his throat. Given Lissandra's careful phrasing, his nervousness made sense. It had nothing to do with me and everything to do with the fact that she represented Arwood.

"Do you have information to share on this man?" she asked.

The jeweler put the bracelet into the cabinet and motioned to Lissandra's champagne as if offering to top it up. When she declined, Waldemar said, "Nothing certain. I am ignorant of Johan's true appearance. They say he always keeps two men beside him as decoys. No one is sure whom out of the three he is, not even those he does business with."

"We've been told Johan may still supply Serbian girls to Ivan. Is this true?"

Anika popped her bubblegum; Waldemar flinched. "My lady, is this your way of enquiring if the Kohnstamms are involved in the recent attacks on your husband and … yourself, I believe?"

Lissandra perched her chin in her hands. I couldn't see her expression, but whatever the jeweler saw made him stiffen. "Word travels swiftly, I see."

Again, his eyes flitted to my collar. *Please.* I just needed the smallest of indicators he'd help me. "Anyone daring to disrupt Arwood's operations gets noticed, my lady."

"Then you understand why it is important we discern who is enabling Johan."

"Absolutely. I recently learned Ivan has increased acquisitions along your borders. *And* established a new shipment route through the country via Austria, something I found most peculiar—that is your dominion, yes?"

Lissandra didn't answer, her wedding ring tapping against the flute stem.

Anika walked along the cases, observing the earrings. She winked at me as she gave another obnoxious *pop,* eliciting another wince from Waldemar.

When Lissandra remained silent, Waldemar tried again, his voice silky. "He may have been using Johan to drive this activity and keep it from your notice. Perhaps the Kohnstamms mean to overthrow you?"

That got a response. "Careful with that conjecture. We don't deal in unsubstantiated gossip."

"Yes, yes." Another *pop.* Another flinch. "You have a treaty to maintain, of course."

Lissandra slowly sipped. Instead of being driven to quell the awkwardness, like I would have been, she used it to maintain control.

My default would have been to make him feel more comfortable. It wouldn't have gotten me anywhere.

Finally, she said, "Do you have names, evidence, to corroborate these claims?"

"Nothing of the sort, Ms. Camardo. Only wishing to alert you to beliefs the Kohnstamm party are no longer satisfied with arrangements, and to potential danger coming your way."

'Camardo' snagged in my mind. It took a second, but when it hit, I swallowed. Situated near Positano, the Camardo crime family had their fingers in many industrial pies and were notorious for dealing in everything from art to weapons to narcotics. My father had worked hard to ensure he didn't fall in with them—or fall out. The Czech Republic had been free of their influence until the last few years, but they planted roots wherever they landed. *Mixing business with the Camardos is a slippery slope,* he'd said. *The house always wins.*

No wonder Lissandra sat there with the feminine equivalent of Big Dick Energy. She didn't *need* Arwood. She and her family were scary enough. My burgeoning girl-crush popped like Anika's bubblegum, along with any hope that Waldemar would help me.

"I know you, Wald. You've thrived between both sides, but make no mistake—it's because we've allowed you to. Your manipulation is not serving you, and I would appreciate it if you ceased at once."

"Yes, yes, my sincerest apologies—"

"Furthermore," Lissandra said, "we've come to learn you've stepped outside the boundaries of your agreement with us. Who are you supplying to?"

"Supplying what, my lady?"

"The gems you're repackaging upstairs."

For some reason, Waldemar shot me a look of such fury I had difficulty comprehending it. "You've heard rumors, have you? I wonder *where.* Well, I fear you are misinformed. I—"

Anika pulled a plastic package of stones from her pocket,

lowering it on the desk the way someone would present the final card in Rummy.

Lissandra nudged it. "We would never place our name behind something so tawdry. You are well-versed in the rule that counterfeit trade of any kind is not approved. That's not what this is?"

Waldemar's chest puffed as much as his waistcoat allowed. "Of course not! I only trade in the highest quality dia—"

"Banshee?" I jumped as Anika addressed me. "Daddy Backhus teach you how to spot a fake?"

Oh no. Oh no, *no*. I shouldn't have been so confident with the white jade in the lab. "I mean, I'm alright at it, but—"

Lissandra reached over, plucking the loupe out of Waldemar's waistcoat pocket.

"My lady, this is not—"

"—it's been months since I've studied a diamond, and—"

"—as it appears, I assure you that—"

"—I'm not sure I'll—"

Between our sputtering, Lissandra must have hit her limit, because she barked "Enough!" and beckoned for me to come closer. She thrust the loupe into my hands. "Are they as he says?"

I blinked, torn, the loupe dangling from my fingers. If I condemned Waldemar, he'd never help me. But if I lied, would Lissandra be able to tell? This felt like a test, especially since she struck me as someone who would know diamonds—or at least, know what *wasn't*.

"I left my glasses at home," she said, as if hearing my thoughts. "Otherwise I'd assess it myself."

I bit my lip, peering through the loupe. It didn't take long. A flip of the gem to vary the angle told me all I needed: there was a double refraction. Given the brilliance and color, it was most likely moissanite. In itself, not a crime—unless you're charging diamond prices.

I tried to keep my face blank as I considered what to do, but Lissandra took one look at me and turned to Waldemar.

"There must be a mistake, my lady!" He extracted a navy

wrapped package. With it came a tangy, metallic aroma I most definitely did not want to smell.

No one commented on the scent, not even Steadman.

"I swear to you, if there are replicas in this building, they are not of my doing. This is my newest approved intake. See?"

He unclasped the box, revealing a pile of individual gems.

The pungent smell grew worse as he defended the cut and clarity. I tasted its familiarity on the back of my tongue: the concrete nightclub room, Arwood's plastic-lined interrogation room.

Death. Danger.

The smell grated my senses. *Move*, the beast urged. *We're not safe.*

Beside me, Anika rolled her eyes at the jeweler's protests. She'd think I was crazy, but she probably already thought I was. I gestured to her, drawing a finger across my jugular.

Anika raised her eyebrows, signaling for Steadman's attention.

Waldemar urged Lissandra to lean closer. "See the way the light reflects—"

And he swung a knife upward, aiming for Lissandra's exposed neck.

CHAPTER FIFTEEN

A CRY OF WARNING STUCK IN MY THROAT AS THE BLADE glinted underneath the overhead lights. One of Lissandra's clasped fists opened, violet flashing across her irises.

A thin sapphire shield bubbled around the knife Waldemar held, cushioning it against Lissandra's neck and protecting her from harm. I gasped. So did Waldemar. He flinched like he'd been burned and tried to shake off the shield like a bug as it closed on his arm. His released knife remained suspended inside the shield, inches below his fingers.

"What in th—"

Lissandra's palm flipped. The shield spread, shifting to coat his hand like a glove. When she angled her wrist backwards, Waldemar's moved in the opposite direction.

The crack of bone accompanied his sudden scream as the shield disappeared. The knife clattered onto the counter. He staggered, cradling his wrist, his gaze darting from his hand to Lissandra like he couldn't believe what he'd just witnessed.

I couldn't, either. Lissandra was an *avertat* like Silas?

Lissandra drove the tip of the blade into the wooden frame of the counter with a *thunk*, the handle wobbling. "I'll ask you again: who is enabling Johan?"

Instead of answering, Waldemar leaped for the counter—to hit a panic button?—before Lissandra tossed him against the wall using another shield.

Footsteps clattered outside, jumpstarting my heart.

"Crap," Anika muttered, popping her bubble gum. "Incoming!"

Both doors flew open, and men entered from either side. I looked at their weapons and dove behind the nearest glass case. Forget finding Isobelle. I was going to die long before we even got *close* to locating her.

Someone grunted. Bone crunched. The doors stayed open.

Steadman was distracted. So was everyone else.

I scrambled up, racing for the room leading to the street. I just needed to get further away—

An arm connected with my collar, knocking me onto my butt. Breath seized in my lungs. Pain lanced my throat as my vision spun. The man who'd coat-hangered me aimed his gun at me.

"Don't shoot!" I rasped, adrenalin spiking through my body as I slid backwards, colliding with the glass cabinet. "Please, I'm not attacking you!"

He paid me no heed; his finger tightened.

Oh my God. "NO!"

The word pierced upwards. The man gripped the side of his head like I'd stabbed his eardrums.

But no wave of pressure released. He wasn't dead. *I* wasn't dead. *What the hell?*

A dagger connected to Steadman's hand painted a crimson line underneath the man's chin. The gun dropped to the ground. Blood gushed. The man swayed, a terrible sucking, groaning sound coming from his mouth.

Steadman spared me the briefest of 'you're welcome' glances before dodging the knife heading straight for his own neck and thrusting an answering blade into his attacker's pelvis.

I squeaked as a dead body folded over my shins. Hysteria lodged in my throat as I shook them loose. On the other side of the room, Lissandra was interrogating Waldemar against the bricks, shields banding like ropes across his chest and arms. She didn't see the burly man creeping behind Steadman or how he clocked him upside the head, throwing him against the wall. Steadman staggered as the man drove a knife toward his face.

Steadman blocked him at the last second, the blade dangerously close to his eye.

"Liss," he panted, pushing against the man's forearm. He matched his attacker in height but not brawn, especially at this angle. "A little help?"

A floating shield appeared above the man. It enveloped his head, constricting. Suffocating him. He jerked, allowing Steadman to wrestle the knife away. The man's fingers scraped against the shield as Steadman drove the knife home and kicked him to the ground.

Blood pooled inches from my foot, drenching the carpet. A phone lay on the ground where Waldemar had stood. Had it fallen out of his pocket?

After all the business they'd done together, he'd have my father's number programmed. I had to get to it.

Anika's cackle bounced from the left as she flitted between two men, their fists and knives missing her at every turn. She swung a piece of metal frame torn from a broken display case; holding it like a baseball bat, she took aim at the man closest.

Thwack. He pinwheeled, falling as the other closed in, firing at her.

With a grunt, I forced myself onto my hands and knees. *Get to the phone.*

Bullets scattered as I crawled. I concentrated on them like milestones. *Just get to the next bullet. Then the next.* Were they missing, or connecting with Anika's skin and falling? Either way, it didn't slow her down. With two swings, she knocked the gun clean out of the second man's grip and made sure he wouldn't have children in the future.

When he doubled over, squealing, she spotted me and rested her 'bat' on her shoulder. "You good, banshee?"

Her words alerted the man getting to his feet. Blood poured from his pulverized nose. Sensing an easier target, he stalked toward me.

No no no. A sob caught as I grabbed at the glass case beside me, terror turning my knees to jelly.

Wait.

Glass. Case.

I tried to visualize like Silas had taught me, but a panicked scream ripped from me. The wave billowed outwards, glass shattering. Lissandra flung out her hand. A shield wall cut the room in half, protecting her, Steadman, and Waldemar from my outburst. On our side, everything breakable broke, and the two remaining attackers flew backwards.

One smacked into the wall headfirst like a wet cloth slapping on cement, and—

Oh, *ew.*

"Nice," Anika crowed as protruding metal framing impaled the other.

Acidic bile gurgled. I retched, trying not to vomit.

Broken lights sparked and popped above us. The ones on the other side still shone, highlighting the perspiration coating Waldemar's hairline as Lissandra stabbed his thigh with the knife he'd tried to use on her.

The shield wall dropped. Waldemar's scream rang clear.

Lissandra pushed his quivering chin upwards with a finger. "Did Johan put you up to this?"

"It's not worth my life to give information on Johan."

"It's not worth your death to protect him, either." Lissandra flicked the knife handle, making him cry out again. "Why, Wald?"

"I will not commit to a sinking ship. Arwood's losing his grip."

"He's losing *nothing*," Steadman snarled.

Waldemar set his jaw as best he could with his lip trembling, glaring at them both. "We've heard otherwise."

I was going to throw up. I breathed deeply, waiting for the nausea to subside while I scanned the crimson carpet. Where was the phone? It must have shifted with my outburst.

"Tell us," Lissandra said, "and it spares you."

"I will not. We fear Johan more than Arwood."

Lissandra sighed, stepping back. "Unfortunately, that was your final mistake. Thinking Arwood is the only one to be scared of."

The shield crept upwards, consuming the jeweler's panicked gasps. Soon, the only sound filling the room was the flinch-inducing discharge of Steadman's gun.

"'Peaceful exchange,' huh?" Steadman murmured as Waldemar's body slid to the ground like a sack of potatoes.

Lissandra rolled her eyes. "Oh, shush, you."

"*Stead!*"

Metal framing clattered. Anika's black-clad figure tore across the room, leaping into the air as a shotgun discharged—right for Steadman's head. The shot collided with her back as she landed on Steadman, arms and legs wrapping around his neck and torso like a child getting a piggyback ride.

She sucked in a ragged breath, her eyes turning black. Bullet fragments fell to the floor as Anika thrust her hand into the side of Steadman's vest. In the time I gave a stunned blink, she'd extracted a throwing knife and sent it careening toward the man who'd slipped through the door, holding a shotgun.

The knife lodged beneath his slack, gaping jaw. His gun crashed to the floor moments before his knees.

Anika slid off Steadman. She pulled his face down and gave him a big, smacking kiss on his cheek. "'Thank you so much, goddess divine,'" she said, her voice deepening comically.

"Thank you," Steadman grunted, shaking out of her grasp. He pulled the knife free from the man's neck. "You said there were five men upstairs."

Anika pursed her lips. "Six is basically five. It's like a tax add-on."

Steadman raised an eyebrow, using a spot on his shirt free from blood to wipe his knife clean.

"I was focused on the gems, Stead."

I staggered to my feet as we listened out for further activity upstairs. A warped piece of technology caught my eye: my scream had destroyed Waldemar's phone.

I almost burst into tears. Another opportunity gone.

"Seriously though, I clocked five. This dude," Anika nudged the shotgun with a sneakered foot, "must have been hiding. Banshee, come with. I need a travel buddy."

Though I wasn't convinced I wouldn't vomit up my dinner, I trailed her out the door, Lissandra and Steadman following behind.

"Even hoarding real diamonds," I said as we climbed the staircase, "why would a jeweler house so many men with guns?"

"Precisely my point, babe," Anika replied. "They wouldn't."

A busy blend of houseplants crowded the upstairs apartment. Music videos in a foreign language played on a wide-screen television beside a window left ajar. The small kitchen featured a table covered in a mountain of gems, plastic bags, and scales. Muffled screaming sounded to our right. One bedroom stood empty, save for a four-poster with black bedding. The other—

"Ah, fuck," Steadman said.

Anika barged past him into the room where six women were huddled on the floor. Filthy hair and tear-tracked skin pinched underneath gags and ropes. Diamonds were branded below their earlobes, like the one on Ferko's neck. My belly swooped as they recoiled from her.

Anika loosened their restraints. She deferred to the least hysterical one, introducing herself. The woman eyed her warily but responded as Anika pulled her phone from her pocket.

"Shit," she murmured, tilting her device. No light shone from the shattered screen. "Stead, can I have yours?"

Steadman passed his phone over and Anika zoomed in on a photo until a girl with long platinum-blonde hair filled the screen. She showed it to the women. They all looked so scared—and there was nothing I could do. They shook their heads, shivering, murmuring too low for me to hear. Anika returned to the doorway.

"They've been here at least a day. No sign of Isobelle here or during transit."

"Nationality?" Lissandra asked.

"Serbian."

"Sounds like an order for Ivan," Steadman said. *"Fuck."*

Lissandra pressed her lips together. "Or Johan could be trying to encroach on Kohnstamm trade. Regardless, we can't afford to linger."

"Leave them."

Anika gaped at Steadman. "But—"

"The police will be here soon," he said as he and Lissandra turned to leave. I was surprised we couldn't hear sirens already. "They'll take care of them."

Anika whispered in reassuring tones to the group. I wanted to do *something*, but I was as helpless in my situation as they were in theirs.

"This isn't your fight, Anika. Let's go."

For that, Steadman received her middle finger. Anika got in his face once she exited the room. "Women like that are *always* gonna be my fight," she snapped. "That's the first and last time I'll walk away from one. Ask me to again, and I'll stop taking bullets for you."

She shouldered past us all and marched down the stairs.

CHAPTER SIXTEEN

ANIKA'S DESTROYED PHONE LAY ON THE CAR SEAT, HER lips cherry red between white teeth. I hated the haunted expression on her face that had appeared the moment we'd left the women behind. Rightly or wrongly, I cared whether she was okay. She didn't look it.

"Is there anything I can do?" I whispered.

Her smirk came thin and forced, like the majority of her thoughts were elsewhere. "You've given plenty. Watching a sex trafficker get skewered like a hotdog bun made my day."

And I was back to feeling sick again.

A familiar sight met us at the mansion. Injured guards. Medical personnel. A vice clamped around my stomach as I searched the foyer for Silas's curls. He wasn't there. What did that mean? Lissandra had handled herself fine with Waldemar, and I knew Silas could too …

Arwood, Steadman and Lissandra stood beside the staircase, snatches of their conversation audible above the movement.

Seven men down.

Johan.

Ambush.

Seven men? The vice tightened. Seven chances it could have been Silas.

Steadman murmured, "Ivan making his move?" like it linked everything together. But did it? After watching him and Lissandra, I wasn't so sure Steadman had Arwood's best interests at heart.

I was horribly tempted to stay out of it. This was *their* circus. Arwood deserved any and all attacks he suffered.

But …

I'd nearly died, too. I didn't want 'collateral damage' printed on my headstone, and every night involved in Arwood's vendetta was another night of being exposed to whoever was targeting *him*. This Johan guy, and the people he worked with, appeared to know our movements as soon as we did. Did they have someone on the inside?

In meetings, my father encouraged his team to say the obvious thing in case it wasn't, in fact, obvious. You can get blinded by the consuming nature of your own reality. Would Arwood appreciate me pointing out the obvious?

I was about to find out.

My hands shook as I approached the trio, but I squared my shoulders, longing for my flattering professional clothes instead of this stupid leather jacket. Jeans that probably made my butt look hideous. Boots which made *so much noise* on the tiles.

At the *clop clop clop* of my interruption, their voices hushed. Steadman turned. Blood was smeared up his temple and into his brown hair.

"Banshee."

I ignored him, addressing Arwood. He was immaculate, like Lissandra. *Teflon.* "How confident are you of your people?"

I waited for Arwood to belittle or dismiss me. He didn't. A good start. "In normal circumstances, very."

"I don't know how your visits to the jeweler normally go, but killing everyone working there isn't my idea of a good outcome. Can we talk privately?"

Steadman raised his eyebrows at Arwood, whatever that meant. I shot him a look of disdain. He may have saved me tonight, but I didn't trust the guy at all.

Arwood excused Steadman and Lissandra. They both walked up the staircase, Steadman's face relaxing into a smile as he leaned closer to Lissandra, laughing at something she said. Arwood wasn't paying them the slightest bit of attention. Seriously? Arwood was way too smart to be this blind.

"Something bothering you, Miss Backhus?"

Here goes nothing. "Waldemar said things are slipping past your notice. Your teams keep getting attacked. You might need to start considering that someone inside these walls wants you to fail."

"Steadman mentioned Waldemar recognized you."

"My father is a client."

"Interesting. Such a small city, Prague is."

Talking with Arwood was like walking across a minefield. Too late, I realized how this must look. "I'm not tipping anyone off, if that's what you're thinking. But it's looking like someone is."

Beside us, medical personnel packed up their belongings. The guards waved them off good-naturedly, like they knew them well— Arwood no doubt had a team of nurses, doctors, probably even cops on his payroll—and helped their injured coworkers to their feet. The front door opened; I hugged my torso to stave off the midnight chill.

"We are taking steps to address the emerging issue," Arwood said. "I appreciate you speaking up, regardless."

Instead of saying, 'Don't you think your right-hand man snaking your wife is the real emerging issue?' I gave him a very restrained, "The sooner we find Isobelle, the sooner I go home."

Arwood's lips tilted, a dimple forming within the stubble coating his square jaw. It softened the harsh lines of his face. How could someone like Arwood look so approachable, so *trustworthy*, rather than the godfather-like overlord he clearly was? "Staying may bring you the answers you're looking for."

I frowned.

"My late wife, Michelle, shared your gift. After she passed, I vowed to learn all I could to better support our daughter."

Wait a second. "Isobelle is a banshee?"

Arwood inclined his head, and this information smacked me hard. I'd wondered at his rationale for abducting me. Yes, a killer banshee was an effective weapon, but so was an *avertat* like Silas. So was bulletproof Anika. Why *me*?

Unless he thought the person who'd stolen his daughter might want me, too.

"That's why you're so sure she was taken," I said without thinking. "You think someone's using her the way you're using me. You want to lure them out!"

The smile forming at the mention of his daughter vanished. "Sometimes we need to think like our enemies to best them."

"And sometimes, in the pursuit of vengeance, you become what you're seeking to destroy."

Arwood's hazel eyes narrowed a fraction—which, for him, equated to a full-blown glare. "There are no depths I won't descend to get my daughter back."

I knew. I'd seen it.

"Isobelle wouldn't want you turning into a monster to save her."

"If your father were presented with the same advantages, do you think he'd behave differently?"

I didn't bother giving Arwood a response. Even though I didn't know what actions my father had taken so far to get me back, it wouldn't be by sinking to this level. I turned and grabbed the wrought-iron railing of the staircase, hoping the conversation was over.

It wasn't.

"I knew your mother," Arwood murmured. "Shay O'Carragher. She was powerful and charismatic. Forsook her Irish heritage for what she thought was love. Did your father tell you how she died?"

My skin chilled like I'd stepped on a landmine. I was *not* talking about this. "Yes," I replied coldly.

"I'm sure Edson was ever so forthcoming with the truth. I assume he explained why she was alone when she had you?"

I whipped my head over my shoulder, glaring at Arwood, but he shrugged, hands in the pockets of his unblemished business suit. I'd poked him, but he was shaking me, right down to my foundation.

"I see. Have a chat with your father when you see him again. In the meantime, employee privileges extend to the library—for the duration you're here, at least. Good night, Miss Backhus."

I seethed on the way to my room. I never walked away from Arwood feeling like I'd won anything, and tonight was no different. If we found Isobelle, I'd find someone else like me. I'd be able to ask how she controlled her beast.

But if we found Isobelle, I was free to leave.

I'd believed Arwood was extending an olive branch. Instead, he'd continued to bait the hook, followed it up with claiming to know my mother, and then attempted to plant doubt about my father.

My mother had been traveling to visit her estranged sister when she'd given birth to me. I'd never asked why so close to her due date; the look my father would get whenever my mother was mentioned wasn't worth the question. Trust Arwood to find a horrible situation and twist it to play games with me.

Except ... what had he meant about forsaking her heritage for what she 'thought' was love?

By the time I opened my bedroom door, the muscles of my back were wound tight and sweat pooled under the collar of my jacket. My reflection did not please me. A cowlick had formed, the baby hairs around my part frizzed, and was that *blood*? On my *shoes*?

I still had no idea where Silas was. I could knock on every door on this floor to see if he was behind one of them, but I'd be caught by the camera stationed outside of my room. How could I sleep, not knowing if he'd made it back?

Damn Arwood, and the dispensable way he treated us all. Damn Steadman and his stupid cactus socks. Damn this whole entire mansion.

I slammed my door, kicking it with my stupid, blood-soaked boots. A thrill shot through me. It felt ... *good.*

A vase of fresh yellow freesias sat next to the Chesterfield.

My father sent freesias whenever he canceled plans with me.

Freesias meant something else had taken priority. Freesias meant a night alone.

I *was* alone, and freesias with their long shelf-life were a cruel reminder. Had Arwood somehow known this, and was messing with me? After everything I'd experienced tonight?

Asshole.

I sent the antique vase soaring across the room. The ceramic smashed against the vertical wooden paneling beside the recessed window and fell into a heap on the hardwood floor. My beast thrilled at the sight.

For a second I did too—then reality kicked in. I held my breath, waiting for movement outside. I'd bargained for this room; what would happen if they caught me ruining it? When silence remained, I approached the mess of broken stems and musty, waterlogged flowers. Someone would clean it up if I left it like this.

But Arwood and Steadman and everyone else in this estate made messes for other people to clean up, too. I wouldn't be like them.

With a sigh, I pulled the toilet roll from the adjoining bathroom and began mopping up the water. I separated chunks of ceramic and stem as cool air tickled my flushed cheeks. For a moment I enjoyed the sensation—

Why is there a breeze?

One of the wooden panels had split and caved under the weight of the vase. Leaning over the mess, I peered across a gap of about two feet. Light shone onto a stone wall.

Which seemed … far.

Another cone of light illuminated the wall, coming from my left. I stood, squinting. How was the light getting through?

My stomach lifted in excitement as I spotted a keyhole partially concealed behind a picture frame, camouflaged by rust and the vertical lines of the panels. The tiniest of gaps separated the panels to the right of the keyhole. I shoved at it with my shoulder. The wall shifted further.

Holy hell, it was a *door*.

Icy air washed across my skin as I held my breath again, preparing for one of Arwood's cronies to barge in. Still nothing. I shoved again. Light poured into a narrow, dark passage.

Floorboards creaked as I crossed the threshold. I met the dust with a sneeze. The passageway ran parallel between the walls of the rooms and the stone of the mansion's exterior, interrupted at intervals by what I presumed were the recessed windows arching overhead. It was wide enough to crouch underneath.

Did every room have a door like this? The mansion was centuries old. This could have been a way for servants to get in and out of the rooms without being noticed by house guests.

Arwood's cameras saw everything inside the house. Anika had mentioned Arwood's late stepmother had renovated many years ago. Did this passageway show up on any current blueprints? Did anyone living here now know this existed? The undisturbed state of the floor waylaid any fears about being spied on; my boots were leaving visible footprints in the heavy dust.

Anticipation dashed up my spine. Did this passageway lead outside?

Did it run behind Silas's room?

I shouldn't go down there. I clearly wasn't allowed to.

Do it, my beast pushed.

Steadman would assume I was trying to escape again.

Do it.

I sneezed. Arwood would ...

Would what? Keep me here as prisoner? Shock my collar? Nothing he hadn't already done or wasn't currently doing.

Needing to learn if Silas was okay decided things for me. I'd started pulling the passage door closed to conceal my departure when three sharp raps sounded from my bedroom door opposite. I had no time to react before the door swung open.

"Damn, banshee. You're a bad girl."

CHAPTER SEVENTEEN

"U**h …," I trailed off. There wasn't any way to** justify what I was doing.

Anika tilted her head, a bottle of whiskey hanging from one hand. Her spiky ponytail was back, and she'd switched out her clothes for an oversize navy sweater and leggings.

"There's a door." She kicked the bedroom door shut with her bare foot. "In the wall." From her smirk, she hopefully wasn't about to dob me in. "I was gonna ask if you wanted to commemorate not dying tonight, but it looks like you're going all Houdini on me."

"I'm not trying to escape." My defensive tone wasn't the least bit trustworthy.

"Oh, no, of course not." Anika peered past me, whistling. "I knew Lady Helena was my kind of woman, but this is something else."

"Who?"

"One of the ladies in the 1800s supposedly visited the earl's brother as much as her husband. This musta been how she did it. Personally, I'm living for the idea that she didn't choose between two men. Not the only time these walls have seen such deliciousness."

I eyed the bottle of whiskey. "You came here … to drink with me?"

"And now we're exploring walls *inside* walls. I love my life."

Which was how I found myself walking down the passage with Anika as she shone a light from her newly acquired phone. I glanced behind, expecting to see Steadman or one of the guards ready to pounce. Goosebumps ran up my arms, along with an urge to whisper *weshouldnotbehere,* and yet curiosity overpowered me. I wanted to see where it led.

I'd been correct in thinking the passageway had access to all rooms in this wing. We crouched under the window panels connecting the interior walls to outside. Blackened keyholes reflected the silvery phone light.

A shaft of amber shone further down, bouncing off the stone— "My room," Anika winked, "in case you need a bedtime story or two"—and a few dark keyholes later, we came to another illuminated from inside.

Through that keyhole—

I gasped, wincing as the dusty floorboards creaked.

"A cleaner dancing naked?" Anika guessed.

"Worse. It's Silas."

At least he was alive. I'd resisted asking Anika about him, figuring questions would draw the wrong attention. The knot in my stomach over his safety eased, dominated by a knot of a, um, different kind.

"*Silas* is dancing naked? That sounds better, not worse." Anika shoved her eye against the keyhole, exhaling roughly. "Hail Mary," she said in an exaggerated southern accent. "He's doin' *push-ups.*"

I shushed her. "We really shouldn't—"

"Uh, yes we really fucking should—"

"But this is an invasion of privacy!" I hissed. *"And* he might prefer to be alone."

"And miss us showing adequate appreciation for *this* display of masculinity? I think not. Here." Anika thrust the bottle at me, ignoring my protests, as she contemplated the keyhole and the handle underneath. "Did yours open without a key?"

At my nod, she grabbed the handle. Ancient hinges groaned, the door shifting inwards.

Silas yelped. He jumped to his feet, hair mussed and damp from exercise, chest heaving from exertion. Bewildered looked cute on him.

Everything looked cute on him. Dammit.

I tried not to notice how the bedside lamp threw muted light over the curves of his exposed biceps, or the way his shirt stretched across his chest. Anika tugged the door open wide enough for us to slip through. She raised her fists in triumph.

"*What the*—"

"—fuck, right?" she finished, inviting herself inside. "Caught Keanna being a little voyeur skulking in the passageway"—my mouth fell open—"so I thought we'd join you."

"I *wasn't*."

Anika gave an exaggerated wink. "This is a safe space, babe. We're not here to yuck your yum."

I glanced at the ceiling. What was the likelihood of it collapsing to save me from my embarrassment?

When it didn't, there was nothing left to do but hold up the bottle. "Night cap?"

Silas pulled on a sweater as he came closer, studying the camouflaged keyhole. Like in my room, it sat flush against a picture frame, embedded into the wooden panels.

"I wasn't spying on you," I reiterated, just in case, "but there's a passageway behind this wall. I'm six doors down and have the same thing. I'd patch this up, if I were you."

"No kidding." He rubbed his face. "*Passageway*, you said?"

"Yep," Anika said. "Steadman unfortunately mislaid this whiskey. Wanna help us finish it?"

Silas grabbed something from the pocket of his leather jacket lying across the arm of the couch. His room, similar in layout and furnishings to mine, was littered with books and tossed clothes. They carried his spicy scent and laced the air with it. "After tonight, I won't say no." He jammed gum into his mouth, chewing, before smushing it inside the hole.

Gross, albeit effective.

"I feel like Arwood would have an issue with us drinking together." There. I'd said it. "*And* Steadman."

"Don't worry, they're distracted." Anika plopped to the ground cross-legged. "Got something to pour this into, or are we all sharing mouth germs?"

Silas plonked down a glass, teacup and mug, taking a seat adjacent to Anika. He pushed a decorative cushion from his unmade bed toward me.

I eyed them as they debated which drinking game to play. Talking like this would be a great way to get more information on Arwood, or Isobelle, or both. But did they want me to stay? Their bond was obvious. Both mages, close in age ...

Jealousy prickled cold under my sternum.

"Sit, Keeks." Silas nudged the cushion again and turned to Anika. "And I'm enforcing a ban against strip poker." I froze as I sank down, imagining having to remove items of clothing in front of these insanely attractive people, only relaxing once he said, "Two lies and a truth, please."

"You're *such* a Sagittarius." Anika poured several inches of amber liquid for each of us and handed the cups out. "Fine. Let's start with childhood hobbies, they say a lot about a person. What did little Silas do—or *not* do—in his lunchbox days?"

Silas's swig was interrupted by her sigh.

"Breaking the rules already. Great start."

He swilled the remaining whiskey in his mug. "Sagittarius, remember? Okay. Growing up, I a) sang in an acapella group"—Anika snorted—"b) participated in a professional parkour championship or c) spent my weekends ballroom dancing."

We locked eyes. His had a knowing gleam.

Anika started playing some music from her phone. "You, my friend, are tone deaf. I vote parkour."

"Are you sure?" I blurted.

"Absolutely," Anika said. "I've seen this guy in action. Parkour. Final answer."

I took a sip, trying to play down my confidence as dry, malty whiskey seared my tongue. I hoped it wasn't misplaced. "I pick ball-room dancing."

"I'd reconsider, banshee," Anika interjected. "*This* guy doesn't dance."

Again, my gaze found his. My pulse raced like we were at the ball all over again, his grip tightening and releasing as he led me through the steps.

I see you, his eyes said.

I suppressed the desire to break out into a Taylor Swift song about red lips and nice dresses at sunset. "I'm keeping my answer."

"I know a lightweight when I see one," Anika said. "We need you lasting longer than the first round."

But Silas smirked, tapping Anika's teacup. "Drink. Keanna's correct."

Anika looked between us, dumbfounded. "Well. Shit." She downed the whiskey, refilling it. "Beginner's luck. Winner goes next."

My chest loosened as Anika waited expectantly. There was no hint of impatience. She really wanted me here.

"Can you give me a subject?" I asked, circling the rim of my glass.

A wicked gleam pierced Anika's eyes. "What's the most impulsive thing you've ever done? Give us your worst."

Thomas, crumpled beneath a shattered hotel window.

Gaping crimson pits where eyes used to be.

I took another sip, ignoring Anika's protest about not drinking too much.

Matej tugging Ri's lifeless body.

Concrete walls smeared with blood.

I forced my mind down a different track. I had to keep things light, or I'd make things awkward for everyone.

"A) I shoplifted a dress I liked even though I could afford it," I said, watching the floor. On top of everything else, I was probably an even worse liar when whiskey was involved. "B) I ditched my security team when I was seventeen to attend a party—and passed out there, or c) I deferred my university degree and left Australia to live here with my father."

The first two were urges I hadn't given in to. I must have been transparent—or predictable—because Silas and Anika chorused without hesitation, "C."

"Am I that obvious? I could have shoplifted."

"How do I say this delicately?" Anika tilted my glass toward my mouth. "You reek of rule following."

Something about the way she said that got my back up. "I'm here, aren't I? You found me sneaking down a hidden passageway."

"And I bet underneath that leather jacket you've been sweating ever since."

I just stared at her, sucking whiskey off my lips because, well … she was right.

Her phone lit up with a shrill tone, interrupting the music. She raised a finger. "ALM Holdings, may I take a message?" she answered, transforming into a spiky-ponytailed secretary. After an *uh-hum* and *yes,* she responded, "We will confirm your appointment within twenty-four hours. Thank you for calling."

ALM Holdings?

Anika waved for us to continue as she typed a message.

Silas leaned closer, lowering his voice. "Your accent gave you away," he said, responding to my initial question. "How long have you lived here?"

Of course. My British accent had adopted an Australian drawl from the years living in Sydney, and provided a constant reminder I'd never found somewhere I felt truly at home. "Just over a year. My father wants to stay in Prague until he's established our new division, then we'll move back to London."

"Does your mother live in Australia?"

An inevitable question. I smiled apologetically to lessen the sting. "My mother died when I was born."

He didn't say sorry, or share platitudes to try and improve a situation that was awful all round. In his eyes I saw empathy. Shared understanding. Who had he lost?

"I used to live in England, too," he said instead. "Born in Sorrento, raised in Chicago. We moved all over when I was younger."

"Hey, save it for the game," Anika interjected. "You two are burning through topics. Finish your drink, banshee, so I can go."

I pointed to her phone. "Do you have a side hustle?"

She resumed the music. "You're looking at the Chief Executive Officer of ALM Holdings."

"It's a registered shell company for Arwood," Silas explained. "The answering service acts as a screening filter for new clients and partnerships. Anika here manages exactly one person—herself."

She nodded to my drink. "I'm hard to manage."

I downed the rest of my whiskey, grimacing as it burned my esophagus. This was the opportunity I'd been waiting for. "What's the craziest thing you've seen, working here?"

"Ooh, I like this one." Anika tapped her chin as she refilled my glass. "How about, a) selling an artifact to a suspected vampire, b) watching a banshee render a roomful of people blind, or c) seeing a witch bind an entire family with a spell?"

Was she being serious? "*Vampires* exist? And witches?" I should have contemplated this earlier. What else was out there?

Anika cackled, taking immense pleasure in my shock. "Maybe. If they *do* exist, I've never met one. But most people don't think banshees exist either." She winked.

I settled back onto the cushion, my brain whirring. "Except I don't make people go blind."

"Isobelle did. Does," Anika retorted as I paused.

"Giving yourself away constitutes an immediate fail," Silas told Anika. "Drink."

"Wait. Wait," I cut in. "Isobelle doesn't kill people when she screams?"

"Not like you, babe."

My dismay must have shown, because Silas said, "Being different isn't necessarily a bad thing."

Except the killing people part.

"Your turn, *avertat*." Anika prodded his shoulder. "Favorite sex position?"

I bit my lip. Thank God I hadn't received that question. I'd suffered a handful of awkward dates throughout high school and my first year of university, and very few of those had led to a kiss, let alone sex. How would I have responded? *Uh, no idea, because I've never done it.*

Silas shook his head at Anika. "You just had to go there, didn't you?"

"You wouldn't let me have strip poker. You get this."

"Well, it's a wasted question." Silas's grin was anything but innocent. The whiskey must have gone straight to my head, because it was … hot. And endearing. "The real lie would be saying any position isn't a good one."

My chest warmed while my beast helpfully reminded me how Silas had looked while exercising. I studied the contents of my glass like my life depended on it, trying to ignore the stirrings low in my abdomen.

"I'm sensing some frustration there. Big shame you can't leave campus to work it off."

"Don't brag about your excursions, *subicite*," Silas replied, drinking. He gestured between me and him. "We get a different set of terms and conditions for being here."

"My condolences to your libidos," Anika teased. Seeing my frown, she explained, "Arwood doesn't allow fraternization among his employees. It's hypocritical as hell, but he doesn't want someone taking a bullet for their lover instead of, say, Lissandra."

I would *not* look at Silas.

"Wouldn't that be tough for him to police?" I regretted speaking as they both stared at me. "I mean, it's a big mansion and there's a lot of, um, rooms."

"Wow, Backhus. *There's* your spine." Anika sounded insultingly impressed at this development. "Look, it's your life. Personally, no amount of getting railed against a headboard is worth pissing Arwood off and him throwing you at the mercy of the Sect."

She'd laughed in front of a loaded gun. Anything Anika was wary of was something to note. "I'm almost afraid to ask what that is."

"The Ripotesta—known colloquially as the Sect—govern mages and other supernatural beings who pop up to say hello."

My lips parted, but nothing came out.

"With what we can do, someone has to make sure we're not exposing ourselves to humans. These mages execute first and ask questions never. Unless you want them to unalive you, staying off their radar is the agreed approach." As if reading my mind, she added, "The fact they haven't come after you yet means they either don't know you're a banshee, or—more likely—Arwood's protecting you from them. May wanna give him a reason to keep it that way."

"How do you know this?"

Anika filled her teacup again. I accepted more whiskey before I realized I'd done it. "Tell her what happened to that guy three months ago," she said.

Silas, too, held his mug out. "A *ferox* mage manipulated the water from the fountains into a tidal wave. He washed away the guards at the front gate and escaped—"

"Technically—"

"—but Arwood caught it all on his security cameras and gave it to the Sect. Less than a week later, the *ferox* was shot on a street in Zagreb."

A tidal wave from a water fountain? That must have been what Silas meant by amplifying the environment. Instead of going down that rabbit hole—I'd have plenty of time for those questions later—I said, "But it could've been retribution from Arwood for desertion. How can you be certain it was the Sect who killed him?" The last thing I wanted was another Big Bad in my world. I already had Arwood. I didn't need a faceless organization to deal with on top of everything else.

"Trust me," Anika said, "I've had a front row seat to what they're capable of. And also trust that I'm not drunk enough for *that* conversation." If her tone didn't shut the subject down, her skipping to the next song did. She visibly brightened and was up dancing before I could protest.

Silas's expression mirrored mine as we brought our cups together to toast our messed-up situations. My limbs tingled like a heated blanket unfurling under my skin.

Anika got sick of dancing alone and grabbed my arm. At some point, somehow, I started dancing with her, self-consciousness ebbing as my body grew lighter, my movements fluid. A controlled sway became spinning around with her, then jumping on the bed to the music, and if part of me whispered I'd regret it all tomorrow, it was drowned out by the buzz from the alcohol and our off-key singing. The lightness in my chest helped my laughter come easy and often. A smile stretched across my face.

Anika pulled Silas into the fold—"So, ballroom dancing, huh?"—moving with him in an exaggerated waltz. Seeing them together unsettled my beast. I ignored her, not wanting to interrupt my bliss with inevitable self-doubt. Silas could dance with whoever he wanted. I turned around and around, until hands snagged mine and I slowed to a stop.

It was Silas. Mussed hair. Eyes sparkling. *Beautiful, beautiful boy.* "Whiskey looks good on you," he said.

It did? "I *feel* good. Like I'm floating."

His laugh sounded far away. "Which means you're overdue for water."

My vision spun, and my knees buckled like they had the structural integrity of a sponge. I sank against the adjoining door while Silas filled up my glass with water from his bathroom sink.

"Here. Garden buddy protocol. We need you functioning tomorrow."

Our fingers brushed as I took it. The grin I gave him grew unabashedly wide. He met it with one of his own, regarding me with the same easy humor as the first night we'd met. Each glimpse of this Silas was something to savor. My fingertips sparked from his touch.

Or the whiskey.

"I heard Arwood got attacked," I said above the music. "I'm glad I saw you tonight. That you're okay. I wouldn't have been able to sleep otherwise."

Warmth rose in his brown gaze. "You don't have to worry about me, Keeks." At my eye roll, he ducked his head to hide a smile. Beats of the song passed as we watched Anika take another swig from the whiskey bottle, singing along to Rihanna. "Though I admit, I was worried about you, too," he said. "Even if you were with Ms. Bulletproof."

My heart beat a victorious *ka-thump*. "I think it's justified. Everyone here is certifiably insane," I quipped, sipping. "I won't make it to my twenty-first birthday at this rate."

He took a matching sip, his tongue flashing across his bottom lip. "I think the same way about turning twenty-four. Not many die of old age in this life."

His full lips always looked soft, but especially so right now. I pressed mine together, remembering how his had felt on my palm at the ball. I bet if I got closer, he'd smell like whiskey. Cinnamon. Smoky remnants of a Prague night. The urge to press myself against the length of his body ran through my blood like a siren call. What kind of kisser would Silas be? Would he lead? Take and give in the same breath? Or—

"Keanna . . ." Silas uttered my name with a breathy groan.

A curl of hair brushed against the sharp swipe of his cheekbone. Hard muscle. Delicate skin. Would he feel like that all over?

I gave an answering "Hmm?" as my beast urged me forward, *forward*.

"You, looking at me like that," he murmured. "I—"

"What's with the side party?" I blinked at Anika's question, my thoughts slow as her fingernails tapped against the bottle. "What am I missing?"

While there was a very valid reason Anika shouldn't find out what we'd been discussing, I couldn't remember what it was. My tongue sat like lead in my mouth while my beast urged me to stay quiet.

Luckily, Silas answered in that deep, unaffected voice of his. "Making sure Keanna doesn't wake up regretting her life choices."

Anika tapped the bottle again, considering. "You feeling sick, banshee?"

Heat of a different kind coursed through me. I drained the last of my water. "I hate that word. I wish you'd stop using it."

"'Banshee?' Why?"

Blood, dripping from hotel room curtains onto the broken body below. The empty silence of stolen life. A beast clambering to be set free.

"It reminds me I'm a murderer."

Silas's expression softened.

Anika shook her head. "What you are, sis, is powerful. I'm respecting that. We both are." Silas nodded, cradling his mug to his chest. Siding with her. "Own it."

Ri's face flashed in my mind. How he'd gone from accepting to terrified.

Silas and Anika locked eyes. Something unspoken passed between them, something I wasn't privy to and never would be. *They knew control. They had each other.*

I had the specter of Arwood's daughter. A graveyard of deaths on my conscience. An attraction to Silas I didn't understand and couldn't share details of with anyone else. An overlord who had nearly gotten me killed tonight and would no doubt endanger my life again before the week was done.

I'd landed in waters I'd never free myself from, my hands stained with blood.

The whiskey had helped me forget, but everything was catching up. God, I was so *tired*.

I placed my glass on the counter. "I think I'm gonna go to bed," I said, heading for the passageway so they wouldn't see me cry.

Anika followed silently. Once we returned to my room, she made a beeline for the bedroom door and slipped out into the hallway.

I skipped my night skincare routine, even though I knew I'd regret it in the morning. I had enough energy to clog the keyhole with wet toilet paper and shrug off my dirty clothes. The cold sheets provided no comfort to my spinning head. I curled into a ball, willing the silence to lull me to sleep.

CHAPTER EIGHTEEN

My mood hadn't improved one bit when I woke the next morning, my pillow smeared with tears. As I got out of bed, memories of the night before joined the party of anxiety already stringing my upper body tight.

Oh God. I'd danced, hadn't I? And if that didn't get any more cringe-inducing, I'd also undressed Silas with my eyes in a way he'd most *definitely* noticed. Just as Anika had taken the metal frame to the guards in the jewelry store, I'd taken a baseball bat to the promises I'd made about protecting myself emotionally.

And I had to face him today.

I got ready, then went downstairs for breakfast. The soundtrack of clanging pots and whirring dishwashers beat my temples like a meat tenderizer. Arwood, Lissandra, Steadman, and others like Matej in their inner circle took their meals in the dining room. The rest of us—supernatural employees like me, the guards, workers of the estate, and Anika if she felt like slumming it—ate at long, stainless-steel industrial tables in the kitchen.

Furtive glances from the guards hit like clicking flashlights; on me, then off.

I perched at the far end of a table. Those nearest to me angled their bodies away. A young kitchenhand presented a dish piled high with breakfast sausages, eggs and toast. As if dispensing an explosive, he placed it in front of me slowly, his attention switching between my mouth and collar.

I exhaled, pressing my fingertips into the tops of my thighs. *Ignore it. Ignore it.*

"Yo, boy. Quit staring, she ain't a circus act," called a guard from the far end of the table, with a thick russet beard and even thicker American twang. He alone met my eyes.

The kitchenhand scarpered.

My stomach churned at the pile of meat and carbs, at the distrustful, wary silence of those around me.

Nope. Facing Silas, *training*, was preferable to this. I bailed, exiting the mansion for the same spot outdoors.

Except Silas wasn't there.

"Morning!" Anika wore her ever-present tights and a sports crop-top with sneakers, looking ready to launch into a high-intensity training session. The sweat coating her hairline made me nervous.

"Morning?"

"No need to look so scared, banshee. Silas asked me to be here. I thought I'd burn off some energy first."

I let the banshee mention slide in wake of my relief. "Is Silas held up? I can come back tomorrow."

Anika stretched her quad, balancing on one foot with ballerina-like grace. "He's not coming. It'll be you and me training from now on."

What? My jaw hung open for a second while my brain caught up. When it did, my empty stomach churned again.

Rejected twice—and before lunch, at that. First the guards in the kitchen. Now, Silas, too, had turned away. Seeing me drunk and mascara-smudged must have changed his mind.

My forehead and cheeks grew hot. Registering that I looked like a stunned mullet—a term our neighbor had used in Australia with regularity, and one I'd appreciated—I snapped my mouth shut, blinking to suppress the knot forming in my throat and the sharp sting of tears against the backs of my eyes.

So, Silas had decided we weren't going to be friends? I could live with that. In fact, this made things easier. A silly crush wouldn't help my conviction to escape.

"I may not be the charismatic equivalent, but I can throw down," Anika said. "Let's have some fun."

I'd never felt less ready to 'throw down', but I pushed it aside. "We didn't get very far," I warned her. *In every sense of the phrase.*

"Visualization." Anika bounced, fists up, imitating a boxer. "I got the memo. Visualize away."

My beast didn't need coaxing. Hurt from Silas, frustration from my conversation with Arwood, and the hours since I'd screamed last, combined into bubbling pressure already rising like fizzing soda. I inhaled, tried to slow it, and let go.

My scream shot toward the battered hedges and straight for Anika.

Like Silas, she remained where she was. Unlike Silas, she went very still, her eyes darkening to black as she inhaled. Absorbing the energy of my scream, not deflecting it, just like the shotgun blast when she'd saved Steadman.

Anika's irises returned to their normal brown as she did a little hop from one foot to the other, shaking fallen leaves off her shoulders. "Spicy," she said, exultant. "Again."

Less pressure weighed on my chest, so it was easier to concentrate on controlling the release. In fact, I could see myself as a fire hydrant. I closed my eyes, imagined turning the valve, and began to wail.

For the first few moments I sounded blessedly normal. At least, as normal as a scream could sound. There's a reason humans have an atavistic response to screaming: it signals extreme emotion, and extreme emotion usually means danger. Gravel vibrated. In the epicenter, I *felt* the pressure ripple around me the way a wave rolls past you in the surf.

Again, Anika's eyes flashed black as she braced, inhaling. A smile stretched across her face like a blissed-out Cheshire cat.

I caught my breath. "You look like you're—"

"—tripping? Because I am. Imagine the biggest rush of dopamine you've ever experienced flooding your body—like you're bathing in sunlight and you've just had the best orgasm of your life—and you'll get close to how it feels."

Her descriptions pulled me up short. It brought forth images of the way Silas had looked in his bedroom and how he'd flushed while deflecting my screams and *I would not blush.* "Like you're on drugs?"

"Don't think I can't hear that judgmental inflection," she said. "We all have our demons. I've been clean three years, but the urge never leaves your bloodstream."

Three years? I blanched, all bashfulness forgotten. "How old are you?"

"Twenty-three."

"But three years means—"

"Told you, first night you got here. I'm here by choice."

Anika's expression told me everything: not all horrors were limited to physical deeds, and whatever darkness she'd suffered, she believed this layer of hell to be an *improvement.* "Anika—"

"I didn't tell you that to make you feel sorry for me," she said. "I'm just reminding you we all have a darkness inside of us, and we find ways to deal with it. My power helps me."

My sheltered upbringing had been horribly unremarkable in comparison, and yet I didn't resent it. My father had given me twenty years of peace and love. I wouldn't have traded that for anything.

As if conjured by the direction of my thoughts, Anika asked, "When did you realize you could wail?"

Her question was the equivalent of a DJ pausing music abruptly. It ran through my mind like nails on a chalkboard as I tried *not to think of that night*—

Empty hotel room.

Supposed to be a safe haven.

Wasn't.

My father had been struggling to source clients for the new Prague branch, stopped at every turn by existing ironclad agreements to other companies. A lot rode on that evening; I'd been so sick to my stomach I hadn't eaten a bite all day and was trembling from lack of food and stress.

I'd tried to hide it, but my father must have sensed it, because he'd allowed me to leave long before the first guests had departed. My father's associate, Thomas, had offered to walk me up to the penthouse suite we'd reserved.

The offer hadn't been strange. The eyes of our security team coated me like a tattoo. To be alone would have been stranger. My father had encouraged it and I'd accepted, because the Keanna I'd been two months ago hadn't had a reason to think why not.

Ten minutes later, I'd learned the hard truth to that question.

Thomas—dead.

Everything breakable within the hotel room—broken.

Life—changed. Forever.

To Anika, I said, "Two months ago."

"No way. You would have screamed before then, wouldn't you?"

"I was raised to express myself in a practical fashion."

She crossed her arms. "That sounds like you were fed some 'women should only speak when spoken to' cereal growing up. With a splash of 'apologize for existing' milk."

"I was not," I snapped. "My father just didn't encourage that kind of behavior. It's undignified."

"I refuse to believe you didn't scream as a child. *No one* has that superpower."

"Of course I did. I don't think it mattered when I was younger. My abilities must have manifested around puberty and I didn't know it."

Anika pushed hair behind her ear. "I see. Well, if you ever drop your dogmatic perspective regarding all this, Arwood has information about banshees you might find useful."

"On Isobelle?"

"Not just that. He's an enthusiast of supernatural abilities. Has been for years. He saw the potential in surrounding himself with people like us."

"Surrounding himself with people to use for his own gain, you mean."

Anika shrugged. "Three years ago, my cousin Lissandra learned what had become of me. She gave me sanctuary here." *Cousin.* Now she'd said it, I couldn't believe I hadn't seen it earlier. They had the same skin tone, a similar facial shape. No wonder Anika was comfortable here. "I protect them, I protect what's left of my family. That's enough for me."

Her words were a timely reminder: I had no allies here. As approachable as Anika seemed, I couldn't count on her to help me the way I needed. I was on my own. Arwood's influence over the estate thickened the air like an incoming storm.

I moved a few paces back. "Ready for me to try again?"

"Always."

❧

I might be stubborn, but when someone presented an alternative course of action to reach my goals, I'd always consider it.

I wouldn't die on a hill where my abilities were concerned. While Arwood used me, I'd return the favor by milking his resources (sorry, *employee privileges*) for all I could, which was how I found myself in his library after my training session with Anika.

The series of adjoining rooms contained tall bookshelves filled with tomes of all kinds: leather-bound classics, worn hardbacks, mass market paperbacks. I sighed as I entered. Belle, from Beauty and the Beast, was my favorite Disney princess for a reason. I tried to ignore the parallels between our situations as I explored the shelves. Eventually I found a stack of books on Irish mythology, and I got to work.

Many of the older tomes were full of traditional myths telling of *bean sídhe*, or banshees, as barefoot, white-clad apparitions of either old crones or beautiful young women with silver hair. They favored true Irish families and appeared as a warning in the night of impending death. Other myths counted them as fairies or red-eyed, weeping ghosts who haunted people following their brutal demise. In short, I found little consensus on how I could be sitting in Arwood's library, very much alive, and looking the way I did.

While the acts of *caoine*—keening—or wailing were mentioned, banshees were supposed to warn or announce death, not cause it. It gave explanation to the sense of *knowing* that arose whenever danger loomed, but no details on how to better control my killing wail.

I moved on to the more modern books and pored over them for hours, expecting Steadman to interrupt and haul me out on another mission.

Instead, I learned that the banshee capability was inherited. A chromosome tied me to my mother, to her mother. The emotion inflating against my rib cage felt as powerful as the pressure before I screamed. It held the sensation of knowledge a whisper out of reach, the way you try to recall a dream once you wake. It was regret, it was relief, it was sorrow for a life, a *family* I'd never known.

My father had told me my mother had a sister, but they'd been estranged for years. My grandmother could be alive, may have sisters of her own.

All my life, a single branch had stretched before me, ignorant of the tree it belonged to. A tree potentially spanning countries—or at least Ireland, where these books agreed banshees lived. Many of the legends originated from the Munster region, the south-west area encompassing Clare, Cork, and Limerick. A core group were said to have established ties to the land, populating the banshee lines over the years; some had entered, others had died off. O'Carragher, my mother's maiden name, was among nine others listed that still—at least, at the time of print—existed. I traced the names.

Holy hell. There could be others like me and Isobelle. Many others.

I shook myself. I'd been staring into space, my thumb and forefinger pinching my lower lip. The cameras I'd spotted in the library were trained on the double-door entrance, but I still straightened my posture. So much information lay in these shelves, and for the first time I didn't feel resentful of my abduction.

When I saw my father again, I'd be able to tell him what I learned. He'd know if my mother had more family. Hopefully he'd know where. If not, Ireland would be a good starting point.

They could teach me how to be *this*.

I returned the books, studying the artwork dotting the walls. An abstract piece—a Pollock—hung above the fireplace between two decorative glass cases. One showcased a pair of daggers with bronze sheaths covered in swirling patterns, the other a sunset-orange shawl with golden threads that caught the light. Travel souvenirs, perhaps?

Beside the shawl hung a series of framed photographs. Most were society photos: Arwood in a group of tuxedo-clad men, he and Lissandra posing at an art gallery, Lissandra shaking hands with other suited women. The one that stood out the most was of two men in combat uniforms. Their arms were around each other's shoulders, stances relaxed but confident. Both were laughing, one staring at something off-camera, while the other blue-eyed man stared squarely down the shutter, his unfamiliar wide smile knocking something loose in my chest. Arwood and Steadman. Both clean-shaven and years younger, but it was definitely them, mud splashed halfway up their legs and across the vehicle they stood in front of like they'd rolled out of a jungle or something.

Their body language revealed a closer relationship than just squad members. They were *friends*.

I didn't know much about the US army, but I knew enough to recognize the sergeant rankings on their chests. Despite being at least ten years younger, Steadman had been in the higher position as Sergeant First Class. Not Arwood. Tenure and capability were the great leveler—especially in enlisted ranks—not age, but I still had to look twice at what was hanging in the library for all to see: Steadman had once been in charge.

So how had they ended up here, in this arrangement? Did Steadman miss calling the shots?

On the heel of this thought came another: maybe he did miss it. Maybe pursuing an affair with Lissandra, the attacks on Arwood, were Steadman's attempts to take over. I searched the glitzy photos again. Steadman wasn't in any of them. Was he jealous of what Arwood had? Had they been discharged only for Arwood to thrive?

As I pondered this, the scrape of a page came from the far corner of the otherwise-silent library. I rounded the stacks to a familiar head of curling hair peeking above the back of a single-seater couch, sneakered feet propped on an ottoman and crossed at the ankles.

Silas.

My humiliation over the night before tempted me to tuck tail and give him the space he so obviously craved. The other side—the side that enjoyed throwing antique vases at walls and shattering entire rooms—urged me to confront him. I deserved to know where we stood.

The latter side won out.

"You didn't strike me as a reader," I said. No doubt he'd seen I was there already, had chosen not to seek me out first. "Let me guess, contemporary romance? Assured happily ever after?"

Silas didn't flinch, confirming my suspicions. That realization hurt, but I was already so annoyed it didn't pinch as much as it should have. "Nothing wrong with a HEA. Life is too unpredictable."

Undeterred, I sank into the couch adjacent to him. It enfolded my body in buttery leather.

"You're avoiding me." The people-pleasing Keanna within quailed, but the reckless one—which I suspected was the beast in my chest—thrilled at my forwardness.

"I'm reading." He wiggled his book for emphasis. Jack Reacher. Go figure. "I didn't realize you were here."

"We don't have to do this." He raised an eyebrow as I gestured between us, taking a deep breath. "This ... this emotionally charged toxic loop where I wonder what you're thinking and why you're ignoring me. I have bigger problems to focus on." I paused, steadying my voice. "This isn't some teen show, and you're not the broody bad boy I'm obsessing over."

The corner of his mouth twitched. "I'm not? Sounds like fun."

"For the angsty love interest," I confirmed, "not the main character. I know I went a little stupid last night. It won't happen again."

"You were having fun. That's not stupid."

Fun? Fun wasn't waking hungover from alcohol and vulnerability. But I didn't let him distract me from my point. "We can co-exist without you doing a bait and switch and forcing Anika to train me. Truce?"

He played with the corner of a page. "It wasn't that. It was more trying to prevent a car crash."

I crossed my arms. I missed the direct Silas I'd met in the garden, the one who hated small talk and wanted to understand what made people tick.

Seeing I wasn't letting him off the hook, he said, "Everything we do and say is monitored. Being around you makes me forget it."

"And?"

"These people have a way of learning what you want—"

"—and making sure you never get it," I finished for him. "So you're saying you can't be yourself because you're scared they'll use it as leverage?"

"Precisely."

I'd been so certain I'd done something wrong, I hadn't contemplated *that*. I sank back and trailed my fingernail over the tufted arm of the chair, unsure of how to proceed. "You're saying we should orbit different circles from now on?" A lump grew in my throat. Like I was saying goodbye. Which was ridiculous, because I didn't know Silas. But I'd wanted to—and I supposed that was the issue.

"I don't like this, Keeks. Believe me, I don't." Our gazes locked, and the prickling behind my eyes intensified at the sorrow in his. "When you're around ..." He exhaled gustily, placing his book to the side. "Shit, Keanna, you are pure sunshine. It's been like that since we first met. But I have people relying on me, and I have to protect them. I'm sorry."

Sunshine. He thought I was like sunshine. I'd thought he was a meteorite. What a pair we made.

I was dangerously close to crying. Timing was everything, and ours was wrong. If we'd met again a year ago, would it have changed anything?

"Why didn't I ever see you, after the ball? I ..." I swallowed, pausing at what I was about to admit, then said it anyway. It no longer mattered. "I looked for you. I hoped to see you again."

Silas played with his ring. My father had so many negative opinions about men who wore jewelry, but Silas's leather necklaces, his silver ring—even Arwood's matte black metal band around his wrist—suited him. Silas wore nonchalance like a second skin; a deep-seated confidence oozed from him. He knew himself. He knew what he liked. His presence drew people. It had drawn me. In a way I'd never been drawn to anyone before.

"My father died that night."

His words hung in the air. I inhaled, pain stabbing me in the chest. He'd mentioned his father was unwell at the ball, but—

"I'm so sorry," I whispered.

Silas shrugged. "It was a long time coming. We just didn't think it would be then, you know? When someone's sick for so long, you keep thinking there'll be another day, another night. You can't imagine it ending, even if part of you secretly knows it's best, because their living increases their misery. It stops being about them and starts becoming about you not wanting to live without them. My father worked for Arwood, but I didn't learn that until later."

He didn't continue. He didn't have to. Arwood must have owned his father somehow. Silas had inherited that obligation ... and responsibility.

I felt two inches tall for striding over here, demanding an explanation for his behavior. I had bigger things to deal with—and so did he.

"I'm sorry," I repeated. "I don't want to make things harder for you." I wanted to weep for his loss. I wanted to cry for this world, where people like me and Silas were exploited by those who could do better and chose not to. I wanted to clutch my own father tight, thankful I had him.

"You're not." Silas's words were unconvincing, especially when he added, "But ... I can't be near you like this, hoping they won't figure out how I feel. I can't afford for them to hold anything else over me."

I inhaled. Deeply. "Okay."

"I wish things were different."

"I do, too," I said, my voice soft.

I rose from the seat. He didn't meet my eyes, so I allowed myself to look at him one last time. The lamplight did beautiful things to Silas. Shadows played across his eyelashes, his lips.

"I promise I'll keep my distance, but I'm here for you. However I can be." I headed for the door before any tears could spill.

Behind me, Silas swore, his paperback bouncing on the carpet.

CHAPTER NINETEEN

S TEADMAN SAVED ME FROM ANOTHER SELF-PITY EPISODE AS
I stormed down the hallway.

"Banshee," he said, halting me in my path. "We need you."
His sharp eyes assessed me, the carved lines of his cheekbones prominent in the afternoon sun. So similar, yet different, to his army
photo. *This* Steadman looked like he hadn't smiled a day in his life.
"You'll have to schedule your existential crisis for later."

What was Steadman's deal? I shouldn't care. It would be easier
to hate everyone here. But the juvenile side of me also wanted to
tug on his sleeve and bleat, 'Why don't you like me?'

Thankfully, my chat with Silas had primed me. While I avoided
politics in the workplace—benefits of being an intern—a solo
Steadman provided an opportunity I couldn't pass up. If he was
trying to sabotage Arwood, then we were on the same side.

In a sense.

I followed Steadman, choosing my words carefully. I needed
to find common ground with him. "How long have you worked for
Arwood?"

"Long enough to know he's not a fan of waiting."

Take two. "Do you enjoy it here?"

"Normally, unless someone is forcing small talk."

My beast flared as I clenched my teeth. "Is this because of what
happened after Ferko?"

He'd deviated from his usual black on black to a crisp white but-
ton-down with rolled sleeves; he glanced at his watch as he strode

ahead, his shoulders tight as he brushed a hand over his face. "A smarter person wouldn't remind me of that."

Had Anika told them about the passageways, then? I'd assumed she'd left last night via my bedroom because she hadn't wanted to tip off the cameras by exiting Silas's room, but knowing her relationship to Lissandra ... "You've had a problem with me since the moment we met. Why?"

Steadman's pace quickened as if trying to leave me behind. It would have worked before I'd permanently swapped to flat shoes. It was no effort to match him, stride for stride.

"I take issue with people who aren't effective," he answered.

Me? Not effective? Defensiveness reared. "That first night aside, I've been a gold-standard prisoner with the death count I've caused. Wasn't this what you and Arwood wanted?"

The sideways look he gave me hinted I'd missed the point in multiple ways. "You're purely reactive, and it's becoming an issue for me. I'm not a babysitter. As for being 'gold standard'—that is so like your generation. You do the bare minimum and expect applause."

"*My* generation?" I gaped. Above a shadowed jawline, his skin was otherwise unlined and supple in a way owing to a healthy lifestyle and youth. Or Botox. "You're, what, fifteen years older than me? At most?"

"For someone supposedly motivated to change your situation, you're not helping as much as you think you are. You're smart, but you're not engaging. I resent dead weight."

I blinked, stunned. I wanted to rebut it with details of how I'd been training, researching, but I didn't want to draw attention to those things. Instead, I said, "I haven't been invited to the staff meetings. You and Arwood abducted *me,* hold me prisoner, and you're saying I could do better?"

"Some things are bigger than you, and, all things considered, you've been treated well. There are people far worse than Arwood in this world."

Yeah, like a right-hand man wanting to usurp him. I needed to be careful, but my mouth wasn't cooperating. I was raw from what Silas had told me, how unfair this all was, and something about Steadman triggered me unlike anyone else.

"I think everyone I've been forced to kill disagrees with you there, and I certainly do too." When Steadman didn't respond, I snapped, "How can you be okay with all of this? You wear cactus socks. There must be a soul inside of you somewhere, even if I haven't been blessed enough to witness your redeeming qualities."

He released a hiss that sounded suspiciously like a sigh, but nothing shifted in his profile. "If you say you're committed to helping Arwood, we're giving you a chance to prove it."

"Prove it how?"

"You're going to one of those meetings you just whined about not being invited to. We're discussing our move on the Kohnstamms. Don't hold back while you're in there."

"I already told you I don't know anything about Johan or the people he works with."

"Arwood has a hunch you know more than you think you do. Now, if you don't mind, I need time with my own thoughts. Your voice is … loud."

C⁀ℯ

Several minutes later, we entered a windowless boardroom. Arwood and Lissandra faced us on one side of the wide, rectangular table, half-finished latte glasses before them. I sat opposite in one of the brown leather chairs.

"I gave her the briefing," Steadman said, taking the seat beside Lissandra. "She's willing."

He called *that* a briefing? I didn't roll my eyes, but I wanted to.

"Your familiarity with Waldemar inspired this chat," Arwood said, turning a remote over in his hand. For my collar? Just as fear spiked my blood, he clicked at the projector. The blank screen perpendicular to him lit up with an image. "We believe your proximity to your father's business dealings this past year may prove useful."

His insinuation about my father fired me up all over again. "I swear, I *don't kn—*"

On the screen, a photo straight out of a society magazine appeared. A man and a woman stood regal. Diamonds winked at the base of the woman's neck and earlobes. Across the single chair they stood behind, like a king receiving at court, sprawled a lanky boy in his early twenties who shared their self-assured pout. His thick black wavy hair matched his mother's. He'd inherited his cleft chin from his father.

I studied the boy's familiar, arrogant form. Leon. I'd met him with his father, Ivan, at our event two months ago, the night I'd killed Thomas and my life had changed forever. My father had petitioned them for use of their ports. My memory of the days that followed were hazy for obvious reasons, but I did recall he hadn't been successful.

He'd tried to strike a deal with the *Kohnstamms*. Out of context, I hadn't remembered their names, but now it came flooding back. My father mustn't have known who they were, or he never would have tried. He'd avoided Lissandra's family only to fall into this world anyway. What a hidden blessing his proposal hadn't worked out.

Either my face had fallen in my shock or Arwood had counted on me recognizing at least one of them, because he said, "Reconsidering your response?"

"We've met," came my tart reply, because really, what else could I say?

"Excellent. What can you tell us?"

I made a show of studying their photo again while I raced to work out how to respond. It was dangerous to enter into any discussions with Arwood. I didn't want to give him details that could hurt my father; that said, if I was going to sell compliance, I had to be, well, *compliant.*

"They attended an event our company sponsored earlier in the summer. I met Ivan and Leon because my father was interested in leasing one of their ports to receive materials for a new property."

"And?"

"They declined." Arwood's smile turned vulpine, and Anika's comments about Prague's neighborhoods came to mind. "But you knew I was going to say that, didn't you? From the sounds of it, your partnership with the Kohnstamms doesn't leave much wiggle room for anyone else to establish an honest trade around here."

"For someone who insists they know nothing, you're proving that not to be the case."

There was no point arguing. "You're certain the Kohnstamms are working with this Johan guy to take you down? Unless I missed something, Waldemar didn't confirm who he was supplying to before he was killed."

"No one else has the resources to conceal her like this," Arwood said with a finality that sounded like he was trying to convince himself of this fact. "And no one else would *dare.*"

Lissandra touched his elbow. "From what we've discerned from other sources, they no longer intend to maintain the truce," she said. "We need to be smart about our response, but we must respond."

Steadman shifted in his chair, looking uncomfortable with the idea. Weird; I'd have thought Arwood going into battle with the Kohnstamms would *help* Steadman with what he was trying to achieve. Instead, he shook his head. "More groundwork is necessary before we—"

"We have enough. Let's proceed," Arwood said. He missed the way Lissandra and Steadman shared a look, but I didn't. "Every year our families host an event as part of our agreement," he told me. "We held ours in February, which is where my daughter met Leon. They were in a relationship when she was abducted. Now that we know their true intentions, we cannot trust the aid his family have provided since, and I suspect he personally played a part in her disappearance. Tonight, the Kohnstamms are hosting theirs. We are obliged to attend, which will give us the opportunity to respond in kind."

I focused on the black hair curling in the center of Leon's fore-head, his arrogant smirk. "You want to question him?"

"Talking won't produce the outcome we're after," Arwood said.

It might take me a while to catch on, but I always got there eventually. "You want me to help you *kidnap* him?" Though I was ignorant of the finer details of their truce, this would break it in spectacular fashion.

"As heir to the Kohnstamm dynasty, Leon is under constant guard, so it'll be a bit hard for you to accomplish that," Steadman drawled. "We just need everything you can remember about your interaction. When they arrived and how long they stayed. If you saw what car they attended in. How many made up their security team. Who they spoke to. Etcetera."

Thank God. But my knee-jerk relief brought another thought: attending this event would give me an opportunity to escape. And if I couldn't achieve that much, I'd be noticed by the attendees. Apart from Ferko, no one who'd seen me with Arwood's team had lived to talk about it, but at a party like this, surely—*surely*—someone there would know my father, know I'd been kidnapped. Prague was large, but it wasn't *that* large. My face could be circulating social media and the news for all I knew. The more I was spotted in public, the better.

Of course, if I'd deduced that, so had Arwood. Which meant I needed a compelling reason to attend that outweighed the risks.

"And why can't I help?" I asked.

"Have experience abducting fuckboys we're unaware of, banshee?"

I ignored Steadman's question, focusing on Arwood. He was the one I had to convince. "Does Leon know what Isobelle is?"

Arwood nodded.

"Well, two banshees are better than one, right? Especially if one has a killing wail."

"And his security?" Lissandra challenged. "How do you plan on getting around them?"

I sat up straighter. "Well, Leon and I have interacted before."

I didn't mention he'd been as arrogant as he looked, and not interested in speaking with me. That was future Keanna's problem. "I'll use that to my advantage to get him alone."

Lissandra's expression didn't soften. "A boy like that is used to the attention of women. He'll see through you."

I tried again. "I could present a case for wanting to defect and work for his family. He won't want anyone overhearing."

Arwood was *not* amused at this idea. "Careful, Miss Backhus. You forget where you sit."

I tried a final time. "I've got a better chance than any of you to get close to him without it looking suspicious. This will be enough to get him away from everyone, and then you can step in."

Under the table, I gripped the hem of my shirt so my nails wouldn't dig into my palms, trying to keep my face blank.

Lissandra leaned back in her chair and took an unhurried sip of her coffee. "It's a risk."

"I don't like it," Steadman said.

Arwood pushed his steeped fingers against his lips. The seconds ticked by while I held my breath. He drew his hands away.

Steadman tried to get another shot in. "Arwood, I think we should—"

"You'd best get ready, Miss Backhus," Arwood said.

Steadman's blue eyes flashed to me like it was *my* fault. I supposed it was. He couldn't say why he was against me going without admitting to my previous escape attempt.

"Anika will provide you with a suitable garment."

Yes. I was on my feet before he could change his mind.

But Arwood wasn't done. "The security team have been quite proficient with updating me on your training sessions."

I froze.

"I'm sure by now you've been informed of who the Sect are and what they do. I would advise against a public showcase of your capabilities tonight, Miss Backhus, through any means other than what strictly benefits this mission. Follow all instructions. Do not speak to anyone outside of our team or Leon, even if you're approached. I will not raise a finger to protect you against the Sect if you cross me."

I have you on camera, his gaze told me. *And I will use it.*

My tongue became a heavy weight in my mouth. I agreed woodenly.

"Excellent. Don't be late."

An hour later, victory still tasted sour. Even my hair curling how I liked couldn't distract from the reality that I'd once again negotiated myself into a bigger, more dangerous cage.

It had dawned on me while applying liquid liner: if I succeeded in aiding Leon's abduction, the Kohnstamms would want me dead for it. If I refused to help in the future or failed in my escape attempt, Arwood would expose me to the Sect, and they'd kill me.

In fact, if I *ever* managed to escape after tonight, between the Kohnstamms and the Sect—not to mention Arwood and the Camardos—there would be nowhere in Prague safe for me to go.

I hadn't vomited into the toilet yet, but it was a growing possibility.

Sharp knocks on the door interrupted my brooding. Anika barged in—really, I was going to have to talk to her about the way she abused her master key privileges—her footsteps underscoring crinkling plastic. I emerged, clutching my robe, as Anika dumped bags filled with bold, jewel-tone dresses on the bed. Sapphire blue, sunset topaz … had emerald green made the cut?

"Arwood mentioned you're a late attendance and wanted me to help you get situated." From the back, Anika's tailored cream pin-striped pantsuit ran professional and demure, but it was a party in the front with the way the double-breasted lapels cut clean down her cleavage to her navel. She'd definitely used Hollywood tape. "This is absolutely a job for me."

"You're coming too?"

"Everyone is. Stand there." She swept up a dress, glancing

critically between the blue material and my figure. Sizing me up. "Arwood doesn't allow it normally, but anything other than full attendance from our side tonight would raise suspicions." She shook her head. Next came a topaz spaghetti-strap slip that would look amazing on the tall, curvy-in-the-correct-places Lissandra but would do nothing for my dumpy frame.

"A condition of the truce?"

"I like to imagine it as two great white sharks circling each other. Checking in, assessing for damage. It's precarious, but it's worked." Again, she glanced between the slip dress and my robe-clad body before chucking it to the side.

"Until now."

"It was never going to last. If Arwood's making a move, he's confident he'll land on top." She lifted up a teal-green dress. It was just like the one I'd worn the night I met Silas, with an A-line silhouette to the floor. I'd need shapewear to smooth the lines, but it was respectable without showing too much. "How do you feel about off-shoulder designs?"

"I prefer this green one—*hey!*"

She threw the dress aside for the red satin one underneath. It had a structured bodice with a deep V, which meant one thing: boobs. "This is the winner. Put it on."

"The green is more my style."

"The green is hiding." Anika ignored the way my mouth opened in protest, cutting me off. "You're a *banshee*, Keanna. Take up space."

Her words made me want to curl into the fetal position. It wasn't *hiding*. People judged clothing choices. It was bad enough I had a black collar I couldn't take off. "If I'm going to talk to Leon, I need to be comfortable."

"I guarantee this red dress will fight half that battle for you. Change."

"Anika, I'm being serious."

"So am I." We stared each other down until she relaxed. "The red isn't your thing. I get it. It doesn't have to be. You're playing a character tonight. We all are. This party is a den of wolves; think of this dress as your form of armor."

My stomach twisted. "Do you have any shapewear?"

"You won't need it."

I grabbed the bag, plastic crackling under my fingers. Of course Anika, with her lightning metabolism, would think that. "Yes. I do."

Sensing she'd breached my limit, she held her hands up in surrender. "Get changed. I'll track down the Spanx."

A few minutes later, I'd armored up, material falling like a watery column from my waist to the floor. As I'd feared, the V-dip bodice revealed *way* more cleavage than I'd historically allowed. I turned. Drapes of silk curtained across my upper arms, restricting their movement, but my boobs felt secure. Self-consciousness prickled the skin of my exposed chest, but …

Dare I say it, the dress looked … *good?* It somehow made my curves look alluring, rather than lumps needing concealment. It brought out the color in my cheeks, highlighted my cascading blonde hair. I would never have picked this off a line-up.

My father would have hated it.

Anika didn't even bother hiding her smug smile. "Told you." Her eyes raked over the leg exposed by the slit running up the side. "Knockout. Let's go cause some trouble."

DURING

Blood and death surrounded my rebirth.

My father found me crying over the broken body of Thomas inside the decimated hotel suite. My beast had woken, announcing its existence by taking away another's.

Afterwards, my father urged for silence. The police were unable to make sense of Thomas's death. Without the variable of my beast, the equation never added up. A death without sense made them uncomfortable, so it became a death they buried.

I wondered why more questions weren't asked. I was relieved when none came. I'd never understood true privilege until I walked from that situation with only internal scars for my actions. Any thoughts of that night joined all other memories laced with fear and failure; the kind that feel like a crude shudder beneath your skin, a tickle at the base of your skull. The kind you can't destroy or forget. The kind you bury.

That night replaced innocence and life with swift, brutal death. A guillotine never apologizes for falling; my beast never apologizes for taking. It just does.

Before tonight was over, it would take again.

CHAPTER TWENTY

PRAGUE IS BEAUTIFUL, BUT AT NIGHT IT'S SOMETHING ELSE. Since my abduction, city lights and darkness had become synonymous with Arwood and his dangerous world. But tonight, as we passed illuminated buildings and their reflections in the Vltava, I took a moment to appreciate it. The romantic flair of baroque architecture mixed with functional communist, minimalist modern intermingled with strong, stark neoclassical. This city, with its soaring hills and narrow, secretive alleyways, had seen decades pass and still stood, all the more stunning for the trials it had weathered. Whatever we did, the night would shrug off our sins and the sun would rise across sloping terracotta rooftops and steep cobblestoned lanes.

Arwood had split up the timing of transportation and arrival to the event as a precaution, so I left with Steadman and Anika in an X7 for the inner east.

The neighborhoods of Prague Three held pockets of wealth but were predominantly a developer's dream, an area my father had frothed at the mouth to get into. It had the seedy ruggedness of Montmartre in Paris, the nightlife an overflowing hub for creatives and the like. My father viewed the aged streets as a ball of dough to be molded and capitalized upon, the proximity to central Prague just another sweetener. Yet we'd never made headway here, and now I knew why: Three was a shared zone between Arwood and the Kohnstamms.

Our car slowed beside a manicured hedge. A formidable ivory building loomed above us as we queued for the valet circle. Lights cascaded down at least six stories of timelessness, geometric windows punctuated by columns and extravagantly patterned, upturned eaves.

Hold on. "We're going to abduct someone in a *casino*?"

Anika grinned at my incredulous delivery. "Sounds like fun, right?"

Not for the first time, I questioned her sanity. "Has no one seen a casino heist movie, like, ever? There's no way they're not going to see we're responsible for this."

"Concealing our actions was never the intention," Steadman answered. "We just need the element of surprise."

I hadn't thought I could feel any sicker, but there you go. I'd been so caught up with what Arwood was capable of, I hadn't dwelled on the Kohnstamms. Any family who could hold their own against Arwood and the Camardos—to the point of a truce being called—weren't people to mess with.

Except we were about to mess with them.

I had to escape tonight. No question.

Too soon, it was our turn. Men in navy suits opened the doors on either side, helping me and Anika to our feet. The driver waved off the valet and pulled away as we followed Steadman up the stairs. Carved above the entrance sat a familiar line drawing of a cat face. Where had I seen that insignia before?

Once inside, security patted us down—"Nothing in this suit except mother-given goodies" Anika told them with a wink—and then allowed us to cross to the lobby. Well-dressed hotel patrons milled around a reception area manned by coiffed staff, while groomed bellboys pushed trolleys loaded with luggage into glass lifts. The interior, accented with chrome and lushly upholstered furniture, smacked of considered, minimalist luxury. If I hadn't been wound so tight, I'd have gasped with appreciation. We followed Steadman. The scent of newly installed carpet mixed with grilled meat wafting from the restaurant doors to our right, making me rue the fact I'd been too nauseous to eat before we left.

Anika met those around us head on with her contagious confidence, nodding, smiling, returning flirty glances. The air-conditioning licked my exposed leg as the silky material of my red dress floated behind me. For a second, it quelled my nerves. I looked like I belonged here. I had a plan to execute. There was no reason it wouldn't work out. Despite Arwood's warnings, I tried to catch the eyes of those I passed, hoping to recognize someone.

"He's cute," Anika murmured, assessing a man across the room with blond hair pulled into a ponytail. He did the same, trailing from her pointed black boots to her cleavage. "Shame," she said as his gaze landed on her black wristband and my collar.

"Because he's blond?"

"Hell no. Blondes are my type," she smirked, tugging on the ends of my hair. "See the mark below his palm?"

He'd turned, sipping beer, but his jacket sleeve had ridden up enough to reveal a line drawing on the inside of his wrist. The feline profile with prominent ears was the same as the carved one at the entrance and—I recalled suddenly—the white plaque at Waldemar's store.

"The caracal is the Kohnstamm mark. You see someone wearing that after our shenanigans here, run in the opposite direction."

I'd gotten lost in the surroundings, forgetting what they represented. "I assume this place is cover for their operations? Laundering?"

"Ah, yes, the standard gangster crap."

"What do they do? You mentioned they're the only ones who traffic?"

Anika nodded. "They're big players in manufacturing, specifically automotive. Like us, they shift anything worth a buck, invest in businesses, and take payments for protection in return. But their biggest activity is moving women and girls across the borders from Serbia, Poland, and Slovakia into the west through Germany. Which is why tonight doesn't upset me in the slightest. Filthy bastards."

"Yeah, right, and Arwood doesn't?"

We passed a set of manned doors leading into the gambling area. Steadman continued, but Anika paused to grab two glasses of champagne from an attendant, handing one to me. "Not that," she said as we resumed. "He crosses many lines, but sex trafficking isn't one."

"Lissandra got attacked at a brothel the first night I went out with Steadman."

"They're ethically run. The girls are paid well and retain their rights and documentation. I wouldn't be here if they weren't. Neither would Lissandra."

An Arwood with moral boundaries didn't compute. I sipped the champagne, bubbles playing on my tongue. The combination of music and gambling patrons rang in my ears, their shouted conversations concealing ours. "So why does Arwood align with the Kohnstamms?"

"The alternative is to try and stop them. They've lived here a long time. So has Arwood's family—his stepmother was Czech, and she owned the property we live in now. Prague used to be a battlefield between both sides, but it's bad for business. Not to mention law enforcement breathing down everyone's necks. Arwood lost his father, stepmother, and older brother because of it all."

I raised my eyebrows.

"Arwood was a team leader in the army when it happened. He returned with Steadman and Lissandra, and they helped settle things and negotiate a truce. Cops tolerate us because we keep the smaller fish in line."

We passed a 'private function' sign into a large, double-story room. A balcony wrapped around the perimeter and framed the chandeliers suspended from the textured ceiling. Guests surrounded gambling tables or lounged in leather seats. Attendants distributed drinks and canapes from their trays. I scoped the closed doors behind the small makeshift stage guarded by security. The exit.

"Wait."

Anika came closer, pretending to adjust my teardrop earring.

She slipped a vial between my breasts—God, they were so *elevated*—and down into the bodice of my dress, arching a suggestive eyebrow. I blushed deep enough to match my crimson lipstick.

"Give Leon the sleepy juice once you get him alone," she whispered into my ear. "We'll do the rest."

Except I had absolutely *no* intention of doing that. I nodded anyway, my pounding heart matching the sultry beats of the lounge music playing over the speakers. "Even if I knock him out, how are we going to get him out of here?"

"Don't worry, we've mapped the building and have a plan. This isn't our first rodeo." Anika fluffed her long bob. She'd parted her hair on the side to showcase a sparkling ear cuff I couldn't have pulled off in a million years. "I'm gonna go play. We'll keep watch on you. When you make a move on Leon, we'll follow."

The butterflies in my stomach doubled. I swallowed, giving a smile Anika didn't buy. She untangled a tendril of hair caught between my collar and clammy neck. "You're doing a brave thing, Keanna. You've got this."

Outside, I looked put together; my insides were frayed seams tugging apart. I pushed down the urge to give her a hug. She exchanged greetings with guests, marching through the crowd. I couldn't see Silas, even though we'd been the last to leave Arwood's estate. My beast wanted to see him, too.

It doesn't matter.

I nursed my champagne, watching Steadman and practicing what I planned to say to him over and over in my head as he circled the room. Steadman had no idea he'd be the one to hasten my escape, and I knew what would make him do it.

It was a change, seeing him in a suit as opposed to the starkness of black-on-black or being spattered with blood. His movements reminded me of the steady grace of a stalking panther. How did Arwood not *see* this? Maybe with my newcomer vantage point such a thing was obvious, but not so for a man preoccupied with recovering his daughter and maintaining control of his territories. Perhaps loyalty to Steadman was Arwood's blind spot.

Steadman came to a stop beside me, clutching a glass filled with amber liquid and ice. I braced myself.

"Red is your color, banshee."

Words piled up behind my tongue like a freeway crash at his approving tone. Was that ... a compliment?

Surely not. Steadman didn't *compliment* people. No doubt his appeal with Lissandra was purely physical, because there was no way this man could be charming. In fact, this might be his way of messing with me, trying to throw me off so he could prove to Arwood I shouldn't have been allowed to come in the first place. I straightened my posture, brushing the cascading folds of scarlet material.

When I said nothing, Steadman asked, "Has Anika communicated the plan?"

"She did." I'd noted the number of circulating security guards, not to mention the all-seeing eyes of the cameras in the black domes between the chandeliers. "I'm not sure this will work."

He took in my vice-like grip on the champagne flute. "Stressing about a little flirtation? From what I've heard about Leon Kohnstamm, he's not the discriminating type."

Asshole. I shot him a withering glare as one of the gaming machines erupted, coins smacking against the aluminum. What I wouldn't give to be on a casual weekend outing to a casino with my father and not doing *this*. "Forgive me for not getting excited over setting a honey trap."

"Arwood expects success here. Get excited."

I gave him another poisonous side-eye, steadying my breath. *Here we go.* "Is being Arwood's lapdog your life goal? Because you're succeeding. Oh. Wait."

Steadman's gaze darted to mine as if to check I was being facetious. Which of course I was. I brought the words home.

"To do that would involve you no longer sleeping with

Lissandra. Tell me, Steadman, how long have you been having an affair with his wife?"

Ha.

Steadman's lips tightened on the rim of his whiskey glass, but he said nothing as he sipped, his eyes roaming the crowd. Always watching.

"You told me once you're strategically forgetful. So am I. Like forgetting to tell Arwood something that will turn him against you. If you agree to help me escape, that is."

Gosh, this was fun, throwing his own words at him. Removing me from their arsenal was an effective way to sabotage Arwood, especially now Steadman knew *I* knew. This made me a variable he couldn't control. Aligning with my plan made sense.

Steadman's searing gaze landed back on me. His expression remained prosaic, like I'd said nothing of consequence. An enviable poker face. I took notes.

"Look at you," he said. "All puffed up. Thought you had a slam dunk there, didn't you? Were you expecting me to fall at your knees in front of everyone and beg for your silence?"

I didn't think Steadman had begged for anything in his life. You had people like him and Arwood, and then people like me and Silas who were vulnerable to their machinations.

"I expect you to help me escape, knowing what I know." I tried to keep my voice calm. He wasn't reacting the way I'd hoped. "Then we both win."

"I disagree."

Perhaps it wasn't a stellar poker face. Perhaps he'd taken one too many knocks to the head as sergeant. I tried again. "I've got a lot of talking to do tonight. Maybe I'll chat with Arwood, too."

"Big words, banshee."

Bluffing. He had to be. He had way too much to lose here. I went higher. Or ... lower, depending on how you looked at it. "Perhaps I'll let it slip to Leon that Arwood's more vulnerable than they think, and it's actually his right-hand man orchestrating these attacks to get rid of him."

He clasped my dress, pulling me toward him, and suddenly I was in Steadman's personal space. His woodsy, musky scent surrounded me. The skin of my neck flushed and tightened—probably from sheer disgust—as I pushed against the hand banded across my back. He held me firm, smiling glibly at those passing us, dropping his voice.

"You understand nothing of your situation." His words reverberated through his chest. I *felt* them, like the thunder of an incoming storm. "The sooner you appreciate that, the safer you'll be. Your interests align with Arwood's. He's the man you made a deal with. Honor it."

An edge had materialized in his voice. I'd rattled his stoic veneer. Finally.

Pity it had meant rattling me too, because being this close to Steadman was messing me up. My pulse throbbed. Knots formed in my abdomen at the movement of his fingers on my waist. I took a deep breath and pasted on a pleasant smile in case someone was watching us.

"And *your* interests?"

"Are not something I'll share with you. I've proven my loyalty. You haven't."

I swallowed with difficulty. His gaze was the kind of intense blue that made me feel transparent. The kind that missed nothing, had already taken notice of the flush rising across my collarbones. Heat prickled under my dress and I desperately needed space, but I refused to fidget; I understood on some level that this was Steadman's way of retaliating for what I'd said. I wouldn't give him the satisfaction of showing my discomfort. "I don't trust a word you say."

"Good." He released me. I exhaled as he stepped away. "It would be the height of stupidity for you to trust any of us, and I don't work with stupid people."

He sipped his whiskey again, like our discussion was over. Except it wasn't. We'd talked a wide circle and accomplished nothing. In fact, I had a bad feeling I'd revealed my hand in more ways than one with nothing to show for it.

"Are you going to help me escape or not?"

"Not. You've got a job to do. Now go do it."

I blinked dumbly. When he didn't move or say anything else, I spun, heading … well, I had no idea. I took the staircase to my left and emerged onto the second-floor balcony. I came to a stop, gripping the banister. Steadman turned back to the crowd like I was no longer a concern.

Fury licked my blood. He—*he*—

My beast threw herself against the bars of her cage, seething. I hadn't just failed, I'd bombed spectacularly. She wanted me to go down there and show him why he should never turn his back on a banshee. Except …

Steadman could. He had. I hadn't considered a plan B if this one hadn't been enough.

Shit.

A spark shot up my spine, warning of a gaze unreturned. I studied the crowd below. There was Matej by the blackjack tables with Lissandra. Anika, clapping from a win at roulette. Arwood, greeting a man wearing a blood-red tie that did nothing for his skin tone. With him—Silas.

A frisson of excitement flitted through me as our eyes met. His lips parted as his stare traveled from my hair to my toes. Even at a distance, his heat-filled expression was everything I could have hoped for. Tanned skin contrasted against the black tie and crisp white shirt under his suit. Seeing him dressed like that again sent goosebumps down my body.

Arwood tapped his shoulder. Silas immediately turned. The curls of his hair glinted in the overhead lights as he approached Matej, passing along a message. Steadman circled the room, reminding me I had someone to search for too.

Dread pooled beneath the vial pressing against my sternum. I regretted every word I'd uttered about Leon. I'd been such an idiot, bargaining my attendance like this.

I was going to have to go through with it now.

I sipped the last of my champagne and sighed to try and disperse some tension. Leon towered above most people, his sun-kissed skin complementing golden eyes. A striking combo, and one I'd see quickly. So far, no luck. I continued to sweep the party attendees.

The velvet curtain rustled beside me; I started as Silas appeared. The tightness in my chest eased. Even two steps away, I felt his presence, the subsequent itch of my fingers to touch him. I stayed where I was, continuing the guise of looking for my target.

"I didn't see any gardens on the way in," I murmured.

He took a sip, his signet ring knocking against the glass. The tang of bourbon hit my nose. "That's a real shame, it being our anniversary and all." The deep tones of his voice, along with the fact he'd remembered the date, made my beast puff up with elation, preening. "Have you found Leon?"

"Not yet." Maybe he wouldn't show. Perhaps he'd been struck down with the flu, or food poisoning? I could hope. "I'm sure I'll see him as soon as he gets here. He's that type of person."

"I spoke to him for five minutes at the last event. It was five minutes too many." From the corner of my eye, Silas took another swig, the curtain shrouding him in darkness.

I went to take a sip, then paused at my empty flute. "Got any of your drink left?"

"Unfortunately not." Ice kicked around his empty glass. "I needed it to cope."

"With Arwood?"

"With you, looking like that."

My grip tightened on the railing. Arwood greeted Gisele and Ivan Kohnstamm. Leon wasn't with them.

"We shouldn't be speaking like this, remember?" I ducked my head. My heart had become a racing thing. "We promised."

"True." His eyes remained on me, caressing like a hand passing atop a flame. "You destroy every promise I make to myself."

Stop talking like this. I didn't want to think of what I'd missed out on by not being with Silas. I couldn't let those thoughts anchor me to a situation I needed to get out of.

"Well, your existence derails my convictions, too." My words came out harsher than I intended.

"Are you okay?"

"No. I really wish I wasn't here." I didn't bother mentioning that I'd asked, nay, *demanded* to attend. I especially didn't mention how my plan with Steadman had spectacularly backfired. I wasn't confident tonight would get better. "I'm not good at this."

"At spotting rich bastards who need a day job to improve their character?"

"Getting Leon's attention and holding it long enough to pull this off." I tried to keep my voice steady around the lump forming in my throat. Part of me couldn't believe I was telling him this—but then again, Silas was off-limits. I had nothing to lose by sharing this. "Arwood threatened to turn me over to the Sect. I can't afford to screw this up. And … I'm scared."

I chanced a look at him. His solemn expression mirrored mine. Silas knew what I was talking about better than most. Feeling trapped by Arwood was his daily reality.

Beyond the balustrade, the chandeliers threw long shadows. His fingers brushed the side of my dress. The smallest of touches, but the equivalent of an embrace for how my skin tingled. "You've had my attention from the first, Keeks. You met me head on and you—" Silas paused, his hand dropping. "You have this combination of wit and warmth that only makes me want to keep talking to you. You're better at this than you think."

His confession thrilled me, my eyes going damp. I blinked tears away—I couldn't mess up my winged eyeliner, especially when I'd managed to get it even—and inhaled steadily. Words of affirmation in my life were akin to finding water in a desert; like a parched woman, I drank them in.

"I miss that night," I said. "I miss dancing with you."

"I miss being able to look at you like I *know* you," he replied. "I hate Leon gets the privilege of talking to you tonight. He doesn't deserve it."

He really wasn't making this any easier for either of us. I was seconds from grabbing him and running for the border, Arwood be damned. "Silas ..." His name crept out, half a moan to keep going, half a plea to stop.

Instead, Silas said, "There he is."

I followed his gaze to a roulette table. Leon had arrived, wearing a gray suit in a sea of black.

Behind Leon, Steadman stood, focused on me. *Double shit.*

I straightened my dress and tightened my earrings, using my wrist to conceal my moving lips. "Stay where you are for as long as you can," I muttered to Silas as I headed for the stairs. "We're being watched."

We always were.

CHAPTER TWENTY-ONE

LEON MAY HAVE BEEN EASY TO SPOT, BUT HIS ACCESSIBILITY was a placebo. From my vantage point, I'd missed the bodyguards stationed around him. The moment I made it clear that I intended to join him at roulette, one halted me, while another got Leon's attention. I tried to lipread, but the language must not have been English because I couldn't make out a single word.

Like the first time we'd met, Leon's eyes slid over me like oil on water. His lips twisted with disinterest, disregarding me with a single negation. In turn, the bodyguard flicked his palm as if to move me along.

My beast reared her head. Outraged my dress hadn't had the expected effect on Leon the way it'd had on Silas, or just outraged in general? Either way, she was incensed.

And me? Well, this was what I'd been terrified of.

I glanced at Arwood. He inclined his head. *Figure it out.*

I wouldn't be able to get past the guards by force unless I screamed, so that option was out. I'd have to talk my way in. Somehow.

With as much grace as I could muster, I smiled at the bodyguard, raising my palms so he knew the message had been received.

"I work for Arwood Sayer. Can you ask Mr. Kohnstamm if he's interested in making a deal?"

The bodyguard could have been a brick wall for all the emotional response I got. He nodded to a taller man standing near him whose midnight black hair sat slicked back with copious amounts of gel. A strand dangled across his forehead as he bent to listen. I longed to prod it back into place as I repeated my request.

I smoothed the folds of my dress as Hair Gel interrupted Leon, laying out his chips. Again, Leon's eyes met mine. He sighed, finishing his bet and scratching his temple like talking to me was the very last thing he wanted to do.

But he agreed.

Giving another generous smile to the bodyguard, I approached the table. Leon had just lost. His opponent chuckled as the dealer presented a stack of colored chips.

"I hear you are a ship searching for a port," Leon murmured in his thick accent, stacking another row of chips in the first third and on red.

I had a minute or less to capture his interest, or I'd be cast out without a second chance. Better use it. "Not the poetic prose I would have used, but not inaccurate. I wish to strike a deal with you."

"Arwood wouldn't send you to speak for him, little girl."

Little girl? A bit much from someone a handful of years older at most. I didn't bite. "Arwood isn't aware of my intentions. Can we discuss this matter privately?" I pointedly glanced at his roulette opponent.

Leon agitated his chips, flipping one over his pointer finger. "I'm in a streak," he said. "And not moving until I'm sure it's worth it."

He must have thought I was stupid, because he'd just lost. Twice. "I'm searching for Isobelle Sayer."

Clack clack went his chips. "You and everyone else in Prague, it seems."

"Do you know where she is?"

The dealer halted bets as the ball bounced into high black. Leon's lips pressed together as the other man whooped again. "You talked of deals. I haven't heard one yet."

"My release from Arwood is contingent on her recovery. You help me find her, I work for you."

He laughed without humor as the dealer spun the wheel again.

Leon put everything in the last third and on black, mimicking the previous bet of his opponent. Everything I needed to know about him was now laid out on the table between us. "No deal. I have enough personnel, and my bed is full." He agitated the chips in his hand again, focusing on my cleavage. "In any case, I prefer my women a little … skinnier."

I maintained eye contact, but barely. Heat rose beneath my collar, humiliation washing down my arms. *Fat. He thinks I'm fat.*

I swallowed, trying to think. Leon wasn't strategic. He copied evidence of success in the hopes for instant gratification, and he'd hit me head on because he was a bully who thought he could get away with it. It was a test, too. He'd never give the time of day to someone who failed to recognize an insult. His comment on my appearance wasn't helpful in achieving my immediate goal, so I tried to ignore it. I'd cry about it later.

My beast wanted to rip his head off. I ignored her, too.

With an air of confidence I didn't feel, I tapped my nails on the glossy wood like I was bored already. "Being in your bed doesn't interest me," I said. "It's your protection I'm after. My value extends further than twenty seconds on your thousand thread-count sheets."

Clack. Clack. "That's an insulting inaccuracy."

"My apologies. Is the thread count higher?"

He paused, his eyes narrowing. Had I gone too far? I pushed on. "Isobelle and I have something in common."

"Being blonde?"

"Our … abilities." His opponent slowed in the stacking of his chips, peering at me like he questioned his hearing. "Have the rumors about me hit your ears yet?" I tapped my collar.

Leon studied me up and down, seeing me properly. Yes. He *had* heard the rumors. "How do I know they're true?"

I came closer. "If you need a demonstration, take me to a room full of people you wish to be rid of and I'll show you."

The man beside me froze.

"You've established quite the tally." Leon crossed his arms. His opponent backed away. "How can I be sure it's not *my* name you wish to add to that list?"

"I'm Arwood's special ammunition. He enjoys utilizing my abilities, but I have no intention of aligning myself with him long-term."

Leon's arms remained crossed. Unconvinced. I played to his ego.

"I petitioned my father, Edson Backhus, to negotiate a deal with you and Mr. Kohnstamm because I respect the way you do business. That still stands. With Isobelle returned to Arwood, I'll be free to work with your family."

They say a watched kettle never boils. The seconds I waited for Leon to consider, then nod to his bodyguards, were some of the longest I'd experienced.

I didn't dare look for anyone as I followed him, trailed by his security, out of the function room and down a cordoned-off hallway. Anika had said they'd be watching me, and I believed her. Leon gestured to an office, barked a bunch of sentences in Czech, and closed the door, silencing the noise from the party.

"You have four minutes to speak." He slid a hand across a glossy obsidian cabinet hosting curved Scandinavian-style vases. "If I don't exit—alive and well—after those four minutes, they've been instructed to enter and pump you full of bullets."

With that, he sat behind the chrome desk and stretched out his long legs, looking every inch an egotistical prince.

I'd never, ever, said the words out loud, but *Holy fuck* rang through my mind so clearly I'd be surprised if Leon didn't hear it. There was no way I'd be able to drug him like this. I'd have to ask him for a drink before we joined everyone again. *And* somehow pilfer the vial out from underneath my tight bodice without knocking my boobs loose or giving myself away.

Hopefully Arwood's team weren't far behind and they had a back-up plan, because I was *not* cut out for this.

"I respect—and expect—an effective contingency plan in an ally. I have no intention of hurting you." I sat opposite, crossing my ankles and settling my hands on my lap in full work-meeting mode. "So. Isobelle."

"I have no idea where Isobelle is."

I held his gaze for several beats, employing one of Lissandra's techniques. He was the first to drop it. "When did you last see her?"

He chuckled, more than my question called for. "Two months ago. I was fucking her, and she screamed so loudly I went blind."

Eugh. He was wasting the precious time I had. "Get to the point, please."

"Just did. My vision came back soon after. She went crazy, saying it was her fault, and left."

"The blindness didn't last?"

Leon gestured theatrically to his face like I'd asked the most redundant question ever. I supposed it had been, but in my shock it had slipped out.

My ability was permanent. Isobelle's was *temporary*. She didn't cause lasting damage when she lost control.

I strengthened my tone. "Had this happened before? How long were you in a relationship?"

"No, and a few weeks." He clicked his tongue. "I don't do relationships."

Except Arwood had thought them together in an official sense. Did I believe the perception of a grieving father, or the arrogance of an overcompensating boy? "No? Then what did you call it?"

"We were hanging out. Not a big deal."

He readjusted on the chair, balancing an ankle across his knee. Everything about this room was impersonally perfect, including the gleaming marble floors. His shoulders shifted underneath his double-breasted blazer as he wiggled a polished shoe. For some reason, the expression '*doth protest too much*' crossed my mind. The only son of a crime lynchpin, surrounded by bodyguards all day and, presumably, fleeting interactions at night. He didn't let people close, but had Isobelle gotten under his skin anyway?

And where the hell was Arwood's team? I was at least one

minute down. No shouts came from the security on the other side of the door. This room was as quiet as a vault.

"Did she make any mention of what she might do after? You said she was upset."

Again, Leon gave a shrug, brushing the contrasting black pocket of his jacket. Balmain? I had a blazer at home with similar lines.

"She wanted to fix it. The screaming," Leon said. "Next I heard, she'd disappeared."

"Some mutual associates are saying she was taken by *you*."

He scowled before he could stop it, schooling his features into neutrality. "Those accusations are bullshit. We've been trying to find her, too. I liked her, and my family respects the fuck out of our truce with Arwood—even if it won't last much longer. Three shipments of girls have gone missing this week alone."

My eyebrows had begun to draw together. I smoothed my expression. "Arwood's not doing that."

"He knows our schedules. He's always negotiating for more territory. My family's had networks here and in Germany for generations. No one else would dare interfere."

His words rang eerily familiar. Urgency flickered, then flared. Our four promised minutes were ticking, but it was more than that: resounding clarity had hit me like a bucket of ice-water.

We were being played. Both sides were. By Johan, or someone else? Was their strategy to manipulate each side into a war? If so, it was working. Each group would be so focused on burning each other, someone could swoop in and take what remained.

I tried to suppress my panic even though I had probably less than a minute left here. Talking things out with Leon wouldn't diffuse the situation between both sides. But finding Isobelle might.

"Did Isobelle mention if she was meeting anyone, or had intentions to go anywhere?"

Leon straightened the buttons lining his sleeve, bored again. "She'd been researching. She left a note saying she would—"

A sharp knock froze me solid.

Before I had the chance to work out how I'd react to two guards entering, guns blazing, the door swung open, revealing Leon's mother, Gisele. Her curvy frame, clad in a silver mermaid-style gown, dominated the doorway, her toned shoulders offset by a cascade of raven waves.

Arwood would be here soon. This wasn't happening.

"We are to welcome the guests. Come."

No no no—

Leon didn't move. "We won't be long, Mother."

She barked a single directive in German, her dark eyes narrowing as they landed on my collar. Leon sighed, getting up. I emerged into the hallway as Steadman, Matej, and several of Arwood's team strode toward us.

"Backhus, there you are!" Steadman grabbed my upper arm, pulling me to the side. "You were not given permission to leave your post." He maintained the charade, not releasing me until the Kohnstamms and their security entered the function room.

I was still reeling from my conversation with Leon. Could I trust Steadman? He'd said he'd proven his loyalty to Arwood. He also could have been lying. But with what I knew, I couldn't do *nothing*. A war would put me in even more danger.

"Got the vial?" Steadman asked. I nodded. "Then you'll try again as soon as the presentation is over."

Applause sounded, drawing us into the room. I clutched the folds of my dress, searching the crowd. I needed someone I trusted to talk to. I needed Silas.

Leon and his mother took to the platform where Ivan Kohnstamm stood. He handed Gisele the microphone, smiling at the audience as she welcomed the guests and introduced the charity this event was raising funds for. Her melodic voice silenced the crowd—

—and a metallic scent flooded my nose.

I inhaled sharply and stepped forward. Steadman tugged me

beside him. "You're staying here, banshee, where I can keep an eye on you."

An attendant passed by, leaning down to offer seated guests the drinks on her tray. The combination of the angle and her movements meant the collar of her shirt gaped just enough to reveal the top of a diamond tattoo on her neck. The same mark seared on the trafficked girls we'd found in Waldemar's building, the same mark on Ferko.

Johan's mark.

I went hot, then cold, as the smell intensified. I couldn't see Silas but could make out Arwood's head near the stage. Gisele opened an envelope, announcing a donation from one of their partners. A smatter of polite applause rippled across the crowd.

Another attendant walked past, his head turned toward Gisele, the tip of a diamond peeking behind his collar. I zeroed in on all the serving staff. Dotted like ants in the crowd, they walked slowly, alert, as if waiting for something.

Or some*one*.

What better way to push two sides into a confrontation than to attack both at the same time—and cause each side to think the other was at fault?

Steadman shook me. "Keanna," he said, in a way that hinted he'd addressed me more than once. "What's wrong?"

My mouth had gone dry; my voice cracked as I bleated, "I need to talk to Arwood."

It filled the room. Unmistakable. Sickening. The smell made my eyes water.

"What's wrong?" Steadman repeated, his gaze catching on the serving staff. His frown deepened as he clocked their behavior.

Death.

No Silas. No Anika. Arwood and Lissandra were too far away. I pushed up Steadman's jacket sleeve. No caracal tattoo.

"Banshee, what the hell are you—"

I pulled his shirt collar to the side. No diamonds.

Steadman shook my shoulders again. "*Speak.*"

A man in a valet jacket steered a silver drink cart stacked with glittering wrapped presents beside the stage as Gisele announced the next donation to another round of applause.

I swallowed. "Something's about to happen."

The serving staff filtered toward the back of the room.

"Keanna?" Steadman repeated. In the steady depths of his eyes, I glimpsed fear for the first time. "What do you—"

"We need to get out of here. We need to get out of here *now*."

He pulled out his phone. While it rang he signaled to Matej, pointing to the front of the crowd.

"Next up, a generous donation from one of our dear friends and partners, Arwood Sayer," Gisele announced, opening the envelope in a flourish. "*Two hundred and fifty thousand dollars,* everyone!" She paused, allowing another wave of applause.

It consumed me. The cloying sweetness of danger flooded my nose. My stomach revolted like I was about to be sick.

Arwood's team converged toward the stage as the silver presents beside Ivan and Leon Kohnstamm exploded.

CHAPTER TWENTY-TWO

THE ROOM SHUDDERED, SPEWING DEBRIS. THE CROWD flattened like a hand had pushed it over. Smoke billowed out and swirled upwards. Pitched screams and a weird popping noise vibrated above the ringing in my ears.

I stumbled to my feet. Steadman yelled something about the exit, racing for where Arwood and Lissandra had stood moments before. Yes. Exit. I could do that. The ringing in my ears intensified as I headed for the double doors, searching for Silas. Anika. *Anyone.*

Ahead, two guests folded to the floor. The popping noise intensified. Something shoved me from the side; I struggled to keep my footing. Smoke pricked my eyes as I turned, my teeth clacking together as the back of my head slammed against the wall. A hand covered my mouth. A thumb pushed against the underside of my jaw. Silver glinted, and something cold came to rest underneath my ear. I blinked, my brain catching up, as a swooping evacuation alarm sounded, overriding the noise of everything else.

The hand belonged to a man in his early thirties wearing a navy valet jacket. Bronze hair waved across his alabaster forehead. Thick black bolts filled his earlobes. I made a muffled squeal of protest and shifted against him—or at least I tried to. His broad body cemented me to the wall. Suffocating me. *Too close.*

My beast reared.

"Don't scream," the man said, staring at my collar. His fingers bit into my cheek. "I'm not gonna hurt you, babe."

Textured wallpaper chafed my bare skin in a smoky Prague

casino, and then I was in a luxurious hotel suite held against a door by Thomas, his hand over my mouth.

Then—back in the casino, peppermint-soaked breath creeping up my nose, screams and alarms ringing my ears and a knife pressed against my throat—

Back in the hotel suite, pleading with Thomas to *stop, stop, what are you doing,* aware of pressure in my chest expanding like I was about to cry/scream/freak out and it was rising and rising as Thomas pulled rope and tape out of his pocket, telling me to be quiet and I was *stuck-confined-can't-breathe-can't-move-have to get out out OUT.*

I knew how it had ended in the hotel suite two months ago. I didn't know how it would end here, now, against the wall with this man. The sharp sting of his blade brought me to the present. My beast keened, wanting him to burn for touching me. *Us.*

"I need you to come with m—"

Crying out behind clamped lips, I exhaled roughly through my nose—

—and a wall of pressure sent the valet man flying backwards. He collided against the filigreed pillar opposite with a smack.

I gaped, stunned.

That had been *me.*

I'd thrown him with the same kind of pressure I emitted whenever I screamed—except he rolled, very much alive. Behind him, a guest fell to their knees, nearly consumed by the smoke, blood blossoming across their shirt. Gunfire. The popping was *gunfire.*

I ran for the doors, sweaty feet slipping in my strappy heels. Sharp pants tore from my throat. I expected to be shot down at any second, for pain to erupt and it all to end. I glanced back; if my attacker had made it out of the room, I couldn't see him.

Somehow, with all the other noise, I heard a husky voice.

"Keanna!"

Silas rushed between the machines toward me. He looked whole. Healthy. "Thank God," he said, grabbing one of my hands.

We ran, the *whoop whoop* of the alarm echoing around us as we sank into the slew of patrons fleeing their gambling nest. The bodice of my dress had reached the end of its tether in terms of support; I held it up, feeling very much a pumpkin after midnight. If I'd known this event would result in gunfire and a bomb, I'd have argued for the green dress harder. And sneakers.

We bolted for the emergency doors flung open to the cars parked outside. Men descended the stairs behind us, caracal tattoos prominent on their wrists as they raised their weapons.

At us.

I forgot all about my bodice, running faster in my stupid heels. "Guns!" I screeched as the Kohnstamm men fired.

A marble planter exploded beside me. I shrieked, ducking.

We're not going to make it.

Silas spun, hands outstretched. A shield erupted as he walked backwards, the barrier unfurling into a thick oval between us and the firing men. "Go!" he yelled over his shoulder. "Get to Arwood!"

I skidded to a stop in front of our cars. Lissandra and Steadman were tugging the poor drivers from the front seats, their throats halved by a gaping, bloody gash. Using the floodlights overhead, Arwood and Matej—both covered in soot and blood—inspected the liquid oozing underneath the driver-side tires. For someone who turned the music up louder if my car ever made weird noises, even *I* knew that couldn't be a good thing.

Vehicles hurtled around the valet circle for the dark road beyond. Except us. Someone had made sure our getaway cars wouldn't go anywhere.

Hurried footsteps came from behind as Anika fled the casino, clutching something. Gunshots followed her. Two SUVs nearby flashed, unlocking. She whistled, throwing us two sets of keys.

"Take Liss," Steadman said to Arwood as they caught them. He'd removed his jacket, his white dress shirt spattered with crimson. "We'll play this like Marrakesh. I'll hang back."

Lissandra rose, palms bloody, glancing at Arwood and

Steadman. The wordless conversation between the three of them lasted long enough for Silas to yell "Incoming!".

Anika pounced on the gunman firing behind a nearby Porsche; bullets fell from her skin as she landed on him like a wildcat, punching him square in the face and wrestling the gun from his grip. More Kohnstamm guards gathered at the foot of the steps, branching out to the sides and trying to pen us in. Lissandra generated a shield of her own. If that shocked the guards, they didn't show it. They kept firing like a figurative battering ram. Lissandra tensed as her shield deflected the bullets, Silas groaning from the effort of holding off the others.

"You two are with me." Steadman pointed to Silas and me. Where were Arwood's other men? Had they made it out? "Anika!" Steadman called, alerting her to the stolen car Arwood, Matej, and Lissandra piled into.

The engine turned over as Anika ran around the shields, cradling the gun to her chest. The heels of her boots scratched the bonnet as she dived for the sunroof. Arwood took off toward the valet circle, Anika firing as Lissandra's shield vanished.

"MOVE IT!" Steadman roared.

I grabbed Silas's jacket, leading him, and didn't let him go until I'd thrown myself into the back seat of the remaining SUV. Steadman took the wheel.

The shield shifted to protect the open doors as Silas collapsed against the leather seat, then winked out as Steadman accelerated. Our wheels crushed flowerbeds as we raced around exiting cars.

"Shield up, Silas," Steadman said as we swung onto the road. A fleet of sedans followed. The Kohnstamms, or Johan's people? Either way, they were keeping up. "This car isn't armored."

As Steadman said this, figures popped up out of the sunroofs of the cars closest to us, barely visible against the night sky. One of our taillights exploded. I flinched. Steadman murmured "Shit" and swung the car into a different lane with a speed that had me securing my seatbelt.

Silas wrapped a shield around the back of the SUV as we screeched onto a side street. Undeterred, two of the vehicles sped up to flank us. The headlights drew closer.

"Silas!" I warned, but he had already brought his palms together as if in prayer. He inhaled. Another shield enveloped both cars, suspending them above the road. As he exhaled, pulling his hands apart, the shield dispersed. The sedans plummeted, momentum sending them sailing in opposite directions. Gunmen flew across the bonnets as the cars plowed into the buildings to either side.

The four cars further back swerved to avoid them, gaining ground.

"Don't let that shield fall, kid," Steadman grated, turning the wheel and hitting the throttle, narrowly avoiding a tram. I nearly faceplanted into the window; an advertisement for a serum and the wide eyes of passengers flashed past.

"I'm a battery," Silas grunted. "Not an infinite power source. We need a Plan B."

"Plans B, C and D are you keeping that shield up until we lose these fuckers. I don't care how you do it."

"If I drain myself to death, *all* shields will fail."

It took a moment to realize what he meant. The amulet around Steadman's neck, protecting him from my scream.

The shield wrapping the car wavered.

"Don't you dare, mage. You know what will happen. And if *they* aren't enough motivation, do it for the well-being of the woman beside you."

Me. He meant *me.*

I locked eyes with Silas for a split second. Had Steadman figured it out? *How?*

The shield strengthened. Silas swayed, shaking his head. He was going to run himself into the ground.

"Silas," I whispered.

The Kohnstamms pursued us relentlessly. As we got closer to the city center, more people and more traffic would slow us down.

Threats or not, Silas wouldn't last much longer. I unbuckled.

"Put your damned seatbelt on," Steadman warned, swerving.

"I have an idea." I turned to Silas. The streetlights emphasized the hollows under his eyes. "Do you have enough strength left to hold me?"

He shot me a bewildered look, nodding. I double checked my bodice—everything was still tucked in, thank God—and manually overrode the lock.

Steadman clued on quicker than Silas. "If you scream inside this car, banshee, so help me."

"I'm not an idiot, Steadman," I ground out. "Right-hand turn when I say to. Silas, I need you to make sure we don't go boom."

"*Shit*," was Silas's emphatic reply. He plucked off his tuxedo jacket, throwing it to the side, and rolled up the sleeves of his dress shirt.

Pulse pounding against my collar, I shoved open the door, groaning with effort. Wind whipped my hair about my face. Silas wrapped the seatbelt around his waist, visibly swallowing as I latched onto his bare forearm.

Steadman swerved again. My arm shook from holding open the door. I shuffled my butt until it almost hung off the seat. Below, the road loomed close, moving *very* fast.

Silas gritted his teeth, extending the shield to deflect the spray of bullets aiming for us. He shifted the folds of my dress aside, shuffling between my thighs. The sight of my bare leg hooking around his torso almost distracted me—until Steadman swerved again.

My butt slipped off the seat.

A squeal lodged in my throat as Silas's hand clasped my waist, gripping tight. I hung, suspended, the backs of my thighs my only anchor to the vehicle and fully at Silas's mercy.

Exhausted Silas, who'd already been put through enough.

"Please don't drop me." I hated how my voice wavered, but the road was *so* close. Falling at this speed would do a lot of damage. Not to mention being run over by the Kohnstamms afterwards.

Silas clutched me closer. "I won't."

Fear flushed my clammy skin, but his unwavering hold—and the intense look in his eyes—helped me push it away. We reached an intersection. Green lights. Cars waited on either side.

"Now!"

Steadman spun the wheel. We veered sharply right, the four cars closing in. The two closest prepared to T-bone us. Our shield dropped. The men standing in their sunroofs aimed straight for me and our exposed tires. Headlights blinded me.

A sapphire shield wrapped around my neck like a silk scarf, expanding as I let loose a scream. On the other side of the barrier, Silas held me while the pressure—with nowhere else left to go but toward the pursuing cars—billowed outwards.

Our pursuers ricocheted. One careened straight for the set of streetlights. Two spun, colliding with cars on either side. The final one blew straight into the front of a store, clipping a pedestrian.

A dropped grenade doesn't discriminate. It just detonates. Civilian cars crashed into each other, accumulating a mess across the intersection.

The shield dissolved to Silas's drawn face. He pulled me back inside, panting. Fatigue folded over him like a blanket; he passed out, head lolling onto the seat.

Arwood's battery, depleted.

My beast settled in my chest, sated. Horror washed me faint, my stomach turning cold, the tears I'd held at bay all night thickening my throat.

In the rear-view mirror, Steadman's steely blue gaze met mine. "Nice work, banshee."

His approval tasted foul on my tongue.

PART TWO

ALL SIGNS
POINT NORTH

CHAPTER TWENTY-THREE

THE BRILLIANTLY LIT MANSION AWAITED OUR RETURN. Arwood met Steadman as he exited our stolen SUV, patting his shoulders. Checking his right-hand man remained intact. He was, with no small thanks to the drained, sleeping mage beside me. I hated to wake him, but it was either me or one of Arwood's men, and I wanted to protect Silas's peace for as long as I could. I gently prodded him and—as the lights in the car's interior faded, concealing us in darkness—dared pass a hand across his cheek, whispering his name.

Silas stirred.

"Keeks," he murmured, his voice a deep rumble that hit me in the gut. "Are you okay?"

"Asks the guy who nearly killed himself shielding us."

His sleepy smile made me wish we were alone so I could sit and share the intimacy of watching him become alert again. Instead, I eyed Steadman directing the guards, pointing to our stolen car.

Silas squinted, then stiffened. "Steadman knows."

Steadman's threats were exactly what Silas had tried to prevent by keeping his distance from me in the first place. He'd hinted he had people relying on him. Who was he protecting? Now would be a good time to ask, but I couldn't bring myself to.

"Maybe he only thinks he does," I said. "We just need to make sure we don't give him any more reasons to think he was right. Stay away from each other from now on."

Even though I'd suggested it, disappointment still took hold when Silas nodded.

"Agreed." He mushed a hand over his face. "I'm sorry about tonight. You shouldn't have needed to do that."

"*No one* should have to do what we did."

If my strained arm muscles and dirty, ruined dress weren't enough reminder of our sins, Anika approached, her pinstriped suit moth-eaten by bullet holes. Reluctantly, I shut the car door to her whooping.

She punched me on the shoulder. "You're *killing it*, Backhus."

Like with Steadman, her approval chafed, highlighting the horrible thing I couldn't undo.

Anika peered into the back seat, her expression turning grim before requesting the guards assist Silas upstairs. I turned, not wanting to watch him stagger, knowing I'd contributed to the reason why. Again.

I followed Anika through the entrance and toward one of the sitting rooms. "What happened to the others?"

She clicked her tongue. "We lost all drivers. Some of our team went down in the function room. We barely got Arwood and Lissandra out of there—ugh, hang on." She wiggled her pant leg. An intact bullet plopped onto the tiles. She kicked it underneath a table holding a vase filled with white roses, straightening the lapels on her blazer. The singed holes in the fabric revealed tanned, unblemished skin. "Thought I had something stuck in my thong. Where was I? Ah, yes, tonight was a clusterfuck, I need a new suit, and we're officially at war with the Kohnstamms. Again."

We'd rounded the corner; Lissandra and Arwood sat on one of the cozy Chesterfields, Steadman opposite. All nursed drinks and evidence—mutinous expressions, sooty, crimson-splattered clothes—of an evening not gone to plan.

Arwood perched his elbows on his knees, the sides of his close-cropped blond hair and chiseled face streaked with blood. Burgundy spread like an inkblot across the collar of his shirt. I'd never seen him look so … human.

"An excellent summary, dear cousin," Lissandra drawled, dabbing the cut on her husband's brow.

"It's what I'm here for." Anika helped herself to vodka from the drink cart. I waved off her offer, not sure I'd be able to swallow past the lump in my throat, and took one of the single-seaters. "What's our next move?" she asked.

"For what it's worth—*hold still, Arwood, I'm not done yet*—tonight provided necessary confirmation that a third party is active, unrelated to the Kohnstamms."

"To the detriment of everything else," Steadman said. "Johan's done a terrific job framing us."

"Perhaps not," Lissandra replied. "The present bomb is Ferko's signature. Neither family has known ties with him."

"Didn't. We *didn't* have known ties with him," Steadman said. "Until I went into his nightclub and killed his men but left him alive. Is it any wonder the Kohnstamms didn't ask questions?"

I jammed my heels into the plush brown rug. We'd killed tonight. We'd killed *many* nights. And Steadman just sat there, acknowledging this with the remoteness of an overworked chef discussing a cut of meat he'd served.

Lissandra swept a white cloth up Arwood's temple. The side-eye and smile he gave his wife had *I hate this but thank you for doing it* energy. Lissandra raised an amused eyebrow.

I immediately looked at Steadman. His lips had curved, but he didn't seem upset or rattled, watching his lady love fuss over another. Steadman might not wear the marks of Johan or the Kohnstamms, he may have genuinely been concerned for Arwood's well-being, but was he truly loyal if he allowed himself to have feelings for Lissandra? Or was this all part of a much larger game?

"It is what it is," Arwood said, wincing as Lissandra pressed on a bandage. "We'll need to instill proactive measures."

Lissandra turned to me. "How did you know about the bomb, Keanna? What did Leon tell you?"

I resisted the temptation to fidget under the weight of

everyone's attention, considering I had seconds to decide how much information to share.

"He mentioned their shipments of women were being intercepted. The Kohnstamms assumed it was Arwood's doing, given we know their schedules." I paused, preparing for someone to jump in, for Steadman to dispel some sarcastic comment. No one did. "I realized both sides were being manipulated into a confrontation. All the attendants were Johan's. And …" I sighed. This would sound ridiculous. "I just *knew*."

Anika plopped a sphere of ice into her cup, refilling it with more vodka. "They do say banshees are the harbingers of death."

"Useful," Steadman murmured. "We'll need that, moving forward." Great. Exactly what I needed—to be *more* useful. I imagined Steadman toting me around like a metal detector to every future altercation, checking, 'Is anyone going to die here?' To Lissandra, he asked, "What resources can we bring in from Positano?"

"I'd rather cut my arm off than seek help from Papa," Lissandra replied after a beat of silence. "I built this city in spite of him; he'll demand recompense for assistance. And we have too much to lose by succumbing to open war again. The Sect *will* draw the line at that."

Her lined brown eyes flashed across everyone in the room, seeking a challenge. The undercurrents of this conversation rolled thick and deep, and I needed to reflect on everything contained within. For now, I focused on absorbing the information instead of dwelling on it.

"I know I'm asking too much of you in this," Steadman said, uncharacteristically gentle. "But we need to consider reinforcing our side as a precaution."

"And we shall do so if all else fails. There's a time for violence— and pragmatism." Resolve tinged her accented voice as she recrossed her legs, her white dress rippling over the rug. "Let's exhaust the latter first. I will reach out to Gisele. Requesting a meeting may give them pause."

"Or she'll take advantage of you trying to make peace."

"I will not proactively command aggression," Lissandra said. "That's what Johan wants. Gisele is a force. She has lost Leon, possibly her husband, too, but even grieving she may be reasonable where Ivan was not."

Leon's dead?

Arwood had been silent throughout their discussion, pressing his thumbs into his chin. At this, he sat up straight. "We're still unclear on whether the Kohnstamms know Isobelle's location."

I jumped in. "Leon swore they didn't have her. He mentioned Isobelle was trying to find a way to control what she is. What if she approached the wrong person for help and Johan has nothing to do with it? What if the Sect has Isobelle?"

"You think that wasn't the first place we checked?" Steadman's voice resumed its usual even cadence as he addressed me. "They don't."

"How do you know?" I pressed.

Arwood shifted, taking the cloth from Lissandra and dabbing at his neck. "The Sect don't suffer individuals with supernatural abilities who go public. They make an example of them, and would have made sure I was witness to anything relating to my daughter."

"But we *did* go public tonight," I whispered. "All of us did."

Anika shot me a sideways look from the drink cart. Distress stamped her features as she tossed back more vodka.

"The Sect possess a weapon that can damage us," Lissandra replied, "just as we possess one which equally damages them in return. While this is fact, and we maintain our scale of operations, they will not pursue us directly."

Arwood's mouth formed a grim line. "And I protect my own. Provided you remain of benefit to me, the Sect will not be a concern for you." I heeded the warning in his voice, even if it wasn't necessary. I hadn't forgotten he had video footage of me. I knew how short my leash was. "Regardless—if they had her, we'd know by now."

"Leon said Isobelle left a note before she was taken. If she was kidnapped, why would she have—"

"Anyone can type a note," Arwood said. "A note proves nothing. It was neither convincing nor detailed enough to be helpful."

"A note proves she may have left willingly."

"Then why hasn't Issie made contact?" Steadman countered. "It's been weeks. She'd know we're looking for her. She wouldn't have left us wondering like that."

His words were a blow to my heart. I couldn't let my father know where I was, or even how I was doing. I was all he had. He was all *I* had.

"Until we reach a resolution with the Kohnstamms, all sweeps are suspended," Lissandra directed. "No one is to leave this estate without permission. Dobromil?"

The guard standing behind us perked up, smoothing his thick russet beard. He'd been the one to defend me against the staring kitchenhand. "Yes, ma'am?"

"Inform the team what has occurred. Prepare accordingly. Any reinforcements we require, I'll arrange."

He nodded, exiting.

Lissandra stood. "Johan must be terminated. Ladies?" She looked between me and Anika. "You're on call for the next few days. Be ready to leave at short notice."

Anika saluted with her glass. Steadman passed Lissandra as they left, brushing the silky curve of her hip in the same subtle way Silas had touched me tonight. Arwood regarded me, missing it all.

"We appreciate your service, Miss Backhus. You're dismissed."

He followed his fabulously dressed, cheating wife out the room.

CHAPTER TWENTY-FOUR

"'You're dismissed,'" I spat, pushing open the door to the servant's passageway. "'Now that you've crossed over to the dark side, it's time for bed.'" Dusty floorboards were the only audience to my hissed words, but saying them out loud made me feel better.

I'd used my abilities publicly, exposing me to some arcane group only Arwood could shield me from. Just when I thought I'd hit rock bottom, I'd fallen further. Been outplayed. Again.

In lieu of a torch or convenient phone, I clutched a battery-operated alarm clock. The white digits cast enough of a glow to navigate the corridor. A ridiculous look, but on-brand considering how out of my depth I felt.

Given that it was accessible, I assumed Anika hadn't told Arwood about the secret passageway. While I still had the advantage, I planned to use it. I needed to win something tonight.

I paused at Silas's door, the keyhole jammed up. No sound came from inside. He was probably asleep. I missed him already, my beast wanting me to knock on the door, join him.

I checked every keyhole I passed. Some were blocked, perhaps by discerning guests or hanging picture frames. Others revealed dark, empty rooms. I proceeded far further than with Anika, reaching a T-section. The thin corridors held the echoes of a hedge maze. They'd never been my thing—I'd always gotten lost in them—so I took particular care as I continued. The library was on this floor, and I hoped it would be one of the rooms I'd find. Defending myself against my attacker had opened possibilities I was keen to explore.

Researching would help ease the heaviness in my chest, but I hadn't wanted to give Arwood the satisfaction of running there after my ordeal like I was trying to comfort myself.

Two doors later, a bedroom caught my attention, the light from the full moon spilling through the recessed window above and across the four-poster bed. A throw rug and illustrated books covered one of the occasional chairs, the floor inside the walk-in closet littered with stilettos and patterned boots. Photographs lined the desk where a laptop sat shut.

A *laptop*, ladies and gentlemen.

I tugged at the door, praying it would open as the others had. The hinges creaked. It swung inward enough for me to insert my hips and butt into the gap and jimmy it open. I cringed against the grating of wood scraping on wood and entered the room. The main door was locked from the outside. I opened the laptop and flicked on the desk lamp.

The screen remained dark. Flat.

After locating the charger and plugging it in, we were in business … until I got blocked by the sign-in screen greeting the owner by name, requesting a password once facial recognition failed.

This was Isobelle's room.

Hopes of sending an SOS email to my father faded. I knew nothing about this girl, much less what she'd use as a password. Surprisingly, *Ih8Steadman* didn't work. One attempt down.

I observed the room, sucking on my lip. It had the messy, lived-in quality of someone with an active social calendar. The walk-in wardrobe was a U-shaped thing of my dreams, with rows of expensive fabrics and shimmery pieces. Designer bags lined the top, logos visible in the muted light. More dresses lay across the ottoman. I moved to the rows of photographs. A selfie with friends, all wearing spa robes. Another of her, younger, with the same girls, the pockets of their blazers showcasing the logo of a prestigious boarding school in England. The one beside it had her pulling a face at the camera, Leon looking down at her, long blonde hair pooling on his lap.

Just hanging out, he'd said.

His expression gave me my answer: Arwood had been right. They'd been together. Happy. Something twisted inside as I spotted another photo with Leon, her cheek smushed against his lips. For the first time since the explosion, I let myself feel sorrow for him. When we found Isobelle, she'd have to deal with his death.

My fingers trailed over her jewelry, handwritten birthday cards. She'd had friends. A boyfriend. And—I took in another photo of her in her boarding school attire, squeezing Arwood in his army uniform—a family. Seeing him smile like that, transforming into a handsome man who would move heaven and earth for his daughter, rooted me to the spot. Made me think of my own father and wonder, again, what he was doing to find me.

I searched her desk, her bedside table, under her bed for a journal, notes she may have left behind of her intentions, but I found nothing except more shoes. I wasn't surprised; surely someone had been here already, seeking the answers I sought now. Disappointment drew my shoulders tight.

Isobelle's room contained evidence of a life enjoyed, a life being lived. My bedroom didn't have these tokens of friendship and love. Before my abduction, my schedule had revolved around staying busy with work and making my father happy whenever we saw each other. She'd found a way to be a banshee and make a meaningful existence for herself. I'd done nothing but hide. From what Leon had said, she'd been trying to find answers. Had her path led her to them, or had she been abducted first?

If I found her, she'd be able to teach me so much.

I typed *Leon* into the password field.

Nope.

With one more glance around her bedroom, I held my breath, typing *banshee*.

The error message remained. I sighed and slammed the laptop

shut again, unhooking the charger and striding from the room without it. If the laptop was my final signal from the universe, I'd received it loud and clear.

I needed to see this to the end. Stay my course. Isobelle was the key to so many things: my freedom. Answers.

Finding her would solve everything.

❧

With the way the night had gone, I could be forgiven for my pessimism, but sometimes the world throws you a bone. Tonight, finding the library was mine. The passageway door I pushed out led into an empty office branching off the main area. I recognized the mahogany furniture and thick shelves lining the wood-paneled walls.

Despite the stillness of the late hour, I tiptoed across the wooden floor and into the adjoining room. Light glowed at the far end, but I couldn't tell if a lamp had been left on for ambiance, or if I had company. I stayed quiet just in case; the people in this house were serious night owls.

I made my way to where the folklore books were stored. Silas had hinted my power may have degrees. Tonight had proven this could be true. Until I found Isobelle, my only hope was to find more information.

As I laid a hand on one of the books, trying to decide whether to hide in the office and read or if I should take them to my room, a wooden creak and a sharp intake of breath made me freeze. I melded against the bookcase, creeping toward the light.

It took a second to register what I was seeing.

Lissandra clutched the outer frame of a ladder. Lamplight washed over the material pooling under her white bustier and the straps of her heels. Tanned legs tightened around a man's waist, holding him close as he thrust into her. Her blood-spattered pearl dress undulated across the rungs. Pitched gasps cut the air.

The man's white shirt strained around his shoulders as he nipped and kissed at her heaving chest, fingers splayed possessively on her hips. Lean build, brown hair, sharp, shadowed jaw—Steadman.

I'd been right.

Holy cow. *I'd actually been right.*

He tilted her. Lissandra released a throaty moan in response. A shiver tore through me.

I stepped backwards into the darkness, grazing the books beside me. Photographs, documents, a pair of reading glasses and half-drunk whiskey littered the desk between us, like they'd come straight here after the discussion in the sitting room. Had they snuck away from Arwood? Was he sleeping, unaware, or dealing with the aftermath of tonight?

The photographs were at-a-distance shots of men walking, like they'd been taken by a private investigator. One of them was the man I'd fought off in the casino.

I recognized the bronze, wavy hair, his frat-boy sneer. Two stood either side with broad foreheads, pronounced noses. One had neck tattoos. Next to these photos lay others of the Kohnstamms, Ferko, and Waldemar.

As Waldemar had said, no one actually *knew* what Johan looked like. Had he been the one to attack me? It seemed likely, looking at these photographs. He'd reeked of authority. His actions to silence me hinted he'd known what I was.

Material rustled, closer this time, bringing with it the unmistakable sound of bodies coming together, the deep grit of Steadman's voice colliding against the smoothness of Lissandra's.

I slunk against the bookcase, holding my breath. The urge to escape warred with the need to understand why Johan had tried to abduct me. Did he have Isobelle? Was he targeting supernaturals and selling them to the Sect? Maybe my abduction was another step in his plan to wipe out both Arwood and the Kohnstamms. It made me wonder if he worked alone, or with a third party as Lissandra suspected.

Heat surged under my skin as I glimpsed their reflection in the adjacent glass case, the sound of their hips colliding. Lissandra lay face-down on the desk, grasping the far edge.

The door opened. I double-checked my position. If the new-comer decided to peruse the stacks, I was *so dead*. What if it was Arwood? And, more importantly, *why weren't they stopping?*

Indeed, the entry of the third person hadn't affected Lissandra and Steadman's, uh, *exuberance* at all. Steadman had pulled her upright against his chest, cupping the side of her jaw. His other arm angled toward the apex of her thighs. Lips and a flash of teeth brushed across her neck as he thrust up and into her with the kind of single-minded focus I'd witnessed on the Prague streets. Clearly, Steadman gave a consistent level of intensity to all things in his life, and from the sounds of it, Lissandra thoroughly enjoyed it.

My beast wanted to sit and watch, amplifying the morbid curiosity that had already caused me to stand there for too long. My pulse raced and my mouth turned dry. I crouched, chancing another look around the stacks and praying the darkness would continue to conceal me.

It was Arwood.

They were so busted.

I expected hasty movement, perhaps pleading protests from either of them for being caught red handed. His footsteps came to a stop as Lissandra cried out. Arwood gripped the edge of the desk, a sleeve of colored tattoos peeking out from underneath his rolled white shirt.

The professional and presentable Arwood had *tattoos*? I had no idea how to deal with this new information, let alone the next thing that came out of his mouth as he stared them down:

"Eyes on me as he fucks you."

Oh.

My.

God.

He reached out, a thumb brushing Lissandra's cheek. "I want

to hear how he makes you feel. Let it out." She gave an answering moan as he clutched her chin, leaning closer. "*Again*, angel."

Another moan.

"She's so close, aren't you, gorgeous?" Steadman crooned in a tone that reminded me of liquid chocolate, which knocked me for six because associating chocolate with Steadman just ... did not compute.

Lissandra's chest strained against Steadman's palm. His fingers flitted underneath her bra in time with her gasps. "Yes, *yes—please, James—*"

Steadman asked, "How do you want her?"

I realized that my mouth was hanging open. My lips clamped shut as Arwood tilted his head to the side, tugging at his undone tie. I had no idea what that action meant, but his right-hand man obviously did. Steadman pulled away, ignoring her cry of protest. They spun her until she sat flanked by both men on either side of the desk. Arwood's reflection showed him pulling Lissandra back against him, capturing her lips in a kiss while Steadman tied her wrists together.

Goosebumps prickled the hot skin under my collar and jacket. I jammed my eyes closed. I'd never been so mindful of how much sound my clothing gave off as I walked or if a floorboard might creak under my boots.

Terrified to move; hating what it would mean if I stayed.

A giggle from Lissandra acted like a lasso. Despite myself, I peeked as Steadman laid the lower half of her body across the desk. Her back arched as her bound wrists—now looped around Arwood's neck—pulled taut. Steadman peeled the rest of her dress down, revealing a dainty white G-string. The swirling black C insignia from the plaque on Waldemar's front door inked the skin beside her spine. Of course. *Camardo.*

Whispered exchanges, murmurs of encouragement, of three people reveling in each other and enjoying being *alive* eroded my shock in favor of other emotions I had trouble identifying at first.

A darkness ebbed at the corner of my thoughts, containing sharp spikes of anger and something else. Frustration? Confusion?

Mewling noises erupted from Lissandra, swallowed by Arwood's lips, as Steadman thrust back inside her. His white dress shirt gaped open, the lamplight dancing across his sculpted torso. My eyes wandered downward—

I shook myself even as my beast purred at the sight.

This was too much. I couldn't stay here. God, *I couldn't stay here.* At some point—how long did this kind of thing last?!—they'd finish, and I'd be in even more danger of being discovered than I was now. The stack of photographs on the desk mocked me, my fingers itching to grab them. I held my breath, retreating a single step at a time. Lissandra's cries reached fever pitch as I shut the door separating the office. My vision tilted and my insides felt molten, a tangled heat bundling in my stomach and accompanying a strange emptiness.

Images of Steadman and Arwood flashed behind my eyes. Of Silas working out, biceps bunching. My beast panted, urging me to go back, to seek out Silas, to do *something*. As soon as I imagined myself laid out on the table in front of Silas, or Steadman—or *both*—their hands kneading and parting my thighs, a warm tongue caressing mine while another trailed down my chest, I violently shook my head.

My beast was always unreasonable. That was normal. My thoughts weren't, but at least I could finally pinpoint my biggest issue with all of this: like an absolute idiot, I'd blackmailed Steadman about Lissandra ... and they were all together, investigating the very attacks I'd accused him of orchestrating.

Did everyone know? Was I too inexperienced, too sheltered, not to have realized this?

I tried to calm my breath, aware that in some corner of my brain I was close to hyperventilating. Steadman had been right. I didn't understand my situation at all. I'd been way off base with him. Assumed Lissandra to be an unfaithful wife and a token extension of her father's empire, instead of a powerful matriarch with her own agency. Not to mention that I'd made an enemy out of the Kohnstamms, willingly killed people, *and* shown Steadman I remained a flight risk in a single night.

I had nowhere to go but forward with Arwood. He'd funneled me to this outcome like a rat and for that, I'd been unforgivably naive. I had to get smarter.

At least I'd had the foresight to keep my near-abduction to myself. Johan was my trump card. While they were still trying to determine who he was, I knew his identity, knew he wanted me for some reason, and I wouldn't give that information up for free.

I stumbled back to my room in the darkness, my beast rattling the bars of its cage and desperately craving a release I wasn't even sure I understood.

CHAPTER TWENTY-FIVE

EITHER FATE HAD A SENSE OF HUMOR, OR IT DEALT BAD karma for snooping, because the next evening Lissandra summoned me. I'd hoped to go a day, perhaps two, without seeing any of them. I hadn't had nearly enough time to process and compartmentalize what I'd seen.

Steadman waited against a black Audi in the halo of light from the mansion's windows, arms crossed over a black jacket that most definitely had a bullet-resistant vest beneath it. No Arwood. We were back to splitting up the trio.

The three of them on the desk flashed, unbidden, through my mind. My neck heated beneath my collar. I avoided eye contact with Steadman as we approached; of all the people to figure out what I now knew, it would be him.

Steadman closed the passenger door for Lissandra and slid into the driver's seat. Surprised, I blurted, "Just the three of us?"

"Technically," Steadman navigated the sedan out of the estate, heading for the city, "there are four of us, but I wouldn't classify the man in our trunk as a willing guest."

"There's a man in the trunk," I deadpanned, looking over my shoulder as if I'd somehow see a limb flailing. "Why is there a man in the trunk?"

Lissandra shifted in the passenger seat. Her blunt bangs framed eyes once again lined and shadowed to perfection. "Because it's bad manners to attend a party without a gift."

She and Steadman shared a coy smile, sending me mentally back into the library all over again—

Aaargh. Stop it, Keanna.

"Who is it? What if they suffocate? Are they hurt?"

Steadman's eyes met mine in the rear-view mirror. "Don't waste your energy being concerned for Ferko. He's been nothing but a pain in our ass from the beginning."

"How did you catch him?"

"Silas blocked off the exits and we dragged him from his club quite literally kicking and screaming," Steadman said. "A little anti-climactic, actually."

Of course he'd think that. "Who would appreciate Ferko in a trunk?"

"We're hoping Gisele Kohnstamm," Lissandra answered.

I'd had a bad feeling that was the case. "And if she doesn't?"

"That's why you're here."

Crap. Keanna Backhus, ready to detonate if required. "How do I tell you if anything changes, um, mood wise?"

"We'll know." Lissandra tapped to the guttural, guitar-heavy back catalog of Dire Straits. "Your face is an open book. It tells us everything."

I froze, the beginnings of a frown starting to form. I hadn't even felt it. *She was right.* "Let's hope it doesn't come to that."

Steadman nodded. "Finally something we agree on, banshee."

We drove past storefronts lining the streets, white plaques with the Kohnstamms' caracal insignia or the Camardo's *C*—or occasionally both—on clear display. I concentrated on spotting them to quell the awkwardness. Well, for me, at least. Steadman's drumming on the steering wheel accompanied our navigation through the stop-start-stop evening traffic, and when 'Africa' by Toto came on Lissandra gripped his forearm, her teeth grazing her bottom lip.

"Are you thinking what I'm thinking?"

A smirk emerged, breaking the hard lines of Steadman's face. "Morocco?"

Lissandra threw her head back, releasing a chuckle. "Thank goodness for sturdy balconies."

"And loaded guns."

Tension-filled—and probably illegal—memories flooded the car, like they'd forgotten little miss third-wheeling me was here at all.

In the trunk, barely discernible above the duet of Lissandra and Steadman's *"Aaaaafricaaaa,"* Ferko's body thumped. Was he even still alive?

What I'd said to Silas was true: these people were *insane*.

And I would never, ever listen to this song the same way again.

∽

The meeting place was in a shared zone to the north beside the Vltava River.

As we pulled up, music now silenced, Steadman murmured, "Plenty of building cover, Liss. Too much. If they renege, we won't know till it's too late."

Lissandra studied the gray communist-style buildings before turning to me. "Stand with James," she ordered. "I must approach alone. If you feel there may be a problem … I'm relying on you, Keanna, to inform us."

My fingers flitted over the padded vest Steadman had given me on the way in. As much as I hated what these people did, if I lost Arwood's protection, I'd be even worse off. I'd chosen my devil; I'd chosen my train. No more stops.

Lissandra strode across the concrete walkway, ducking her chin into her bronze scarf, the hem of her navy coat fluttering in the breeze. Distant car horns combined with the gentle sloshing of river against brick, the repetition pricking at my skin like a torn clothing tag. A vehicle arrived a minute later. Three figures emerged. The woman left the two men behind, making her way toward Lissandra.

Gisele had twisted her raven hair into a stylish knot at the crown of her head, her leather thigh-high boots peeking between the folds of her beige trench-coat. She'd hidden the evidence of any grief underneath porcelain makeup and burgundy lipstick.

The two women greeted each other, showing their palms as if to prove neither were armed.

Lissandra spoke first. "My deepest condolences regarding Leon. How is your husband?"

Gisele studied Lissandra as if trying to detect insincerity. "Still critical. I'll be cleaning things up for weeks."

"We regret what happened."

"I bet you do." Gisele's gaze locked on my collar. Seconds dragged on before she released me. I resisted a sigh of relief. Like a sniper's laser, I felt marked. "You bring a banshee but talk of peace?"

"You bring five men instead of the agreed two and wonder why I brought a banshee."

My head snapped up. I couldn't spot whom Lissandra referred to, but I supposed that didn't matter. She'd seen what my untrained eyes hadn't. I'd locked my beast down last night, ignoring her all day; I let the walls fall. Her hackles were up. She'd been warning me there were others, hidden out of sight, the entire time I'd stood there.

I'm sorry. How could I explain that I'd been fearful of how she'd made me feel, the things she'd made me want?

At this, my beast turned on me in a huff.

"I assume everyone on your side is accounted for?" Gisele asked.

"Yes."

"What a relief for you."

"I understand your anger, Gisele," Lissandra said. "And suspicion. We had no knowledge the attack would take place."

"Hmm. You said you have the culprit?"

Our trunk opened to reveal Ferko, wrists and ankles zip-tied so tight that blood dribbled beneath them. He panted around his gag, eyes bulging. Steadman sliced his ankles free and forced him to stand on shaky legs. He delivered Ferko to the Kohnstamm men.

Lissandra and Gisele watched as they subdued him and slammed the trunk shut on Ferko's tear-slick face. I clenched my fists to keep my expression smooth. Steadman returned, eyebrows raised in question. I shook my head. I could only smell briny river water and the faint whiff of sewerage.

"He's funded by Johan Matousek," Lissandra said. "An associate of yours?"

"Was. Ivan ejected him for embezzling."

"I also understand you've had shipments go missing. We, too, have suffered losses on our side."

Gisele said nothing.

"It is our priority to terminate Johan's network before it takes hold," Lissandra continued. "Do you know where he operates from?"

"If I'd had it my way, I wouldn't have let him live. I made sure to keep tabs on him just in case."

Gisele listed addresses and associates she believed Johan was affiliated with. Steadman nodded to the Kohnstamm men, reaching inside his vest. They started, weapons rising, until his hand emerged, clutching his phone. He typed the information given, his focus darting between the screen and their pointed guns.

Occasionally, a street name Gisele provided tugged at my memory in the same maddening fashion as trying to remember the name of someone you vaguely recognize. When nothing transpired, I eyed the rooftops. Did those men have guns trained on us, too? My gut remained settled. No metallic scent laced the wind. How much warning would I get if things went wrong? It had appeared moments before the bomb detonated at the casino, filled the room at the nightclub as we'd arrived. Did it only occur once a decision was made that resulted in death? How much notice would I get if Gisele or her team decided to kill us?

"You have to know, Lissandra, that I've always supported what you and your family do. However, in light of recent events, I'm reconsidering this arrangement. My men are out for blood. I can't promise I'll stop them next time."

"Let us settle things with Johan as a demonstration of our commitment to the treaty." Lissandra gestured to their Porsche. "For now, you have the man responsible for the death of your son."

Gisele held Lissandra's gaze. My body locked up, waiting for when things would change, for us to be gunned down, our bodies thrown into the Vltava for Arwood to find.

Finally, Gisele gave a single nod, striding toward her car. My heartbeat sounded in my ears as they pulled away, headlights disappearing around the corner.

With a final glance at the rooftops, Lissandra joined us, relief evident in her flushed cheeks.

I'd never been so happy to get back in the car and head south for Arwood's estate.

CHAPTER TWENTY-SIX

LIFE ESTABLISHED AN UNEASY CADENCE. MID-MORNINGS were spent with Anika, trying to recreate the soundless pressure wave that had saved me from Johan. When it didn't work, she taught me basic self-defense, or we trained in Arwood's gym. Afternoons I'd hole up in Arwood's library, bruised but focused, reading banshee folklore and trying to connect whatever dots I could. Nights often found me assigned to Arwood or Steadman, acting on the leads provided by Gisele. Though we came into contact with more of Johan's network, the man himself proved as slippery as oil. Arwood lost members of his team; I killed Johan's in return. Prague became a circular chessboard with no checkmate in sight. Throughout it all, I kept Johan's abduction attempt secret, a card in my back pocket I patiently waited to play because I had no idea *how* to.

September became October. Some days I did well to work with my beast instead of against her, growing stronger with every training session. Others, I contended with the grief of missing my father and despair that we'd never find Isobelle.

Today was the latter. Sometimes, routine is our only salve.

The metal bar rested cold in my palms, muscles engaged after what seemed like a million—okay, ten—bench presses. Above me, Anika slid large circular plates onto either side of the bar. Her spiky ponytail flopped about her ears as she hummed to the music filtering from the gym speakers.

Arwood and Steadman stood in the opposite corner, the

repetitive smacking of their boxing gloves underscoring gusty exhales from nearby guards releasing rope pulleys and barbells.

"I barely felt that," Steadman gruffed, agitating the foam pads on his hands. "Again."

Sweat coated Arwood's shirt, his tattoos on full display as he threw his weight behind another one-two combo like his sanity depended on it. A boxing Arwood contrasted jarringly to the Tom-Ford business suit Arwood I'd met. It was hard to believe they were the same person.

Arwood gave another *thwack*. "Status from last night's ambush?"

"Bohdan discharged this morning," Steadman said, dodging Arwood's swing. "They're gonna take Jack's leg."

Arwood's barrage of punches came harsher, harder.

Steadman's nods of approval with each *thwack* turned into a frown, as if sensing Arwood teetered somewhere dark. "Break. *Break*." Steadman took a step back, shaking his wrists. "We're gonna pin Johan down soon. We'll find her. We've been fucked way worse than this in the past."

"No, James," Arwood heaved, brushing sweat off his forehead with his arm. "Not like this, we haven't."

Fingers snapped in front of me.

"I, too, appreciate a masculine despair vortex, but eyes back here," Anika said. I blushed. She tapped the bar. "You've got sixty pounds suspended above you, and I need some reps."

Two sets later, and with sweat forming on my upper lip, Lissandra entered. She strode for Arwood and Steadman, clutching an envelope.

I might have gotten better at managing my expressions, but Anika still dispensed a sly smile as she added extra weight. "Finally figured it out, I see."

I would die before admitting how. "Are Arwood and Lissandra legally married?"

Anika tapped the bar again. I got the hint, tightening my core. As I completed my next rep, she said, "As legal as it gets. Fifteen minutes in a courthouse. She wore a white Valentino Garavani jumpsuit for the occasion. I want to be Liss when I grow up."

Details I appreciated while lifting heavy things. "How did they meet?"

"Lissandra wanted a foothold in central Europe to establish a territory on her own terms, Arwood needed Camardo resources to build out his operations. 'Twas an effective match on that alone. You could say they're … business partners. With benefits."

Seven. The tension cording my chest made me pause. Anika's fingers hovered near the bar, fluttering encouragingly. *Eight.*

"So she's with Steadman?"

"The same way she's with Arwood. Come on, you've got two more in you. Keep breathing."

Lissandra gave the envelope to Arwood. He loosened the wrist straps of his gloves with his teeth, tossing them to the side.

"For fuck's sake." Steadman's voice carried across the room. "Anika!"

I paused. Anika shrugged, looking as surprised as I was. Seeing us approach, Arwood turned on his heel, exiting with Lissandra.

Steadman passed the photographs to Anika. "That insignia what we think it is?"

I peered over her shoulder. It took a moment to work out what we were seeing—a dead body. I gasped, recoiling.

A flayed black dress exposed Gisele Kohnstamm's chest and the bloody insignia burned into her skin: three ovals with thick lines stacked vertically, the smaller oval sandwiched between two larger ones.

"You asked how we knew that mage was taken out by the Sect?" Anika said, referring to the *ferox* they'd mentioned during our drinking game.

A feather of fear trailed down my back.

She pointed to the mark. "That's how."

Steadman plucked the photograph from Anika. "They

smothered Ivan in his hospital bed. Same mark. Do you think this is retribution for their part in our exposure at the casino?"

The feather of fear became a wing closing around my shoulders. "But the Kohnstamms aren't mages," I whispered.

"Proximity to us still counts," Anika said. "It's in line with what I've seen before. They saw an opportunity to wipe them out and took it."

With a shake of his head, Steadman, too, left. Anika bit the inside of her cheek.

"What does this mean for us?" I asked.

She stared at the doorway, cracking her knuckles one by one, like a memory held her hostage. Then she blinked, shaking her head. "The longer this situation with Johan carries on, the more vulnerable we're gonna become. A few well-placed attacks made the Kohnstamms weak enough to end up like this. This is the Sect's reminder that they're waiting for the chance to move in on *us*." Anika met my eyes. "Time ain't on our side, banshee."

࿐

Silas and I had retreated from each other as much as possible in the weeks since the casino bombing. The unseen danger of the Sect had materialized for me this afternoon and served as a brutal reminder of how only Arwood and his operations stood between me and something much worse. I couldn't risk jeopardizing my bargain with him.

Still, my noble intentions offered little comfort. The distance infuriated my beast. The distance hurt *me,* had become a papercut that wouldn't heal.

Which was why, upon spotting Silas cooking in the kitchen that night, I halted and ducked back behind the corner. His melodic, husky voice broke up the productive racket, a bark of laughter sending a frisson of longing up my spine. He stirred a large silver pot, offering instructions to another chef and singing along to the song playing from the speaker.

I peered around the corner to watch his hips sway from side to side to the music.

My fingers curled as possessiveness enveloped my chest. I wanted to protect this version of him, the one who found something to laugh about even with everything else going on. I wanted to bask in his energy and share it with him. I hated having to watch this from afar. I hated the constant surveillance of the estate. Each day passed with and without him. I kept telling myself enduring this parallel existence was better than nothing. Today I wasn't so sure.

I entered as the song ended, taking a seat at the communal table.

Silas averted his gaze the way he had for weeks now. A fist captured my heart, giving it a squeeze. The room grew busier around me as kitchenhands dispensed gnocchi with lamb ragu. Despite my mood, I couldn't stop a smirk from pinching my cheeks. I glanced at Silas through my eyelashes as he distributed dishes on the other side of the table.

"Chose lamb tonight, I see."

His lips curved. "We were out of sage."

"'Gotta have the sage,'" I echoed. Our eyes met and cut away.

Dobromil, one of the senior guards, sat beside me and started tucking into his dinner. One by one, the table filled. Over the weeks, repeated exposure had diluted even the most paranoid guard to my presence, and most barely noticed me anymore.

The ragu was as delicious as Silas had said. Many of the guards made noises of pleasure, smacking the table or giving the thumbs up. Silas remained at the far end of the table between two scarred guards, their pink puckered flesh like paint strokes across canvas. Not for the first time, I wondered if wounds covered their whole body. Were they burn marks? They looked like they'd been pelted with a hot whip. From head to toe.

With my theories about Steadman humiliatingly contradicted, I'd taken to observing the staff, wondering who among them worked against Arwood. So far I hadn't been successful in spotting any evidence, but that didn't dissuade me. If the mole was obvious, they'd have been discovered by now.

"Hard to look at, ain't they?"

I focused on my dinner. "Oh, uh—"

"All good," Dobromil gruffed. "They're used to it."

"What happened to them?"

Dobromil practically inhaled his glass of water. I resisted lecturing him about diluting his digestion. "Shrapnel," he said, wiping his mouth with his thumb. "Whole bunch of 'em were in the same platoon. Third tour in. One of the vehicles hit a roadside IED and *bang*. Half dead instantly, other half in hospital nursing those conversation starters."

"Is that why they were discharged?"

He gave a *sort of yes, sort of no* shrug. "Steadman was their platoon sarge, but he and Arwood were pretty close. The IED was the start of an ambush on half their squad. Steadman defied orders and went back after the captain wrote 'em off. He and Arwood saved as many as they could, made sure they got taken care of. Did neither of 'em favors with those up top though."

I blinked, filing this information in a drawer called 'Facts hard to believe about Arwood,' alongside 'has tattoos' and 'is sharing Lissandra'. How could the person who ordered a bullet into someone's head also be a person who couldn't leave a man behind? Then again, the thieves he'd executed had gone after what was his first.

So perhaps Arwood wasn't that complicated. Either you were on his side and for his cause, or you weren't. Was Arwood the best of the bad bunch in this city, trying to stabilize a world encouraging instability?

"Arwood got called back here to take over, so he reached out to the teams," Dobromil continued, not needing any encouragement to gossip. "Steadman lost his platoon over the whole thing and got buried in paperwork bullshit, so Arwood made sure he had a place, too. They've all followed him ever since."

"And where do you come into it?"

Dobromil chewed, lips smacking in appreciation. "Needed a job. Got a mother with early-onset Alzheimer's in care and an alcoholic father who don't know what day it is, so someone's gotta keep the money coming in. I was between contracts, Arwood was hiring, and the pay's better than sitting in some desert, wondering what the point of even being there is."

"Amen to fucking *that*," the guard beside him muttered, raising a glass.

Dobromil brushed a hand over his russet beard. "Got a room and meals, too, so can't complain."

"You all live on site?" As I said the words, I realized this should have been obvious. The house was big enough, and it made sense to have a team on call. "Where?"

I gave my best wide-eyed, curious expression, hoping they wouldn't see past the blonde-haired-young-innocent-female thing. This was additional leverage I'd been hoping for: chatterbox guards willing to talk to me. I might have an agreement with Arwood, but I was getting a crash course in the importance of strategy and diversification—the more back-up plans I could create, the better.

From Dobromil's enthusiasm at relaying a story no doubt everyone else already knew, he didn't suspect anything was amiss. "Not here," he drawled, swallowing a mouthful of lamb and gesturing to the floor. "East side, bottom floors."

"Surely not everyone? Wouldn't it get crowded?"

"Nope, plenty of room for us all. Most aren't local. We got short-term contracts with the option to renew. Works for everybody."

"Wouldn't that make it difficult to relax, if you're always here? Do you get time off?"

Again, no flicker of suspicion. Either Dobromil was a little naive, or, to him, I wasn't worthy of suspicion. Perhaps both. "Oh, yeah," he said. "Arwood's got things locked down tight, scheduled for coverage day and night. The nights we go out on sweeps is best, though. Gets us out of the estate while newer recruits get stuck here. Like this guy." He nudged the guard sitting next to him, who rolled his eyes.

"Say it louder, yeah?" the guard said. "Gimme a few more months on the perimeter."

I gave him a generous smile. "You have to start somewhere, right? If I ever find my beloved Romeo, I'll let him know requirements for a midnight visit are via the front door."

Silas looked up, having heard my comment. Our eyes met then tore away again.

"With ID and an invitation from Arwood, or he won't make it far," Dobromil winked.

"He could slip over the west corner," the other guard added. "Steep drop, though. Natural barriers—more effective than any of us."

"Ah, yes," Dobromil said, entertained by the thought. "Can this guy levitate?"

Chatter dissolved as Steadman and Matej swept in. Their hands landed on the shoulders of a guard two down from me. With a single nod from Steadman, they marched him out of the kitchen, leaving his half-empty bowl behind.

"Poor guy. Shit's gettin' real," Dobromil breathed.

I had a feeling I already knew the answer, but I still asked. "What are they doing with him?"

"Tryna' plug the leaks, miss. Ain't making for a good working environment, but we're enjoying losing people less."

Appetite ruined, I excused myself.

Closing my extravagant filigreed bedroom door, I slid to the floor. A heavy, dragging sensation covered me like a wet blanket.

Isobelle remained out of reach. Training with Anika might be making me stronger, but I wasn't any closer to unlocking what I'd done the night of the casino. I'd been a hamster in a wheel these past weeks, soothing myself with the illusion of action while the walls drew closer.

Missing my father made me feel like my heart was about to

burst out of my chest. I longed for the insulated days inside my estate, my theoretical discussions with Zeina. Since my abduction, life held colors I never thought I'd see. I wanted to hate everyone around me. I *should* hate everyone around me. How often I forgot this made me uncomfortable. The girl with smoothie on her legs would've wondered what the hell my problem was. The girl with her back against the door, with over twenty deaths to her name, had nothing to say.

Eventually, despair and inaction got old. I entered the bathroom and did all the things old Keanna had found comfort in; I exfoliated. Shaved. Conditioned my hair. Tried to address the irritated, flaky skin underneath my black collar. It was red and itchy and another sign I'd been here too long, that this thing should have been off *weeks* ago.

My attempts to utilize the cortisol cream I'd swiped from the first aid kit in the kitchen proved pitiful, but it was all I could think to do. Unless Arwood suddenly felt charitable, this thing wasn't coming off. Frustrating minutes passed while I nudged lotion underneath the metal, hoping I wasn't just making the irritation worse.

I was almost thankful for the interruption of a knock. Giving up, I pulled my bathrobe tighter around my body. Hopefully it wasn't Steadman playing fetch. In my current state, I wouldn't be ready for at least thirty minutes, which would piss him off to no end.

I opened the door, frowning. No one was there. Another knock came from the wall behind me.

The servant's passageway cracked open.

CHAPTER TWENTY-SEVEN

I SHOULD HAVE KNOWN IT WASN'T STEADMAN. THE KNOCK had been subtle and hesitant, two things Steadman wasn't.

"Can we talk?" Silas whispered, nudging the door open further.

My hand went to the waist tie of my bathrobe as I agreed, my pulse picking up speed.

"Did I interrupt something?" At my questioning expression, he pointed to the tube of cortisol. Oh. That.

"Some neck TLC." I sat on the edge of my bed, continuing to prod it under my collar to give me something to do. And to give the impression I didn't care a boy was in my bedroom. Door shut. At night.

Another first.

"I got that when I first came here, too." He shook the wrist with the black band. "Do you need help?"

This made my beast *way* too excited. "I think I've got it. What did you need to talk about?"

He mussed his hair, casting a glance around the room before sitting on the Chesterfield. "I hated tonight."

"The ragu? You're too hard on yourself. The lamb wasn't that dry."

"You look like you're joking, but—"

"Of course I'm joking. I can barely cook toast, you won't hear me dispensing culinary critique."

He narrowed his eyes playfully, then turned serious. "I hate ignoring you like this. You seemed upset, and I couldn't ask you why without worrying someone would notice."

"I'm fine. It's just …" I gestured to the walls, my collar. Anywhere that wasn't him. "Our daily existence. Thank you for checking, but I'll be alright."

"I'm not. Alright, that is. With any of it." He plucked at the hole in the knee of his jeans. "I … I've been thinking, and I figured if I was going to put myself through this, you should at least know why."

Put myself through this. Silas being raw, vulnerable, was like witnessing something sacred. I wanted to hold on to moments like this forever.

"You don't have to tell me if you're not comfortable," I said. "I understand why you have secrets."

"It's *because* you understand that I want to tell you. But it's dangerous information to learn, so I wanted to give you a choice."

Was he kidding? It sounded like he was giving me keys to the kingdom. "I won't say a word." I paused. "Garden buddies for life, right?"

He gave a small smile. God, he was beautiful. The low light from the lamps beside my bed threw a glow over his olive-toned skin and gave a honeyed hue to the brown curls of his hair.

"Arwood has my mother and my sister. He's kept them off site, in the basement of one of his office buildings, since I started working for him." He nodded at my slack expression. "They're … they're as comfortable as they can be, locked in a room with supervised bathroom breaks and designated mealtimes."

I blanched. Those three days stuck inside one of Arwood's cells with no option to leave had been borderline traumatic. Silas had started working for Arwood *eleven months ago.*

He shifted to the front of the couch, leaning his forearms against his knees. "It's okay," he assured me, even though we both knew it wasn't. "My father was a member of the Sect, swapping information for funding from Arwood. That's why he was supposed to be at your party, scoping out your company." Seeing my face tighten, he said, "I had no idea. I promise. That was the kind of stuff my father did for Arwood. He accepted money to keep his restaurants afloat, made poor investment decisions, got deep in debt. We didn't know about it, of course. Not until it was too late." He fidgeted, nails dragging over his stubble.

"Because of that, I started working for Arwood, doing what my father used to do. Protecting him, that kind of thing, in lieu of paying back the debt. The amount my father owed would have ruined us otherwise. But Arwood's not an idiot. He knew he needed to convince me to do the right thing. I mean, I could *not* ignite a shield"—his devilish smile vanished as quickly as it had appeared—"and he and his team would be dead. So he took my mother and sister."

If my father had been taken, I knew there wasn't anything I wouldn't have done to keep him safe. I thanked the stars Arwood hadn't done it. "I'm so sorry, Silas."

"I rebelled early on, let some of his men get shot. They survived—it wasn't life-threatening," he added, seeing my eyes widen. "I just wanted to prove he didn't own me. But ... he does. He kept my family in the dark for two days without food."

He fell silent. I wanted to wrap a blanket around him, shelter him from the world. I also wanted to run from this place screaming.

I couldn't help but snapshot the Silas and Keanna from the garden. Him in his suit, me in my beautiful green dress. Shiny. Young. Flirting and full of promise. A far cry from the shirt and ripped jeans he wore now, the bathrobe and collar contrasting against my pale skin. We'd had no idea what was coming for us. We'd had no one to protect us.

"For a while there, I was staring down the barrel of lifelong service, but a few days ago things changed," Silas continued. "Arwood told me if we found his daughter, he'd let me and my family go. Debt repaid."

I sucked in a breath. That was *my* deal. I could imagine Arwood rubbing his hands together with glee as he pitted Silas and me against each other. "I've made the same bargain with him. Do you think ..."

"He'll recant?" Silas said, hearing my change in tone. He contemplated my question, his nail running over his lip. "Arwood is a man of his word, despite everything else. Months ago, I wouldn't have put it past him to play games to keep us both under his thumb, but he's desperate now." The knot in my chest eased. Barely. "Besides, he's smart enough to understand the more people are motivated for his cause, the better off he'll be."

Okay. That made sense. And fell more in line with the Arwood playbook I'd observed so far. From my conversation with the guards, he wanted loyalty. Preferred people choosing to work for him. What a dichotomy. For someone who valued choice, he had no reservations taking it away. "We track down Isobelle, we both go free?"

"Sounds too easy, doesn't it?"

"You don't think we'll find her."

"After the things I've seen this past year … I don't think the world is a good place anymore."

The hopelessness in his voice hurt. Pressure built in my chest, my beast rousing from her slumber. Not incensed, like when I was in danger. Instead she sat wary, watching my tears form. I couldn't let them fall. This wasn't about me. "The longer you work for Arwood, the more you damage yourself."

"It's the least I can do. My family are having enough trouble keeping themselves mentally intact without knowing what's going on here."

I'd watched Silas pass out more than once. A battery, charged then depleted. The air of defeat lingering around him said, more than anything else he'd told me tonight, that we were running out of time. Eventually, Silas would have nothing more to give.

"Did your mother know about the Sect? Could she help with Isobelle or Johan?"

"He kept a lot from us. I've never asked her."

I could barely breathe from the pressure building. I bent my head and reached blindly for the cortisol. Around me, a buzz matching the one within swelled. The hairbrush on the writing desk rattled next to a rocking lampshade; an abstract painting jittered on its hook against the wall.

Silas leapt to his feet. "Are you alright? Here, let me help you."

I shook my head as I tried to swallow the lump moving up my throat, tried to suppress the intensity of the storm brewing inside of me. I'd never be able to explain why I'd screamed in my room, or why Silas had been there to begin with.

"Seriously, let me help. You're okay."

But *he* wasn't.

I was scared if I protested I'd start screaming/crying/a combination of the two, so I kept my head bowed. The mattress dipped behind me as he sat, plucking the tube from my loose grip. His proximity doused the worst of the pressure. I took a deep breath through my nose, trying to calm myself.

The rattling stopped.

Silas gave a soft laugh. "Well. That was new. Training is paying off." When I didn't respond, he asked, "Keeks? Can I move your hair?"

His knee brushed my hip, distracting me further. I swallowed painfully, nodding.

Light fingers grazed the terry material of my robe. I stilled, hyper-aware of how he gathered my wet hair, moving it to one side. At least I no longer needed to concentrate on keeping my scream suppressed. Silas dominated my attention.

"Try and relax. Tensing makes it harder to move."

I exhaled, squeezing my knees as he touched me, pushing the collar upwards as far as it would go. Goosebumps erupted. I focused on breathing evenly; I kept holding it, anticipating when he'd touch me next.

He loosened a sigh, no doubt at the ugly red band of skin underneath, then cool relief hit my neck. I shivered.

"Relax," he whispered. I lowered my shoulders, realizing they were up near my ears. "I'm sorry if it's hurting. A few days of this and it should clear up."

I didn't correct him, too embarrassed to admit it wasn't hurting at all right now. Opposite spectrum. My abdomen tightened.

"I hate that he makes you wear this," he said.

"Does yours shock you, too?"

"No. That's why yours is so inhumane. Ours is a signal to the people of the city. Who we belong to. I guess it's better than tattoos. We have a hope of removing it."

My fingers danced across the blunt edge of my collar. The people who understood studied it with a strange combination of intrigue and fear. I was a deadly chained animal. Arwood held my leash.

Yet … he hadn't forced me to scream in weeks. He hadn't even been with me when I'd decided to blow up our pursuit. Worse, the satisfaction of watching the cars career over themselves had reached beyond my motivation. My beast had enjoyed death coming to those endangering us.

"I'm scared I'll become something I don't recognize," I whispered. "I've done so much damage already. I'm not sure what I'll do if I can't get away from him."

"You're trying to change your situation." His hand moved to the front of my throat. My breathing turned shallow. "That counts for something. We'll find Isobelle, and then you can go home to your father."

"And you can go home with your mother. And your sister."

The bed shook as he nodded. "I also have an older brother. Gabriel."

"Where is he?"

"I don't know. He worked for Arwood, too." His tone sharpened. "I … I think he's dead. I haven't seen him in months. No one I talk to has, either."

"What's Gabriel like?" I used present tense deliberately.

Silas didn't. "Everything you'd want in an older brother. He was a better person than me. Kind. Always pushed me to do what was right." His fingers curved around the top of my shoulder. I could sense he was done but for some reason wasn't moving. I didn't want him to. "He and Arwood never got along. They clashed too much to be productive, and once my father died there was no one to stand up for him."

I made a sympathetic noise. Silas's hand tightened, stopping me from turning. "Please … please stay as you are. This is easier if you're not looking at me."

I understood what he meant. It was like confiding to someone in the dark. "Why do you think Gabriel might be in trouble?"

He resumed rubbing along the back of my collar. Not done, after all. "Being *maspotem* is hereditary. If a parent is a mage—either side—it's all but guaranteed you'll transcend. My father was a *ferox*, and a good one at that, so it was a given. But Gabriel's time came and went without it happening. In our circles they called him a *nil*. That's it. 'Nil', like he had nothing better to offer." Silas sighed. What was he thinking? What memories tormented him? "I transcended on my nineteenth birthday."

"Were you worried you wouldn't? That your parents would …"

"Would what?"

"Be disappointed."

"My abilities don't define me," he said. "As long as we're healthy, they would have accepted any outcome. We don't know why it never happened for Gabriel, and it has to have bothered him, but he took it in his stride and made his body a weapon instead."

My abilities don't define me. I wished I believed the same. "You talk about him like he's for certain dead. What if he's escaped?"

"He's dead." His hand slipped to my shoulder. "I can feel it. I just wish I knew how. And when. I'm scared I'll never find out."

I touched first my fingertips to his, then my whole palm. Warmth flooded down my arm. My heart maintained a steady, pounding beat. My beast was calm. So was I.

I'm a firm believer that you have a path in life to follow. Not predetermined, exactly, but occasionally the universe throws you a thumbs-up. Moments of internal stillness, a peace and rightness you can't describe past a lightness in your chest and an assurance in your soul you're on the correct path, that all signs are pointing north. I knew, despite everything else, that this was where I needed to be. With Silas. Our fingers were barely threaded together, we weren't even looking at each other, and I felt more connected to him than I had to anyone else in my whole life.

Somewhere along the way, Silas had become important to me. Somehow, it didn't scare me. I wanted to be his ally. If we could be nothing else, that was enough.

I was all in.

"I'm on your side," I whispered. Silas was right—this *was* easier. Not seeing his expression made me braver in my quiet declaration. "Always. I promise."

Silence.

Had I talked out of turn, scared him off?

He moved my hair aside further. Tickling breath hovered above the curve of my shoulder. His lips connected with the sensitive skin there.

I sucked in a breath, my eyes drifting shut. My skin sparked beneath his touch, electricity traveling down my body and pooling low in my abdomen. *Holy hell.* I swallowed the moan threatening to rise.

"I don't trust in much here, but I do with you," he murmured. "I always knew I could, as soon as I saw you in that garden. You *are* sunshine, Keanna. You lit up my life then, and you still do."

I pivoted. My heart had broken for him earlier; now it was racing. His eyes dropped to my lips. So many reasons we shouldn't be this close, this alone. I couldn't think of a single one.

A shared breath released as our lips came together.

His scent filled my nose. I turned further, and our legs tangled. The roughness from the stubble on his chin met my smooth skin. My chest swelled with excitement—and fear. Self-consciousness over my lack of experience darkened the corners of my mind, slowing my response. I should have thought about this earlier, prepared somehow. How would I know if I was doing this right and not making an idiot of myself?

Silas planted a kiss on my lower lip and then the corner of my mouth, moving slowly like he sensed my hesitancy. "Is this okay?" he whispered.

No judgment, no expectation marred his voice. Despite my insecurity, safety warmed me. This was Silas. He knew me. He saw me. Somehow, he liked me anyway. The desire to feel his body against mine enticed me forward. I curled my hands around his neck, entwining my fingers through his soft hair as our lips met again and again. Fleeting panic at my lack of experience gave way to natural, rhythmic instinct. My beast—or both of us—sighed as I sank further into his arms.

I clutched him tighter, straddling him, my tongue brushing his. He gripped my hips, pulling me against him, blazing kisses in a path across my cheek. His lips went to the space behind my ear, shooting heat straight to my abdomen and plucking a gasp from me. My pelvis moved of its own volition. For a moment I feared he'd find my hips and thighs too big, too awkward, but a moan rumbled in his chest like he enjoyed how I moved against him.

Of course he does, my beast admonished.

He rolled us to the side, my head falling against the pillows. A hiss escaped as his lower body settled between my thighs. My bathrobe gaped open, revealing the swells of my breasts and the valley of my torso. Silas paused, breathing ragged as he took me in, awe coloring the way he whispered my name. The friction of his jeans against me was a reminder that a single layer of material separated us. With another tug of my bathrobe, I'd be exposed. Was I ready for that?

Picking up on my indecision, he kept the bathrobe where it was. Instead, he explored the exposed parts of my chest and neck, leaving a trail of fire and robbing me of my sanity. I wanted him to kiss me *everywhere*, but I had no idea how to ask for it.

"Does this feel okay?" Silas asked, his teeth tugging at my lower lip. The calluses of his palms smoothed across my naked legs as he hitched my knee over his hip. His hair framed our faces, cocooning us against the world.

A quiet—very quiet, very far-off—part of me wondered if we were moving too fast, careening toward an edge we couldn't come back from. The rest of me didn't care in the slightest, lost in the heady sensation of his body stretching across mine, our matching heartbeats. My beast had no issues. She howled in delight as I felt him hard against me.

My answering "*Yes*" caught on a sigh as Silas kissed me deeply. He began a slow grind against my pelvis that tightened my body like a coil and brought a keen up my throat. His hand cradled my butt as my fingernails dragged under his shirt and oh—it felt so good, *he* felt so good. I wanted him, all of him. Against me. Inside me. Pressure built within my chest, spiking my blood.

Careful, my beast warned.

Silas paused, panting. I realized belatedly I'd tensed up.

"Keeks?"

Jamming my eyes and mouth shut, I released a steady breath through my nose.

I'd become so worked up I'd nearly let a scream loose.

I didn't dare imagine what would happen to Silas at such close proximity. Would he have the chance to produce a shield? A sickening churn kicked up in my stomach, washing away the heat.

"We should stop." I willed myself to calm down. My beast sat quietly, like she *wanted* me to relax.

Silas rolled to the side, tying my bathrobe closed. I murmured an apology—how could I even begin to explain what had just happened?—but he shook his head. "Don't apologize. I got a bit carried away there."

"We both did."

His smile turned playful. "I promise I didn't visit with an agenda."

"You mean you didn't plan to get me on my bed in only a bathrobe?"

"Imagine if I applied myself."

Silas didn't need an agenda. He just needed to look at me, touch me, and I was his. What did that say about me? Was I making up for lost time, or was it my reaction to *him*?

His smile faded. "I should go. They might do a sweep."

I'd dreaded this. This moment held a fragment of the universe we could control. Some things are precious in their brevity, like a sunrise or a sunset. Just as the clock ticked beside me, what we'd shared in this room was slipping away.

"I'll pretend not to see you tomorrow," I whispered.

Silas opened the passageway and, with a small smile that said everything, slipped out.

CHAPTER TWENTY-EIGHT

I WOKE THE NEXT MORNING TO ANOTHER SCRAWLED NOTE from Silas wedged beneath the door.

Meet me in the garage at midday.

Thrilled I would see him again so soon, but also concerned, I dressed and plaited my hair into twin braids. I paused in front of the mirror. Before all of this, I'd never deemed workout gear appropriate for daily wear—yet here I was in sneakers, yoga pants, and a waterproof jacket to combat the cooler autumn days. I'd forgone foundation in favor of tinted moisturizer. Makeup and nice clothes had been a balm, an armor. I had no idea what was coming for me today, but a flawless complexion wouldn't change how I'd handle it. And, I was starting to realize, I *could* handle it.

A haunted awareness of the world now clashed with the glow of secrets shared last night. How Silas had felt, clutching my naked hips. Pink spots sat high on my cheeks. I looked excited. Hopeful.

Being around Silas was like standing in a humid electrical storm, air thick, sparks flying. Scary in its intensity, in how it provoked feelings I'd never experienced before. I'd spent hours after Silas had left thinking about my reaction to him and what it could mean in the future. If I'd be able to control myself enough to dare to go further. I wanted to. Could I trust myself enough to try? Would Silas? Despite his admissions, part of me worried he'd view my response to our intimacy as another setback in our relationship—perhaps one setback too many—and a sign to walk away. His note, at least, soothed some of those fears.

I detoured to the kitchen for breakfast before attending my training session with Anika. Once midday hit, I made my way to the garage to see what Silas had in store.

The vehicles glinted beneath fluorescent lights like headstones. Silas entered with Dobromil, Matej, and two other guards, his easy smile generating one of my own. Perhaps it was wishful thinking, but his dark circles looked a little lighter today.

"What's going on?" I asked, voice low, as the guards moved toward the fleet of nondescript black sedans.

"Do you trust me?"

I didn't hesitate. "Yes."

"I negotiated your presence," Silas said. "We're visiting someone."

I followed him to the car on the far end. Dobromil opened the door for me like a chauffeur. I sat in the back. The strong smell of leather hit as Silas joined me. Locks sounded as Dobromil and Matej took the front seats. I gave Silas a questioning look—being in a car with Matej would always trigger me—but he relaxed, raising a finger to his lips.

We exited the garage, heading for the front gate.

Silas shifted closer. "Once a month, I get to visit my family," he whispered.

My eyes nearly popped out of my skull. "That's where we're going? Right now?"

"Yes." At my expression, he sobered. "It was what you said last night, that my mother could have information on Johan. It's worth a try. This morning I convinced Arwood you might know what questions to ask."

Shallow of me, but that hadn't been my initial concern at all. "Silas, I'm not appropriately dressed *at all*. I can't meet your mother like this!"

"She's not going to care in the slightest what you look like."

My hands went to my braids in a pitiful attempt to smooth them down. "That doesn't make me feel any better. I'm not even wearing makeup!" So much for thinking I could face whatever today would bring me. "Why didn't you tell me earlier?"

"Arwood didn't want it to get out that we were leaving the estate. I checked, and you won't be required until tonight. The attacks have knocked share prices, so they're in meetings all day."

Another sedan followed behind us. "Isn't Arwood worried we'll try and escape?"

"Shoot-to-kill orders if we step out of line."

That made me relax in a weird way. Arwood knew what Silas was doing. He wouldn't get in trouble.

"I'm sorry," Silas whispered. "I should have checked if this was something you were comfortable with. Did you want to stay here?"

"No, I'm glad I'm coming." Yes, things were complicated and we couldn't be together in the traditional sense—but I still wanted to be involved in his life, and this compromise made the knot in my heart loosen.

I sank into the seat, brainstorming topics in case any awkward silences occurred. I gave up when the only icebreaker I thought of was whether they'd started meditation to deal with incarceration.

"Relax," Silas whispered. "You'll be fine. Talking to people you don't know is your specialty."

Not like this. "Not parents," I admitted, shooting Silas a wary glance.

The smile he gave filled me with light. "You've marched into buildings with armed men waiting for us. This will be the easiest thing you've done in weeks."

Thirty minutes later, we descended into an underground parking garage near the river. We were escorted from the vehicle, searched by a set of security guards, then taken through a service door and up two flights of stairs. Just as I was certain Silas had made a mistake and we were about to be murdered in the cold underbelly of some unnamed building in Prague, we passed a swipe-access door and entered a room halved by bars set in concrete.

Dobromil and Matej stopped at the entrance, nodding to Silas.

Beyond the bars were two beds, a circular wooden table with two chairs, and a beige two-seater couch facing a television mounted into the concrete wall. The room was sparsely decorated with generic paintings, but carpet covered the floor and the temperature was comfortable. A window, set high into the wall, spilled light across a shelf of books, a treadmill, and piles of yoga mats and cushions.

While the two women started from their respective positions—one reading on the couch, another completing a puzzle at the table—only one rushed toward Silas. The older woman reached for him through the wide bars, resting her forehead against his in lieu of a hug. I waited in the doorway, not wanting to interrupt, the push-pull of warmth and melancholy igniting my chest at the sight.

The young woman—presumably Silas's sister, who had hung back—alerted them to my presence. "Who's that?"

Three sets of eyes focused on me. Silas smiled invitingly. "Mom, Layla, this is Keanna."

I bit my lip. Breaking up their reunion was the last thing I wanted to do. The beginnings of my murmured protest were drowned out by his mother summoning me.

"Come closer, love. Let us see you."

I did, feeling three feet tall, my sneakers scuffing the floor. His mother and sister were dressed in structured beige loungewear—slacks, oversized thin knits—which complemented their olive-toned skin. I had workout clothes and an itchy, flaky neck. I didn't even have earrings in. I wanted to apologize for my appearance, but also didn't want that to be the first words out of my mouth; his mother and sister lived in a *cage*. Instead, I tried to smile and removed my fists from my jacket pocket.

"Hi." I smiled, activating my default greeting. "It's lovely to meet you."

A wide grin erupted above his mother's pointed chin,

excitement dancing in eyes that matched Silas's for color. Dark brown hair cascaded in tight curls around her heart-shaped face.

"Oh, Silas." His mother squeezed his hands. "This is wonderful. Do you live in the mansion too?"

"Yes," Silas said. "She's a fellow … associate, you could say."

"We both work for Arwood," I clarified. "We're friends."

His sister, Layla, shot us a *yeah, right* expression, but remained otherwise silent as her mother bubbled in front of her.

"You're Edson's girl, aren't you?"

"Yes." Part of me wanted to stop intruding on them, and the other half basked in the parental love streaming from the other side of the bars.

"I saw you at the party last year." His mother's gaze softened as I stepped beside Silas. "Nasty business, that, but you'll rise above it. I keep assuring Silas we are not the sins of our fathers—"

"Mom." Silas shook his head. "Not a good time."

I frowned. She ducked her head in the universal signal for *whoops*. "I apologize, Keanna. I'm just so excited to meet you."

I pushed my questions aside for the moment. "I'm so sorry. You don't get much time with each other. I'll go and wait outsid—"

"Nonsense. Silas has never brought someone home before. If this is how it has to be, I'll take it. You're staying right here."

This was a first for him, too? Silas shrugged unapologetically at my questioning glance.

"Keanna and I struck a deal with Arwood," he told them. "Her release—and ours—is contingent on finding Isobelle."

His sister's eyebrows rose. "She's still missing?"

"Yes."

Layla scoffed. "She's probably dead in a forest outside of Prague—"

"*Layla*—"

"—so wouldn't it be smart for Arwood to direct his *considerable resources* there instead?"

"That's enough," their mother hissed.

Layla retained her mulish expression.

Her mother sighed, turning back to us. "I fear for the poor girl. Arwood hasn't heard anything at all?" Silas shook his head. His mother's mouth formed a thin line. "Hmm. Still, the deal is a promising development."

"We're running leads to ground," I said. "I've been wondering if the Sect might have taken her. Silas mentioned your late husband was involved with them?"

She nodded at my apologetic tone. "The existence of banshees is known to the Sect. They tracked a large clan down in the County Clare area years ago."

There *were* banshees in Ireland! Arwood's books had been right.

"Arwood thinks the Sect would have killed Isobelle if they had her," I said.

"If she'd given them a reason to, yes. It's not their style to capture and ransom. They keep things black and white to maintain the threat of their existence."

I sighed. I'd been so sure Arwood had missed something. "There's another player called Johan Matousek. Have you heard of him?"

"Awful man. I thought he trafficked for the Kohnstamms?"

"Not anymore." Silas explained how the Kohnstamms had been bombed at their own party, and Gisele and Ivan assassinated by the Sect.

Her lips pursed when she realized Silas had been present at said bombing. "He's a ghost," she told us. "Johan's identity is a mystery, which was always part of his appeal for Ivan, I suppose. I'm not surprised you're having so much trouble. This may be a contentious suggestion, but you could ask your father."

"*My* father?" I bleated out in knee-jerk fashion. I tried to soften my tone—this was Silas's family, and I wanted to make a good impression—but I couldn't keep the bewilderment from my voice. "Why would he know?"

"I heard a rumor last year he was courting the Kohnstamms and their associates. He may have come across Johan then."

Oh. That. My shoulders sank. Old news.

"That was a mistake," I said. "We were so new to the city when my father approached them, but nothing eventuated, thank goodness."

Silas's mother didn't look convinced. "Are you sure? I heard he was brokering a property deal in that circle."

What is she talking about?

"*Anyway*," the warning in Silas's voice broke through, "we got a bunch of leads about Johan from the Kohnstamms. One could track us to Isobelle. And if it does …"

"Yeah, sure. Let's keep shooting for that pipe dream."

"*Layla!*"

But Silas's sister stubbornly set her jaw. "No. I'm beyond over this. You say you're working hard to solve things, but we've been here for nearly a year. Don't just visit, parading around with your girlfriend, promising things will get better. *Prove* it."

Protectiveness reared. *We're trying*, I wanted to say. *It's bad in here, but it's bad out there, too.*

"Layla, that's enough. If you can't be civil, be quiet," his mother spat. "Go. Sit. Over there."

Layla flared her nostrils, frustration dancing in her glare, but she did as she was told without another look at her brother.

I squeezed Silas's hand. My touch calmed his face for the briefest of moments before it hardened to stone. I released him, hoping the guards hadn't noticed.

"I'm sorry," his mother whispered. "It's … it's been—well, we're doing what we can. And so are you, I know it."

Silas nodded.

"Now," his mother went on, her tone turning determinedly upbeat. "Are you looking after yourself?" Silas sighed, to which she tutted. "You look tired. You're using, aren't you?"

"Do you want the truth, or the answer I wish I could give?"

His mother brushed her fingers across his cheeks. "My gorgeous boy. But," she pulled back and tutted again, this time with humor, "honey. That *shirt*. You'd look so much nicer in the new ones I bought you last year."

"I'm raging against the system," Silas said, plucking at the faded black material. "But comfortably."

She rolled her eyes, dropping the subject. Her voice lowered as she pressed closer to the bars. "Have you heard from Gabriel?"

Silas shook his head.

Her lower lip trembled. It was small, but I caught it. So did Silas.

"No, it's okay, Mom. He'll be fine," he said, gripping her hand tighter. "Arwood has teams all around the Czech Republic we don't even see. And the Camardos have operations across Italy. He could be anywhere."

Silas was telling his mother the things I'd told him, things he didn't believe himself. A lie, but a kind one, I supposed. Seeing them in their cage, I understood why he kept things from them. There was nothing they could do, and nothing breaks you faster than a problem you can't help solve.

Dobromil cleared his throat. Silas's mother glanced between us with glistening eyes. "I'm so glad you have each other. Really, I—that helps. To know he's not alone in there. I'm just so …"

"Mom, honestly," Silas murmured, his tone a mixture of embarrassment and pain.

Dobromil cleared his throat again.

Understanding that the guard was giving the equivalent of Oscars wrap-up music, I stepped away, allowing Silas and his family some final minutes of privacy.

Matej still stood in the hallway. Murmurs from his conversation with security wafted through the crack of the door. Beside me, Dobromil shifted. "Bathroom, miss?"

At my questioning glance, he pointed from one eye to the other. Oh. Did I look that awful? I must, if a *guard* was telling me to fix myself up.

Dobromil opened the door. "Matej will escort you. We'll catch up."

I followed Matej down the narrow corridor and waited as he opened a plain white door. He searched the toilet stalls and banged around, checking for weapons or convenient escape routes. Once satisfied, he returned.

"I'll stand here," he warned, pointing to the entrance.

"Fine," I murmured, letting the door shut and heading for the sink. Okay, so I was a little puffy—probably from lack of sleep—and my eyes were a tad bloodshot. I didn't think I was that bad, but my standards for presentation had obviously fallen to horrific depths. I splashed water onto my face, then grabbed paper towels from the dispenser. A contrast on the ceiling drew my gaze.

A square black hole interrupted the plain, industrial white ceiling tiles above the toilets.

I spun against the sink at a muted thump. I'd no sooner sucked in a breath when a stall door opened, revealing a woman with hooded brown eyes, severe chin, and absolute no-nonsense attitude in a black jumpsuit.

"Oh!" I gasped, running to her.

It was Zeina. My bodyguard.

CHAPTER TWENTY-NINE

HER SURPRISED PAUSE LASTED A SECOND. STRONG ARMS roped around my waist. I'd never hugged Zeina before, but I clung to her now, inhaling the men's deodorant she always wore because she said it was less invasive and she preferred the smell. The musky scent reminded me of safety.

It reminded me of home.

"I can't believe you're here." I drew back, tears burning my eyes, looking between the hole in the ceiling and her harness. "You're okay!"

"I'm fine." The jagged scars above her eyebrow that contrasted with her smooth, tawny skin suggested otherwise.

"What happened?" One of the toilets clicked; I darted a glance toward the bathroom door to check it was still closed. Matej's gritty timbre sounded on the other side, but the handle didn't move. "You were there on the street and then you were *gone*."

She gave an eye roll, which for Zeina was the tempered equivalent of smashing the soap dispenser on the floor. "Arwood's team detained me until they secured you. But that's not important." She pulled me into the stall and shut the door behind me. "We've got minutes at best, so let's be quick. I know you're being held at Arwood's estate."

She did? I blinked away tears, swallowing my questions. "Yes. There's security but it's not infallible. Guards are stationed in the east wing, bottom floor. They have a full complement, day and night, on rotating shifts—but the rookies often patrol the estate perimeter," I whispered, eager to show her what I'd learned. "West corner, where the greenhouses are, has a drop-off on the other side. It isn't as heavily guarded."

"Excellent. Our primary contact's been selective about their information since Arwood realized he has an informant."

I preened beneath her approval. So there *was* someone— multiple people?—inside his estate working against him. Was it Dobromil? Matej? Both? "Who's the mole?"

Instead of answering, Zeina turned my head side to side. "This. What does it do?"

"Shocks me. Like a dog collar."

Her eyes narrowed. "Disgusting. Any other features?"

"I hope not." What could be worse than shocking someone into submission?

Zeina pursed her lips. "I don't like this. It's a variable I'll need to investigate. It looks like it's locked with a customized key."

"Arwood has it," I said, remembering the key chain he'd slipped beneath his suit all those weeks ago. And who had stood next to him afterwards. "*Mariel!* Mariel turned me in, she was with Arwood the day I was abducted."

"We know," Zeina all but growled. "Listen to me. Take this." She pushed a small phone into my hands. "It's silenced. Keep it that way. Don't use it, just make sure it stays switched on. The battery should last. Show no one you have it, keep it on you. It has a tracker, so I can find where in the estate you are. We will get you out, but it won't be today. My team needs to scope the information you provided. Are you safe there?"

I clutched the phone like a lifeline, unable to believe I was talking to Zeina while a single door separated us from Matej. *I'll be home soon.* Elation swelled in my chest, along with a strange jolt of … something. "Yes. He's not hurting me."

"Good. I'll message when we come for you. But remember: tell no one. I mean it. There are eyes and ears everywhere."

"How did you find me?"

"No time." Zeina cupped my face. "You must go out there

looking upset, so they don't question why you've been in here for so long. I need a gold-star performance from you, Keanna."

I'd already cried upon seeing her; keeping the tears coming wouldn't be difficult at all. "I can do it."

She squeezed me. "Yes, you can. Wait for my message."

She reached around me to unlock the stall door. A bubble of panic rose. "How long?"

"By the end of the week." She stood on the cistern. "You'll be home before you know it. Remember," she said, voice as serious as I'd ever heard from her, "*no one.*"

I moved to the sink and splashed more water on my face as Zeina tugged on a rope, vaulting herself into the ceiling and replacing the tile.

With nowhere else to store the phone, I shoved it into my sports bra, and double-checked it wasn't poking out underneath my jacket—it wasn't; my boobs helped with camouflage—as the door opened to an impatient-looking Matej.

I jumped, tears falling. His severe expression became a degree more sympathetic. "We must go," he said.

Silas stood with Dobromil in the hallway. His damp cheeks shimmered in the fluorescent lights as we were shepherded back into the car.

The phone poked my sternum. I was hyper-aware of its presence as we drove down the freeway, anxiously entertaining myself with what would happen if Arwood or his team discovered it or my contact with Zeina.

My stomach plummeted with the strange combination of excitement and apprehension again. Beside me, Silas slumped against the seat, like the visit to his family had added to the weight on his shoulders.

I grazed his hand, shifting my body sideways and concealing our fingers with my legs. Gave Silas a small smile, trying to tell him without words how much it meant to be introduced to his family.

He'd shown me he trusted me. Circumstance had built a brick wall between us, but this tiny tether helped.

We stared at each other for a long time. In the depths of his brown eyes, I saw many things. Guilt. Fear. Frustration.

I would be rescued soon … which meant leaving Silas behind.

My belly swooped again. *No one*, Zeina had warned. Almost as if she knew about Silas. Perhaps she did. When I next saw her, I'd ask the questions swirling in my mind, the biggest one being: how long had she known where I was? Why hadn't my father come for me sooner?

For now, I concentrated on the heartbreaking reality of leaving Silas. But how could I? We were a team. If we found Isobelle, we'd both go free. If I escaped before that happened, I'd be abandoning him to deal with this. Alone. His health would continue to decline. His mother and sister would remain locked in that awful room …

I pushed down the painful swell in my chest. Zeina had indicated my rescue wouldn't come until the end of the week. I had time. *We* had time.

Trepidation lay thick over me as we drove back to the estate.

Zeina's rescue loomed like a ticking clock once we returned. I headed to the library, determined to make the most of Arwood's knowledge while I had it. Much of the information I'd discovered in the past month had proved validating, like how a banshee's first wail triggered her 'maturity' and thus the rest of her abilities—most notably, the ability to sense openings into the plane of the dead. Learning this had explained so much. The awakening of my beast. My keen sense of smell and ability to sense death. Why these things had followed that horrific night with Thomas.

Several minutes in, I learned something new. And unwelcome. The book open in front of me explained how banshees were identifiable by their silver hair, a transformation which indicated their full maturity and capability.

I reached for my braids. At first I didn't see anything out of the ordinary, but a shift into the light and a closer look confirmed my fears. Threads of silver glinted back at me—threads that hadn't been there several months ago. I bit the inside of my mouth. I loved my blonde hair. It was one of my best features. How soon would I lose it?

Another item added to the ever-growing list of things unfairly out of my control.

With a sigh, I pushed that down. I couldn't afford to get distracted.

An hour later, I'd still found no precedent for my screams. According to the books, there were no records of deadly banshee wails, let alone a soundless one. Would Arwood know? I resisted the idea of asking him anything; he'd use it as ammunition.

"Found anything useful?" Silas murmured, sitting beside me. His arm brushed mine, and a spray of warmth traveled across my skin. My beast relaxed. With a sigh, I rolled my shoulders and nudged the book toward him.

"Your mother confirmed a lot of things in these books to be true, but I can't find evidence of banshees killing people. Even by my own kind's standards, I'm a freak."

Silas nudged the book away. "Books aren't a universal source of truth. Do *you* write everything down?"

Ugh, he had a point.

"I'm having a pity party here," I said, still sore over my hair. Why *silver*? I'd look sixty before I was thirty. "And your logic isn't helping."

"Sorry, I'm fresh out of goodie bags." His lips tugged to the side, his cheek dimpling, but it was a weak effort.

"Are you alright?"

He spun his ring around his finger, trying to look unaffected. I didn't buy it. "It's the best and worst part of my month," he said. "My mother adored you, by the way."

I'd mulled over his mother's words, wondering what her quip about 'nasty business' meant. Silas hadn't been keen on the conversation then, and something told me he wouldn't be now, but time was no longer a luxury for us. "What was she talking about, regarding my father?"

"Sorry. She gets overexcited."

"That's not what I'm asking."

Silas shot a furtive look beneath his eyelashes. "Yes, she knows him."

"And?"

"And what? She said it herself. Fathers aren't a reflection of their children. Mine was a decent father only when it suited him, a terrible husband, and an overall selfish person. That's not on me."

I jerked, taken aback. "You shouldn't talk about your father like that."

"Doesn't release him from accountability. My father lectured me on using my power every day after I transcended. Most parents tell their kids not to drink alcohol or party. My father pushed me to use just enough to train. Just enough to learn. Meanwhile, he's working for Arwood and doing it at every opportunity. Like a junkie."

"Maybe he had to."

"And maybe he didn't. It's addictive, and he rode the high. Living large while burying the rest of us six feet under with his shitty decisions." There was so much venom in his voice; it brought color to his face. "He crashed, wasting away from an illness, but it took months for his body to actually quit breathing."

Although it hurt to see him so angry, I understood why. Silas risked his life daily working for Arwood, putting his own well-being at stake to keep his family safe, dancing the tightrope of addiction and trying not to succumb. What kind of internal battle did he wage every day?

"I'm sorry your father let you down." I wanted to reach out to him, but I kept my hand where it was. The last thing we needed was someone walking in on us. "You should be able to rely on them to be your compass when you're lost. To be your north. But I have no idea how this relates to *my* father."

He sank into his chair, giving a heavy sigh. "From what I've heard, he's as bad as Arwood is."

I groaned. First Arwood, now Silas? "I understand you're upset, and I can't begin to imagine what your family is experiencing in that cell, but please don't drag my father into this."

His jaw hardened with skepticism.

"Sounds like your father trained you to the letter. Cages come in all forms, Keanna."

Hot anger surged. "Says you," I spat. The depths of my rising fury took me by surprise, but I held my ground. I'd been there for him, and he wanted to repay me by acting like this? "You're always on me to train and change my situation, but do nothing for yourself. Your mother and your sister have been imprisoned for *eleven months*. Until I got here and bargained a deal with Arwood for Isobelle, you were content to angst around and treat yourself as dispensable. You're so preoccupied trying to keep them safe at any cost to yourself, you'll die before you free them!"

Silas gave me the coldest look I'd ever seen from him. "Don't. Say. That. To me."

I was aware on some level that I should stop talking, but Silas criticizing my relationship with my father had struck a nerve. "But it's true, isn't it? You're too paralyzed by fear. Don't attack me, Silas. I see what you're doing."

"And I see *you*. A spoiled girl who only started living a few weeks ago. Who hero-worships a father who prefers to control you. He raised you to hate yourself, rather than help set you free."

Spoiled? I flinched, that particular dagger driving deep. Deep—because it was true. "Wow. Tell me how you really feel."

A single disagreement had deteriorated the fragile pyramid of promises and understandings we'd built together. Perhaps it was better I was leaving.

Hurt, puffed up on righteousness, and with *spoiled girl* echoing in my head, I stormed out of the library.

CHAPTER THIRTY

THE NEXT MORNING DAWNED SLOW. ALTHOUGH THE TWO coffees I'd choked down at breakfast had yet to wake me up, I headed to training with determination. Spurred by my fight with Silas, and his mother confirming what was known about Johan—or rather *not* known—I'd woken with a plan.

Though I wouldn't admit it to him, once I calmed down I realized I'd accused Silas of the very thing I'd done myself: wait for a solution. Just because a rescue was coming didn't mean I couldn't accomplish everything I needed to first. Escape didn't solve the danger of the Sect or Arwood turning me over to them; finding Isobelle would do that.

I'd sent a message via a housekeeper requesting an audience with Arwood. Given it was the first time I'd sought him out, I hoped he'd be intrigued enough to respond quickly.

I arrived at my 9am training session on the dot as Anika finalized a message for 'ALM Holdings.' "We will confirm your appointment within twenty-four hours. Thank you for calling."

"Does Arwood pay you extra for the secretary services?"

She tossed her phone to the side. "You bet. Looks great on the resume. Gotta think long-term in this economy. You mentioned you wanted to progress faster?"

I nodded. I was getting better at isolating the moment my scream became a killing wail, but I hadn't been able to do anything about the wail itself. It was still just as deadly—something Anika had confirmed herself, 'feeling' the intensity as she absorbed it.

Pressure was what erupted from me. Pressure that shifted

people, did things to their insides that killed them. Sound was pressure, but after the casino, I wondered if it was my scream that created it, or if degrees of pressure could exist without the sound.

It was a hell of a chicken or egg situation, and one I needed to determine. Fast.

Anika unraveled a bundle on the ground. It was a collection of weapons I'd seen in movies. And museums.

She placed her foot on the pile. "We rarely find out what we're capable of in controlled circumstances. I didn't know I could neutralize a bullet's momentum until someone shot me." She grabbed a knife, flipping and catching it.

I watched her hand. "Someone *shot* you?"

"Tried to." Without warning, she threw the knife at my head.

All I could do was flinch and shriek. My scream knocked the knife off course; it clattered onto the white gravel. It was the length of my shoe, and would have caused serious damage had it collided.

"Want me to continue?"

I must have been crazy, signing up for more intensive training. But to understand what I was capable of, I needed to indulge in a little crazy.

Before I finished nodding, another knife hurtled toward me. I ducked and rolled as a third bounced off the gravel. A fourth. I rolled again, scrambling to my feet. Anika launched a punch. After several weeks of self-defense training, it was easy to dodge—

"*Oof.*" I stumbled backwards, winded, as her other fist landed in my gut. Served me right for getting cocky. Anika didn't stop; huffing, I deflected a jab to the throat, sidestepping her knee.

She left none of the usual breaks, her assault relentless. "Anika, wait—"

Another blade glinted in the sunshine as it swiped toward my outstretched arm.

I let loose a scream, the pressure wave rippling outwards and taking the knife with it. Anika stood her ground, her eyes transitioning from their usual brown to black and back again. She sighed as if sampling a fresh ocean breeze.

"Still full power, banshee. That was delightful."

My pulse raced like I'd run a marathon. "I meant it to be. It looked like you were about to stab me."

"I would have. You protected yourself. Top marks. But that's not what you're wanting to achieve, is it? Remind me how the soundless wave happened."

I told her how I'd been threatened with a knife against the wall, how he'd kept my mouth shut. Naturally, I omitted who. Considering she hadn't tattled about the passageways, I didn't think Anika would run to Arwood and get the jump on me, but I'd learned the hard way about making assumptions.

"I've got an idea. You're probably not gonna like it."

Oh boy.

She lunged, then gaped at something behind me. "What's Silas doing with Matej?"

I whipped around, forgetting I was trying *not* to openly care about Silas. The path out of the garden was clear. Where was he?

Gravel crunched. I'd barely turned before Anika's fist connected with my jaw. My teeth clacked together. Fury surged, thick and fast, both from the pain and the humiliation of Silas—my clear weakness—being used against me.

A blow to my temple knocked me off balance. A kick to the back of my knees sent me to the ground. Tears sprang into my eyes. It *hurt*. I was so stunned I couldn't move.

"Asshole," I hissed, losing another micro-battle with myself. Black spots dotted my vision as I winced against the sunlight.

A knee lodged underneath my chin. The unmistakable sharp coolness of a blade settled against the side of my neck. I inhaled through my nose, unable to open my mouth.

She was trying to recreate my attack.

I struggled against her, wincing. Her leg on my chest made it hard to breathe. With a neat pivot, her sneakered foot crushed my wrists, pinning me to the ground like a butterfly with its wings caught.

The knife broke the skin. At first I presumed it was accidental—she was crouching *on* me—but the pain grew, tracing the top of my collar.

"Make me stop, banshee. Think this hurts now?"

She pressed harder. Light-headedness kicked in. I couldn't *breathe*, couldn't take the spinning; I jammed my eyes shut, concentrated on the heaviness building from the base of my skull.

I exhaled roughly as my beast screeched. Pressure burst from me like a wave, her weight shifting.

I sucked in a lungful of air. I thought I'd managed to blast Anika off me, but no—she'd absorbed it like my other screams and stood, releasing me. Blood trailed down my aching neck. I'd be bruised tomorrow.

I was mad. And I wasn't.

"That's what happened in the casino," I gasped.

Anika raked her raven shoulder-length hair back. "I *would* apologize for my methods ..." She shot me a smug grin. "If they weren't so darn effective."

⁓

Arwood's request to meet came soon after. I patched up my neck— my jaw would turn purple soon—and headed to the boardroom. Arwood, Lissandra, and Steadman sat spaced as far apart as I'd ever seen, their grim features and stiff postures contributing to the tension lacing the air. Now that I understood the dynamic between the three of them, I had no idea why I hadn't seen it from the start. Respect, loyalty, and the utilization of their individual strengths had constructed a delicate ecosystem to help them weather the harsh landscape of this world.

"Miss Backhus," Arwood said as I sat opposite him. "You wanted to see me?"

My eyes darted to the picture on the projector screen. "Another attack from Johan's team?"

"One of my distribution centers. Five dead, ten injured."

That was as good a segue as any. "Are you still having difficulty identifying him?"

Arwood's hand bristled over his close-cropped blond hair. If I swapped his business suit for camo gear, he'd look just like his army photo. "I'm not in the mood to entertain theories."

I'd obviously chosen a poor time to do this. I steeled myself, squaring my shoulders. "Johan tried to abduct me at the Kohnstamm casino." I pointed to the profile shots lying on the table, the shots I'd seen on the desk in the library. "He's one of those men."

"You IDed Johan that night?" Steadman demanded. "And you only think *now* to tell us?"

"You never asked."

The thunderous displeasure on both their faces sparked the urge to fawn, but I held strong, maintaining eye contact. Lissandra's lips quirked. She, at least, seemed amused by my audacity.

"Well?" Arwood snapped. "Which one of them was it?"

"I'm offering an exchange: I tell you which one is Johan, and in return you remove my collar."

I wanted to win this for myself. My collar symbolized more than just being his weapon, and we all knew it.

Arwood clasped his hands together, looking like he wanted to put them around my neck. "Do better, Miss Backhus. Removing the collar is a large concession on my part."

I gripped the hem of my shirt, assessing the room while I tried to work out what to say next. I'd banked on their desperation being so great they'd accept whatever I had to say.

The picture of the distribution center had knocked a memory loose in my head, a memory couched in the undertows of dread and inevitability. "Do you have a map of where we've tracked his associates to?"

The initial silence to my question broke when Steadman

grabbed the laptop and plugged it into the projector. Prague showed on the screen. Lissandra identified the affected areas. One by one, circles generated on the map. Some were in clusters.

"If you're looking for a pattern, you won't find one," Steadman said, echoing my thoughts. "We've been over this."

Lissandra shushed him. "Let her think."

I couldn't see which streets the locations sat on. "Do you have a list of the actual addresses?"

I loved puzzles. Pre-abduction, Sunday mornings had meant long breakfasts and Sudoku. Sometimes my father would join me, and we'd work together to solve the crosswords in the paper. But puzzles had rules. Johan's people did not.

Except . . .

Two addresses itched my brain. Both were located in Karlin, an area of redevelopment after flooding two decades ago. My father's company had bought up big in the neighborhood, and a few months ago listed a portfolio including office and apartment buildings. As an intern, I'd assisted in the sale while they were on the market, but they'd sold as part of a larger deal that included properties all over north and east Prague. Arwood's distribution center had been an asset we'd tried to acquire without success—no surprise why.

The two addresses had been locations in that sale. In fact . . .

There was Waldemar's jewelry shop filled with the trafficked girls. A property in Prague Seven I'd physically visited to help assess. They'd *all* been sold by my father's company.

But not every property in the deal was featured here.

"There should be two others."

"You're mumbling," Steadman said.

I swallowed a retort, filling them in on the sale. "Two are missing from this list."

"Where?"

"Give me a minute." I tried to suppress the icy, sick feeling rising. You do due diligence when going into business with someone, but I doubted the same had occurred here. People buy and sell real estate all the time without necessarily knowing what the other party is tied up in, right?

But as much as it hurt to admit it, evidence was starting to stack up. I just didn't want to believe it. I resisted the urge to touch the phone hidden in my bra, pushing it all aside. I'd have a crisis over my father's ethics later.

I focused on the list, willing my memory to trigger. I'd worked this sale. Photocopied documents, listened in on the meetings. "If I could access my work emails—"

Steadman didn't even let me finish. "Not a chance."

Yeah, I wouldn't have let me, either. I stood, facing the projection. The shadow my figure cast blocked out most of Arwood's territories, but I wasn't looking at them. I mentally recounted the reports I'd proofed, the emails I'd drafted. I'd seen the addresses over and over. I just had to remember what they were.

I gestured to the map. "Is there a list of all addresses for that area?"

After perusing the list in silence, I tapped on two of the locations: a secure parking garage, and an industrial warehouse. They hadn't been included in any information we'd reviewed so far. My instincts told me I was on to something.

"If you still think Johan will lead you to Isobelle, then these buildings are our best bet." I addressed Arwood, trying to keep my face passive. "Johan's location and confirmation of his identity. For my collar." *There. I did better.*

"Let's move," Arwood said. "I want us out there tonight."

Steadman shook his head. "Not tonight. Going in without—"

"I don't care. Make it happen. None of this matters if I don't get her back. I want her found."

"I do, too." Steadman's tone was calm. "But we have to keep perspective here. What if this Johan fuck isn't the guy?"

"He is." The desperation Arwood kept hidden from me, perhaps everyone, bubbled to the surface. Cords in his neck protruded below a tense jaw. The grip on his glass tightened, but his tone turned soft, like a benediction. "It *has* to be him."

"We need more time—"

"We aren't in the field anymore, James. Tonight, or I'll find a different person to lead them."

Steadman's expression went stony. The tension between them didn't just make me uncomfortable—it hurt to watch.

"Arwood." Lissandra's tone cut across the table as she removed her cat-eye glasses. "Take this offline. *Now.*"

He cleared his throat, plucking at his tie—and just like that, Arwood was a businessman again, discussing a proposal and not his daughter's life. "Good work."

Finally, *finally*, I felt on equal footing. "My collar?" I prompted.

Heads either side of the table swiveled to Arwood.

"Deliver Johan tonight, Miss Backhus, and it's gone."

⌒⊙

Late afternoon sun filtered through the open windows as I walked to the kitchen, overwhelmed from the day.

And it wasn't even over yet.

Those in the room were sworn to secrecy about the operation. The guards accompanying us would be told of the job and timings, but details of locations wouldn't be shared until the last possible moment. I'd waited for Dobromil or Matej to approach me since Zeina had made contact, but neither had done so. Regardless, I was convinced one of them worked for my father—or they at least knew who did. I'd left Steadman and Arwood as they debated who would take the warehouse, given we'd likely find trouble there. I'd be going irrespective of who led, so I took the opportunity to eat.

I flinched as Silas sat beside me.

"I'm sorry for what I said," he whispered.

Borrowing some bravery from the boardroom, I ate a large bite of risotto while Silas watched. The night we'd met, I'd thrown my food in the garden. My, how far I'd come.

"Define your statement, mage," I deadpanned.

Silas smothered his smirk, leaning closer. I checked the kitchen. We were early to dinner; the chef and his kitchenhand stood by the grill, not paying us the slightest bit of attention. "Calling you spoiled. The things I said about you and your father. It was a dick move. I'm sorry."

I mined his gaze. I saw contrition there. He *was* sorry. His words still stung, and I needed to reflect on why, but Zeina's ticking clock urged me to give the smallest of smiles. Despite my anger, I wouldn't forgive myself if I spent the time I had left with Silas fighting with him.

The time I had left. That thought twisted my insides.

But I couldn't resist one last dig. "You *were* a dick," I agreed. "My father is the most important person in my life. I'll never not defend him."

"I get it. Family's off-limits."

I swallowed the apology that rose; I wasn't sorry about what I'd said to him.

"This mission worries me," Silas murmured. "Johan's dangerous. More dangerous than Arwood anticipates."

"You've been assigned?"

"With you and the warehouse team. Something about it makes me nervous. Steadman isn't the spontaneous type, and it all feels too last-minute. I don't want you there."

"I don't want you there, either," I said, not bothering to tell him that Steadman had been overruled. It wouldn't change anything. "I'm in this with you. I'll watch your back."

Underneath the table, our knees brushed. Material separated us, but a shiver stole down my arms. The kitchen filled until we were once again surrounded, bodies turned away from each other, knees still touching.

CHAPTER THIRTY-ONE

I T'S FUNNY, THE THINGS THAT STICK IN YOUR MIND WHEN you're heading for danger. As we exited the car a block from the warehouse, piling out onto a sidewalk slick from recent rain, I clocked today's date on the dashboard. In a few hours, I'd be twenty-one. Last year, I'd woken to a room full of balloons and presents and worn an obnoxious tiara all day. This year, I'd mark the occasion surrounded by heavy artillery.

Zeina's phone pushed against my chest, secure under my sports bra, a reminder that this would all be over soon. I just had to keep myself safe and find Isobelle.

My gut twisted as the team milled around us. I let out a sigh at the trash-filled street illuminated in amber from the lamps over-head. It wasn't only the tang from the dumpsters filling my senses. Something was off. Anticipation we might corner Johan tonight? Fear we wouldn't? Whatever it was, my beast reacted with similar discomfort.

For the first time ever, I asked her a question: *Do you think this is a mistake?*

My beast didn't hesitate. *Absolutely.*

Steadman communicated at intervals with the other team. I'd overheard Arwood being relegated to the second location with Anika as protection.

I took the opportunity to make my thoughts known.

"What was that?" Steadman's breath steamed in the frigid air.

"I have a bad feeling about this," I repeated.

I watched him assess my posture, the grimace on my face. Once, he would have met my words with derision. Instead, he gave something strangely akin to … respect. "Now?" he asked, fingers tightening around his phone. "Or where we're going?"

"The warehouse." His shoulders relaxed. "I could have been wrong about where he is."

"And you could have been right," Steadman replied, gesturing to the team to get their attention. "Back yourself."

It was the kindest thing he'd ever said to me.

Silas quirked his lips. *I'm here.*

His presence made me all the more nervous. If this went badly, he'd be caught in the crossfire.

"Let's go," Steadman said.

Ahead, the warehouse stood like a slumbering giant, its metal roof like cut glass tearing the night sky. The last of the car doors slammed, vehicles peeling away as we sank into the shadows. A prickling sensation rolled across my skin.

Something wasn't right. But the problem was, I couldn't pinpoint *what*. A cloying metallic sweetness laced my tongue and filled my nose.

People were going to die tonight.

Matej, who'd downloaded the blueprints that evening, had talked over the entrances in the north and south of the warehouse on our way in. The south led into a storage area with materials and machinery, the north to the offices. Half would enter on one side, while the other half would take any potential heat from security.

A peaty combination of smoke and gas mixed with roasted meat from a nearby restaurant as we filed down the alley. Empty milk crates and broken wooden pallets rested against the exposed brick. Footfalls scraped across cobblestones. Ahead in the darkness, a single red light was suspended from the side of the warehouse.

"Security systems?" I asked Matej.

"Almost certainly," he responded, his accent cushioning his words into one long hiss. "Be careful tonight, little lamb. Anika needs her training friend."

I stumbled at the unexpected nickname from my kidnapper.

Steadman already had a phone to his ear, conversing with the person overriding the security systems. The camera light went dark.

I didn't match their confidence, but I matched their strides. My beast sat watchful like a meerkat. I reached for her, placing figurative hands against her cage. Talons closed around my fingers.

Silas and I hung back as the team blasted open the small entrance beside the industrial metal roller door. Like a swarm of insects, helmet-wearing guards funneled inside.

Steadman nodded to us. "Watch yourselves." We followed him.

The interior of the warehouse contained a series of wide, industrial shelves. They towered at intervals between concrete pillars, holding rows of plastic-wrapped pallets. The rusty tang of metal strengthened as we followed the assault of guards around forklifts and toward the wall separating the shipping area from the offices beyond. A long, dark rectangular window overlooked the ground floor. I kept my eyes on it as we approached the doorway, expecting movement. There was none, but I couldn't get past the feeling we were being watched anyway.

Ahead, light arched through a series of open doors. The shouts of those responding to the first half of the team led us like a beacon.

We entered a large, square room. The bare, white walls and generic furniture reeked of temporary intentions. Plastic chairs surrounded a long metal table, and along the perimeter of the room stood filing cabinets and cupboards. At the table lounged three men, dressed in jackets and jeans. Half-drunk coffee sat in front of them, newspapers and phones scattered under their forearms.

The man on the end started at our entrance. The other two observed us with the calculating look of a snake before it attacked. None moved as our team circled them.

Guards searched the other rooms in the building, their shouts of 'clear!' echoing down the hall. Steadman pushed to the front, meeting my eyes. I gave a subtle nod toward one of the seated men, my heart rate increasing.

Johan was here.

"Matousek?" Steadman addressed the trio.

"You're talking to him," said the man on the end, taking a sip of his drink with forced casualness.

"Bullshit. Silas, Matej." Steadman gestured around the room. "Start searching. Take anything that looks useful."

Silas brushed past me, his fingers squeezing mine. He and Matej began rifling through the cabinets.

The younger man on the opposite end sighed, sipping his coffee. His thick bronze hair curled at the ends, framing his wide nose and thin lips. Like at the casino, thick, bolt-like earrings took up both pale earlobes. "This is how Arwood Sayer says hello, huh?"

"Be glad that's all we're doing at this point," Steadman replied. He kicked one of the chairs to the side and sat.

Johan shuffled, getting comfortable, his movements laced with a level of confidence I paid close attention to. I hoped Steadman had taken notice. Something definitely wasn't right.

"Who's your boss?" Steadman asked.

"Don't need one." Johan's finger ran over the edge of his cup. An American accent dueled with an unplaceable European one as he said, "I'm entrepreneurial as fuck."

"Your connections are too broad to come from just being a client of the Kohnstamms," Steadman said. "Who are you working for?"

Behind Johan, Silas kicked aside a box with his foot, shaking his head at Matej, and tugged open another filing cabinet. The nervous man on the end twitched at the movement.

Johan raised an eyebrow. "You can quit stomping around my office, dude. You're scaring my men."

The opening of the next drawer scraped louder than the last.

"We'll stop when we get what we're looking for." Steadman showed a photo on his phone. "Isobelle Sayer. Where is she?"

Johan eyeballed Steadman and proceeded to knock back the rest of his coffee. "Don't know her."

"I wouldn't expect a man of your ilk to remember all the women you traffic, but I doubt she would have passed your notice—given who her father is."

"They look the same to me. The price they fetch on the other end is the differentiation."

Steadman's response was the hollow echo of a gun discharging. I jumped as the nervous man to Johan's far right slumped lifelessly in his chair, his expression one of shock.

Johan didn't even flinch. He could have been painting his nails. "That changes nothing. I don't know what I don't know."

"You've been interfering with Arwood," Steadman said.

"I've been *paid* to interfere with Arwood." Johan studied us. Though I was partially concealed by the guards, his beady eyes landed on my collar. I bet if I asked him after tonight, he'd be able to relay every detail of the room and the people within it. Someone that meticulous wouldn't be here alone with only two men—sorry, *one* man—and no backup. What were we missing? "I'm not lying when I say: I don't know who or where she is. And," he said, his thick accent lingering in the air, "you and your Arwood can go fuck yourselves."

Steadman grabbed his gun, pointing to the man beside Johan.

Tattoos lined the man's throat, diamonds stamped under his ear. He stood, chair squealing against the concrete floor, his eager expression the opposite of what you'd expect from someone staring down a weapon.

Steadman fired.

The man's eyes flashed gold. The bullet paused, turned in trajectory—

—and Matej dropped, clutching his neck.

"*Ferox!*" Silas yelled.

Panicked shouts filled the office as Silas's roar of "Don't shoot!" quickly drowned under gunfire. Shields erupted—but Silas wasn't quick enough. Guards fell, their own bullets shot straight back at them, the rest fleeing down the hallway. Two seized me. I was submerged into a wave of padded vests.

Leaving Silas behind.

"Silas!" I screamed, unable to see past the panicked guards. We emerged into the warehouse.

"Outside!" The command came over thumping footsteps and shouts—then I stopped thinking, because a ball of fire shot straight for the pallet I stood next to.

I dived to the side, slamming into a metal aisle beam and the dirty, uncompromising concrete floor.

Searing heat flashed across my face as the pallet erupted into flames. I coughed, scrambling backwards down the aisle. The tattooed *ferox* came into view, his gaze sweeping the stacks. A gun discharged. He waved a hand, diverting the bullets away from his head and sending it straight back into the shooting guard.

I wheezed, chemicals cloaking my lungs. The *ferox* clicked a lighter, cradling the single flame. It grew into a shivering, shifting globe of molten heat. Golden eyes locked onto my collar, then my face. My breath caught. *This is it.*

I'd die, alone and cowering in a warehouse I had no business being in, on the eve of my twenty-first birthday. Zeina wouldn't find me. I'd never see my father again.

My life—over before it had really begun.

These spiraling thoughts were interrupted by the impossible: the *ferox* fired in the opposite direction.

I didn't wait to find out why he hadn't pulverized me on the spot. I heaved a cough to clear my lungs, scrambled up, and fled down the aisle. A suffocating cloud of smoke had formed like a fog throughout the warehouse, bringing with it the scent of melting plastic. My beast keened, wanting to wail, but I suppressed her, trying to block out the screaming ringing my ears. Who had succumbed to the fire? Was one of the pained, panicked cries Silas? Had he even made it out of the hallway?

Fear propelled me faster. I reached the end of the aisle and turned left for the entrance, searching the flickering orange for Silas. The temperature ratcheted as the smoke increased, sweat beading at my temples. It scorched my nose. Everything was a mess of flame, of fireballs …

… fireballs flying from the outstretched hands of not just the tattooed *ferox* who had left me alone, but Johan, too.

Johan's confidence now made sense. He'd been assured of his safety the whole time. It had been *us* in danger—an ambush we'd walked right into. In our haste for Isobelle, we'd missed the critical consideration that we might not be the only supernaturals in Prague.

A fireball hit the pallet to my left. I skidded, diving behind the metal shelving.

Johan approached, his wavy hair backlit by flames. "Stay where you are, girl!"

Mere steps separated me from the next aisle. If I could stop him from throwing fire, I had a shot of making it.

I raised my palms in exaggerated surrender, calling his bluff. Johan nodded. "Yes, co—"

I ran, ignoring his holler for me to stay still. Another fireball hit the aisle I hid behind. The metal shelves groaned, rattling.

A hand jerked me backwards as the plastic wrapping on one of the pallets split. Bricks poured through the gap, smashing onto the concrete floor where I'd stood moments before.

I gaped, stunned, as fingers dug into my arm and tugged me behind the next aisle. Fingers attached to a man smeared with blood, sweat, and soot. Blue eyes shone with adrenalin. Steadman. He'd escaped the room. Had Silas? Wordlessly he assessed me, then, satisfied I wasn't physically hurt—mentally was a whole other story—guided me toward the exit with trained precision.

"Where's Silas?" I yelled, then coughed. Steadman either didn't hear me, didn't know, or chose not to respond, because he said nothing.

His grip tightened on my upper arm as we dove for the next aisle.

My face warmed as another fireball shot in front of us. Arms went around my waist. Steadman hauled me behind the shelves. Fire pillowed against the concrete wall to our right, disintegrating into black singe marks and smoke. Sweat dripped down my forehead as Steadman peered around the corner. My chest tightened as our eyes met. His throat bobbed before he grabbed my arm again, nodding at the exit. It was fifty feet away. Three aisles.

Behind us, Johan and the other *ferox* appeared, fireballs forming. Steadman swore, pulling me with him. We weren't going to make it. Cornered against a cement wall and within range, we shared a heartbeat of solidarity. He could have left me and saved himself, but he hadn't.

Steadman was human, powerless against supernatural creatures like Johan. I wasn't.

I sucked in a breath and screamed.

My beast tensed, ready for my go-ahead, and something inside *clicked* as I released her. My wail swept upwards in pitch. Pressure exploded from my body.

A shield folded around Steadman. In the distance, through the fire and darkness, more shields erupted. Some guards were still alive! Two lay on the ground, injured. Johan and the other *ferox* rolled behind a concrete pillar, avoiding my outburst. The two fireballs they'd thrown soared toward us, combined into a single incoming inferno, but with my scream it deflected upwards—

—and straight into the ceiling of the warehouse.

CHAPTER THIRTY-TWO

O H. *SHIT.*

I sucked in a breath, cutting off my scream. Above, metal and fire met in groaning unison. Beams shuddered. Windows and lights shattered, glass shards plummeting straight for our exposed heads.

Another wave exploded from me, soundless this time, blasting the glass sideways into the crackling fire.

Steadman swore again, grabbing my wrist, sprinting for the exit. A dark figure rushed us from the side.

A scream caught in my throat when I recognized his curls. *Silas.*

Cleaner than Steadman, he'd hiked his shirt up over his nose to protect against the smoke. Soot gathered along his hairline, but he was alive. Relief surged without opportunity to bask in it. The ceiling cracked over the roar of the fire. I wasn't experienced in warehouse structural integrity, but my novice assessment? We had to get out. Now.

Steadman released me. "Get to safety, both of you!"

Silas tugged his shirt down. "Aren't you coming?"

"Getting my team first." Steadman faced where the shields had erupted—thirty feet away, and in the dead center of the warehouse.

"James." Silas blanched. "Don't be stupid, this—"

"Get out of here, kid."

Steadman took off, staying low as the ceiling groaned forebodingly. Thick smoke smothered the warehouse and everything inside of it.

Silas grabbed my hand. I wavered at the exit, searching for Steadman, until Silas pulled me through the door.

⁓

The warehouse stood like a black skeleton with fractured orange skin. Sirens laced the air. Flashing lights reflected off store windows.

The police.

"Let's go," Silas said.

He was right. I doubted the police would believe men had thrown fireballs at us and that my scream had accidentally set the roof on fire. Arwood probably wouldn't even bother releasing us from jail—providing the Sect didn't get to us first.

The full emergency response entered the vicinity. We kept our pace until we lost sight of the smoke, the sirens grew weaker, and we entered the tourist-heavy bubble of Old Town.

My feet ached as we plunged into the crowd filling the cobblestoned square. I tugged on Silas's arm, slowing us to a stop and collapsing against a stone wall. The cool night air crawled across us as we panted, regarding each other with shell-shocked expressions.

I voiced the commentary running through my head, which had been in the cheerful vein of *'holy crap holy crap holy crap'*. "What are we gonna do?" I coughed to clear my lungs, gathering up my hair. It curled wildly and clung to my neck. Movie stars were always unruffled while running from danger, their hair perfect and free of cowlicks. I felt ripped off. "Can you contact Arwood and tell him what happened?"

"Nope." Silas joined me against the wall. "I wasn't allowed a phone, either."

Zeina's device remained secure underneath my clothes, even with all the running. Could I use it to call my father? How quickly could he organize a rescue? I ran the risk of exposure, but if it worked, I wouldn't have to wait for Zeina. I could go home *now*.

But if I went home now ...

I looked at Silas. An elaborate perpendicular streetlight hung above him, highlighting the crease forming between his eyebrows as he watched tourists milling beneath the astronomical clock. The circles under his eyes were more pronounced than ever, but he was with me, alive. For a few moments, I'd feared I'd lost him.

We were *both* alive. And, for now, free as well. The weight of Arwood and his team—gone. Contemplation over whether I should contact my father or not faded, sheer relief bubbling. Without warning, I started laughing. Tonight had been a *fucking disaster*. We were no closer to finding Isobelle and—bonus—we'd nearly been incinerated by Johan and his tattooed decoy.

Silas shook his head incredulously, as if sensing my thoughts. "Who knew we were hunting *feroxes*? Those two did a lot of work exploring their limits."

Lighters, fireballs, changing trajectories of bullets—no wonder Arwood had used Silas's father for all he was worth.

"I'm thankful they didn't think to catch your scream. Man." He shook his head again. "Arwood is going to lose it when he learns we were ambushed."

"Do you think Steadman made it out of there?" I asked.

"He led Arwood in the Middle East. I think he's got a better chance than most."

A strange twisting sensation rose in my gut when I thought of Steadman dead. A second passed as I regretted our decision not to stay, until I reminded myself that Steadman, and Arwood for that matter, weren't worth dying over. Silas and I had been lucky to escape with our lives.

Two people nearby posed for a selfie. It derailed my musings and brought me to the present. "It's my birthday," I told Silas, watching their phone screen. It had hit midnight. "We nearly perished in an inferno—and now I'm twenty-one."

A smile bloomed across his face. "Before all this, what were your birthday plans? A bar? Ballet performance?"

Another gurgle of laughter escaped. God, this *night*. "You're correct on the last one—tickets tonight to *Giselle*. I've never drunk in a bar."

"Never?" Silas glanced around the square, grabbing my hand again. "Let's go."

I frowned. "Shouldn't we stay here? Just in case?"

"They'll track us down," he said with a certainty that made him hard to argue with. "If not Steadman, it'll be Arwood."

I didn't budge. "And if they don't? They might think we're trying to escape and send the Sect after us."

"If we run for the German border, maybe. Don't worry. They'll find us. They own half of this city."

I bit my lip. Rule-abiding Keanna—even rules put in place by an awful man—had sweaty armpits at the prospect of just ... running off. Arwood had so much hanging over me. *And* Silas.

"Keanna Backhus," Silas said, placing a kiss on my palm. "We have an unspecified window of freedom. Will you accompany me to celebrate you? I promise I can be responsible *and* incredibly charming."

The idea of exploring the streets was tempting. "I don't know if we should. You have your family, and ..."

"They'll find us," he repeated. "Right now, all I care about is that we nearly died tonight, and we finally have time together without them breathing down our necks. I don't want to waste it. Come with me."

I let him pull me across the square and toward the lights and sounds of Charles Bridge. We cut through patrons lining up for a multi-story nightclub bathed in bright lights and submerged into the crowd crossing the river. A busker joined in with the beat coming from a nearby bar, violin strings pulling sharply to create a rustic atmosphere completely at odds with the techno music and calls from vendors standing at food carts. Euphoria rose in my chest. A manic response to surviving, possibly, but no less precious.

For a glorious moment, my beast was at peace and I was *free*.

I laughed, releasing Silas and twirling like a little girl in a princess dress. To a passer-by I would have seemed drunk, but that didn't bother me. In a way I *was* drunk: drunk on the atmosphere of those milling around us, on the disbelief of being *here*, of the craziness of the night and how it had led to this. Silas must have felt it too, because his grin stretched wide, eyes sparkling. He spun me like a dancer. Then I was in his arms, one of his hands snaking around my waist, the other dropping to cup my cheek, and his lips landed on mine.

Warmth washed over me, a current surging to my toes. I sighed as I sank into Silas's spicy, musky scent, the smoke of the warehouse clinging to our clothes. Felt the velvet touch of his lips, the roughness of his chin, the silky hair at the nape of his neck.

His mouth pressed against mine, taking, and then it turned gentle, inviting. Warm. Exciting. Safe. The sharpness of the violin matched the electric hum under my skin, the staccato thumping of my heart.

Revelers knocked us off balance. My eyes opened as Silas grabbed me again.

"Come on," he said.

On the other side of the bridge, we continued down a narrow lane and into the depths of Lesser Town. I had a leap of panic as we approached security guarding a door—we had no money, no identification—but he eyed the band around Silas's wrist and the collar around my neck and stepped aside, allowing us to pass underneath the white plaque emblazoned with the Camardo C insignia.

Down and down we descended into a dim sub-level nightclub, a suffocating mixture of low ceilings, tangy liquor, and loud house music. We passed people clustered around tables, sharing buckets of cocktails with oversize straws, more still lining up at the bar. Silas made a beeline for a vacant spot at the far end, squeezing me between the wall and the wooden bar top. With a flash of his black wristband, the bartender heeded Silas's shouted request, pouring shots.

"I know I'm new to this nightclub stuff," I yelled over the music, "but don't you have to pay for these?"

"They know we're Arwood's." Silas nudged a glass toward me. "They won't ask questions."

I'd never done shots before. I had rules about shots. From my observations, where shots began, bad decisions followed. It figured that a night starting with fire and death would also include broken bargains with myself. His arm wrapped tight around my waist, influencing my decision; what was another rule obliterated?

We clinked our glasses together and threw our heads back. Liquid fire consumed my throat. I gagged, eyes watering. It was awful.

I wanted to do it again.

"That was for surviving tonight"—Silas signaled for another two—"and these are for celebrating."

They went down in another burst of fire.

Silas's lips brushed my ear. "Happy birthday, beautiful."

My smile was nothing short of stupid. I shifted my palms across his chest, feeling dips of muscle underneath, then hooked a finger on the hem of his shirt and eased his face down for another kiss.

He tasted of sweet liquor and smoke. His hands passed up my hips, skirting the sides of my breasts. I surrendered to the intoxication of his hard body folding against mine. A curl of heat unraveled from my abdomen and flared outwards, seeking more.

The repetitive music and orders from patrons in Czech and English flooded my ears. Everyone else was too close. Silas wasn't close enough.

I broke away. "Is there somewhere quiet we can go?"

Silas held me, considering. I fell into the depths of his gaze as he measured my countenance, my posture. Then, like something had come to mind, a mischievous grin emerged.

"Absolutely."

Two shots had wreaked havoc on my sense of direction. I was fully disorientated as we arrived in front of a building I recognized.

"What are we doing?" I whispered, following Silas. The street we ventured down stood graveyard still, with a high perimeter wall on one side and no movement within the rows of polished apartments opposite.

"Avoiding the security cameras," he replied. And, yes, we'd given the front entrance a wide berth and clung to the darkness caused by the wall, but that didn't answer my question. "Here," he said, stopping in a spot shrouded by sidewalk trees. "Let's move quick—we'll miss it."

Miss what?

Silas generated several small shields. They smoothed into rectangular shapes, levitating against the wall. He used them as footholds, climbing up.

I placed my boot on the first one. It decompressed like a sponge but held as I rested my weight on it. "Isn't breaking and entering Anika's thing?"

"I decided to add another new experience to the list." He reached for me as I climbed to the top.

A spectacular view of inner-city Prague greeted us, the breeze tossing my blonde hair. I would have stayed longer, but every second invited unwanted attention. My heart pounded—how did Anika *do* stuff like this?—as I followed him over the other side of the wall using another set of conjured footholds.

My feet hit grass—and dammit if I didn't fall even harder for Silas.

We were standing in the garden we'd met in.

CHAPTER THIRTY-THREE

FAMILIARITY TICKLED MY SENSES AS WE KEPT TO THE SHADOWS and out of sight of the cameras facing the repurposed opera house. We passed the sprawling staircase leading from the terrace, the one I'd walked down before meeting Silas for the first time.

"You're really fulfilling our 'garden buddies' pact, aren't you?"

Silas laughed, his breath puffs of fog in the air. He led me past the rows of hedges, bleached chrome by the moonlight.

A year hadn't changed anything. There were the bushes I'd thrown my half-eaten pastry into. The ivory stone bench we'd sat on while exchanging banter about plants. Though the large window-panes in the building remained dark, it wasn't too hard to imagine champagne light cascading over the flowerbeds and the tinkle of instruments floating across the emerald grass.

He pulled me to a stop, laying a finger on my lips and tapping his ear.

A frown puckered my forehead. Above the repetitive clicks of crickets …

… the closing strums of *Giselle*, the crescendo barely audible through the thick walls of the theater next door.

I shut my eyes and sucked in a breath—one of the deepest I'd taken since my abduction, cradling his hands in mine and savoring the last of the strings. My chest swelled, but it wasn't with pain or pressure. The demarcation between the Keanna who first stood in this spot and the Keanna I was now weighed on my soul. A tear crept out from under my eyelashes. I let it fall.

"Damn," Silas murmured as the vibrations reduced to silence.

"I should have thought of this earlier. I was hoping you'd get more than that."

He's ...

"How did you know they were still playing?"

"The night we met, they had a performance running late. I took a gamble that would be the case tonight."

... perfect.

There had been so many times where I'd believed I wouldn't live to this birthday, would never again appreciate the beauty of the city or the rousing swell of an orchestra. Never stand with Silas—let alone in a garden, *our* garden—his presence grounding us in the eye of the storm consuming both of our worlds.

Words didn't seem sufficient to communicate how I felt. I didn't bother trying.

Like two magnets, we came together. I sank back into the embrace of his lips and arms, hoping he could feel my gratitude for his thoughtfulness, for just—*him*. For trying to make my birthday special with the few means he had. For the incredible irony that the darkness of the last few months had paved the way to how I felt now, standing on my tiptoes, pulling him closer.

Silas walked us until the vine-covered wall met my back. He deepened the kiss, his wide shoulders forming a canopy and blocking out the light from the moon. I tuned out the sirens and purr of traffic beyond, letting his heady, spicy scent and body cradle me as I angled myself into him.

Two strong hands secured my hips, lifting me. My beast purred with delight. Leaves crunched against my leather jacket as my legs found their place around his waist; it was like being back on the bed, and with it, familiar urgency returned. My arms circled his neck. I squeezed my thighs to pull him closer. The firm planes of his torso pinned me against the wall and his tongue moved against mine, relentless. With each stroke, my breath turned shallow, and heaviness built in my lower abdomen. His hardness pressed against my jeans, which in turn pressed against—

Ohh.

I tore my lips from his, releasing a hiss that shuddered through me. Spurred on, Silas molded his pelvis against mine, moving in an intoxicating rhythm. His shifting movements tightened a cord that formed a direct line from my abdomen to my center as his tongue grazed the sensitive spot behind my ear.

"You have no idea how much I've been wanting to do that again." His hot breath laced my skin and he shifted his hips again, eliciting another sharp inhale. "Can I touch you, Keeks?"

I'd deny him nothing right now. I nodded, clawing at him. I needed—I needed—

Carefully, he lowered me to standing and continued his assault on my senses, dragging his lips over my neck and slipping a hand between us. The pad of his thumb pushed against the seam of my jeans, rubbing up and down. A moan released from deep in my chest as I scrabbled at the valley of his back, sinking my fingers into the flesh of his backside, moving to touch him through the constrictive layer of his jeans. His breath caught, body tensing.

We balanced on a precipice. The cord within tightened to almost unbearable levels. I didn't want him to stop. I'd go insane if he stopped.

His calloused palm delved under my sweater, passing over my sports bra and teasing the peaks of my nipples. I bit my bottom lip, clamping down on another moan. It felt incredible. He did it again, nudging the hard plastic of Zeina's phone—then paused, his brow creasing.

Lust whipped my thoughts, wicked, impatient. "It's okay." I kissed him and moved my palm against him in a similar rhythm to what he'd done for me. I didn't want to think about my father and my rescue, nor the repercussions of tonight's events. Regardless of what it cost me later, I wanted to stay suspended in this fragment with Silas. I might not get another chance to. "It's okay," I repeated. "I'll explain it later. *Please don't stop.*"

He relaxed at my choked plea, groaning into my touch. Lips

tormented the curve of my neck, his fingers working me into a frenzy I couldn't come back from. My beast urged me on. I arched against Silas, his name a breathless benediction.

"Tell me, Keeks," he murmured. "Tell me what you want."

Words proved difficult. What *did* I want? I wanted him. I wanted this. I wanted these stolen midnight hours, hidden within Prague, to be something of our own. I wanted to know what coming together with Silas would feel like.

Please let me have this, I pleaded to my beast.

"I want you," I choked out. "I want this with you."

His chest heaved against mine. "Are you sure?"

Trepidation surged like an undercurrent, but excitement overwhelmed it. I bunched up his shirt, exploring the expanse of skin and shifting muscle beneath. He felt *magnificent*.

"Keanna?"

"I'm sure. Do you …?"

A curdle of fear broke the lust. What if *he* didn't? But his kiss turned claiming, consuming. "Yes. Absolutely." His teeth tugged on my bottom lip. "I've wanted you since we met. Never doubt that. But I don't have anything on me."

It clicked what he was referring to. "I'm on birth control." That damned rod in my arm, finally delivering on the benefits. "Please, Silas."

His groan vibrated against my neck as his lips carved a path south. He sank to his knees, his hands trailing down my legs. At my nod, he pulled my boots off, along with my socks, before pausing at the waistband of my jeans. Silas peered up at me, the moonlight washing his dark features a shade of purple. His gaze roamed, steady, taking me in. My hair would be sitting wilder than ever. Did I have soot on my face? I smelt of fire and sweat and—

Silas undid the button and zip, his thumbs smoothing over the skin underneath as he peeled my jeans off. I wanted to cover my thighs, conceal them somehow, but inhaled at the look in his eyes. The way his fingers hooked around my underwear, the way he slowly drew them down, placing kisses to the inside of my knees, suppressed the insecurities that rose. Heat fused in the pit of my belly. It took everything to stay still at the play of his lips rising higher and higher. My hands went to the soft curls of his hair, tightening my grip. A sigh collided with a shiver.

Casting around a glance, Silas sat on the ground, his back against the stone bench. I straddled him within the protective circle of his arms, bare from the waist down and more naked than I'd ever been with another person. He shrugged off his jacket and wrapped it around my hips to keep me warm—then clutched me tighter, holding my gaze.

"You're beautiful, Keeks," he whispered.

It felt like a fist had squeezed my heart. I smoothed my hands across the goosebumps on his bare arms, weaving them into the hair at the base of his neck.

"So are you," I replied. I wanted to say more, but again, I couldn't find the words.

One kiss, then two, became a persistent, pulsing rhythm of demanding lips and shifting hips. His fingers moved down, gently parting me. One slipped inside. I'd become wet, heated, and electricity strung my body tight as his thumb danced over where I was most sensitive, his tongue moving within my mouth in time with his hand below. I moaned, jerking, as he slipped another finger inside. If I hadn't been clutching his hair, I would have melted.

My panting breaths were the only thing I could hear above the muffled chatter of departing patrons from the ballet performance and their exiting vehicles. I rode his fingers, alight, surging, seeking an end that felt inches from reach. It was almost too much.

Pressure built. I swallowed. *Please,* I whispered to my beast. I mentally reinforced her cage walls, leashing her down.

Was the cage strong enough? Was I?

"Hold on," I whispered, nearly whimpering as his fingers drew away. "How quickly can you generate a shield?"

Silas searched my expression. "Seconds," he replied. "Less, if I'm prepared."

My heart hammered. "My beast. I … when we were last this close, it felt like I was going to scream. I'm worried I … I mean, I've never done this before, I don't know what to expect …"

Stop talking, Keanna. No doubt he could already tell from the clumsy, untutored way I'd grabbed at him against the wall. Though he didn't look surprised, his features softened.

"This is enough," he reassured me. "Being like this is enough. We don't need to go further."

His offer cemented my determination to continue. "I want to. I think I've got a handle on her, but just in case …"

"I trust you."

"But I don't know if *I* can trust me," I pleaded. "Promise if I lose control, you'll use your shield to protect yourself. I can't hurt you, Silas."

Time crawled as he gazed into my eyes. What was he looking for? Finally, he cupped my neck.

"We'll go at your pace, Keeks." He pressed a kiss onto the curve of my chin. "We can wait if it means making sure you feel comfortable."

Warmth enveloped my heart. He wasn't just saying this. I knew he meant it.

Just like I knew—without a doubt—that I'd fallen for him. I couldn't imagine life without him in it. I'd walk away from this night irrevocably changed.

"I'm ready." My words almost matched Silas's for their huskiness.

His fingers teased me while I undid his belt. His thumb passed over me, again and again. I'd combust soon for *sure.*

I worked his jeans down, freeing him. He straightened his spine against the bench, hissing at my tentative, then firm, touches. If I'd thought him hard before, he became harder still underneath my hand.

I'd explore him later. I couldn't wait any longer.

"Stay on top." Silas positioned me so I sat poised above him. "Let's keep you in control."

I'm really doing this.

Trying to relax, I inhaled, lowering until I felt the tip of him push inside. I sank down—

Pain sliced upwards. I gasped. His jaw hardened as he cupped mine, passing his thumb over my parted lips, working between them. I caressed it with my tongue, biting gently as I breathed through the stinging, burning, stretching sensation. My beast hated how much it hurt, but otherwise allowed me to slide down, taking him in completely.

Silas breathed in a slow, measured way that I mirrored. His hands trembled, the rattle of his exhales hinting at the effort it was taking to keep himself still. He rained kisses over my cheeks and the exposed parts of my neck around my collar until the pain lessened. Until I could focus on him inside me, underneath me, his flecked brown eyes watching the changing landscape of my expressions and making sure I was alright. Looking at me like he couldn't look away. It halted the self-consciousness that bubbled, the automatic fear I was doing something wrong or taking too long.

"You're doing so good, baby. You're amazing."

His affirmation joined the heat lancing my abdomen. Pain transitioned to pleasure as I moved my hips, our limbs entwining further. The rough material of his jeans rubbed the backs of my thighs. Grass slid underneath my knees. His soft hair tickled my fingers.

Silas continued to whisper encouragement while cradling my face, the safety net of his hands ready to catch us both. Thumbs brushed my cheeks, my lips. He studied me just as I studied him. The constellation of moonlight-bleached freckles under his eye entranced me, as did the minute changes in the set of his jaw. His breath became mine as our jagged gasps filled the garden. My beast remained a contained—but enthusiastic—spectator. She no longer lurched at my throat and stayed where she was, waiting for my summons.

She doesn't want to hurt him, either.

With this realization, I relinquished the tight hold I had on her. Checked with every step back she wasn't about to take advantage of her freedom.

She didn't fight. Didn't even move.

My entire focus reduced to *him*: his scent, the firmness of his chest. The pressure of his hands as he guided me. His kisses marked me, tormented me, cherished me. These past weeks Silas had woven a shield around my heart. Protecting me. Protecting us both. He'd become my safe haven, my fortress.

The tightening sensation rose higher and higher. With a staying motion at my beast, I ignited from within, shattering around him and muffling my cries against his shoulder. He released a gravelly moan that tightened my abdomen all over again, grabbing my hips and driving up into me. Somehow, this prolonged the pleasure soaring through my body. My pulse thundered. He gave a final hard thrust and stilled, his forehead finding the crook of my neck as he loosened a groan.

I held him tight as he exhaled, long and slow. I'd never felt this light. Vulnerable. Connected. Our breaths steadied, cheek to cheek, aftershocks rolling under my skin.

And I'd stayed in control.

Awareness of my surroundings returned in degrees. The persistent percussion of traffic beyond the wall. The smell of cut grass and woodsmoke. The cool breeze playing through the trees.

"Are you okay?" Silas whispered, kissing my forehead.

Okay? I was amazing. My chest felt like it was about to burst—in the best way. I understood why people sacrificed everything for *this*. What the songs and movies and books meant.

I love him.

"I wish we could stay here," I replied.

The corner of his mouth tugged up wickedly. "I hear there's beds back at the estate."

I shivered, both from the cold and the thought of being with him inside the cocoon of bedsheets. Navigating every inch of his body. Exploring how to make him moan like that again ...

"My appreciation for the passageway behind our rooms just increased tenfold." I pressed lazy kisses to his lips. Doing this again and again … oh, I wanted to. So much. I tightened around him. He gave a noise of agreement, hardening again inside of me—

Soreness blossomed between my legs. I winced.

Silas caught it, giving a soft smile and kissing my palm. "We should go."

Another moment, slipping through our fingers like sand. I wanted to hold Silas forever, but he was right. Our absence wouldn't be missed for long. We had to find a way to reconnect with Arwood and the team.

I giggled at my jelly legs as we stood. I was a glorious mess: grass punctured my knees. Moisture coated the inside of my thighs. Sweat pooled under my sweater. The slight soreness became a radiating dull ache.

And I didn't care.

Silas helped me dress, then held my hand as we returned to the wall we'd snuck over … but not before drawing out one final, languid kiss. I clambered up the footholds in a sated, lovestruck bliss—

My beast keened in warning. I halted Silas at the top of the wall.

A few feet away, leaning against a sidewalk tree, stood Steadman with his arms folded. The moonlight cut across his face, illuminating murderous angles.

Silas went very still. So did I.

How long had Steadman been standing there?

I dropped Silas's hand, even though the damage was already more than done.

Steadman strode for the parked car on the other side of the street, not even waiting to see if we would follow.

Icy trepidation replaced the lingering heat in my chest, curdling my stomach into queasiness. It was hard to pinpoint what made me sicker: that Steadman had seen us mussed, holding hands and *together*, or the repercussions for him finding us here, so far from the warehouse. Immediately, my mind went to Silas's family, Arwood's blackmail, and the Sect. We'd jeopardized our standing with all three.

In my wanting, *I'd* jeopardized all three.

I descended unsteadily. The streetlights bathed Steadman in yellow as he thumbed a quick message on his phone.

"You two have an interesting interpretation of 'get to safety,'" he said, tone dripping in condemnation. From the neck down he was filthy, blood-spattered in places, his bullet-resistant vest singed. Only his face was wiped clean. He'd escaped. Had he managed to save his team? I knew better than to ask.

"We didn't know where else to go. We had no way of contacting anyone …" I trailed off, my thoughts sluggish from the whiplash of emotion, my excuses pitiful. I quit before I dug a hole I couldn't come out of. "How did you find us?"

Steadman gave me a look that inferred I was too stupid to live. "We track our assets, *banshee*." He gestured to my collar, then turned to Silas. "And you. Your compliance should have been warranted. I have half a mind to make a call."

No!

"I—"

"It's not his fault," I jumped in. "It's my birthday, and I haven't been out in Prague yet." Words fell out of my mouth, instinct hijacking my tongue. "I *made* him take me here."

Steadman's eyes narrowed. "His inability to keep his dick to himself *is* his fault. But"—he ignored Silas as he went to speak again—"I honestly don't give a shit. It's my job to get you both back. Come."

The driver sat alone inside the vehicle. Matej wouldn't join us ever again.

"I kept telling Arwood he couldn't put two kids together and expect them not to fuck around." Steadman opened the door. "Get in, and if either of you so much as breathes wrong, the other will die. Got it?"

We got in.

CHAPTER THIRTY-FOUR

FOUR GUARDS HAD MADE IT OUT OF THE WAREHOUSE. *Four.* Steadman had managed to save two before the roof caved in. The other two had escaped while Silas and I made a run for it. As we approached Arwood's manor, one died in the hospital from her injuries, bringing that measly number down to three. Steadman's anger was so electric it practically rolled off his shoulders as he hung up the phone. He acknowledged the security at the gates, his icy blue gaze meeting mine in the sun visor vanity mirror.

Honestly? I'd be furious with me too. I'd repaid him saving me with chasing me all over Prague when he should have been taking care of his team. My father would have yelled until he knew I was sorry. I almost wished Steadman would yell too. Anything was better than the thick tension of waiting for him to expose me and Silas.

Our car doors slammed. Steadman dismissed us. I wavered at the foot of the stairs, glancing between Silas and Steadman's retreating figure. Behind us, Arwood's team arrived.

I could go upstairs and sit in an anxious pit of doom for the bomb to drop. The urge to shove my head in the sand was strong. The need to protect Silas—and myself—was stronger. Placing my fate with James Steadman didn't sound appealing to me or my beast.

So I followed him, giving a parting nod to Silas in what I hoped he interpreted as *I'll find you later.*

I didn't have to look far for Steadman; he'd chosen a room based on the criteria of 'immediately available liquor'. He was gulping mouthfuls of whiskey like it was water, sweat tracking lines down his sooty neck. A warning finger rose in my direction as he poured another glass and drank again.

As soon as his finger dropped, I spoke. "We wouldn't have found Johan tonight without my information."

Steadman exhaled, no doubt soothing the burn coating his throat. "Your point, banshee. Make it."

"The benefits of keeping me around far outweigh the negatives." At this, Steadman shrugged off his singed padded vest and barked a laugh. It wasn't an amused one. It was more, *is this chick for real?* I didn't let it stop me. "Johan tried to take me again."

"Good for him." He tossed his vest onto the seat. "I'm considering holding you over the gates by your hair until he takes you."

Weeks ago, this threat would have sent chills up my spine. Today, it barely flickered my pulse; if he meant it, he'd have done it already. "Use me to draw him out again. If he's tried twice, he'll try a third time."

He still wouldn't look at me, peeling off his jacket. His face twisted as melted fabric stuck to the black long-sleeved thermal he wore underneath. I cut my gaze away from the thin material stretching across his upper body, forcing memories of the library from my mind before they took hold.

"Send someone out. Have them offer to swap me for information on who is paying him to mess with Arwood," I said.

Steadman closed his eyes and sat on the arm of the couch like he was beyond over what I was saying.

"And then your team can—"

"Stopping you right there." He punctuated his words by jamming the rim of the glass against the bridge of his nose. "I'm sick of losing my people, so whatever plan you're cooking up won't include them."

I pursed my lips, quelling my protest to let me speak. My beast tugged the back of my shirt, urging me to observe the rounding of his posture, how he held the glass in a death grip. I didn't pretend to understand Steadman, but the frost cleared momentarily, allowing a glimpse behind his mask. Tonight had unsettled him more than any of the others.

Seeing him like this made me want to comfort him. I stayed put, burying that urge. Sympathy was a dangerous, slippery slope when it came to Steadman.

"Then use me as bait," I said, softening my tone. "I'll stand outside those gates and yell out for him if I have to."

"Didn't realize you had a death wish."

"No, this is me warning you to think before you go to Arwood and tell him what you thought you saw." I hated how I sounded, but fear for Silas obliterated any moral codes I subscribed to. "I'm the best chance of Arwood getting what he wants. If he turns me over to the Sect, you'll be back where you started, and your team will have died for nothing."

The look Steadman shot me was incredulous. I'd never seen him so animated. "'*What I thought I saw?*' You can fuck right off with that gaslighting bullshit," he spat. "And don't insult the memory of my team by pretending you care about them."

"I *do* care. I know you're upset—"

"Don't patronize me—"

"—but I really am sorry about tonight. Silas had nothing to do with my choice to run off." He drank again, refusing eye contact. "We saw the police were coming, and I was so overwhelmed with what happened I needed the distraction. It meant nothing, and neither does Silas."

The lie seared my tongue. The room fell silent while I seesawed between pleading my case further, or giving up and letting Steadman take the wheel of my fate. I had a bad feeling I'd made everything worse.

Then Steadman said, "Do you know what burnt flesh smells like?"

A question like this wouldn't lead anywhere good. "No."

"Pray you never learn. I had to choose who to leave behind

tonight because I couldn't carry two people at the same time. I have no room for your excuses."

There it was again: that urge to comfort him. I *was* sorry about the guards, but seeing Silas's family in a cage gave painful perspective. I clung to it. "You and Arwood started this. Whoever hired Johan, they have it in for *you*. You stole *me*. You're going on about my decisions, but if you keep choosing Arwood, you choose what happened tonight."

Steadman placed his empty glass beside the canister. "The same thing that drove you in here is the same reason I don't leave Arwood."

I realized what he meant: my loyalty to Silas, and willingness to protect him. Steadman hadn't bought what I'd said for a second.

"You're lecturing me on choices, but you've forgotten two things: your abilities have repercussions, regardless of intent. And," he crossed his arms, staring down his nose at me, "you're useful, but not irreplaceable. My advice? Don't forget who you work for, and what you're trying to achieve. That should be your sole focus. Think Silas will want much to do with you once he learns what you did to Gabriel?"

Gabriel? As in Silas's older brother? For a moment, I feared he'd been one of the faceless men I'd killed when we'd interrogated Ferko in the nightclub, or one of the thieves in the plastic room, but Silas had been with me both times. He would have found a way to protect his brother.

Still, Steadman's tone gave the impression of a gavel about to slam down.

I swallowed. "I've never met Gabriel."

"You came here with him."

I frowned. Surely, I would have remembered if I'd met—

Wait. No.

No.

Brown curls. His similar gait. That familiar smile.

Ri. *Ri.* Gabriel. He'd smirked as he'd said his name. Like it was a nickname—

I sucked in a breath, going hot, then cold.

Ri. How hadn't I put it together earlier? The man who'd comforted me during my abduction. The man who—holy hell, he'd even *looked* like Silas. An older, stockier version, but—

"What's going on here?"

Arwood stood by the door.

"Debriefing," I choked out, my eyes stinging.

Arwood concentrated on Steadman. If I didn't know any better, I'd say the faint crease between his eyebrows was concern for his right-hand man.

"You're excused, Miss Backhus," Arwood said.

I barely heard him.

His name was Gabriel.

Numb, I trailed out of the room. As I rounded the corner, Arwood touched Steadman's shoulder, pouring another drink for him and murmuring a low, "Where's Matej?"

Monsters. Both of them.

I ascended the stairs slowly, my boots scuffing the carpet.

Gabriel.

Silas's beloved older brother. The brother he'd feared was dead.

He *was* dead.

I'd been the one to kill him.

༄

I made it to my room before the tears came. Big, choking tears that stole my breath. My mouth hung open on a silent scream.

My beast keened inside as I doubled over. Zeina's phone pushed against my chest. With a sob, I pulled it out and threw it on the bed.

Silas would never forgive me. It didn't matter that I hadn't wanted to kill Gabriel. How could I expect him to view his brother's death any differently because I'd tried not to cause it? As Steadman had said: repercussions, regardless of intent.

Tonight, Silas had treated me with reverence, looked at me like I was who he'd been waiting for. I'd recognized it, feeling the same.

He'd had sex with his brother's killer, and he hadn't known it.

The collar around my neck suffocated me. I wanted to scream, *but that was what had gotten me into this mess in the first place.* I sank beside the bed and grabbed a pillow, jamming my face into it. How had my world built to an ecstatic high, only to break so quickly?

I cried until my voice grew hoarse, until I gasped for air. Until the phone lit up on the bed. I pressed the side button as I had routinely done since seeing Zeina, expecting an empty screen.

Except there were two messages.

I read both in disbelief. One sent hours ago:

5am. Be ready in your room.

And one sent seconds ago:

Confirm.

5am was mere *hours* away. Dread threatened to pull me under, but habit had me thumbing a response of 'confirmed' to Zeina. I tried not to panic.

Send a photo so I know it's you. Hold up three fingers.

Great. I took a photo and sent it. The mess I felt inside was reflected in my bloodshot eyes and tear-streaked, blotchy skin. Zeina, ruthlessly efficient as always, didn't comment.

Stay where you are.

I waited for another message, but nothing came. My lips trembled as I succumbed to a fresh wave of tears, heaviness leaching from my stomach to the rest of my body.

I'd had five days left! 'By the end of the week,' she'd said.

But even in my panic, I knew I'd assumed what I'd wanted to believe. Zeina's message made me want to throw myself on the ground, hug the furniture, and kick my legs like a child at a playground. I couldn't go. I needed more *time.* I had things to do, people to find, and … I couldn't leave Silas. Not after what I'd just learned about Gabriel.

Zeina's message sat there, stark. Like it or not, in two hours, the cavalry would come for my rescue.

I'd never wanted anything less.

CHAPTER THIRTY-FIVE

"K EANNA?" S ILAS WHISPERED, HIS FACE PALING AT THE expression on my own. He let me into his room, closing the passage door. "What happened?"

What *hadn't* happened? Despair had stolen precious time, the hour ticking over forcing me into action.

"Steadman hasn't said anything," I assured him. *Yet.*

It was a sheer testament to my emotional turmoil that I took in the expanse of his bare defined torso and worn gray sweatpants with only the smallest of pulse elevations, especially after all we'd shared. The black leather cords around his neck contrasted against his tanned skin, muscles shifting as he wiped my tears. When more appeared, he led me to the couch, kicking the ottoman to the side and pulling me onto his lap. The heat of his bare shoulder was a siren call for my cheek; the scent of the soap he'd used clung to him.

His bedsheets were twisted like the damp ends of his hair. Books and clothes scattered every surface. When I'd last been in his room, I'd danced. Drunk. Wondered what it would be like to kiss him. Fearful of my feelings, worried at their intensity, presuming a lack of reciprocity.

I hadn't had nearly long enough with this intimate, rumpled version of Silas. Time was stealing him from me.

He drew away the hair stuck to my wet cheeks. "Please tell me what's wrong, Keeks."

Zeina had ordered me to stay put, but I couldn't *not* tell him. Leaving without an explanation wasn't an option. Words falling in a rush, I told him how Zeina had found me in the bathroom when we'd visited his family.

Silas's eyebrows crept higher and higher up his forehead. As I finished explaining the situation he sank against the couch, running a hand through his hair, smoothing his fingers across his mouth. He tightened his grip on my waist. "That's—that's terrific." His tone was a pitch higher than usual.

"Is it? Because I don't agree with you."

"You've been hoping for this."

"That was before our deal with Arwood. Before …" I trailed off, hoping he understood what I was getting at. Before *us*. Before the garden. Before I met his mother and sister. I put my hand on his chest, my fingers intertwining with the white jade amulet hanging there, reveling in the play of warm skin and taut muscle beneath my palm. "Come with me."

Hope rose on his face, quickly smothered. "I can't." He nudged his ring around and around. "I have to free my family first."

"We can do that together." I stilled his agitated movements, bringing his hand between both of mine. "My father will help us. I promise."

His brown eyes were soft. Too soft. "You can't promise that, you know you can't. And you know what'll happen if I escape."

I did, but I shook my head anyway, my heart racing. "I can't leave you. I won't."

Silas ducked his head, bringing me closer. His tone changed again. Gentler, more urgent. "Yes, you will. This place is killing you. It's killing *me*." He ignored my shaking head and tightening grip, pressing on. "The amulets are useless without your wail. I feel them trigger, even when I'm not there to see it. It'll be one less thing draining me." The dark smudges beneath his eyes were more pronounced than ever. A constant reminder of his weakened state, what my ability did to him every single day. My vision blurred as he continued. "It'll be safer for the both of us if you leave while you can."

He wasn't supposed to say this. I'd fantasized that he'd agree, and we'd escape together. Always together. I needed time to tell him about Gabriel, then more time still to earn his forgiveness and try and win him back. "Silas—"

"Please. You might not get another chance. Your father'll keep you safe. You can forget this place and start to heal."

"I don't want to forget, and I don't care about healing. I care about *you*. I can't stand what they're doing to you here." Tears plummeted. I made no move to wipe them, forcing words through my swollen throat. "I can't leave knowing you'll be subjected to that."

Silas's fingers brushed languidly over my lips, my chin, as if memorizing my face.

Like he'd given up.

He was saying goodbye.

"They own me, but … you have my heart, Keanna." I went still as he cupped my cheeks. "You're the north my compass points to. Always."

I cried harder. It wasn't fair I could escape this. He deserved freedom, too. He deserved his family safe, and autonomy over his body. *Be careful what you wish for.* In a few short weeks, this boy, man—*Silas*—had become everything to me.

And I hadn't told him about Gabriel. I needed to. But if I told him, he'd want to take those beautiful words back.

"You have to go," Silas whispered. "Steadman saw us. I can handle anything they do to me, but nothing else matters if you or my family are threatened." He pulled me closer, his hands splaying over my hips. I cradled his neck, pleading silently as the resolve in his gaze grew stronger. "If you leave, we have a chance. If you stay, we'll both end up dead. You know this."

"This is so unfair."

"Go with Zeina." He pressed a fleeting kiss to my brow, bringing our foreheads together. I breathed him in, counting the seconds. The muscles in his jaw tensed as if he was contemplating his next words. "I knew you'd be important to me when I found you on the window seat. I knew I was falling for you at the casino. And I knew I loved you on that bridge tonight. And because I love you," he whispered, "I need you home and safe."

How could he say that and expect me to walk away?

I tightened my grip on him, protectiveness washing through me. Inside, my beast rejoiced, but my stomach hardened, a reminder not to get caught up in elation. He couldn't love me, because he didn't know the truth. "But I may never see you again," I murmured.

"You have to believe we met in that garden for a reason. We'll find each other."

I love you, too. The words hung on the edge of my tongue. I couldn't release them without telling him how Gabriel died. Selfishly, I wanted to hold his declarations close. Keep it and this moment pure. But what if I truly never saw him again? He deserved to know, even if it destroyed the fragile thread between us.

"Silas, there's something else."

His eyes darted to the clock on his bedside table. "Come on." We rose from the couch. He pulled on the sweater hanging from the edge of his bed. "Let's get you to your room. You don't have long, do you? Tell me there."

I let him drag me, because he was right.

Once returned, doors locked securely, Silas asked, "What is it?"

He looked at me with such trust. Such ... *love.* I squeezed his hands, trying to draw it out. I couldn't leave him. I couldn't tell him.

I had to.

"I found out what happened to Gabriel."

His eyes widened. I released him, staring at the carpet.

"The day I was abducted, I met a wonderful and kind man named Ri. They put *this* on," I plucked at my collar, "and put us in a room together and ..." I broke off, the air thickening between us. Ri's face haunted me. I could never undo what I'd stolen that day. "I couldn't—I tried not to, but ..."

Silas stepped back, lips parting. He took a shuddering breath and half-turned, angling himself away from me.

"I'm so sorry, Silas."

He stared into the corner of the room, his chest the only movement in his otherwise frozen body.

When I couldn't stand the aching silence any longer, I bleated, "Please say something."

Silas laced his fingers around the back of his neck, bowing his head. "I need—I need a second."

He took another step toward the window, another step away from me. I felt every inch of our separation; my body yearned to close the gap. My beast urged me to latch on to him, tell him I loved him, force him to reconcile with what I'd said.

My beast didn't understand how unfair that would be.

When Silas spoke, it sounded like water running over the edge of a knife. "How long have you known?"

"Tonight. Steadman just told me."

He may as well have been in a different room for the distance now between us. It was what I deserved—but that didn't make it hurt any less. A heaviness grew in my chest, making it hard to breathe.

The window Silas stood next to splintered, crashing inwards. I yelped as a figure in a black jumpsuit landed on the broken glass.

My rescue had arrived.

CHAPTER THIRTY-SIX

"**M**OVE." Zeina didn't waste time asking who Silas was or why he was there. Once he stood aside, she brandished a harness. "Here."

I told you no one was to know, she admonished via her sharply raised brow. I stepped my jean-clad legs through the holes and she tightened the straps around my waist.

Panic surged as she placed her hand on the small of my back, pushing me toward the open window. I grabbed her forearm. "Wait, Zeina—"

An explosion rattled the picture frames on the walls.

"Was that a—"

"Move, Keanna. That's our cue."

"Wait, I can't—"

Silas stepped forward, addressing Zeina. "Where's your exit?"

"I'm not telling you anything," she shot back.

"You can trust him," I said, trying to catch his eyes. He was focusing on anything in the room but me. If it weren't for Zeina, I'd have run to him, tried to reach him somehow. "I promise. Tell him."

Zeina pursed her lips. "West."

"I'll say I saw you head south," he said.

"Silas," I pleaded.

He paused at the threshold, the pain within his gaze shuttering as it landed on me. Swallowing, he murmured, "Go, Keanna." Then he was gone.

The slamming of the door tore my heart like paper, and the sound I released from my lungs barely sounded human.

Zeina gave my harness a sharp tug. "Keanna! Focus, please. Have you got everything you need?"

No. He'd just run through the door. And away from me.

She pushed me a final time. "Let's go."

◦∽◦

We rappelled down the side of the building, our ropes supported by black-clad figures on the roof of the mansion. Upon landing we ran, gravel spraying, for the estate boundary. More figures hoisted us up the wall. A familiar russet beard came into view.

Dobromil extended his hand.

I glared at it. For some reason, betrayal bubbled instead of validation.

"West corner, huh?" I jabbed, letting him pull me up. "You don't look like a levitating Romeo to me."

"Over the wall, miss," he said, reconnecting my harness for descent. Vehicles waited for us on the other side, interior lights on and doors wide open.

The ground shook with another explosion. Above the mansion roof, an orange cloud flared. Arwood's guards swarmed toward the commotion. If I wasn't mistaken, my rescue had just blown up the office building with the plastic-lined interrogation room. Any pleasure at this realization died as the figure beside me removed his ski mask, bronze waves springing free.

"Yee-haw, motherfuckers," Johan said with relish, eyeing the carnage.

Gasping, I darted back and nearly slipped. Zeina steadied me as the ground shook again.

"Move," she urged.

I gaped at Johan as he lowered me and Dobromil down the other side, my brain struggling to catch up with what I was seeing.

Once we landed on the grass, Zeina pushed my hair back,

shoving spongy material between my collar and my neck. Dobromil did the same in front of my throat. I recoiled from his touch, poking the material. It sank underneath my fingers. Rubber?

"Hold her hair up," Zeina instructed. "Keanna, I need you to stay very still."

She secured clasps on my collar. A winding, whirring sound turned into a grinding screech. I held my breath as the skin above the rubber insulation heated. The whirring stopped. Zeina unlatched the clasps. "We can't remove your collar tonight," she said, taking the rubber layer. "But that should fry the tracker."

"I'll try and secure the master key." Dobromil checked his watch. "Time to go."

Johan gave a thumbs up, his grin widening as I glared at him. "Good thing chokers never go out of style."

We marched to the Jeep. Zeina sat next to me, slamming the door. Johan hopped into the front passenger seat and slapped the driver on the shoulder with frat-boy cheer. As we picked up speed, the obnoxious seatbelt warning dinged inside the car.

Johan nodded to my lap, tugging on the bolt in his earlobe. "Safety first. Would be a shame to perish in a car accident, yeah?"

I set my jaw and buckled up, pivoting to Zeina. "What is Johan doing here?"

"Your father hired me," Johan answered instead. "Told you I'm in demand."

"That's unfortunate, because this man nearly killed me tonight. *And* attacked me a few weeks ago."

Zeina's head whipped toward him, but Johan waved a hand. "Not at all. I was trying to get you out. *You* ran away."

"I wonder why. You were the one shooting fireballs, remember?"

Johan skipped the song playing, settling on a country tune. "Not at you. At the uptight fucker working for Arwood."

Too late, I realized he was right. The tattooed *ferox* leaving me alone now made sense. "Why were you trying to start a war?"

"Destabilizes operations quicker than you think. Your father's idea. Some solid boomer genius."

Surely I'd heard him wrong—but a glance at Zeina confirmed his words. She looked straight ahead, her lips in a grim line.

"My *father's* the one paying you? This whole time?"

"How do you guys say it? Spot on, *mate*. Ah!" He turned up the volume. "I love this part." He clicked along to the twanging guitar.

"Turn that damned shit off," Zeina snapped.

Johan shushed her playfully.

"But …" We were speeding along the dirt road, the forest on either side of the Jeep a dark blur illuminated by the headlights. "Those ambushes killed people," I said. "Civilians."

"Necessary collateral damage. Besides, I've seen what you can do." I regarded Johan warily; a smirk twisted his profile. "You shouldn't throw stones."

I didn't want to think anymore. I jammed my eyes shut until we slowed, then stopped, gravel crunching beneath the wheels. The purple pre-dawn sky highlighted the familiar outline of our estate.

Johan threw me a saccharine smile. "Home sweet home, baby girl."

♋

I'd imagined reuniting with my father constantly since my abduction. It had become my coping mechanism, believing each passing day drew this closer.

Just as I'd pictured, he stood on our front steps dressed in navy slacks and a cream sweater. His face split into a smug grin as the car pulled to a stop.

My answering smile was generated from obligation rather than joy. I'd kept correcting my posture in the car, trying to dissolve the tension from my upper body. My stomach hurt. Everything mirrored my expectations … except for how I felt.

The rays of my father's satisfaction cascaded over me as I approached. For a moment, the uncertainty lacing my limbs gave way to comfort as his arms came around my waist. The familiarity of his kiss on my temple and the rumbling timbre of his voice calmed the racing thoughts in my head. Something released inside my chest. I sighed, sinking into him.

After a small eternity, we pulled back. He smoothed down my hair over and over in a way that told me it sat wild, then wiped my streaming tears.

"You're home, darling," he said, his voice low and soothing. "You're safe. You're okay."

The lump in my throat choked off any possible response. I clutched his hand while Johan gave my father the rundown of our escape. Surreal, when just hours ago I'd watched him verbally spar with Steadman. I hated souring my homecoming with questions, but all the things I wanted to say built up, ready to unleash at first opportunity.

When Johan paused, I dove in. "Dad? I need to talk to you."

"Of course," my father said, his hand running over my hair again. "We have so much to catch up on. I've organized a beautiful brunch later to celebrate you being home."

"Can we go somewhere private? Please?"

A devilish smile emerged on Johan's face as he passed his tongue behind his bottom lip. I suppressed the urge to shove him so he'd fall backwards down the stairs—but I considered it for several seconds longer than the old Keanna would have.

"Oh." My father glanced between me and the amused *ferox*. "Well. I am needed to finalize matters. And you must be so exhausted."

"I can wait for you."

"Alright, darling. I'll come by as soon as I can." He led me toward the front door.

"But this is important—"

"Hush, Keanna."

He'd practically forced me inside. Was he trying to get me away from Johan for my safety, or because he didn't want me around to listen? I clung to him. "Please tell me you're not going to continue dealing with this man!"

Johan threw a *can you believe this?* look at the men gathering beside him. Like I was a child refusing to be put to bed, and they were waiting for me to be dealt with so the 'grown-ups' could chat. It boiled my blood.

"Darling—"

"He's *dangerous,* he—"

"That's *enough.*" He plucked his arms out of my grip. "Zeina."

"Dad—"

"Shh," Zeina hissed into my ear. "Pick your terrain, Keanna. Regroup when he's willing to listen."

My father shut the front door, his face like stone. *What's happening?*

"What if Johan does something to him out there, Zee?"

"He and your father have an understanding, Keanna. You'll find he's quite safe."

An understanding. Had I taken a knock to the head during my escape? It would explain why everything felt so surreal, like the blurred edges of a dream. My father had slammed the door on me figuratively—and literally. I recounted the things I'd said, how I'd behaved. Had I been unreasonable?

No. He'd pushed back against my questions as soon as I'd asked them. He hadn't even given me a chance to speak.

The residue of his anger chilled me. I shuddered, clutching myself tightly as I followed Zeina into the white and orange sanctuary of my room.

It was as I'd left it. Four-poster bed, covers pulled up tight, with rows of European pillows and cushions placed just so. Laptop on my desk beside a planner, open to the day of my abduction over a month ago. The door to my walk-in wardrobe stood ajar, revealing neat rows of clothes.

My boots—covered in ash and blood—nudged faux-fur slippers as I sat staring at my reflection in the mirror opposite: black jeans. Black jacket. Bruised from training. My hair curled wildly. Light from the bedside table cast my face into shadow.

I didn't recognize her.

This room didn't recognize her.

"Should I call for some assistance?" Zeina asked from the doorway. She was still here.

Her question sank in. "No." Even to my own ears, my response sounded unconvincing. I tried again. "I'll be okay." When Zeina didn't move, I said, "Perhaps I just need to be alone."

"I don't think that's best."

My fingers brushed over the throw, barely registering the texture. I caught myself staring at the white bedspread and blinked. "My father will be here soon?"

We'd talk. He'd have an explanation for everything. Then things would stop feeling so …

"Well, yes. As soon as he can be."

… *weird*.

"I'll wait."

She wavered, grabbing the door handle. Her pause lasted a minute, during which I went back to staring at the bedspread.

"I'm glad we got you home, Keanna," she said. "You're going to feel strange for a while, but you'll be okay. Feel what you need to feel. I'll check on you soon."

My room was a cozy sweater I'd worn every day. I'd put it on to find it had shrunk a size too small. These walls hadn't seen what I'd seen. My sanctuary didn't understand me anymore.

The knowledge my father would arrive soon encouraged me to clean up. Like wading through thick tar, I plodded into the shower. The last twelve hours laced my clothes and skin; I peeled the night away. A sob caught at the copper smudge between my legs, the ache, the scent left behind. Another sob escaped as remnants of the garden washed down the drain.

Hot water ran cold. Wet hair clung to my collar. Silk pajamas chafed like straw. I sank into bed, shivering. My beast sat silent in my chest with nothing to say.

A tight knot pushed against the base of my throat, making my head throb. I should be relieved. Comforted. *Something*. I should be laughing, dancing around my room. I was *free*. Home. No more negotiating. No more guns. No more fear.

And no more Silas.

The hours stretched without meaning. I watched the sun rise.

CHAPTER THIRTY-SEVEN

ROUTINE IS A FUNNY THING. LIKE RUTS IN THE ROAD, falling into a routine can happen without realizing it. Some routines perpetuate positive habits and set you up for success. I used to have a killer morning routine: wake up, exercise, stretch, breakfast, then study or work. Small things every day naturally became bigger things. Every book I read said the same thing, and I consumed them like vitamins for my mind.

But routines are fragile things and break easily. The new routine I'd developed with Anika was no longer accessible—or necessary.

Thoughts of Anika kernelled in my already nauseous stomach. I hadn't said goodbye. During the hours staring at the ceiling, I'd wondered how long the explosions had distracted Arwood's team. More fire, perhaps more death, closing out an already horrific night. Steadman, trembling over his whiskey, came to mind. Had anyone lost their lives so I could escape? Unfortunately, I didn't put that possibility past Johan.

Johan, who'd been working with my father all along.

The implications of this would snowball until I spoke with my father. I needed confirmation he was unaware of the truth about Johan, that his pursuit to recover me had blinded him to all else, just like it had for Arwood. Though the dregs of who I'd been quailed at making him angry again, anger of my own bubbled. I needed answers more.

Of course, that meant getting up.

Zeina knocked, interrupting my spiral. If she was surprised to find me still in bed, squinting from lack of sleep, she didn't say so.

"The wheels on the bus: are they on, or off?"

"They're on." The automatic lie left my tongue before I considered responding otherwise.

"Your father said he came by earlier, but you were asleep."

I let her words pass without comment. Had I slipped off to sleep after all? My crusty, burning eyes suggested otherwise.

"Are you ready to join him for brunch? He's been caught up on a call, otherwise he'd ask you himself," she said. "Do … you need help getting ready?"

Her tone sounded nurturing, almost maternal. It contrasted against the sharp suit she wore, her no-nonsense bun. Soft from Zeina was unusual, just another thing knocking my grasp of reality.

I clutched the covers closer. "I'm alright, Zee. You don't need to stick around, I'm sure you have a million things to do."

"I'm staying here." Her voice gave way, turning hard again. "I lost you on my watch."

Oh. *Oh.* "I was abducted," I assured her. "*After* Arwood captured you. That's not your fault."

"That's irrelevant."

Somehow, I pulled myself from the bed, and somehow, I got dressed, gravitating toward a pair of lounge pants instead of my usual pretty dress or structured two-piece set. My head pounded. My body was sore, muscles strung tight. What day was it, anyway?

Zeina stood over me like a sentinel. She wasn't a master at hair, she told me with a smirk, but she could braid thanks to having two sisters back in Jordan. Her gentle fingers tamed the snarls out of my hair, brushing my collar more than once. "I'll get this off you as soon as I can."

I picked absently at one of my cuticles until it bled, crimson mixing with the now-ruined dark polish manicure Anika had given me last week.

"That boy meant a lot to you, didn't he?"

They own me, but you have my heart.

I met Zeina's eyes in the mirror as tears pricked my own. The mention of Silas lanced my chest. Why had I told him about Gabriel? His remote expression when he'd told me to leave overrode everything else we'd shared.

The sweetness between us turning sour would have been too much to bear on top of everything else at Arwood's estate. I couldn't have gone back to pretending he didn't exist. It was better I'd left.

It was better I was here.

"It doesn't matter," I whispered. "He doesn't feel the same."

Not anymore.

"That's not what it looked like to me. Something big happened with him, didn't it?"

I'd given him *everything*. Including my heart. And the means to break it. I sniffed in reflex, giving myself away.

With a sympathetic murmur, Zeina wrapped an arm around me. The hug finished as quickly as it had started—she straightened before she could be busted for breaking protocol—but I relished the momentary comfort anyway.

I considered telling her everything, but decided against it. Sharing with Zeina before my father felt wrong. And conversations about Silas wouldn't help me cope with the next few days, or the next few weeks. Understanding what had happened here with my father would. Returning to my old life would.

So I inhaled, swallowing my tears, and echoed Zeina's words. Tried to believe them myself: "That's irrelevant."

⁂

Sunlight streamed through the glass ceiling of the conservatory, highlighting my father's proud nose and the gray budding at the sides of his neatly combed blond hair. He sat, ankles crossed and posture-perfect, at a table nestled between a row of green plants and floor-to-ceiling windows overlooking the rolling hills beyond our estate.

"Darling!" He set aside his book, his tone containing an edge I couldn't place. "How did you sleep?"

"Well," I lied. He kissed my cheek and I joined him, inhaling the musty scent of the room. Outside, the leaves had turned sunset colors; winter would be here before we knew it.

"I'm sorry if Zeina pulled you from bed. Did you want to get changed?"

The colorful breakfast spread was a jarring contrast to the protein-heavy plates I'd become used to. A bowl of cut fruit sat beside a green smoothie. I picked up the smoothie, wiping the condensation with my linen napkin. "Oh, this is fine." He frowned, taking in my oversized sweater and chipped nails. His gaze lingered on my braids; I smoothed them down. Could he see the silver streaking my hair? My pulse spiked at his expectant silence as I hastily added, "I'll get dressed properly later."

"Wonderful."

The performative cadence of his tone finally hit: he was speaking to me like a prospective client. But why?

He reached for something at his feet, plucking out a large black shopping bag covered in tell-tale white letters. My gasp enhanced his indulgent smile as he presented it to me. "Happy birthday, princess. You didn't think I'd forget, did you?"

Happy birthday, beautiful.

The shots I'd drunk at midnight with Silas felt like a lifetime ago.

"I didn't expect—"

"Go on, go on."

I unwrapped the two ribboned boxes, trailing a hand over the soft leather of my new bag and shoes.

"These were the ones you wanted, yes? I had to organize for them to be shipped from Paris, but it was worth it."

They'd been *exactly* what I'd wanted. Two months ago.

My knees bounced under the table while my skin crawled under my collar. The heaviness in my chest wasn't from my beast, or anything else I could name. Zeina had said I'd feel strange; I felt like a stranger in these clothes, in this room, as out of place as those first days in Arwood's estate. I had no idea how to communicate this in a way that wouldn't grossly offend my father, so I overcompensated with a large hug, whispering a thank you in his ear.

"I'm sorry I wasn't here for your birthday," I said as I pulled back.

"And today is hardly a celebration for yours. However …" With a flourish, he presented two tickets. "I secured seats to *Giselle*. In Stockholm. At Christmas. To make up for what we both missed. Shall we?"

I nearly sobbed. This time, my enthusiasm wasn't forced as I thanked him. *There he is.* The wariness I'd heard in his voice must have been nerves. No guides existed to navigate this kind of stuff. Once I understood what was going on, my stomach would stop feeling like a wrung washcloth. How could someone who cried when Albrecht knelt at Giselle's grave be a bad person? My father wasn't a bad man. He'd made some bad choices—but everyone did. I'd made plenty.

"How about I excuse the chef and we cook dinner here tomorrow night?" he asked. "Watch a movie?"

"Just us?"

"Absolutely."

See? I told myself. *He's fine. We're fine.*

The chef bustled out with sauteed spinach, tomato and mushrooms, setting it down. The small plate didn't match the hunger I felt. It had been *hours* since I'd last eaten. "Good morning, everyone!"

My father peered at his phone screen, winking. "Afternoon."

"Ah, yes. Good afternoon, Keanna." Her smile remained fixed.

I smiled up at her. I'd missed her, too. "Will you be making bacon and eggs? Toast?"

Her pleasant expression froze, eyes flitting to my father.

"I thought you'd appreciate a bit of a detox, darling," he said, excusing her with a lift of his finger. "Get you back on track. God knows what they forced you to eat this whole time."

Smoothies, soups, and light salads it would be for a while, then. I hadn't checked the scales recently, but obviously my training with

Anika hadn't done squat. I prodded my jawline. Any weight I gained always went there first.

"It wasn't too bad." I sipped my smoothie, hoping to dispel the haunted look in his eyes. "They didn't starve me."

"I can see that." Exhaustion had slowed my reflexes; my face fell before I could stop it. "Don't take it like that, princess—I meant you've been through such a traumatic experience. I'm trying to be mindful of this, help you transition. Think of the pretty dress you'll get to wear in Stockholm."

I swallowed a blueberry with difficulty. We were going to *Giselle*. Things would go back to normal soon.

He reached for me. "Are you alright?"

I'm safe. I'm home. I forced myself to smile, interlacing my fingers with his.

He watched me warily over the rim of his espresso. His features were more pronounced, sharper. *He'd* lost those last kilograms—at the cost of his peace.

"I'm so glad you're home," he said. "It was unbearable, having you gone."

"I was worried about you, too. Have you been sleeping?"

This earned a smile that highlighted the faint lines around his eyes. "As much as you from the looks of it, princess."

I waited for him to ask what I'd done while trapped with Arwood, but the question never came. Imagining and knowing were two sides of a coin. Some people find comfort in ambiguity, others in absolutes. I'd come to realize while my father was the former, I was the latter. Staying within safer boundaries like work and fashion would keep things light, but it wouldn't make me feel better long-term. I'd have to tread lightly with what I wanted to ask next.

"Arwood has a library," I began. My father's lips thinned. I glanced over my shoulder to check we were alone; a vacuum was whirring, but it wasn't coming any closer. "It's full of information on supernatural creatures. I used it to research banshees and what I can do."

"Arwood is a master of manipulation. No doubt he fed you lies to keep you busy and reliant on him."

It wouldn't be helpful to rebut this, so I changed tracks. "Did my mother ever talk about her family when she was alive?"

"That's an unexpected question."

"I ask because the folklore said banshees originated from County Clare. That's where she grew up, right? I thought"—I sped up at the forlorn expression descending over my father's face, his default setting whenever my mother was mentioned—"perhaps she still has family there? Surely they'd look past old differences if they knew about me. Didn't she have a sister?"

"This is too much for your first day back." My father's gaze landed on my collar.

I drew my fingers away, realizing I'd been touching it. "I can handle it."

"You never wanted to know any of this before."

"I didn't want to accept what I was before. That became a liability while I was gone." Silence fell between us, his displeasure as sharp as glass. I continued carefully. "I found her family name, O'Carragher, in the texts. This can't be a coincidence."

"Keanna—"

His sigh warned of conversation shut-down. Weeks ago, I'd have let my point go in favor of retaining peace. An idea unfurled. "Where are my mother's old photo albums? I haven't seen them since we came here."

"In offsite storage."

"Do you think I could arrange access? I remember seeing in one that her sister's name is ... Kerri? No, Kara?"

His lip twitched.

"Karen?" I guessed.

The muscles in his jaw shifted.

"Hang on. It was Kate," I declared. "Definitely Kate."

"*Katherine*," he exhaled, frustrated. "And there's no point seeking those out. That storage container isn't accessible at present."

"Oh. Okay." I hid my triumph behind another sip of my smoothie. As much as he'd wanted to stop talking, he hated blatant inaccuracy more, and I'd counted on it. "That's fine."

Katherine O'Carragher.

My father inhaled on the other side of his admission, like he regretted speaking. "Look, darling—"

The shut-down. Here it came. Prickling fear budded along my spine, along with a slight tingle of exhilaration. The kind I experienced whenever I won something with Arwood. "How long have you been working with Johan?"

The skin between his eyes pinched as he blinked, long and slow. "For goodness' sake, I just got you home. It's been *weeks.*"

His words squeezed my heart. One side clutched the ballet tickets, reminding of the things we shared. His love. His protection. It emphasized my father's avoidance as a way to keep me safe, separate. Unfortunately, the weeks with Arwood, the things I'd seen and heard, cast a cynical light on his motivations and left me seesawing between both extremes.

Regardless of why my father wanted to drop the topic, I couldn't. The Sect wouldn't wait for me to settle in. Arwood might have turned me in already.

"Arwood threatened to expose me to the Sect if I escaped," I blurted out, a familiar rush of adrenalin thrumming in my veins. "Have you heard of them? I'm—"

"You're not to concern yourself with them any longer, Keanna. I will manage that risk moving forward with Johan."

So he did know about them. What else did he know? "*Johan* could be the very person who draws their attention to you. They wiped the Kohnstamm family the moment they could, and they were only humans exposed to magic. If they hear you're working with—"

"Enough. This is upsetting you." His voice developed that damned professional edge again. It made him feel so far away from me. "I'm managing it."

"I'm not upset—" I started, but he *tut-tutted* me silent.

"After everything we've both been through, all I wanted was a lovely meal with my daughter, and now you look ready to burst into tears." He sighed again. "I'm trying here. You've done nothing but badger me in return. What more can I do to make you happy?"

I grabbed his hand. *Tell me Arwood was wrong,* I wanted to plead. *That Silas was wrong, and you're a good man stuck in a bad situation.* "I just need the truth—"

He tugged it away. "No, you need Dr Ambroz. He, at least, might understand where all this is coming from."

Goosebumps descended over my arms. I'd started seeing Dr Ambroz after my attack all those months ago. Our discussions had been largely useless, given I couldn't talk about being a banshee, and the psychologist could tell I was keeping something from him. We went around in circles in our sessions and both left unsatisfied. I'd have the same problem with talking about my abduction. "I … I'm not sure if I'm ready to see him yet."

My father stood, nudging his chair with his legs. "Let's allow Dr Ambroz to make that assessment."

He strode from the room without looking back.

◌〜

Over the following days, three things happened.

I spent the next night alone in the kitchen waiting for my father. After an hour of staring at the vase of freesias, I had to accept he wasn't coming and instead dined on the half-answers and anger he'd left behind.

The lounge pants and oversize sweatshirt I'd worn that first morning, plus any others like it, vanished from my closet drawers.

And I Googled my mother's sister.

CHAPTER THIRTY-EIGHT

THE DAY I RETURNED TO WORK FELT A LITTLE LIKE THE first day at a new school. I slept badly, woke sluggishly, skipped my morning routine, and dithered in front of my wardrobe. Pressure in my chest built steadily, like water against a dam wall, but I didn't fear it anymore. It was a reminder of what I was, of how much of myself and my world I had yet to understand. My lack of preparedness for working matched my determination to learn what my father had done to get me back.

I settled on a foolproof black pencil skirt, beige heels, and a white structured button-up. Boring, but would do the job. I tamed my hair into a bun, trying to ignore how my skirt pulled tight even with shapewear underneath. The ill fit added to the sweater-sensation of my old life colliding with the present. In fact, most of my clothes no longer fit right. Shirts that had sat *just so* now cut across my shoulders and biceps. No wonder my father had looked at me the way he had when I'd returned—something had changed. I hadn't realized how, because training with Anika had made me feel better somehow, more comfortable in my own skin.

Zeina escorted me to the office building behind our house. I'd used it in the months after my attack, and the scents of hardwood and furniture polish brought forth curdling undertows of isolation from the aftermath of Thomas. I'd leant on Zeina's presence before my abduction. It was comforting to have her with me. I still had the collar around my neck, but there was nothing to be done for it; it was so tightly fitted my father had deemed cutting it too dangerous and treated that option as a last resort. Zeina had tried to jimmy the lock open, but we'd deduced that only Arwood's master key would work. At least with the tracker pulverized inside, Arwood's team wouldn't be able to follow my every move.

Had they located Isobelle yet? Would Arwood try and steal me back if they hadn't? I felt so disconnected, wanting to ask my father about it all. He'd avoided me since our disaster of a breakfast days before, our text string a lonely row of my unanswered messages.

I'd no sooner dropped my things off at my desk when a woman I didn't recognize bustled in. "Mr. Backhus requires you in the boardroom," was all she said, firing off emails on her phone as we walked. She must be my father's new assistant, which meant …

"Where's Mariel?" My mouth went dry as I spotted a diamond above the collar of the women's white blouse. She was Johan's.

"She's been redistributed."

I'd have heard the lie even without the experience of the last month.

Any hopes of spending time alone with my father were dashed as she ushered me into the boardroom. Suited men sat around a table, backlit by the windows overlooking a cascading wall of plants. Thankfully, Johan wasn't there.

"Ah, excellent." My father tapped the vacant seat beside him. "A welcome back to my daughter, who has returned after her horrific ordeal."

The men chorused their greetings. Two of them I knew, one I didn't. The Chief Operations Officer, Keldan Malina, patted my forearm as I sat.

"I heard it was Arwood Sayer who had his greasy paws on you," he said, his forehead conspicuously unlined beneath his short, styled chestnut hair. "How terrible. Thank you for returning so soon to help us."

I nodded, unsure of what to say, of how much the people in this room knew.

My father propped his chin on his hand, his fingers skating the edges of his lips. He looked better today, his pale skin tone even, green eyes clear and steady. "Always prepared to go the extra mile, she is," he said. His approving tone untwisted some of the knots in my stomach. "The timing is perfect. Keanna, darling, we need your assistance."

At my questioning glance, Keldan took over. "Sayer is a cancer. Thanks to the disbandment of the Kohnstamms and a recent injection of funds and personnel from the Camardo family, Arwood's foothold in Europe is set to strengthen. Understanding his operating model will further our strategic objectives moving forward."

I darted a look to my father. "What do you want to know?"

"Everything you can tell us about his network and estate," Keldan answered, swaying his chair side to side. "His associates, affiliated businesses."

I shifted in my seat, running my damp palms across my skirt. "His primary focus is locating his daughter, Isobelle. She was kidnapped two months ago." My father's expression didn't change. "He believes Johan is responsible. Do you know where she is?"

"If I did, I wouldn't share that information with Arwood," my father answered, lifting his brows in jest at Keldan. "Whoever it is, if they have any sense, they'll hold her forever just to watch the bastard suffer."

Frigid dissatisfaction slid under my skin at his words and Keldan's *haw-haw* laugh. "Dad, that's not ... it's killing him. Why would you wish that on someone?"

"He hurt *you*, princess. Taking you was a direct insult to me. It abolished our ceasefire the moment he did it." My father swilled his espresso, looking mutinous. "He and his entire fucking family, including his little whore of a daughter, can burn alive for all I care."

"Dad!" I'd never heard him speak of another person like that. Ever. And what was this regarding a *ceasefire*? "What are you talking about?"

"Nothing that concerns you, darling." His dismissive words grated, the endearment ringing like a warning. "Now, who makes up Arwood's inner circle at present? What are their names? Anyone we can leverage?"

"What about that wife of his?" Keldan asked, wrapping his knuckles on the polished table. "Keanna, what's her name?"

I could imagine the look on Lissandra's face, being addressed as 'that wife'. "Dad, can we—"

"No," my father's Chief of Finance cut across me. "She's a Camardo. Too entrenched. Possibly his friend, the younger one who does his dirty work?"

"Think he can be bought?" Keldan asked.

"If we push hard enough," my father said.

I stood. "What did Arwood *do* to you to make you hate him this much?"

My father sighed, pulling his navy tie free from the folds of his lap and heaving himself from the chair. "One moment, gentleman." He gripped my upper arm, leading me into the attached office. The tops of his ears darkened in displeasure as he released me.

"Keanna." He closed the door, his voice leached of all warmth. "You're embarrassing me in there. I need you on task."

"Dad." I hated how the word came out like a plea, but it was. My arm ached from where he'd held me. "I don't understand. Arwood mentioned you were both business partners. What happened between the two of you?"

"What else did the bastard say?"

"Nothing! No one is telling me anything. Not him. Not you. Why do you need to know these things about him? Can't we move on?"

My father barked a laugh, leaning against the door. "A man

doesn't just *move on* after someone spits in his face. He took you. He's going to pay for it."

The venom in his voice made me wince, his clipped tone warning we were approaching the cliff of his temper. I needed him calm and rational. "I'm home safe and unharmed. I didn't help Arwood get what he wanted. Johan has caused enough damage. He hasn't won anything over you. Retaliating further isn't necessary."

My father's steely gaze held mine. "It's the way of this world, Keanna. I know you don't understand, but that's why you're here today. I want you to understand. I want you involved in what we're doing here."

I'd thought I *had* been involved before my abduction. "Tell me what happened between you and him. Please?"

"We *were* business partners, building a network here in Prague while Arwood's father ran the overarching operation. A decade ago, I discovered Arwood had established side ventures outside of our arrangement. There was an … altercation. He started it. One of the bullets hit his wife. A horrible accident, of course, but once Arwood woke up in hospital and learned of Michelle's death, he went on a warpath."

I bit my lip, studying the cream carpet. My intuition rang. My father had no reason to lie, and yet something about his explanation made me feel as if he was—or, at least, not telling the full story. Weeks of listening to Arwood and the straightforward way he and his team spoke with each other shaded my father's words in a different hue. Especially the 'established side ventures' part. It sounded like something a politician would say.

"What was this about a ceasefire?" I asked instead.

"There was a difficult period following his wife's death. Neither side benefited from the constant fighting. We agreed we would no longer interfere with each other."

"Was that why we moved?"

"He enlisted, and I decided to nurture my affairs far from his influence. But Prague was my city, too. Since I've returned, he's strangled attempts to regain the ground I'm entitled to. *You're* entitled to. This is your future he's trying to destroy."

I paced the small room, my heels sinking into the carpet. "Arwood kidnapped me because someone took his daughter. He came to believe it was Johan. He didn't realize Johan was working for you."

The ambushes. The explosions. How many lives had been lost because of their misunderstanding? Something about the timelines didn't make sense, either. My father made it sound like the ceasefire had broken once I'd been abducted, but I'd been abducted *because* of what Johan and his team had been doing in Prague long before that. Their actions had been enough for Arwood to think they were responsible for taking Isobelle. Had my father engaged with Johan only after my capture? Was there a chance my father remained ignorant to the depths of Johan's depravity, that he was unknowingly funding girls being trafficked and God knew what else? Had he simply been as desperate as Arwood?

"Johan's a mercenary willing to do anything for a paycheck," my father said, blowing my musings about his ignorance to bits. "And there are others like him unsatisfied with the way Arwood and the Camardo dynasty hold this city in their grasp. Investing in Johan puts us on the winning side."

This made me sicker than anything else he'd said so far. "You need to stand down, Dad. You're the better man here. Rise above it."

"You're too new to this, darling. To stand aside now would show weakness, and not just to Arwood." My father straightened his suit. Unruffled, even as we talked of such awfulness. He'd kept this side of himself hidden from me. What else?

"What happened to my mother? Was she involved in this life, too?"

He pushed away from the door. "Not now."

"Then when? I have so many questions! I know it hurts you to discuss her, but we have to. Why was she alone when I was born? Was she really trying to visit her family if she hated them so much? Why weren't you with her?"

"*Enough.* I haven't the faintest clue what's gotten into you, but you've lost all decorum and I won't stand for it. I raised you better than this."

His disappointment burned, but I kept my shoulders back and chin raised. Once, I'd have done anything to appease him, hated the tension building, but his continued avoidance ignited the anger Arwood had sparked. Treating me like what I wanted didn't matter, just like Arwood had.

"My asking questions isn't the issue here, Dad."

"You're acting like Arwood's puppet. I didn't think you'd be so easy to manipulate against me."

I inhaled, his words skewering me. "That's not true. I love you and I'll always put you first."

"Pretty words with no substance. Exactly like Arwood."

Don't cry. I swallowed, wishing I could pinpoint where we'd gone so horribly off course. Since Zeina had rescued me, everything had felt wrong. This bloodthirsty man wasn't my father. He couldn't be.

Mistaking my silence for compliance, he pointed to the door. "Now. We're going back in there, and you're going to answer every question you're asked. Everything you learned, everything you saw. No details are unimportant. *Do you understand?*"

I opened my mouth. He raised his eyebrows in challenge. I pressed my lips together. There was no point fighting him further on this. Giving him what he thought he wanted wouldn't help diffuse the situation, and going to war with Arwood would only end with more death. I needed to bide my time and wait for an opportunity to make him see reason.

The eyes of the other men heated my skin as we returned. I tried to ignore my embarrassment and clung to anger. For the next two hours I maneuvered another minefield, answering questions with outdated information or details that would lead them to dead ends. For those I couldn't work around, I'd play dumb and pretend not to remember. Once it was over, bile sat at the back of my throat. Steering my father astray was the best thing for him, but it was still lying. I hoped my snap omissions would protect Silas and Anika and not hurt them further.

My father excused me. "You'll be escorted to your desk. Stay there until I return for you."

Something about his directive didn't sit right, but I did as I was told. Initially.

When Zeina went to the bathroom, I sent her a message stating I'd gone to the house for my lunch break. It would confuse her long enough to cover my absence. I considered traveling down the main corridor, but it had cameras. Instead, I navigated to the boardroom through a side hall connecting our unused offices.

Keanna Backhus didn't break the rules, but today Keanna Backhus had vacated the building. Or finally woken up.

The boardroom door was closed, the waiting area otherwise silent. The office where I'd argued with my father had a second entrance into the kitchen and reception desk to allow for catering, and I stood on that side of the room. A camera hung from the ceiling, aimed toward the boardroom. If I stayed against the wall until I reached the reception desk, then dropped low, I'd make it into the office without being caught.

I slunk across the carpet, clutching my heels. Then, with another considering look at the camera, I clambered over the reception desk, gritting my teeth, trying to stay silent. I paused, listening for movement behind the boardroom doors. Material ripped somewhere within my pencil skirt. I dropped to the other side, hugging the desk wall. Again, I checked for the camera. I had no idea how wide the lens capture would be, but I could only hope it wouldn't show me crawling into the office.

I crept over to the opposite door leading into the boardroom, assessing the gap above the carpet.

My deliberation was swift. I'd come this far, and my desire to eavesdrop overturned the distaste of mushing my cheek to the floor. I placed my heels to the side and sank down, hoping they'd shampooed the carpets at some point in the last year. I couldn't see them, just the shifting light across the floor as one of the men walked between the table and the window.

It took a few seconds to pick up the thread of the conversation, but when I did, my stomach bottomed out like I'd plunged downward on a roller coaster.

They weren't talking about business.

They were discussing *me*.

CHAPTER THIRTY-NINE

"IT'S ARWOOD'S MO TO SHOWCASE WHAT'S HIS. AT LEAST HE broke her in. We can always repurpose it when we send her out."

My father's voice, but it sounded nothing like him. *Broke me in*? What the hell was he talking about?

"How long till she's on board?" Keldan asked.

A seat squeaked, followed by the rattle of a trolley. "Give her a few weeks to get over it all," my father replied. "Some more Louis, gents?"

"Is that even a question?"

Laughter ensued, along with the clinking of drinking glasses and murmured acceptances as my father issued the cognac. After a momentary silence—presumably while they drank and congratulated themselves on their brilliance—the CFO said, "She can really kill people by screaming? Sounds like something from my daughter's comic books."

"Yes," my father answered. "Anyone in the immediate vicinity. The pressure she releases works like a bomb. Effective and makes their deaths hard to trace, but she's learned control." My fingers tensed on the carpet. Another thing he'd learned—but how? From Dobromil? "I'd prefer not to force her, so I'll need to warm her up to the idea."

Ice slipped from the back of my neck to the base of my spine. I stayed motionless, holding my breath for stretches at a time. As if, by not moving, I could stop the words coming out of my father's mouth, stop a voice I knew so well and no longer recognized at all.

Keldan jumped in. "You foresee that being an issue?"

"Not at all. Keanna does what she's told. It's just easier if she thinks it's her idea."

This wasn't my father. It couldn't be. Maybe I'd mistaken his voice for someone else, perhaps the unspeaking fourth man. I was sleep-deprived and traumatized; how much did that affect comprehension? Surely a lot.

An email tone cut off my cyclonic thoughts. "Just got another one, Eddy. Barb Richards is sniffing. Wants more money."

"She got five hundred," my father snapped. "That was the agreement."

"She's threatening to talk if we don't up it to a million. Says she'll tell the media you 'set her husband up to die.' Quote unquote."

Her husband? My eyes widened. *Thomas* Richards? The associate who'd attacked me in the hotel room that night? The first man I'd killed? Betrayal locked my limbs down.

"Bloody hell," my father groused. "Give Johan one hundred to go over there and shut her up." He let loose a long-suffering sigh. I held my breath again. *This isn't my father. It can't be.* "I can see why Thomas was such a 'yes' man. Shouldn't have kept her alive to begin with."

Keldan murmured his assent.

A swift knock interrupted them.

"Sir?" came the cultured voice of my father's new assistant. "He has arrived."

"Speaking of loose ends," my father muttered. "Let him in."

Heavy footsteps filled the silence as the door closed.

"Dobromil, my man!" my father said, his tone changing; jovial, almost conspiring, as if he and Dobromil were in on a secret. I was so thrown by what I'd heard I couldn't muster the appropriate surprise that Dobromil was here. "What's happening?"

"I'm compromised, sir. Too much heat from the escape."

"Ah. And you decided to come here."

Dobromil cleared his throat. "You said you'd double payment when she was delivered to you."

"Correct," my father said. "I said nothing about you coming with her."

"Can't go back, sir. My partner's still alive. My exit's taken attention off him for now. I assumed I'd be more useful staying this side."

"And with that enterprising attitude, what's to stop you from returning to Arwood, telling him everything you hear today, and tripling your fee?" my father quipped, his jovial tone gone.

"I wouldn't do that, sir."

"Because I can depend on your word and loyal character, can I?"

A cruel silence followed, in which the only sounds I could make out were the squeaks of a chair, another set of footsteps. Dobromil's word of protest dissolved into a strained, muffled grunt and a repetitive thumping, like a foot stamping. I edged closer. What was going on?

The noises slowed as a minute passed, and then ... nothing.

A metallic scent I knew too well crawled underneath the door.

I recoiled, then flinched from the thump on the floor, like a sack being thrown. A voice I hadn't heard before—the silent fourth man?—spoke, his words assured, like he did this frequently.

"Disposal, sir?"

I clamped a hand on my mouth to silence my sharp inhale, thoughts crashing into each other and bubbling like sea foam. One rose to the top: *they'd killed Dobromil.*

Numbness poured down my wilting body, gluing me to the floor. In my head two Keannas were screaming at each other, demanding my attention. One was convinced I'd somehow misunderstood everything. My father wasn't a murderer. He wasn't any of those things. He was *Dad.* The man who protected me, watched bad movies with me, loved ballet, and sang Sinead O'Connor off-key in the car. The other Keanna reminded me of the things Arwood and Silas had said I'd determinedly ignored, waving their warnings like picket signs and demanding I quickly come to terms with the reality of what I'd heard and *get the fuck out of here.*

I didn't move.

In the boardroom, it was business as usual. "The best insurance policy is silence, I'm learning," my father said. "Apologies you had to witness that, gentleman."

The executives gave affirming murmurs.

"Use whatever resources you need to clean this up," my father directed. "No one will miss him enough to look, but wipe the security footage of him entering the estate anyway. Call whoever you need to."

"Understood."

I gripped the carpet, breathing shallow. I couldn't feel my arms or legs. My chest was a cold thing. Inside, both voices united, forming a single dialogue that sounded suspiciously like my beast, warning me to get back to my desk. *Now.* In the end, bargaining with myself was the only way I could move. If I got back to my desk, I could excuse myself to the house, complaining of period pain or a headache, and go to pieces there. It would take five minutes. A time-specific, achievable short-term goal.

My beast yelled at me again. I stood.

The noise behind the boardroom door threatened their imminent departure. I retained enough sense to avoid the camera while retracing my steps over the reception desk and down the side hall, slipping on my heels. My shoes could have been on the opposite feet for all the notice I gave.

Zeina found me moments later.

"Keanna! Why did you leave without ..." She ducked her head, trying to meet my eyes. "Keanna?"

When I didn't reply, she took me back to the house, muttering things under her breath I barely absorbed like "too soon" and "should have warned Edson."

The familiarity of my bedroom undid me. Heavy heaves plucked from my soul.

She embraced me on my bed, rocking me. At some point I registered that Zeina believed me to be in shock, succumbing to the trauma of my abduction. She'd been waiting for me to break down. I let her comfort me anyway, because I had no idea what to do or how to process what I'd heard. I couldn't trust her, or anyone else. My universe had shifted off-axis, with no way to tilt it back.

My father had been my equilibrium, and I'd lost it.

I hadn't known my father.

I didn't know anything.

∽

I ate dinner alone, a piece of filet mignon and steamed vegetables that crumbled like ash in my mouth. My father was home—I'd heard him arrive and frozen, anticipating he'd join me—but after twenty minutes I'd realized he wasn't going to. He was still angry with me.

Loneliness built like a silent scream, chipping at the numbness. An afternoon of crying had deflated me like a wet paper bag, self-doubt taking hold. What I'd overheard—what I *thought* I'd overheard—had been too shocking to be real, to the point where I wondered if it had been. Wasn't there a psychological condition where people suffering from trauma hallucinated?

"Keanna? You're needed in your father's office."

Zeina stood at the doorway. Her face betrayed nothing, but my heart kicked up anyway. Regardless of whatever had happened this afternoon, I needed to make sure my father didn't suspect I was falling to pieces. I schooled my expression, keeping my features soft but unaffected. Loosened my shoulders, too.

Another man sat opposite my father, a square metal case beside him, his haircut and features as generic as his black sweater and shoes.

"Ah, yes. Keanna, please sit," my father said. "We need to inspect your collar."

I suppressed a sigh of relief. It was coming off, just as he'd promised.

Plain Face walked a circle around me, then opened his case. I'd expected tools—a screwdriver, perhaps, or a magic knife that could cut through anything—but he extracted a camera. I couldn't quell my frown as he took photos from all angles, lifting the collar to capture shots from underneath.

My gaze met Zeina's. As always, she watched on, her brown eyes filled with something I hadn't expected: concern.

I found my voice as Plain Face prodded my neck. "Are you able to work out how to take it off?"

The man didn't answer. My father shook his head, pressing against his temples as if pushing away a headache. "Unfortunately, no. This was my last resort while we wait for Dobromil"—I tensed at his name, then smoothed out my fists—"to obtain the master key from Arwood. We can't risk there won't be a failsafe in something so customized." He nodded to the man. "Thank you."

Just cut the thing off! I wanted to scream. Instead, a "thank you" of my own echoed as Plain Face packed up his camera.

Dobromil, my beast urged. *Ask him about Dobromil.*

"Have you heard from Dobromil?" My father frowned. I amended the tone of my voice to sound younger. Pitiful. "It's … it's just *so* uncomfortable."

"I'm sorry, princess. He's working to keep his cover intact. He'll resurface soon."

Except he wouldn't. Because I'd heard him die.

My palms grew sweaty. "Please. Can't this man do something? I've seen what Arwood is like. Dobromil might not return."

"Have patience, darling. I'm doing everything I can."

Back in my room, panic threatened to consume me. I hadn't been hallucinating. Somehow, this parallel universe I was suffering *was* reality.

Safe with my father, I'd never been in more danger.

⁓

When I'd searched my mother's sister on social media, focusing on matches to women situated in Ireland, I hadn't thought anything would come of it. O'Carragher may not have been the most common last name, but it was an old one, and there had been many results. It was also flawed rationale—her sister could have changed her last name with marriage. But it was all I could think of with the resources I had, and so, not wanting to tip off my father, I'd disconnected from the Wi-Fi and used phone data to send numerous polite enquiries to the most likely results, asking if they'd had a relative by the name of Shay O'Carragher. In the days since, I'd received all types of responses.

Most people had seen my message and said nothing. Not unexpected. In the age of online scams, I'd ignore me, too.

Another responded with yes, they did know a Shay O'Carragher, but she was ninety and ensconced in a nursing home in Sligo. Was that who I meant?

But one—one was promising. From her redacted profile and grainy image, this Katherine O'Carragher appeared to be mid-to-late forties, situated in Ireland, had studied in Dublin. Yes, she knew a Shay, she'd said. Her sister. Why?

It was probably stupid, but—reeling from everything I'd overheard and at a complete loss for what else to do—I told her. I justified it by assuming that if she was the right Katherine, then she might be a banshee too.

So I wrote how Shay was my mother and she'd died in childbirth. How I'd spent my early years in London and Europe, later raised in Australia, and was currently situated in Prague with my father.

And that I needed help.

CHAPTER FORTY

I STAYED LOCKED IN MY ROOM FOR THE REST OF THE NIGHT after the meeting with Plain Face. Zeina insisted on my being left alone. A blessing, because I had no idea how to function.

Silas had been right. My father *was* cut from the same cloth as Arwood. Perhaps worse. He hadn't killed Dobromil in self-defense, or because he'd been wronged. He'd done it to avoid delivering on an agreement. And he'd arranged for Thomas to attack me, then paid off his family. Had he known it would be a death sentence for his employee? Had he done it to see if I'd inherited banshee capabilities? He seemed intent on using me for them now, like Arwood's abduction had merely stalled the inevitable.

It proved nearly impossible to reconcile these thoughts with those of my father, but I knew I somehow had to. The realizations inside my room kept coming in waves, along with a hard truth: I'd *never* been safe here. I just hadn't stretched far enough to touch the bars. I'd found them today, a cage waiting to close around me.

This was what I'd desperately wanted to return home to?

I'd gone from one monster to the next—except here, I had no allies. Zeina, for all her concern, was contracted to my father, and to him her loyalty would remain. Everyone with the resources to assist me was at Arwood's estate, but I couldn't go back there, either. Arwood would surely kill me for my part in escaping, or use me relentlessly until we found his daughter before turning me over to the Sect.

I turned my phone around and around, reflecting on what I knew about Silas. Not his last name. Not a phone number. But even if by some stroke of luck I managed to contact him, he wouldn't want to hear from me anyway. Not after Gabriel. And I couldn't blame him for it.

They own me, but you have my heart.

It hurt so much to think about him that my hands gravitated to my chest. Tears splashed down my arms.

He was gone.

And I was on my own.

As I cried, Katherine O'Carragher replied. She was rightfully suspicious of me but said that if I wanted to meet, we could do so in Dublin. For security, she told me to wipe my internet history, create a new email address not synced to any of my devices, and to use it to contact her moving forward. Damn. I should have thought of that myself.

Could I stay? If I stayed, I'd have to pretend nothing was wrong. If I stayed, I'd soon be pulled into whatever my father had planned for me.

I cast my eyes around my perfect room. My beautiful cage. Before my abduction, I wouldn't have fathomed leaving this behind. But I'd survived without it at Arwood's estate. I'd adapted. I could do it again.

In the end, my choice was easy. I couldn't stay. But I had to be smart. I'd get one shot at escaping.

Lissandra had warned me of my inability to hide my emotions; to get out, I'd need to put on a performance. Convince everyone I was fine, nay, *thrilled* to be back home. My father believed me too naive and conflict-averse to see through his lies, and that would be my advantage.

I set up a new email address and keyed a response to Katherine, telling her to stand by. I didn't trust her, but if she really was my aunt and could offer some answers, that was good enough for now. It gave me an initial plan while I formulated a better one.

Ireland would be my life raft while I weathered this storm.

An anxious gut became my constant companion in the days that followed, but my intentions and seething anger kept me anchored. I transacted money from the account I used for shopping in small increments, stashing the wads of cash beneath the padding of my bras. I built lists in my head, too scared to write them down, of things I'd need. I exercised. Dieted. Attended work under the watchful eye of my father. I played the part of the wide-eyed Stepford daughter—and waited.

"I'll be in Milan this weekend," my father announced during a mid-week dinner of oven-baked salmon. He'd been discussing one of his deals, and I'd nodded along, my trembling hands concealed in the napkin on my lap and lower back aching from my stiff posture. "I'll depart Friday evening and return Monday after breakfast."

This was it. As my father had quoted so often over the years: opportunities are like sunrises, and if you don't take action, you'll miss them.

His departure for Italy was the window I'd been waiting for.

I kept my expression curious, even slightly eager, saying something I knew past Keanna would have asked: "Could I go with you, help in some way?"

He smiled, taking a sip of his red wine as if contemplating my question. He wasn't. He'd been vague with details, but this made my act more convincing.

"Maybe next time, princess. I'll ensure you have the full complement while I'm gone. Zeina won't let you out of her sight."

I forced a simpering smile as I ate a bite of fish. It had the consistency of sawdust. "Fine with me."

"What?" my father jested. "Not sick of her yet? I've been expecting you to ask me to tone it down."

It would make escaping so much easier. "She's been wonderful," I replied. "I feel so much safer having her here."

"I've been receiving favorable reports from Dr Ambroz."

"I'm doing a lot better," I said, digging my nails into my thighs. "You were right to suggest returning to work. It's been helping."

"Good to hear, darling," my father said, skewering asparagus. "You're welcome to attend some meetings with me next week, would you like that? They're night appointments, but we can schedule your workload around it."

"Who are we meeting with?"

"Ah." He waved his fork. "Some new investors. I'll receive full briefings on Monday once I return. It'll be good for you to shadow me."

"Looking forward to it." New investors? Night appointments? Before, I wouldn't have thought anything of it. Now, I could only imagine what he had planned—and why my presence proved necessary—and it cemented my resolve. "Perhaps we could go out for dinner next weekend?" I offered. Making plans was a sure-fire way to create the illusion of security, wasn't it?

"Perhaps. I'll be on the back foot from Milan. Let's see how things go?"

After dinner, I locked my bedroom door, and, with a sigh of relief, ripped off my pretty dress and the shapewear underneath. I kneaded the tight cords of my neck as I eyed my wardrobe. The rows of dresses and skirts were every bit as appropriate for the office as they were inappropriate for escaping. Time to change that.

⌒

"Tell me again why the shorts you already own aren't sufficient hiking attire?"

The bags in Zeina's hand rustled as she followed me into our third department store for the day. My father had left for Italy the night before, and I was shopping up a storm.

"Bike shorts," I said, weaving around customers who had stopped at a perfume display, gripping my own bags closer so they wouldn't bang into their legs, "are not appropriate hiking attire for winter, which, I'll remind you, is *weeks* away. Fleece-lined tights are where it's at."

Zeina followed dutifully, keeping her composure while I used her as a glorified coat-hanger and exchanged some of the bags she held for tights and thick coats.

"I appreciate you," I told her, smirking as she tried to keep a straight face. "It's just been so long since I shopped. I'm trying to be efficient about it."

"At least you're feeling like yourself again."

My bravado must have fooled her, because underneath my layers I was sweating buckets. The crowds of people and the noise of the busy store were overwhelming after the weeks in our estate, and I kept checking my coat was buttoned to conceal my collar.

We walked to the changing rooms. There were two exits, and the cubicles were mostly empty, but Zeina lumped my clothes into one and asked me to wait while she investigated the others. Once satisfied, she nodded. I gave her the purchases from other stores I didn't need—"I have to check everything matches," I said, gesturing to the ones I kept hold of—and shut the door, assessing my pile. I breathed deeply, trying to calm myself, as I pulled my jacket and shirt off.

"Oh!" I yelped. "Oh no …"

Zeina stood on the other side of the door immediately. "What is it?"

"Uh …"

"Keanna."

"My period. I … oh no." I pulled my hair into a knot at the base of my head and slipped a beanie on.

"Do you have tampons?"

"No, it's come early, I didn't think—do you have any?" I asked, knowing full well that due to surgery sparking early menopause, Zeina hadn't had a period in years.

She'd shared that with me in confidence months before, but didn't remind me of it as she issued an apologetic, "No."

"I saw a pharmacy in the mall on the first floor." I slipped a thermal shirt over my sports bra. "Would you be able to get some for me?"

"I'm not leaving you."

"But—*oh*, I'm so embarrassed. And I'm wearing *white*." I replaced my pristine coat with a navy hoodie. "Please, Zee. I'll stay here."

She mulled over my request while I moved items into a slim backpack.

"Please." I added another sweater and some shirts, plus the extra pairs of underwear I'd put on this morning under my jeans, and the extra layer of socks under my sneakers. "I promise. I won't move."

"Fine. What kind?"

"If they have the organic ones, that would be best." Into the backpack went my passport and two plastic Ziploc bags of cash I'd stuffed inside my bra. I kept my wallet in my handbag and threw my phone on top of it, murmuring a silent goodbye. No point making it easier to track me. "Oh, and can you get some painkillers too?"

Zeina warned me to stay quiet and keep the door locked. Her footsteps faded on the carpeted floor.

I counted to ten as I hoisted the backpack over one shoulder, then raced for the opposite exit. I slowed my pace, dawdling by a display near the exit to throw off the security guard. I didn't have time for a bag search, and the receipts for the items with tags were back in the changing room. They wouldn't believe I'd already purchased them, and the last thing I needed was to be accused of shoplifting.

I kept calculating. It would take Zeina a minute to descend two floors and exit, and a further two or three traversing the aisles for the tampons and painkillers. Including payment and return, I had five or six minutes at most. I'd used one already. I forced myself to stand there for another thirty precious seconds, smelling a candle, before meandering to the exit. I shot a smile to the guard, who let me pass without inspection. Once I hit the street, I ran for the metro stairs.

My heart sat in my throat as I descended, running my fingers over the jagged edges of notepaper in my pocket containing written instructions. *Take the metro B line to Florenc station. Board the coach to Paris.* I weaved through the sea of passengers on the platform, hunching in case Zeina had followed me. It was a Saturday, and I'd scheduled my escape for peak hour just after lunch.

I stayed submerged within the crowd as we boarded, allowing myself the smallest of sighs as the train departed. Step one complete. I shifted my bag to hug it against my chest and stood beside the doors, head bent. When the doors opened at each stop, I melded against the train wall, expecting a surge of activity down the carriage, for my father's team to board and capture me. My knuckles turned white from gripping the backpack and the handrail. The moment we arrived at my station, I ran down the platform.

Crawling paranoia sent me straight to the bus station bathroom. I switched the navy hoodie I wore for the gray one stuffed in my backpack, feeling as if I had an 'X' marked on my back. The minutes I stood in line to purchase a ticket, then perched on the edge of the seat, waiting, felt like hours.

Only once I'd sat near the center exit on the coach and begun the thirteen-hour journey to Paris did I sink against the headrest, pulling my beanie low over my forehead, concealing most of my face beneath the hood of my sweater. Heat blossomed beneath my eyes as the lights of the city flashed past, but I refused to cry. I'd cried enough. I'd cry when I was safe. Hopefully I had enough of a head start to make it to Ireland. In this age of technology I'd never be able to throw them off my trail completely, but I hoped with my recent behavior, the mess in the department store change room, and the fact I'd left my phone and wallet, they'd believe me abducted again. At least at first. It would buy me some time to disappear once I got to Ireland.

Despite my resolve, the further the coach drove, the heavier my chest became, until all I could concentrate on was the wrenching sensation within, like an elastic band being stretched. My soul trying to cross the borders between myself, Silas, and the life I'd left behind, a magnet searching for its likeness.

Loneliness rode with me as I boarded the train at Gare du Nord bound for London. As I traveled across Welsh landscape. As I caught the ferry to Ireland. As I headed for Dublin.

Being alone was a strange skin to wear. It was one I'd have to get used to.

IRELAND

CHAPTER FORTY-ONE

I FOUND ST STEPHEN'S GREEN EVENTUALLY, THE MEETING place Katherine had specified in her last email. I'd arrived in Dublin the evening before and promptly holed up in a small laneway hotel perpendicular to the famous temple bar district and the River Liffey. Close enough to central Dublin, but cheap enough to stay for a night or two. The woman at the counter had taken in my hair—which had frizzed the second I'd hit damp Irish soil—and pinched face and made such a maternal fuss about finding me a room that I'd nearly cried fat, gulping tears all over the mismatching Persian rugs in the lobby. Instead, I'd shuffled up the tight, creaking staircase to my room on the fourth floor.

I hadn't wanted to wander far, both for safety and logistical reasons, so the pub attached to the hotel—named after a madam burned at the stake and later thought to be a serial killer—felt like an appropriate place to lick my wounds. I ate my first proper meal in days, the hot soda bread and thick stew soothing my hunger while I sat in the corner, avoiding even the friendliest of locals looking for a chat. The bells of the nearby church woke me the next morning, and I'd had a bad moment peering out the matchbox window across the wet rooftops, but I gritted my teeth and concentrated on the plan: find Katherine, get some answers about my mother, and then …

Well, then I'd have plenty of opportunity to think, because I'd be a free—and hopefully educated—agent, wherever I chose to settle. And if dark uncertainty clawed at the bottom of my stomach while I crossed the cobblestoned streets toward the park, I tried to ignore it. I'd wallow in self-pity later.

I wiped the seat overlooking the small lake—wet from a sudden, vicious downpour on my journey which had sent me scurrying for the eaves above someone's front door—and tried to practice being present while I waited, watching a mother and her small children delighting over the birds by the water. The cuteness of it all distracted me enough from my nerves and waylaid the urge to throw up on the grass. Such a step would no doubt complete my descent into the 'homeless youth chic' vibe I courted, and if I didn't look the worst I'd ever been in my life, I wasn't far off.

"Don't understand the appeal of birds. They're unpredictable. Can never tell if they'll swoop you or not."

I tensed. Beside me towered a woman comprised of angles: sharp nose, cocked, jean-clad hip, pronounced shoulders filling out a worn brown jacket. Steely confidence coated her long limbs. Watchful gray eyes assessed me beneath thick, well-maintained dark-blonde eyebrows.

"Katherine?" I observed her hair, so silver it was almost white, and so thick she'd braided it back into a single plait. "You're my mother's sister?"

"I wasn't sure you were Shay's, but I am now." Laced with a thick Irish accent, her voice held a higher melodic pitch than I'd expected, belying her tough exterior and making her sound far younger than she looked. "You're so much like her." She nudged her face. "Got the family nose, too. Suits you better than me. What's your story?"

I blinked. "Could you be more specific?"

"You look like you haven't slept well in days."

"I haven't."

"Ah." She lowered herself next to me, slinging a leg over her knee. Her eyes landed on the children beside the lake, and she flinched in distaste as one of them squealed. "Where ya staying?"

"Here, near Dublin Castle. Where are *you* staying?"

"Not here." The child ran straight for a flock of birds. Katherine ducked as wings flapped overhead. "Who'd ya run from? You never said."

I mirrored her position on the bench. "Did you know my mother was a banshee?"

Her features didn't change apart from a single raised eyebrow. "Answers my question. You share the gift?"

"I wouldn't exactly call it that. Do you?"

"Yes. But I won't be speaking of it in the open like this."

"But—"

"Later. Tell me how you got to Dublin. You take precautions?"

I recounted how I'd avoided planes for their security protocols, how I'd switched between trains and coaches and paid cash. Short of being impressed by my resourcefulness, Katherine pursed her lips. "At least you muddied your trail. Any trouble on the road?"

My beast *harrumphed*. "I'd like to see someone try."

We locked eyes. She was the first to break it.

"Come." Katherine stood, gesturing for me to follow.

I stayed where I was. "Where are we going?"

"You'll see."

"No. I've had enough of people making decisions for me. If you can't help, I'll keep moving." And if I quailed inside my hoodie while I said this, at least Katherine couldn't tell.

"To where?"

"Anywhere. I'm not going back." It started spitting again. Icy droplets hit my forehead. "Can you prove you knew my mother?"

She sighed, tugging a battered leather wallet out of her pocket, and extracted a folded photograph shoved between euro bills.

The fold left white cracks down the center, separating two sun-faded women around my age. The one on the right in a high-waisted floral bikini was definitely my mother. I saw myself in her long, flowing silver-blonde hair, the widow's peak, in the smile that took up most of her face. I traced it with a finger. *This* was the version of her I'd held in my mind growing up. Eternally smiling. Eternally beautiful. The woman beside her was a younger version of the one standing before me; the years had melted her softness.

Katherine broke me from my trance. "You're needing to eat, so do I." When I didn't make a move to follow, she added, "Let's talk about Shay over lunch. I'm not eager to get wet so early in the day."

The rain decided things for me. I had limited clothing, after all.

She sent a text as she walked ahead. I followed, watching for movement around us. The pub she led me to was like any other I'd seen in Dublin so far: low ceilings, dark wood, green stained glass. The scent of stale beer hung in the air.

Katherine greeted the bartender by name, asked for "the usual," and directed me to a booth in the corner away from other patrons. I perched on the edge. Katherine stretched out opposite, crossing her ankles on the green cushioned seat.

"Relax, Keanna. Unless you hate lamb, I'm not gonna hurt you."

I shifted onto the seat proper, but not without reservations. There were plenty of breakable things near me, and I'd be able to handle myself if someone attacked me—but Katherine remained a question mark.

"What's with the choker, by the way?"

As she asked this, the bartender served lamb stew and crispy French fries onto the table. Katherine dragged her beer across the wood, observing me above the glass. I stuck to water.

"An insurance policy in case I didn't do what was asked. It had a tracker in it." Seeing her expression, I added, "But it's been fried."

"You sure?"

"I made it here, didn't I?"

"They coulda been waiting for you to stop."

I thumbed my collar. "The person I'm running from now isn't the same person who gave me this."

"Well. Feck." Katherine tilted her beer in my direction in a 'cheers' motion and took a swig.

I slid the folded photograph across the table. "When was the last time you saw my mother alive?" My stew smelt delicious and I was hungry enough to wolf it down, but couldn't relax enough to do so.

Katherine peered into her beer, taking another sip. "She was six months pregnant with you. Bleedin' happy." At my head tilt, she elaborated. "It's difficult for us to have children. Not impossible, but harder than most humans. If a pregnancy sticks, it's always a girl, and they always share the gift. One child is tough enough. Two is a miracle."

She watched me do the math in my head, smirking.

"Me mam was a paragon," she said, answering my question. "Shay and I were twins. Anyways, Shay met your father while traveling through France. Married him quick. We fell out of touch a bit, but she seemed in love, content." She shoveled some fries into her mouth, gesturing to my empty water glass. "Want anything else?"

I shook my head, eager for her to continue. At her pointed look, I ate my stew. Once I was a few mouthfuls down, she went on.

"A week before she was due to have you, she contacted me in a panic. Kept saying she'd made a mistake trusting your father and was going to try and escape." She nodded at my stunned expression. "She wouldn't tell me anything else over the phone. We agreed to meet in Scotland. She didn't want him following her to Ireland. But she never made it to Oban."

"Why?" I croaked.

"Went into labor early. Had no one to help her except the people who owned the bed and breakfast she was staying at. Last I'd heard, she'd died, you with her, and your father took your bodies back with him."

Thinking of my mother, scared and alone, clogged my throat. "You didn't know I survived?"

"Not until you sent that message."

I tapped my empty glass, my stomach cold. I was losing my father in degrees with every revelation. How had I been so blind to him? "My father said she was traveling to visit family and got there too late to help her."

"He the reason you're here?"

"He wants to use me."

"How?"

I lowered my voice. "My scream kills people. At first I couldn't help it"—Katherine pulled away, gaze darting around the pub—"but I've started learning control."

"I need to get you back." Her voice had hardened. I didn't like that one bit. "A killing wail is bloody rare. Shay's the only banshee thought to have had it." Katherine stood, waving some euros to get the bartender's attention as she placed them on the table. "No wonder he kept you hidden."

I didn't move. "Tell me where we're going."

"I belong to a clan south of here near Ennis. You'll be safe there."

"Why didn't you say that earlier?"

She nodded to someone behind me. A woman in a high-collared jacket with a messy silver bun and shaved undercut had entered the pub.

"Needed to talk to you first," Katherine said. "For all we knew, you were a plant to draw us out. This is Chloe. We'll travel back with her."

"We're clear," Chloe said to Katherine, holding out a hand to me.

I sized up the new woman, returning her handshake. She was five to ten years younger than Katherine, sunburn emphasizing her freckles and tinging her alabaster skin red. They looked normal enough, but then again so did I. Their silver hair lent legitimacy. Going with them might be the best move. My father would never find me, and it would solve my problem of not having anywhere to go. I'd taken some jewelry with me to sell in case I ran short of money, but that wouldn't last forever. If Katherine's story about my mother was true, she'd trusted her sister to protect her. The need to belong *somewhere* made the choice to leave an appealing one.

But if they were lying, I could be walking into even more danger. Frying pan. Fire.

As if sensing my indecision, Chloe's rough voice broke the silence. "We gotta get moving. D'ya know about the Sect?"

I wondered if the Sect knew how regularly their name was

uttered in tones of dread and fearful respect. It felt like everything I'd learned about them so far had been against my will. "They regulate mages and keep supernaturals a secret from humans," I said.

"Then you understand they barely sanction our existence, and only if we're discreet—and stay that way. If what you were saying is true, you're already exposed," Katherine said. "Your best bet is with us."

"You don't have to stay," Chloe added. "But let us shelter you while you consider your options."

Stuck between a rock and a hard place, I conceded. Potentially dead if I went, probably dead if I didn't. My beast stirred, reminding me I wasn't alone. If they led me to trouble, they'd have a fight on their hands.

I followed them to a white 4x4 parked down the street. I'd packed my backpack with everything I had that morning and taken it with me, so we were able to leave immediately. We navigated the Dublin streets, heading west, and eventually industrial buildings gave way to rolling landscape dotted with livestock.

"Chloe here"—Katherine nudged her in the ribs as she drove—"is our tracker. Watches the news and nurtures our contacts within the Garda. She scans for banshee activity and dispatches Eilinora—you'll meet her soon—if we suspect there's an untrained banshee in the open."

"What's your role?"

"If you didn't notice, I've got no patience for recruitment. Eilinora brings 'em in. I train 'em. We take new recruits for at least two to three months. No contact with the outside world, just full immersion so they can walk away with the skills they need to live life as they please."

We spoke off and on after that. I kept my eyes glued to the passing green hills. The compact towns, narrow bridges, and running streams soothed me. I'd always wanted to visit Ireland. Was it my heritage calling to me, my beast yearning to be around her kind? Whatever the reason, the rain-drenched countryside, lilting accents filling the car, and never-ending, moss-covered stone walls kept me entertained enough. For a moment, I forgot my situation.

After a few hours, Katherine turned, holding a piece of fabric. "Do I have permission to blindfold you, Keanna? We can't afford to be found."

A black collar.

Now, a black blindfold.

"I vow on Shay's soul if you choose to leave, I'll be granting you safe passage wherever you want to go," Katherine said, her eyes unwavering on mine.

I agreed, putting it on.

From there, time stretched—it could have been thirty minutes, it could have been an hour—across bumpy, winding roads that made my butt slide on the seat. We slowed to a stop. The rustling hum of trees swelled as the doors opened. Katherine dragged the blindfold off my face.

"Come meet everyone."

On the drive, I'd wondered what a banshee clan would look like. Where they'd live, *how* they'd live, how many of them there'd be. The wood-paneled house we pulled up beside sat within a forest clearing; the sharp, ash-colored slanted roof was more Eco-lodge than the gothic, overgrown stone manor I'd imagined. Bright light shone across the plush grass from the floor-to-ceiling windows on both levels, and inside women milled around the kitchen bench and wooden table, talking and drinking. At the slam of our car doors, several waved in greeting.

I sucked in a breath, nerves mounting. I climbed the short flight of stairs to the deck and followed Chloe and Katherine through the sliding door.

Down the communal table, someone yelled, "Finally! We can eat."

"Not yet. Everyone"—Katherine gestured to me—"welcome our newest arrival, Keanna."

The attention of approximately forty banshees in the room

flattened me like a tidal wave. Hair of differing shades and textures was accented with varying amounts of silver that glinted underneath the circular ceiling lights. I smiled as best I could, smoothing my own hair with a hand. The woman closest to me wore twin silver braids that contrasted against her flawless deep brown skin. She approached with an enthusiastic smile, giving me a hug in welcome.

"I'm Aoife." With her thick, breathy accent, her name sounded like 'ee-fa'. "Pasta?"

She piled a plate high, leading me to the table. Voices washed over me. One by one, introductions came my way, names I forgot once I recognized the woman sitting at the far end.

A banshee poked her. The woman waved distractedly and yelled her name.

That cemented it for me. Disbelief and irony froze me to the seat.

"You've got to be kidding me," I whispered.

It was Isobelle Sayer.

CHAPTER FORTY-TWO

ISOBELLE SAYER WAS *HERE*.

She'd been in County Clare all along, slurping spaghetti and laughing like a member of a *fucking sorority house*.

I had no idea whether to laugh or scream.

A few indecisive moments later, I decided on neither. I pushed my chair back noisily and headed straight for her, ignoring Aoife's yelp of surprise at my sudden exodus.

"Isobelle Sayer?"

Isobelle waved as she chewed, blissfully ignorant. "Keanna, right?" she garbled with her mouth full.

I exhaled through stiff lips. "You have no idea how much trouble you've caused in Prague. Have you told your father you're here?"

After that, naturally, the table went quiet.

⁓

"I knew he'd be upset," Isobelle said for the tenth time, "but I did what I had to do. I left a note! And Ellie's been letting him know my progress and when I'll be home."

My question had the effect of a stink bomb. The others dispersed, leaving Isobelle, myself, Chloe, and Katherine facing each other over the kitchen island. Eilinora, who'd excused herself to the bathroom before my conversation with Isobelle, hurriedly returned.

"Tell them, Ellie," Isobelle said to the statuesque banshee leader. "I left him a note, didn't I?"

I cut off Eilinora's reply. "No one believes you wrote it." *You eejit.*

"Well, what about the texts?" Isobelle tried again. "Show her! The ones you've been sending for me. Show her your phone."

Eilinora clicked her tongue. She crossed her booted ankles, perching against the timber bench housing the whirring dishwashers. "Technically, the texts I showed you were sent, but they never went to your father. The number you saw me program wasn't his."

Isobelle sucked in a breath, tears budding in her expressive brown eyes. "Oh. *No.*"

Eilinora had the grace to sound apologetic, her crossed arms tightening. "We can't risk messages being tracked."

The anger that had ignited upon seeing Arwood's daughter was now diverted to the three banshee leaders. "Do you have any idea what you've done?"

Chloe stepped forward, palms outstretched. "Here, Keanna darlin', give us—"

"Don't 'darling' me," I snapped. "There are people being held hostage because Arwood believes she's been kidnapped." I flung a finger out, my tone climbing in octave. "I was abducted off the street because he thought I'd be able to help find her!"

"You said you'd run from your father," Katherine said. Warning.

"*After* he rescued me from Arwood," I corrected her, pointing to my collar. "Arwood gave me this. I've been pulled like a ragdoll between two psychotic men, and all the while Isobelle's been *here!*"

"It's for her own good," Eilinora said, unmoved by my outburst. She looked the youngest, and her Irish accent rang weakest of the three leaders; her words carried predominantly American undertones. "Left untrained, the Sect would have found and killed her. Isobelle knew this. It's why she came with us when we approached her in Prague."

"Disappearing without a trace was *never* the deal," Isobelle argued.

Ellie shrugged. "I'm sorry we misled you, Is, but we take no chances."

Isobelle moaned in frustration, dropping her face into her hands.

"Arwood Sayer is too dangerous," I murmured. "She can't stay here, either."

"Until she's trained, we can't be letting her go," Katherine said.

"I *nearly* am—"

"She has to go back," I pressed. All I could think of was Silas. His mother, his sister. "He's killed people—he's made *me* kill people—because he thought they might have taken her. He's blackmailing a mage by holding his family hostage. In a cage. Arwood won't stop killing, he won't let them go, until he has Isobelle back."

"*This* was why he needed to know I was okay! Ellie—"

"Stop," Katherine commanded. "I'm not minimizing what you've gone through, Keanna, or what you've told us. But we three never make decisions alone or without consideration. Give us twenty-four hours to discuss."

I didn't want a delay. I wanted a decision *now*. Twenty-four hours wasn't long in the grand scheme of things, but every day ticking by meant more death, another day of Silas being trapped.

"Twenty-four hours, now," Katherine repeated, watching me closely. "In the meantime, I recommend you both try to get some sleep. Keanna, there's a spare bed on the second floor, second door on the left. Breakfast is at seven."

Seething, I followed Isobelle's bobbing silver-blonde ponytail up the flight of stairs. At best, the leaders would deliberate and see reason, but that meant waiting a whole day. If they decided to do nothing, was I really in a position to bite the hand currently feeding me? Where would I go if I didn't stay here until I found my feet?

In the end, I knew what I had to do. I'd seen too much, done too much, to ignore what had transpired countries away.

We paused on the landing. Isobelle's arms were linked across her stomach. Bracing herself. Like her father, she had tried to solve a problem without paying mind to collateral damage.

At least she seemed guilty about it.

"You knew your father was capable of these things?" I asked.

She raised her chin even as she clutched herself tighter. "He's … he's made difficult decisions the last couple of years. He's needed to. But he's been a good man most of his life."

"'Good men' can be another person's villain."

I gained no pleasure in the way her face fell as she focused on my collar. She bit her bottom lip, staring at her bare feet. Pastel blue toenails matched the clothes she wore.

Isobelle stood taller than me. Thinner than me. Prettier, too, with thick lips and long eyelashes. The picture-perfect daughter I'd tried my whole life to become, yet the urge to compare felt less intense than I'd expected. Ingrained, negative, pervasive thoughts—*if I'd been like her, my father might have loved me better*—rose like an instinct, demanding space and sanity. But the cold reality of my situation had taken over.

What good are long, thin legs when you can't control what you are and you kill people because of it? What is the point of counting calories when you have no idea where your next meal is coming from?

With these realizations came the harsh, unrelenting truth I'd forced myself to acknowledge each day since I'd left: in any form, I wouldn't have been enough for my father. I needed to remember that.

"When Eilinora contacted me, I knew my dad wouldn't let me go if I'd asked," Isobelle said. "None of them would. But I was sick of being scared of the Sect, and if I kept screwing up I knew it'd only be a matter of time before they overwhelmed my family and came for me anyway."

This echoed Leon's thoughts, even as I inwardly winced. *Leon.* Unfortunate pun aside, I should have dropped that bomb on her there and then, but I decided just as swiftly I wouldn't be the one to deliver the news.

Her father would. When I united them.

"Do you have a phone?"

Isobelle shook her head. "Cellphones aren't allowed for anyone except the leaders. Too much of a security risk." There went my plan to try and bribe one of the other banshees. She peered at me in the dim light. "Why?"

I'd been trying to work out how to get word to Arwood without exposing the banshees. At first I'd considered finding Anika on socials—out of everyone, she struck me as the type to have them—but I didn't know if her last name was Camardo, and the plan was dependent on her even having an account and checking it regularly—

Hang on.

I *did* have a way to reach Anika.

Could I confide in Isobelle? She watched me in a manner reminiscent of her father, assessing my posture, observing my defiance. If she told on me, the banshees would never trust me, and I'd ruin my future here with all of them.

But if the leaders decided not to let us go—entirely possible, they appeared rigid in their utilitarian convictions—they'd be on the lookout for what I planned to do. Tonight, I might have the jump on them.

"Prague is becoming a warzone," I whispered, watching her expression. "Your father sends people out, night after night, searching for you. To any end." Isobelle bit the inside of her cheek, but didn't interrupt as I went on. "The Sect are closing in. They're just waiting for an opportunity."

She tilted her head, her gaze sharpening. "Whatever it is you're thinking, I'm in."

I whispered my idea. Eagerness filled her face; she was nodding before I'd finished.

"Is there a way we can access one of the leader's phones?"

Isobelle shook her head. "I've never seen them leave one lying around."

"Laptops?"

"There's a bunch on the top floor for those who work remotely."

"Would they be connected to the internet?"

"Pretty sure they would be. Like, they do investments, virtual assistant work, translation services, that kind of thing. But it's always locked down of an evening."

A frustrated exhale escaped. "Any other ideas?"

She pointed over the landing. Across the oiled floorboards, a landline phone lay tucked in an alcove between the window and a packed bookcase, balancing atop a thick, gnarled yellow-paged book. A phone directory, Isobelle told me.

"We're in the middle of nowhere. Reception's terrible here," she whispered. "I've seen them use that phone loads."

We formed a plan in hushed whispers.

A giggling fit erupted behind one of the closed doors as we ascended the next flight of stairs. Laughter rose and fell like the tide as Isobelle opened her door and slipped inside.

I went to my room. My bag lay against the pillow on the bed closest to the threshold. Three other beds crammed the space, the floor filled with cushions and paperback books in varying pastel shades. Dainty fairy lights were strung across both walls and framed a thick paned window. Three banshees sprang upright on their beds as I entered.

Aoife padded over in her knee-high bed socks, introducing the other two. All three had trained for several years and decided to stay with the clan. Aoife assisted Eilinora with recruitment, and the others worked with Chloe locating new banshees.

I dodged well-meaning but invasive questions about where I'd come from. They got the hint, leaving me be. I changed in the communal bathroom before ducking under the covers, pretending to sleep. One by one, whispers ceased, and murmurs of "goodnight" faded into the soothing draw-drag of slumber.

Isobelle's door opened. Footsteps rushed down the hall. Soon came what I was waiting for: Katherine and Chloe's concerned whispers as they attended to Isobelle's 'panic attack.'

I listened for disruption from the banshees around me as I exited the room, creeping past Isobelle's muffled faux hysteria and the comforting tones of the leaders.

Pausing at the bottom of the stairs, I listened out for Eilinora. She hadn't attended the meltdown. Was she still awake?

As I tiptoed to the landline, my beast reeled. I halted, spinning into a crouch next to the bookcase. Outside, chrome-tipped trees swayed under the full moon, the belly of the forest empty and unmoving. Again, my beast cautioned me to pause.

Metal flashed—

A tall pale woman with a thick silver ponytail peeled away from a tree. Darkness coated her as she flipped a knife, the blade catching the light. Eilinora. Her gaze stalked the depths of the house, watching for movement through the windows. Lurching moments passed as I clung to the bookcase. Finally, she turned.

How many others were out there, on patrol? I darted a glance around, making sure I wasn't visible from any other angle aside from the window directly in front of me. I'd have minutes, perhaps less, before Eilinora was replaced with another banshee. I pivoted the landline, preparing to grab the handset, when something glinted beside it.

A single silver strand of hair lay underneath the receiver, poised to fall to the ground as soon as it was disturbed. If not for the moonlight, I'd have missed it.

The length of the strand matched my hair—and Eilinora's.

I should have expected they'd have a sneaky way to check if the phone had been used without their consent. They housed and protected teenage girls, after all.

Eilinora remained turned, but her presence sent chills up my spine. I gingerly secured the strand of hair between my fingers and opened the directory, crouching behind the bookcase and stretching the cord as far as it would go.

When the dial tone hit my ears, I exhaled, thanking Ireland's reliance on old-school technology. Thanked every deity existing in the universe that the company name I searched for was listed in the snarled, curling tome. I also thanked anything else worth thanking that Anika was a night owl even with the time difference and would most likely answer.

Several clicks later, it rang. And rang. Then, words I'd been longing to hear:

"ALM Holdings, may I take a message?"

CHAPTER FORTY-THREE

BREAKFAST PASSED WITHOUT INCIDENT. ONCE THE rostered kitchen clean-up dispersed, I wandered to the vegetable gardens where some banshees toiled, huddling in my hoodie against the morning chill. Steam rose from my coffee and the sun-drenched dirt beside me. Beyond, Aoife and a slew of others trained together, a mishmash of accents and wails floating across the grass. Isobelle hadn't joined them—she'd stayed upstairs, nervously waiting. If the leaders decided we could go, I'd take Isobelle to Dublin. If the leaders decided we must stay, we'd find a way to steal around the nightly patrol and head to Dublin anyway. Either way, we would meet Anika in the city, but I'd slept better after the phone call having put something in motion.

Clad in workout gear, the banshees swapped between running laps, sparring, doing burpees—an exercise that was the root of all evil and made me thankful I wasn't participating—and throwing knives at targets. Aoife had mentioned at breakfast the Sect and other supernaturals held such a threat over the future independence of banshees that training was a given. I'd done *something* right, getting a head-start with Anika.

Guilt over my plan with Isobelle kept me where I was, as did my killing wail. Would they die if I screamed, or did they have some kind of resistance as banshees themselves? Until I spoke further with Katherine, it wasn't something to risk. I was finally among my own kind—and still as apart from them as I could be.

After seeing the banshee operation, I understood why my father had moved us so far away for so long. They would have found me if we'd stayed in Britain or Europe. I was equal parts grateful and resentful for my normal childhood. My abilities could have been nurtured all this time. I'd have learned to control them in a safe space. My ignorance wouldn't have been exploited.

I wouldn't have killed anyone.

"Morning, Keanna."

I flinched, bringing my coffee cup close, realizing I should have offered to distribute the soil or something. From the way some had cooked, cleaned, gone upstairs to work, or ventured outside to train, every banshee appeared to have a role.

Eilinora approached, clutching a cup of her own. Her hair descended from a high ponytail that slid across her shoulder like pale silk. Vanity had tainted my perception of silver banshee hair, but seeing everyone here, I realized how wrong I'd been to fear it. Silver meant transition. Strength. Embracing our power. It wasn't weakness—far from it.

I prepared myself now with my own strength of conviction. Had Eilinora figured out I'd painstakingly reset her booby-trapped phone?

She came to stand beside me. "We didn't get a proper chance to chat last night. How are you today?"

"Better. Worse," I admitted, sipping to keep my hands busy. "Have you made a decision regarding Isobelle yet?"

Eilinora's midnight blue gaze studied mine, intense but clear. As if she often analyzed the world and those around her and came away rarely surprised. Before Arwood, talking to someone like this would have terrified me. I kept my face as neutral as possible and my posture relaxed, like I had nothing to hide.

"Not yet," she said. "You shocked us all. It sounds like you've had a brutal time of it."

"Relatively speaking."

"Did you leave anyone behind?" Eilinora asked as Katherine and Chloe joined us, each holding baskets of eggs. Chicken feathers clung to the damp hems of their jeans.

"I don't want to talk about my father," I said.

"Not him," Eilinora said. "There was a sadness in your eyes when you mentioned the mage. Do you miss them?"

I looked between the three women, expecting judgment and finding none. An urge to change the topic to literally anything else bubbled, but my body had also become a knotted tapestry of regret and pain. I'd longed to discuss Silas with *someone*.

"It's like I left half of myself back in Prague."

Eilinora raised her eyebrows. "You Matched?"

The lurch inside had nothing to do with my coffee. "Do I want to know what that means?"

"There's no fancy way for explaining a Matching," Katherine said. "Most simply: we're drawn to men most biologically suited to pass along our banshee gene."

The light breeze ruffling the trees surrounding us could have knocked me over. "You're saying how I feel about Silas is only, um, banshee hormones?" It explained my immediate, magnetic attraction. Why I'd felt like a piece of paper being torn in two when I'd left him. I mean, I'd assumed hormones had something to do with it. I was a young woman, and Silas was Silas. But I hadn't realized it was ... *hormones*. "It's not real?"

"Bang on," Chloe cackled. "Biology, baby."

This made me want to cry more than ever. Was *nothing* under my control?

"Don't listen to Chloe," Eilinora said. "She's a cynic."

"After three failed Matchings I'd expect you to be more of one too, Ellie."

"No, it's been four, and yet I still don't hate men as much as you do."

"They have their uses, but you can't be blaming me for also wanting the tender touch of a woman. Kathy gets it." Chloe winked, grazing the shaved hair at the back of her head as she tugged two garden hoses across the ground. She handed one to me and gestured where she wanted me to aim. My guilty conscience drove my eagerness to comply. At least I could do something constructive while I spiraled.

"You've never Matched?" I asked my aunt, pointing the nozzle at a row of carrot sprouts.

"Oh, I felt the tug, but I've never swung that way," Katherine said. "It's a flawed system—"

"It's not flawed," Chloe cut in. "You don't have to love a man to get impregnated by one. Think of a Matching like your personal homing missile to quality dick."

I choked on my coffee, setting the cup aside.

Eilinora thumped my back. "Classy, Chlo."

"Does he …" I cleared my throat. "Do they go through it too? The Matching?"

"Nope," Chloe said, popping her lips around the *p*. Something within me loosened. It was bad enough Silas had given words of love without knowing about Gabriel; the idea I'd done anything to influence him against his will had been an icepick to my soul. "Would be grand if they did. Poor Ellie here has suffered unrequited situations since puberty."

Eilinora sipped, pinky finger extended. "They never stick around, but at least they delivered heaven in their bedsheets."

"Trading good sex for a broken heart is stupid. You have the worst taste in men," Chloe retorted.

It hurt to swallow. "So what you're all saying is I feel like this about Silas because of the Matching?"

"Yes," Katherine answered. "And no. Only *you* can decide what you feel. The Matching isn't love, and love isn't everything. Love alone doesn't sustain. Your mother loved your father dearly, but he made bad choices. In the end, he wouldn't do better, and she had to leave him. You always have a choice, and love doesn't abolish those choices just because it exists."

I stared into the garden, lost for words, the steady stream of falling water and the shouts of training banshees filling the silence.

Chloe coughed. "*Awkward.* Keep up that intensity and Keanna'll run from here screaming."

"Speaking of screaming—if I did it now, would I kill you all?" I held my breath but relaxed when Chloe snorted.

Katherine shot her a sideways glance, saying, "Banshee immunity is a beneficial thing. We'd find it tough to wrangle newcomers otherwise."

"Why am I different?"

"Why does someone have red hair, while another has brown skin? Genetics."

"But if you're all the same, then why—"

"We're not all the same." Katherine pointed between herself and Chloe. "When we both scream, it knocks people unconscious. Whereas Ellie here, well, her screams only immobilize—"

"*Only* immobilize? My screams disrupt *neurons.*"

My aunt winked at Eilinora, before turning to me. "You said you'd learned to control your wail. It took Shay years, and she lived here."

A small flutter of pride rose, doused by shame. "I had to. They were using me to kill people."

The three of them shared a look. Chloe rubbed her nose on the back of her hand, focusing way too hard on watering the parsnips. Eilinora gave my shoulder a squeeze. I appreciated that they didn't ask questions. They seemed to sympathize with what I carried.

"The Sect devastated us many years ago, wiped out several of our bloodlines," Eilinora said. "They murdered our eldest. Our mothers. Some of our sisters. We've had others come for us since. That's exactly why we hide, why we train. It's taken years to restore our numbers. Like you've experienced, in the wrong hands, we're weapons. I hope you understand now why we prioritize caution."

A cry ripped through the clearing from the depths of the trees. It hooked into my skin, impossible to ignore. Chloe and I shut the nozzles off, dropping the hoses to the ground.

"What was that?" I asked as Chloe and Eilinora took off, sprinting across the grass.

"Our clarion wail," Katherine said. "Something's wrong."

The women around us pulled their gloves off and threw their tools down, swarming toward the banshees converging at the tree line. Aoife broke away.

"What happened?" Katherine demanded.

"Intruder," Aoife gasped, her brown skin flushed. *"Maspotem,* we think. They have produced a shield, but—"

A mage? With a shield?

Silas.

I heard nothing else, my feet propelling me faster. He couldn't be here. If he was, something had gone horribly wrong.

My heart whispered: *please.*

"Let us through!" Katherine barked. The crowd parted. I stopped, gaping at the woman before us. Banshees held her forearms. A stark, granite-colored collar sat around her neck, above one of Silas's amulets.

"Zeina?" I breathed. Collar? Amulet? Had she been captured by Arwood somehow? Bruises coated her chin, and a gash had torn her bottom lip in two.

The banshees all turned, accusing glares finding their target—me.

CHAPTER FORTY-FOUR

THE BANSHEE LEADERS PUSHED PAST.

"You can't hurt us," Katherine said to Zeina, "so I wouldn't advise aggression." To the women holding Zeina, she added, "Release her."

They did, reluctantly, while the others closed a tight ring around us.

"You know this woman?" Katherine's voice cut sharp.

"She works for my father." I wanted to get closer to Zeina, to offer her some comfort, but I knew that wouldn't help the situation. "Zee … what happened? Did Arwood get you? How are you here?"

Zeina's eyes flitted to the throwing knife Eilinora spun.

"We're not leaving," Eilinora said. *Spin. Spin.* "If you have something to say, say it."

"Your father sent me." Zeina spoke slowly, as if every word was an effort. "He says you're to return with me."

Heads swiveled in my direction. Had my father somehow started working with Arwood to track me down? The idea was *so* unlikely, but after these past few months … "Why do you have a collar on?"

"Edson recreated them and needed a test subject. I let you get away, you see."

My gut turned to ice. With Zeina's experience, I should have realized I hadn't given her the slip.

And she'd paid for it.

"I'm so sorry, Zee. If I don't come back?"

"He's got this clearing surrounded and advises if he must take you by force, he won't hesitate to take the rest of you as well."

Immediately the banshees scanned between the trees. The trunks towered overhead, casting long shadows, with canopies so dense it blocked nearly all sunlight.

Katherine gestured to Eilinora to get her attention. "Initiate protocol two." Half of the banshees broke away, hurrying to the house, Eilinora leading them. She turned back to Zeina. "How'd you find us?"

"Her collar."

I clutched at the metal wrapped around my neck, the others' distrust spearing me. "That's not true. You fried it when you broke me out. You said the tracker would have stopped working."

Zeina's head was shaking before I'd even finished speaking. "We underestimated the technology Arwood used. There was a secondary activation." Blood seeped from her lip. "Edson left for Ireland when you escaped, believing you were headed for this area. We had one guard remaining inside Arwood's estate. Once Anika alerted Arwood you were here, your father obtained your position."

Cries of dismay erupted. I wanted to vomit.

"Keanna." Katherine's voice went deadly soft. "Did you lead them here on purpose? Answer me."

"No!"

I caught snatches of condemning sentences seasoned with words like 'liar'. Even Chloe looked uncertain.

"I didn't. I swear," I pleaded above the stinging barbs from the banshees. "I called Anika last night using the landline and said I'd meet her in Dublin with Isobelle." Several banshees gasped. "I *never* told her where I was. On my mother's grave."

Katherine faced Zeina. "How long?"

"Arwood isn't far behind."

Another cry of dismay. Katherine silenced it with a frustrated wave of her hand.

A quiet voice said, "My father's coming?"

Isobelle. She pushed her hair behind her ears, her face red and swollen. "I felt … I saw you were all here, I thought …"

Katherine began barking orders. "Chloe, take the rest of the girls to the house. Make sure they lock down our resources, then enact protocol one."

"What're we gonna do about Keanna?" Chloe asked, as if I wasn't standing there.

Debate erupted, the banshees falling into two camps. One side urged to turn me over to my father, Arwood, and even the Sect. I'd brought nothing but bad fortune on them all.

That hurt, even if they had a point. I hadn't earned my place here. I could be turned out as quickly as I'd been taken in, too much to help. And I *had* brought this upon them. *Repercussions, regardless of intent.*

The other side had embraced me as part of the sisterhood, and argued that 'an affront on one is an affront on all.' When Aoife finished defending me, I jumped in.

"My father and Arwood capitalize on opportunity. Trained banshees are a windfall they won't walk away from. My leaving with them won't make you safer. They know where you are, and they can always come back. We have to end this."

I kept my focus on Katherine, trying to ignore the hisses from my detractors. Her opinion seemed to be the one that counted. Even Chloe, a leader on equal footing, waited for her to speak. *Please. Please don't abandon me.*

The disappointment in Katherine's eyes killed me. Anticipation slowed each passing second, like listening for a leaking tap to drip again. She turned to Chloe. "My order still stands. Enact protocol one."

The remainder of the banshees left with Chloe. Only some shot me dirty looks; it seemed the majority accepted Katherine's ruling. I inhaled deeply, relief wracking my body.

"What's protocol one?" Isobelle asked.

"Defense," Katherine said. To Zeina, she said, "As you've no doubt discerned, Keanna will not be returning to her father. Will you be staying with us to defend her and our family, now, or going back to your employer?"

Zeina lifted her chin as best she could. "My loyalty is to Keanna, not power-hungry, exploitative men. Let me help however I can."

I clamped down on my bottom lip, swallowing tears.

Katherine stared at Zeina. "How does a human enact a mage shield?"

"One of Arwood's mages created amulets that channel his power. This was Dobromil's."

Katherine, of course, had no idea who Dobromil was, and didn't bother sticking around for an explanation. She strode for the house.

"If Arwood is coming," I told Katherine, hurrying to catch up, "there may be more people with amulets like this. You'll need to fight them differently."

"Then let's hope Zeina's presence works to our advantage."

Behind me, Isobelle bit her nails, darting glances back at the forest. A flight risk if I'd ever seen one. She'd no doubt run into *my* father instead, which wouldn't help anyone. I locked eyes with her, nodding. *I'll help you.*

Wafting between the trees, seasoned with pine and musty earth, came the unmistakable scent of death. It latched onto my shoulders, overwhelming my senses and seizing my stomach in a vice.

The other banshees shivered, as they, too, felt it.

A rhythmic spray of gunfire broke the steady silence of the forest. A fireball soared across the clearing, dissolving on the damp grass with a hiss. Clarion wails filled the air.

My father was here.

CHAPTER FORTY-FIVE

I'D BECOME REMARKABLY GOOD AT RUNNING TOWARD trouble. Worryingly so.

Ahead, hot air blew between trees, embers soaring. Two banshees dragged a third on the grass, red sprouting across her chest.

"Stay close," I said to Isobelle. Her brown eyes reflected the carnage before us. "As soon as your father arrives, I'll get you to him."

"Let's go!" Katherine roared as we neared the house. A row of banshees assembled in front of us. Most carried wickedly pointed knives; others shouldered loaded guns like they did this every day.

"The mages without shields are *feroxes*," I yelled, securing the knife Eilinora passed to me. She stood at an open box, giving out weapons like newspapers. "Don't shoot them. They'll only send the bullets back."

Katherine grabbed a gun from Eilinora, facing the armed men prowling through the trees. Johan flanked the far-right side, lighter in hand.

"Most of these men have never seen a banshee before today," Katherine said. "Let's make 'em regret coming here."

The banshees split, curtaining either side of the house and running for the forest like a wave closing around a patch of sand. Eilinora and Chloe ran behind them, knife blades gleaming, while Katherine and two others stood like sentinels on the front stairs. Katherine ordered us to stay in the house. We were the least trained of the lot, not to mention that *I* was the one my father wanted.

Correct in theory, but hiding and letting them fight for me wouldn't solve anything. I'd started this. I had to help finish it.

Once Katherine moved out of earshot, I said, "Keep your eyes peeled for someone from your father's side. The quicker we find Arwood, the quicker we remove one of the threats." I passed Isobelle a knife from the weapons box. She bit her lip as her fingers closed around the hilt. I didn't know how to use a gun, so I left those where they were.

"Unless … do you think Arwood will help us fight?" I asked.

"I hope so."

Her uncertainty made me pause. "I heard you disrupt vision when you scream."

"Temporarily," Isobelle corrected me. "I *temporarily* disrupt vision."

Banshee screams accompanied the sounds of gunfire. Their wails swept high, thin and piercing, sending chills across my arms and ending in a full-body shudder. The sound triggered every human instinct I had to run, hide, escape at all costs.

"Works for me," I said. "Let's get you home."

⌒⌒

I'd never fought beside a banshee before, and I made a vow to do it again in the future because, as Anika would say, it was 'fucking empowering.' We slipped out of the house via the back stairs to avoid Katherine's notice, entering the forest further down. Like the other banshees, we flitted from tree to tree, using them as cover.

We spotted our first intruders. Isobelle wailed, her brown irises disappearing behind a film of translucent gray.

Silas and Anika had never told me that happened. They'd never said, "Oh, hey, when you scream, the color creepily leaches from your eyes." No wonder people looked at me the way they did.

The guards flinched like they'd received a blow to the face. Some fell to their knees, dropping their weapons and clutching at their ears. Others staggered, blindly trying to find purchase. One loosed a spray of bullets.

Without thinking, I jumped in front of Isobelle. A silent

pressure wave released from me. Bullets soared. Bodies and guns flew backwards. Those who collided with trees went down and stayed down. The remainder rose, blinking, eyes refocusing. Their grip on their guns tightened.

Eilinora appeared, releasing a wail of her own. The guards fell like discarded puppets, twitching. She winked at us as she passed, racing off between the trees.

"I want that trick," Isobelle pouted.

I laughed, adrenalin thrumming within my veins. We ran for the next group. The trunks thinned. Sunlight filtered down, highlighting the bullet-resistant vests of our attackers. They carried themselves with steady military discipline. Where the hell had my father found these people?

Wails continued to pierce the air as we spied banshees and our attackers. Some fought in hand-to-hand combat or dodged the bullets ripping through the air. Loud explosions revealed Johan's location. I hoped Katherine and the others at the house had managed to fight him off. Guilt at defying orders rose, but determination doused it. I hadn't seen my father yet, but knowing him, he'd most likely hang back where things were safe.

Isobelle and I shifted into an offensive pattern. She'd wail first, disarming the primary sense our attackers relied on. My silent scream propelled them backwards and, most of the time, they'd be knocked unconscious by whatever they collided with. I could have wailed properly and ended their lives, but I held back. These people had been hired to do a job. Killing when I had another option crossed a line, and it wasn't something I'd do lightly.

We made a great team, disarming about a dozen guards before another wave wearing helmets converged from a different direction. Isobelle stepped forward, releasing a wail. The amulets around their necks glowed. Transparent, sapphire blue shields erupted.

Arwood's team had arrived.

"I have Isobelle Sayer!" I called. They gave no heed, training their guns on us. The woman leading the group jerked her barrel toward the ground, ordering us to surrender.

I grabbed Isobelle's wrist. "Your father's here," I yelled. "Let's go."

With nothing else at my disposal, I hurled my knife at the woman and took off, not waiting to see the outcome. We tore through the trees, ignoring their shouts, and gave the team a wide berth as we moved in the direction of their arrival. Smoke and death saturated the air, so thick it nearly choked us. We stumbled into men without helmets, disarming them. No amulets. Pleased we could identify the difference between teams, we continued deeper into the forest, damp leaves brushing across our cheeks.

Minutes later, I caught a glimpse of a figure running parallel to us. I released a silent scream. A hand extended beside the tree trunk, a sapphire shield erupting around them.

Filtered light from overhead glinted off a silver signet ring.

"Silas?" I skidded to a stop.

The shield blinked out, and he emerged from behind the trees.

I thought I'd never see him again, and here he was, confidence clinging to him like the musty, smoke-filled air. His faded navy shirt stretched across his shoulders just like I remembered. Curly hair brushed his neck in a way that made me long to touch it. Ashen skin pulled taut over the planes of his face, the repeated use of the amulets taking their toll.

His eyes widened as he saw Isobelle beside me.

My hand fell from her wrist as she, too, gasped. "Silas? What are you doing here?"

I was stunned for a second, but of course Isobelle knew who Silas was.

He swallowed, chest rising and falling. "I can't believe you found her."

A garble rose, a combination of *I'm sorry/here she is I didn't forget my promise/I love you/please don't hate me.* It was so overwhelming I swallowed, clenching my fists tight.

My beast keened, pushing to close the distance between us, but I'd frozen, my heart lifting in elation and body tingling with awareness of him. Since learning of the Matching, I'd despaired that my emotions were not my own. Seeing him, I knew the truth—they were. My feelings for him the night we'd first met were a whisper to the intensity I experienced now. They'd blossomed under the most unlikely of circumstances, tempering the darkness, encouraging growth in all the ways that mattered. I loved him, regardless of what was to come.

Silas answered Isobelle's question, unaware of the monumental shift I was experiencing. "Arwood sent me in with the team, hoping I'd draw you out." *They know*, his gaze told me. *They know about you and me, and I'm bait.*

Tears surged, hot and violent, at his remote tone. I had to remind myself that this was Silas's coping mechanism, removing all evidence of his emotions.

And it still hurt, so much.

"My father's here," I croaked, gesturing to the sounds of gunfire. "Can you lead us to Arwood?"

"You escaped for a reason, no point undoing it. I'll take Isobelle back—"

"No," I interrupted him. "I'm coming with you. I have to see this through."

If I'd hoped for anything else from Silas, perhaps a look that told me, I don't know, we were okay, or he was happy to see me—*something*—I was sorely disappointed. He spun on his heel, speaking into a radio and alerting Arwood he'd found us both.

We made it three steps when the tree beside us exploded, sending us sprawling into the dirt. Behind falling burnt leaves stood Johan, fire forming in his hands.

CHAPTER FORTY-SIX

"**H**ey, friends." Johan's grin split his face. Wooden slivers from the decimated tree pelted us. "You're going the wrong way."

The unmistakable sound of a fireball erupting—and the responding scream of a banshee—came from nearby in the forest. Johan's grin widened below gold eyes as he pitched his hand forward.

Silas sprang up, violet flashing across his irises. A shield enveloped the three of us. Isobelle shrieked, dropping her knife and flattening against the ground as flames rippled against the sapphire barrier. The shield wavered. Panting, Silas let it fall the moment the fire disappeared.

A twig snapped. The dark-haired, tattooed *ferox* from the warehouse approached. A fireball lit up in his hand, ready to launch toward Silas's exposed back.

Reason fell away. "No!" I yelled, grabbing Isobelle's knife and scrambling upright. My silent scream deflected the fireball; it disintegrated, surging upwards into a swirl of hot air. The *ferox* flew backwards, hitting the tree. I hoped it would keep him down.

It didn't.

He rose, clicking his lighter again. I threw myself at him, swinging like a wild thing. My knife nicked his chin, but he managed to dodge most of the blade, catching my fist and squeezing it. He swept his leg across the back of my ankles. I landed on my back, air whooshing from my mouth. Wet leaves and muck squelched underneath as he straddled me. Tattooed hands reached for my neck.

The pressure in my chest matched the pressure spiking up into my head. I wheezed, choking. His weight smothered me. Blood dripped from his chin. Isobelle wailed and he shuddered in response, losing his vision. His grip tightened. I braced myself, releasing another silent scream, knocking him backwards.

Behind me, Johan pelted fireball after fireball at Silas. Isobelle cowered between us. Fire crept to the treetops, creating an umbrella of heat and falling embers. Johan was stalling—either the fire would get us, or they would. Silas groaned from the effort. Once the fire dissipated from Johan's onslaught, he dropped his shield and doubled over. I dragged myself to my feet, palms sweating and legs shaking. Lighters clicked either side of us.

Silas and I locked eyes. I nodded, warning him.

My beast hissed in elation as I began to wail. With a click, I released a wave of pressure that would liquefy organs, shatter bones—and kill the two *feroxes* intent on destroying us.

I hadn't counted on the trees. The *feroxes* dove behind the thick trunks closest to them, avoiding direct impact as my scream spread outwards, heading straight for Silas.

Silas stood his ground, his eyes flashing a fiery *ferox* gold—*gold*, not the violet I'd become used to—and cupped his hands as if catching a football. A shuddering translucent orb formed between his palms, as if he'd *caught* my scream. He pelted it over my shoulder as the other *ferox* reappeared.

The tattooed *ferox* flew backwards, convulsing then stilling, landing in a heap.

Dead.

Silas sank to his knees. Isobelle shrieked.

Johan stalked toward us. Pure, animalistic protectiveness propelled me before Silas, preparing to scream again—

Anika leapt in front of us both, knocking us into the dirt. Fire collided against her back, tendrils contracting into curling wisps of smoke as she inhaled, closing her black eyes.

Exhaustion and gratitude stunned me silent. I'd never been so relieved to see *anyone*.

Johan whistled, looking like all his Christmases had come at once. "Never seen a *subicite* in action before."

Anika flashed him a sugary smile. "I'm the only one worth meeting. Wanna try that again, fuckboy?"

Johan's response—something along the lines of buying her dinner and a new shirt—became a gurgle as a knife sank into the side of his neck. He stumbled, eyes widening in shock. Steadman emerged from behind him, kicking the lighter from his hand and pushing the knife in deeper. Johan fell to his knees.

Steadman pulled another knife from his waist as he faced Johan, blocking our view. A strangled gasp caught on another gurgle. Johan's body thumped to the ground.

I dived for Silas. He trembled, breathing shallowly. I grabbed his arm and slung it around my neck, using my shoulder as leverage to get him standing. Anika shook her limbs as if throwing off the residue of the fire, before doing the same on his other side. Her black shirt had a massive hole in it, the edges crusty and warped, the skin underneath perfect.

"Just had to show off, didn't you?" she said to Silas.

"Shut up," Silas murmured, his olive complexion the palest I'd ever seen.

Steadman turned, his gaze settling beside me. "Issie."

Isobelle gave a guttural sob and ran for Steadman. He tightened his arms around her, then moved her hair aside as if checking her for injuries. "I've been so worried about you, sweetie. Are you okay?"

Sweetie? Had the stoic Steadman just called someone 'sweetie'?

I coughed to conceal a laugh as Isobelle made her assurances, beaming. "Keanna, this is James. He's like an uncle to me."

"We've met."

She frowned at my tone, as if she couldn't fathom that James Steadman, her 'uncle,' wasn't a lovely person to everyone ... after he'd slit a man's throat.

The fire continued to grow. We traveled in the opposite

direction, trying to get as much distance as possible away from the flames. Death sat under my nose, a reminder we weren't safe yet.

"I've got legs," Silas said as we supported him over a fallen log. "You don't have to babysit me."

"It's our job, boo," Anika cooed. "I'll take payment in a hearty Sangiovese followed by an even heartier rubdown from an attractive blonde. Any gender will do."

My spine straightened as a *whoosh* rang through the air. A throwing knife hit squarely in the eye of one of my father's guards—I hadn't even seen him approach—at the same time another knife embedded into the tree next to Steadman's ear.

Eilinora stepped out from behind a trunk, her hair a contrasting mess of blood, leaves and dirt. A shallow cut marred one of her temples, but she otherwise stood strong, fingers skating over the knives strapped to her torso and thighs.

She assessed Steadman and his hold on Isobelle. "This man known to you, Is?"

Can I stab him?

"He works for my father, Ellie. He's safe."

Eilinora traipsed over to them, tugging the knife from the tree. She paused, trailing her gaze upwards from Steadman's feet, her face inches from his.

"Appreciate you missing with that thing." Was it just me, or had Steadman's voice deepened?

"Appreciate you recognizing I missed on purpose," Eilinora replied. Her eyebrow arched as she tucked the knife beside the bloody one he'd sheathed at his waist. "Here. Something to remember me by."

A clarion wail ripped through the trees, disrupting … whatever that was.

"Arwood's on the other side of the clearing," Eilinora said to Isobelle, her eyes flitting to the blaze behind us. "North of the house. Y'all right to get her there? Quickly?"

We confirmed we could. Eilinora took off. Steadman and Isobelle led the way while I kept an eye out for my father's team.

Every step with Silas felt like a journey across a minefield. I monitored his minute grimaces, waiting for him to fall unconscious. It physically hurt to see him so weak.

When he stumbled, my hand went to his waist for extra support. Our eyes met. For a moment, it didn't matter we were surrounded by intruders in a burning forest. Wordlessly, I tried to tell him everything I couldn't say. That I was sorry. That I loved him. That I'd continue to care for him, protect him, even if he couldn't forgive me. Especially if he couldn't. That I was thankful for this time with him, even if it would be the last time. Isobelle was back with Arwood, meaning Silas would be free, and that was all I cared about right now. I'd deal with my father later. Somehow.

I tried not to be disappointed when he only nodded in response. It was the equivalent to being left on 'read' after sending a long, emotional message. A spiral of self-pity loomed until he touched his lips against my hairline, pressing a kiss across my brow.

I sighed, electricity passing over my skin.

We'd almost reached the tree line when multiple gunshots punctuated the clearing. Ahead, Steadman staggered then dropped like a stone. My mouth went dry as Isobelle cried in dismay, falling to her knees beside him.

My father, gun in hand, headed straight for them.

CHAPTER FORTY-SEVEN

MY FATHER ACTED RAPIDLY. HE HELD ISOBELLE AT gunpoint while she cowered on her knees, clutching the granite-colored collar he had slapped around her neck. Anika and I hung back in the trees, indecision stalling us both. Motionless bodies—my father's team and Arwood's—were strewn across the clearing.

Steadman lay prone on the grass. I couldn't see where he'd been hit. The suffocating sensation rising up my throat was similar to when I'd watched him disappear into the flames at the warehouse. I'd thought I hated Steadman; I couldn't stop looking at him, hoping he was somehow alive.

Arwood blanched as he broke through the tree line opposite and took in the scene. Four of his team filtered around him, pointing their weapons. The team at my father's side responded in kind.

"Glad you showed up," my father sneered at his ex-partner, pressing his gun into the back of Isobelle's head.

With a click of a button in my father's hand, she gave a bone-chilling scream. A shudder shot down to my toes as a sapphire shield encased my father, an amulet glowing at the base of his neck.

Silas groaned. I tasted bile, my bones aching with the memory of the pain.

My father released Isobelle from the shocks as Arwood ordered his team to stand down. Dissatisfied, they lowered their weapons.

"What do you want, Edson?" Fatigue and wariness weighed on Arwood's posture, his tone weak. He threw his gun onto the grass as he approached, his face falling further once he saw Steadman.

The king of crisp white shirts and tailored vests, now broken with humility. "Name it. You can have it."

"You knew I wanted Prague, yet you stole it from me anyway. I want all of it. Anyone in the territories loyal to you become mine."

Isobelle's screams filled the air, a short burst that cut off quickly.

Arwood nodded, raising his palms. "It's—please, just release her."

My father's eyes gleamed, his smile triumphant. Isobelle screamed again.

He wasn't going to stop.

I'd hidden for too long in the trees, frozen by my fear of him. My nose seared with burning wood and the ever-present scent of death. I had to do something.

I tapped Anika's hand, passing Silas's weight onto her. "Don't leave his side. He'll need you if you're attacked."

Anika clutched him tight.

Silas resisted, shaking his head. "Keeks, *no.*"

I prized myself out of his grip.

My father was so busy tormenting Arwood, he didn't notice me creeping up to Steadman's body. I sank beside him. He twitched at my touch, his pulse fluttering beneath my fingertips. I gave a sigh of relief until I spied blood pooling on the grass. A crimson-coated rock sat next to his forehead.

Shit.

"Steadman? Are you conscious?" I couldn't roll him over to see his bullet wounds without attracting attention. "I hope you're awake, Sarge," I whispered. "I might need your help soon."

He gave a moan. His gun lay a few feet away in the grass. He was lucid. Maybe.

I shoved the gun into his hand, then continued toward my father.

Two steps, four steps. I called out to him.

Distaste flitted across my father's features as he absorbed my wild, disheveled appearance. "Thank you for taking your time, princess."

The endearment sounded poisonous on his tongue. I pushed

down the flutter of panic that rose. "Please let Isobelle go. Arwood's agreed to everything."

"*You* caused this," my father told me. "You made me come and get you. Anything that happens here is your fault."

I kept walking, taking his words but not holding them. I saw the lie in them the way I wouldn't have before.

"You're making your own choices, Dad. And you can choose to do the right thing. I'll come with you—just let her go back to Arwood."

My father's calculating gaze swept over his ex-partner and the banshee at his feet. "You've just made a critical misstep in your negotiation, Keanna. I have no confidence in your deal. What's to stop Arwood retaliating once he gets home?"

Arwood shook his head, rebutting my father's words. It wasn't needed. I saw him clearly, like I could see my father. Arwood had let us all witness the depths of his desperation. Had relinquished his pride for his daughter's safety. And unlike my father, he'd walk away, if it meant getting Isobelle back.

"He won't do that, Dad," I said.

"Because after a month, you're an expert on Arwood Sayer?"

"Better than you."

My father's jaw tightened. He gave an exasperated sigh. "This man stole you, used you, *degraded you*, yet you defend him? You betray me with your weak convictions." His lips thinned. "The fickle girl you've become sickens me."

I could tell myself he was wrong, but his comment still dug into me like a shard of glass. I sucked in a breath. "You betrayed me first. You *paid* Thomas to attack me—"

"And I'd do it again. You wouldn't have reached your potential without it—"

"—and I overheard you were going to use me!" I cried, the shard driving deeper at his lack of denial. "I *had* to leave—"

My father cut me off again. "Wake up, Keanna. It's better to be useful. You'll live longer. It's the reason Arwood kept you alive; it's why I've come for you now."

Pressure swelled within my chest, a cold flush coursing down my arms. Acidic tears filled my eyes. I couldn't believe he'd just said that, and yet …

I could. Because I didn't know the man standing before me. I'd hungered for slivers of his approval my whole life, dined upon them, thinking they nourished me. I would have died, starved by his poison, believing it to be happiness.

My father had been my world. He hadn't deserved an inch of it. I loved him, but like my mother, it wasn't enough. Love had never been enough for him. Would never be.

At my silence, my father tugged Isobelle's hair cruelly, making her sob again. "She'll stay with me until Arwood fulfills his promise, and *then* I'll consider letting her go. You, however …" He sneered, gesturing to my collar. "Take that off her, you bastard. She's not yours to shackle."

To Arwood's credit, he didn't retaliate with 'Pot, meet kettle.' Instead, he fished the chain from beneath his shirt. I drew my hair to the side, exposing the back of the collar. Watched my father's face light up as Arwood came closer, unarmed and unprotected, pushing the key into the lock.

"For what it's worth," Arwood murmured, his chest brushing my shoulder, "I'm truly sorry for taking you, Keanna. Forcing you. And …" He paused, swallowing. "Thank you for finding her. I'll never forget it."

I hadn't expected an apology from Arwood. His words left me speechless.

It was because I was staring at my father that I noticed him give the tiniest of nods. It wasn't the nod that clued me in, but the contentment on his face. It was the look he got in the boardroom when he'd secured an advantage.

My collar clicked open. Cool air rushed over my neck as my father's team moved, a ring of black artillery closing around me and

Arwood. One of the men broke ranks, aiming his gun at Arwood's head.

"No!" I released a silent scream as the man pulled the trigger, sending half of the group falling backwards. The bullet veered into one of my father's men; he collapsed onto the grass.

My father raised Isobelle to standing by her collar and pushed her toward us, shouting another order to his men. Arwood gave a strangled sound, embracing his daughter.

The team reformed a tight circle around the three of us.

Above their shoulders, my father locked eyes with me, shaking his head. Fury had blinded him to reason. To him, I'd chosen the wrong side, betrayed him, publicly disrespected him a final time. I didn't want to believe it, but death rolled across my tongue.

My steady inhalation echoed in my ears as guns rose.

We were about to die.

Me. Arwood. Isobelle.

I spun, searching beyond the wall of black. Silas stood, mouth agape. Steadman had risen to his knees, blood streaming from his temple.

Fingers squeezed triggers, narrowing my threshold of choices to one horrific option.

A powerful, killing scream burst from me as bullets went flying. Silas's protective shield appeared beside me, Arwood's amulet glowing.

Death consumed my senses as my wail stole the lives of every circling guard without an amulet. Which was all of them—except my father.

Once the shield dropped, Steadman tossed his gun across the radius of fallen bodies. Arwood caught it single-handedly, taking aim.

The field fell silent, save for one final, foreboding gunshot.

AFTER

Blood and death surrounded my freedom.

My beast and I watched on, separate and the same, our maelstrom of emotion reduced to a choked inhalation as my father fell across the broken bodies of his men. Departing this world in a single, ragged exhalation of violence.

CHAPTER FORTY-EIGHT

THE REMAINING MEMBERS OF MY FATHER'S TEAM FLED INTO the sections of the forest not currently on fire, leaving behind the body of their leader.

A body I refused to look at.

My heart plummeted to see Katherine sprawled on the front steps of the house. Zeina stood in front of her protectively, weapon at the ready, lowering it once she realized we were approaching.

Banshees fought the fire spreading to the house with garden hoses. Silas, with the last of his strength, used his *ferox* abilities to amplify the streams of water into a wave, dousing the flames within the house and the trees. It was amazing to watch, and left more than one of the banshees gazing at him with heart-eyes.

We'd lost five banshees, including one of the leaders. Chloe. Five that shouldn't have died, five adding to the weight on my conscience.

Katherine had taken a bullet to her thigh, so we set her up on the kitchen table—thankfully, that side of the house hadn't been affected by the fire—with Zeina using her belt as a tourniquet to try to stem the bleeding. Pain medication wasn't taking the edge off, so Katherine clutched a bottle of Jameson, taking repeated swigs between shouted orders.

On one of the couches, Eilinora treated Steadman's head wound and broken ribs, his padded vest—decimated by bullets—lying discarded beside him. Grief over her fallen sisters tracked lines across her dirty cheeks, but she focused on trying to keep him upright and conscious with a debate about Irish versus American whiskey.

In the corner sat Arwood and Isobelle. He cradled her hands in his, foreheads close as they spoke, tears of relief falling from both sets of eyes. The sight of the two of them together speared my heart, a reminder of what I'd lost—and what I'd never had to begin with.

Katherine took a large mouthful of Jameson, heaving a cough. Zeina fussed over her, bringing her water to chase it.

"Thank you for protecting her," I said.

Zeina shrugged off my words. We'd located the key to her collar and removed it along with Isobelle's, and its absence revealed the extent of Zeina's bruises.

My tears were barely held at bay as I clutched Katherine's hand. "I'm so sorry. I'm sorry about the girls we lost. And Chloe." Remorse built like a surging sea in my chest.

Katherine gave a weak smile. "She loved a good fight, and she went down in one. She'd call that roarin' luck." She swigged again. "You alright, Keanna?"

"I'll deal with everything later."

And my father's body. I need to do something about his body. The realization nearly broke me.

"*We* will deal with everything later," Katherine corrected me, gripping tight. "You're not alone. I'm not going anywhere, now. And you don't have to leave, if you don't want to."

"I can stay? After what happened?"

"For as long as you like." Katherine's weak smile strengthened. "Shay wouldn't have listened to me and hidden in the house, either."

My eyes misted.

"Bus wheels off or on, I'm here too," Zeina said, squeezing my wrist.

Darkness threatened to rise up and consume me. I tried to push it down. I *would* fall, and fall hard—later. Katherine sat through the minutes it took to compose myself, her steady presence soothing me.

Branches snapped as three identical black SUVs emerged from the smoking forest, cutting off all conversation. At first I thought it Arwood's fleet we were waiting on, until half a dozen men and women dressed in head-to-toe black piled out. The woman leading them wore high-waisted trousers and a blazer the same shade as her golden-brown skin. They followed her up the front stairs, assessing the damage. The woman spotted Katherine as she entered, her black asymmetrical bob swaying as she stepped over broken floorboards in her polished black shoes.

"O'Carragher."

Katherine shifted herself to sitting. "I'm happy to report we managed on our own."

She gave Katherine a mild smile. "I trust the matter is resolved?"

Katherine's lips twitched. "O' sorts."

"Exposure?"

"Minimal." Another swig of Jameson. "Group of civilians hired by Edson Backhus. The survivors fled into the forest. Won't be too hard to find. Two rogue *feroxes* worked for him. Both dead."

The woman gazed about the room as if admiring the speckled wooden decor. She glanced at Arwood and Steadman more than once. "I see."

Intimidating presence? Subversive discourse? The way everyone in the room had frozen as if expecting a gavel to fall? This woman had to be from the Sect.

"Could only imagine how effective our defense would've been if we'd had your resources at our disposal," Katherine added.

"It *is* regretful we were at capacity today." The woman gave a casual shrug. "I wish you a swift recovery, and look forward to witnessing your continued efforts in maintaining your operations here."

"I've got it sorted. You don't need to be threatening me."

Another mild smile. "And yet our trackers follow reports of a banshee causing chaos in Prague. Perhaps it's not as sorted as you say."

The sensation of free-falling overtook my body. I sucked in a breath, holding it, gripping the tabletop.

Arwood stood, eyes now dry and features neutral. "I assume you refer to the banshee under my employ?"

The Sect woman turned to him. "Their name?"

I didn't dare move. Arwood had Isobelle. My father was dead. He had no reason to protect me—

"That's none of your concern."

Steadman was as unreadable as ever beside Eilinora. Neither he nor Arwood so much as glanced in my direction.

I released a careful breath.

"Is the banshee … present?" The Sect woman scanned the room again, observing everyone's hair. A chill rushed down my spine as we locked eyes. I didn't look away.

"The one you seek perished during the altercation," Arwood said.

She observed the tear-streaked faces of my banshee sisters. "We do not tolerate the way you and the Camardo family conduct your affairs. You'd do well to remember that."

Arwood's dimple appeared, lips quirking above his proud chin. He crossed his arms like they were discussing a dip in the share market. "Your displeasure is noted. Vesha."

Come and get me, his gaze challenged.

Neither Vesha, nor those accompanying her, moved.

A squirting of hand sanitizer broke the tense air. Anika wandered in, rubbing her palms together, then blinked, startled, at our company.

Incredulity crept across Vesha's face. "*You*," she said, drawing the word out. It reminded me of a shark circling prey. "How lovely to see you, looking well. Alive. Does your mother know you're consorting with banshees these days?"

I gaped at Anika. *Mother*? In all our interactions, she'd made it seem like Lissandra was her only relative, that she'd been alone in the world before working for her.

Anika's tongue poked the inside of her cheek as she shifted from foot to foot. "She doesn't. Think you can keep a secret, Vesh?"

Vesha's expression remained predatory. "This situation with your mother and father—"

"*Step*-father—"

"—was always so deliciously amusing. I will mind my tongue, but I can't guarantee my team will."

The color drained out of Anika's cheeks.

Soon after, the Sect vehicles departed, replaced by Arwood's. They took Katherine, Steadman, and the injured banshees being attended to in other rooms. Zeina and Aoife accompanied them.

Arwood paused at the threshold, giving me a final nod before exiting.

Eilinora stood beside me as they drove away, swiping at her tears as if annoyed they kept appearing. Chloe's absence created a noticeable void. Most of the banshees gave me a wide berth; I couldn't blame them for it. My fingers passed over my naked neck, reminding myself the collar was gone, what it had cost.

Minutes ticked past until Eilinora, who'd stared out the window unblinking, shook herself. "I'm going to bed for a bit. Are you right to cover?"

"I'll be here."

She paused at the base of the staircase. "Blue-eyes. What's he like?"

"Steadman? It's … complicated. And he's taken."

Eilinora sighed. "I had a feeling he was spoken for. There's always a catch. I'm like a bull, running for red flags."

"Don't be fooled by his mellow behavior. The guy hit his head on a rock. He's usually more onerous."

"Fate is a fickle piece of shite," she said. "I'm off to bed before I Match with another gorgeous criminal."

⌒૭

Silas was asleep in one of the upstairs bedrooms when I checked on him, his hair a riot against the white pillowcases. My heart swelled at the endearing way he gripped the blanket to his chin.

I sank beside him, leaning against the headboard. As if sensing my presence, he rolled, propping his head up on my thigh like a pillow and throwing his arm over my knees. My beast—and I—gave a sigh of contentment. His sleeping face looked misleadingly innocent, like he hadn't had to make difficult decisions daily to keep his family safe.

When he woke, he'd no longer have to.

I brushed hair from his forehead, touching him while I could.

"Oh, stop it," Anika whispered as she entered the room, pulling a sweater over her bra and wet, shower-soaked hair. "You're too adorable."

"Decided not to follow Arwood?"

She sat at the end of the bed, crossing a leg under her butt. "Been thinking I should go solo. Captain my own ship, as they say."

"What's the deal with Vesha? Is that why you're leaving?"

Anika screwed up her nose. "The Sect finally tracked me down, so I gotta bounce. Prague was fun while it lasted."

I didn't buy her bravado. "Will you be okay?"

"I've been on the run for ages. Provided they don't catch me, I'll be peachy." The heel of her boot bounced off the floor, shaking the bed. "I gotta apologize, Backhus. I fucked up."

"You told Arwood I'd found Isobelle, didn't you? You didn't wait."

"Guilty as charged." The sarcasm in her voice dissolved as she bit her lip. "I jumped the gun. Things were falling apart. And then *you* called."

"I would have been found eventually." Today smacked of a certain inevitability I still had difficulty reconciling with. "This started long before Isobelle."

Silas sniffed, rousing, gripping my thigh.

Anika winked. "That's my cue."

The door closed behind her as Silas murmured my name in a thick, husky whisper that tightened everything from the waist down. It was ridiculous how much he affected me.

"Where's everyone?" he asked.

"It's all over."

Silas frowned as he dragged himself upright against the head-board, taking in the silence and otherwise-empty bedroom. "It's really done? Arwood's gone? My family's free?"

"He's gone. You're free."

His gaze caught his empty wrist. Tanned skin surrounded a pale strip where Arwood's bracelet used to sit. Moisture sprang into his eyes as he inhaled jaggedly, concealing his face. His sigh of relief dispelled slowly.

The silence stretched. He'd soon be fully awake and alert, and no doubt remember my reason for being wary. "Would you like me to leave?"

He dropped his hands, frowning. "Why would I want that?"

The purple elephant had grown to exponential size. "Because I killed Gabriel."

Silas watched me for a long time. I'd apologized, I'd shown I cared for him—but was it enough? It was unfair to hope that of him.

But I still hoped.

He cleared his throat. "Gabriel … Gabriel was done for, long before he met you."

"What do you mean?"

Silas rubbed the bridge of his nose, staring at the sheets. "He was terminal. He didn't know about the cancer until it was too late. It was even later when he told us. He'd hoped to keep Arwood away from me, but …" His voice wobbled as he cleared his throat again. "At least … at least we now know when. And how. I didn't think I'd ever find out."

'You're doing me a favor,' Gabriel had said that day. I wanted to throw myself on the ground and scrub myself from head to toe, to go back to the plastic interrogation room and beg for forgiveness from him all over again.

Silas weaved his fingers through mine. "How … how was he?"

My response came out shaky. "He was so kind. He stuck up for me against Arwood. I—I think he even flirted with me a little bit?"

"I bet he did. Guy could never help himself."

"Sounds like someone else I know."

He squeezed my hand. "I've got good taste."

Silas slowly closed the gap between us. His lips caressed mine. Careful. Sweet. Heat shot down my spine at the contact. In his kiss, he told me we were okay. In his fingers, brushing the hair from my face and passing across my bare neck, he told me I was forgiven.

The tears I'd been holding back fell. His palms smoothed them away.

"How can you forgive me when I can't forgive myself?" I whispered, seeing Gabriel in my mind. I always would.

Silas rested his forehead against mine. "Because what happened that day wasn't your fault. Because you don't blame the victim, Keanna. You don't ever blame the victim."

My tears continued to fall for Gabriel, for Silas. For being prisoners. For being set free. For the crevasse in my heart my father had carved, for the emptiness I felt now. I floated like a kite with cut strings. He'd been my tether to this world. I had no idea how I'd adjust without him.

Silas held me close until my tears stopped coming. I breathed him in, my cheek against his warm shoulder.

Speaking of heat …

"Since when are you a *ferox* too?"

He smothered a grin. "Yeah. About that …"

"How is that even possible?"

"It's rare, but it happens. I transcended with both. My father didn't tell anyone, so I came to Arwood identifying as an *avertat*. Arwood missed my father's abilities. I knew he'd do nothing but run me into the ground."

And he didn't have to worry about that any longer. I ran a finger up and down the swell of his bicep. "Your mother and sister will be so happy to see you. Arwood wanted me to tell you they've been moved to a hotel in Prague."

"I'll need to go to them soon."

My hand stilled. I knew he'd have to leave. I just didn't want him to.

"Will you come with me?" he asked.

Yes, my beast crooned. My fingers drifted to his lips. They parted underneath my touch, his breath tickling my skin. "I want to, but I can't," I said. "I have to set right what happened today, take responsibility for my part in it. Katherine needs me here."

"For good?"

"For now, yes. Long term … I have no idea."

Silas's grip went to my waist, shifting me until I straddled him. My neck warmed at the familiar position, but in it I also found comfort. The scent of woodsmoke surrounded me as he buried his face into my hair. I wrapped my arms around him, nestling into the crook of his shoulder. For several minutes, we just held each other.

"I meant what I said that night," Silas whispered in my ear. "Nothing's changed in how I feel."

I clutched him tighter, relief rushing through me. When I didn't reply, Silas nudged me, his tone teasing.

"You can say it back. Any time now."

Flush against him, there was nowhere else I wanted to be. There was no one else I wanted to be with.

I'd do anything for this man. The least I could do was be honest with him.

I smiled, my fingertips fluttering on his chest. "I love you, too."

EPILOGUE

SEVEN WEEKS LATER

LUTCHING AN UMBRELLA, I RAN ACROSS WET cobblestones as I departed Trinity College, heading for the pub where Silas and his family waited.

He was the first person I saw, his hair curling adorably around his ears. I set my umbrella aside, ducking beneath snowflake garlands hanging from the ceiling, and ran over to him.

"You guys are gross," his sister, Layla, declared from the table as Silas greeted me with an unselfconscious kiss. A harsh assessment, given he'd at least kept his tongue to himself.

I'd stayed with Katherine and the banshees until two weeks ago, making the move to Dublin to resume my business degree. While I'd offered for Zeina to come with me, she'd opted to remain with Katherine. Their swiftly built but powerful romance was comforting and had me missing Silas more than was healthy.

We'd seen each other twice in the last two months while he and his family relocated to England, and it had never been long enough. Today, they'd traveled to Dublin, planning to stay for several weeks while Silas awaited the outcome of his job applications. He'd decided to go back to being a chef. I hoped he'd be placed near me.

His mother rose once Silas and I broke apart to issue a hug and a kiss to my cheek. Her carefree smile and relaxed posture lightened my soul.

"How are you settling into school?" she asked. I spent several minutes filling them in on my classes.

Sharing such details felt like a dagger to my heart, another reminder of the things I could no longer tell my father. My chest had ached constantly since his death, since his funeral, since the PR cover-up of his 'tragic, accidental death.' Every day, I woke to the inevitable, slamming realization he was gone. Every day, I worked to disassociate the man who'd died in the clearing from the one I'd believed him to be. The one I wanted to remember him as. Comfort or denial, I pretended they were different people. I'd lost more than just my father that day.

Silas's family had settled into their new house on the outskirts of London. They'd been destitute upon their capture because of debt, and Silas had feared life would be difficult as they started over, but Arwood had delivered payment for Silas's service, giving them enough to relocate very comfortably and *very* far away from the Camardos. Otherwise, we hadn't heard a peep from Arwood. Rumors had circulated for weeks that he'd scaled back his involvement in Prague to be with his daughter. Lissandra maintained operations, but it hadn't been a clean transition. Between this and the dissolution of the Kohnstamms, plenty of holes existed for someone to fill.

Silas's mother shared their plans for the holiday season, wine coloring her cheeks as she finished a glass, gesturing enthusiastically for another.

"You'll join us, then?" Layla asked, her tone casual and a degree kinder than I'd expected. She'd had the hardest time reconciling my involvement with Gabriel's death—understandably so—making this admission a promising development in our relationship. "We can watch a crappy Christmas movie and eat ice cream or something."

I wanted nothing more, and I told her so as Silas pulled me close. The weeks without my father hadn't lessened the pain, but I embraced the warmth of their love and acceptance with an abandon I wouldn't have thought possible six months before. With Katherine a pillar of strength to the south, and Silas beside me, I felt grounded, secure, my compass pointing in the right direction.

I was home.

The End ... for now

BONUS

Want to know what happens next?

Download the bonus chapter here:

Please leave a review!

If you enjoyed this story, it would mean the world to me if you could leave a review on any of the platforms—Amazon, Barnes & Noble, Goodreads, etc—so it can find other readers in the future. You'll receive an unlimited supply of palm kisses from Silas as a thank you*

*Actual results may vary

Review on Goodreads:

Review on Amazon:

ABOUT THE AUTHOR

Sarah is an award-winning author of slow-burn, high-stakes fantasy romance.

Born and raised in Australia, she spent her hot summer days inside reading, saving money on SPF, and being an overachiever at school. These days, Sarah's a serial cookie-in-tea dunker and Spotify playlist curator and adores writing paranormal & urban fantasy romance filled with morally grey characters you'll fall in love with (against your better judgement), forehead kisses, and the occasional explosion.

She graduated from the University of Queensland with a degree in Communications and—when she's not travelling—resides in Brisbane, Australia with her partner, a stack of TBR books she promises she'll read someday, and a growing array of indoor house plants. They're still alive. She thinks.

You can reach her at authorsarahlrichhelm.com

ACKNOWLEDGEMENTS

Writing may be a solitary task, but creating a book takes an army. This is going to sound like the most long-winded Oscar's speech ever, but I truly couldn't have done this without everyone who supported me along the way. Make some tea and treat yourself to a cookie or two because there's a few people to mention.

Eternal thanks to my partner Hamish, who supplied countless cups of coffee, cooked dinners, and made sure I went outside on occasion while I toiled over every draft. Despite not being a reader, you threw yourself into understanding what it takes to get a book out there, and you always encouraged me to show up for myself. I'm *your* biggest fan.

To my family: Mum, Dad, my sisters Danni & Ali, my grandmother. Thank you for gifting me the books that helped make me a writer. You've been there from the beginning, you've always encouraged me and believed this would happen, and I appreciate you all for it so much.

To Taylor Ferguson, my OG critique partner, and one of my first ever beta readers: Thank you for loving the first version of this story and for helping me see the potential in it. Becoming your friend was one of the most unexpected and delightful gifts the online community brought me.

To my international critique partners and the first official readers of this story. It's hard to put into words how much you all mean to me, but I'll try:

To Lindsay Elizabeth and Michelle Garcia: Thank you for the *hours* of iMessages, Google Meets, laughs, sobs, feedback, hype ups, thirst traps, and niplets. You both made me a braver, better writer, and gave me the confidence to tackle this series. Writing alongside you is one of my greatest joys. You're both made of stars.

To Christina Rann: Thank you, my fabulous word witch, for the song shares, the rabbit holes, the rambling voice memos, your courageous critiques, and championing my story and my characters.

To Sarah Brinley and Arielle Janvier: Thank you for welcoming me into your corner and being early friends. Your passions for storytelling are unparalleled, and the gentle grace with which you support us all makes me ugly sob.

The best choice I ever made in this whole writing thing was joining the Instagram writing community. You all make the Pacific Ocean feel smaller. Silas palm kisses and Daddy Arwood tattoos for you all (but you'll have to share Steadman with Taylor. Sorry ladies).

To my Australian critique partners: Deb, Shaz, and Jo. I love how we transcend genres and prove time and time again the universal truths (and struggles!) of writing stories. Video calls and writing retreats with you all warm my heart.

To my beautiful soul friends: Tammika, Amelia, Kelsea, Jayde, Pascale, Shennae, Sarah V. You are such bright lights. Thank you for supporting me from the moment I announced I wanted to take this hobby seriously. You've always shown interest and supported how you could, and I can't thank you all enough. I am so lucky to have found such an empowered and empowering corner of the universe.

To my beta readers: AJ Lexa, Aynia Noever, Briana H Louis, Davona Mapp, Emma Hausfeld, Rebecca Frank, Lacie Erickson, Mandi Kontos, Melanie Pickering, Melanie Woods, RC Reyn, and Steph Talarek. Thank you for running through the woods with me, seeing potential in all the seasons, and helping make this story what it is now.

To the ladies in the Romance Writers of Australia (RWA) community, you're all amazing. Thank you for welcoming me into the fold and supporting me. Thank you to the judges who listed this story as finalist in the Emerald Award for 2024, and for your kind feedback.

To my editor, Emma O'Connell at @emmas.edit, thank you. You made this manuscript a million times better with your attention to detail, your crackships, and wrestling those em dashes out of my hands. A few made it through our tug-of-war; any that aren't structurally or grammatically correct you can assume are my fault.

To Kirsty Inic at @kirsty_inic, thank you for helping make my opening pages shine.

To my proofreaders. Sharon Strahand, your grace and professionalism always makes me feel like I'm in safe hands. I can't wait for our next cup of tea together. Amelia Long, thank you for championing this book from day one.

Big thanks to the following for my research questions. Any mistakes made in the text are my own: To Sir Kenneth, who assisted me with US Army technicalities. To Val (@kay.does.ballet), Michelle R (@onewanderingmuse), and the other Prague writers on the IG community. To Pampage and Pants, for humouring me. To everyone I queried on Europe logistics, crime, armoured cars, and everything in between.

Massive thank you to those on my ARC and Street Team not mentioned above. You've all made my debut so special, and I'll never forget it.

Thanks to Taylor Swift for 'Enchanted', the song that inspired the meet cute between Keanna and Silas. To Nikki White, for the song that became the unofficial soundtrack to this book, 'Fought & Lost'. And also to the band Kosheen for being my muse for this project. Apparently, I reached the top 1% of their listeners on Spotify while drafting this story. Like the overachiever I am, I'll wear that badge proudly.

To anyone who supported me through the iterations of this story, whether you knew it as Project Prague, All Signs Point North, Control My Night… or any version in between, you're the best.

And most importantly—thank you, reader, for picking up this story. It means the world to me to finally share this with you.

SHATTER MY NIGHT
4 November 2026

When fugitive mage Anika finds sanctuary—and a new job as
a supernatural bodyguard—in a warded historical manor, she
soon realizes that whatever lurks within the house may be more
dangerous than anything she is running from on the outside.

**From award-winning author Sarah L Richhelm comes
another high-stakes new adult urban/paranormal mafia
fantasy with an excruciating slow-burn rivals-to-lovers
romance between two bodyguards trying to protect their
client at all costs. *Shatter My Night* is the second instalment in
the interconnected standalone Shadow Cages series mixing
mafia vibes with romance, action, and spice in a reimagined,
modern-day Europe.**